CAPITAL CITY

CAPITAL CITY

BY MARI SANDOZ

UNIVERSITY OF NEBRASKA PRESS
LINCOLN AND LONDON

First Bison Book printing: 1982
Most recent printing indicated by the first digit below:
1   2   3   4   5   6   7   8   9   10

Library of Congress Cataloging in Publication Data
Sandoz, Mari, 1896–1966.
    Capital city.
    Reprint. Originally published: Boston : Little, Brown,
1939.
    I. Title.
PS3537.A667C36   1982   813'.52   81–14656
ISBN 0–8032–4130–5   AACR2
ISBN 0–8032–9126–4 (pbk.)

Reprinted by arrangement with the Mari Sandoz Corporation,
represented by McIntosh and Otish, Inc.

A few men and women who have played some part in the history of our times are mentioned by name in this novel. These apart, all characters are fictitious and all scenes are imaginary.

FOREWORD

IF a man place his hand flat on the map of our country, the crotch of it at the mouth of the Missouri, his forefinger will reach up along the Mississippi towards Canada and his thumb out towards the Spanish Peaks. Between them will lie the newer lands of America, with the blood of the vanquished Indian scarce dry upon their golden grasses, the rutted trails that followed the buffalo up the great rivers still plain in the spring cornfields and the green of the summer alfalfa. Here, in the region that required far over a hundred years to settle, with all the nations of the earth contributing, I have placed my state of Kanewa, with the high white tower of its capitol encircled by a stone frieze dedicated to its citizens, the frieze of the Peoples of the World.

CAPITAL CITY

CHAPTER I

In the evening sun of September the capital city lay along the bed of the Little Grand River like a cluster of lice along the vein of a yellowing leaf. On both sides of the alkali bottoms the breaks climbed away to wide farming tables, their canyons pushing deep through the fertile pasture lands, gullying the sun-browned stubblefields, washing the rich corn ground to the clay. The scattering of old trees along the fence lines were peeling, many of the weathered farmsteads stood bleak-eyed and empty. But past them the smooth and white-lined highways swept the traffic in from all the state of Kanewa: from the pavements of the Lower Grand River, and the Lasseur and the Wakoon; from the gravel and dirt roads of the middle counties; and from the rutted trails of the farthest reaches of Wild Horse Plains — swept it all in towards Franklin, the capital city on the Little Grand.

Today there was no thought at all here of the impoverished earth of Kanewa, of short crops and low farm prices, or of the winter coming. Tonight the city would be celebrating. Already the hot, dusty streets were thick with cars all the way from Grand Vista Country Club out on Boulder Heights down to Silver City, the Coney Island of the Middle West; from the prairie villas along Blue Ridge across to the squatter shacks in Herb's Addition. Empty lots were filled with hot-dog and souvenir stands, with campers, trailers, and big revival tents. Every corner in the flag-hung business section had its accordion-playing blind man or its pencil-selling cripple; every doorway its pitchman spieling to the gathering, sunburnt crowd. Days ago the dine-and-dance places began to bustle with extra girls, who followed fairs and celebrations like wheat tramps the harvest. Some of the more experienced trailer and cabin-camp women didn't bother with jobs at all, depending upon themselves and perhaps a leg man loose in the crowd for their customers.

Not even the sky was free of advertising this evening. Off to the south the anchored Silver City balloon rose and fell above the old ferris wheel. High over the town itself the white puffs of a sky writer's cigarette advertisement rippled to beds of cotton while below him two smaller planes circled, trailing banners advising the public to DANCE AT EL TROC and to STOP AT JOE'S CABIN CAMP. But from the center of the city the tower of the state capitol building rose tall and remote as always, a slim white pinnacle lost against the pale sky of the flatlands of Kanewa.

As the evening settled down the highways towards the city darkened to solid, flowing belts of cars, the late sun glinting along new tops, flashing against back-tilted windshields that paused for no crossroad. But at the railroad tracks they stopped, and as the noisy paralysis spread miles back, two long streamline trains, one from the north and one from the south, slipped out of the breaks into the city. With short, hoarse whistles of warning they swept past the blocked highways toward the smoky old depot, running easy and smooth as oil — the special trains for the Fall Festival and the annual coronation of the emperor and empress of the land of Kanewa.

Not everybody was hurrying into the capital city, particularly not the squatters of Herb's Addition, on the slope of Grandview Hill overlooking sluggish Little Grand River and the city beyond. Two men leaned against one of the shacks, a special one, all the same kind of tar paper and with a little screened stoop in front, almost like a house. Smoking, they watched the streamliners tootle in. Hamm

Rufe, passing forty and shabby-neat in old suit pants and a laundried grey shirt, was like his mother's people, clean-jointed, lean-flanked, men of decision and action. His thick hair, greying vaguely to the color of tarnished sterling, stood up vigorously from a brown wall of forehead. The scar that cut across his left cheek and through the bridge of his nose, the stiff wrist broken by the same blow — these also belonged to the man of action. But even the scar and the break had come to him as a spectator.

Beside Hamm Rufe hunched the long, folded figure of the Coot, who built the first brick kilns in Franklin, over sixty years ago. When the building boom died down he put his money into the coming business of the capital city, banking. Until the hard times of the nineties closed the door of his bank, he stamped every one of the pink checks of the Farmers National with his full name: Asa Bruce Harcoot, President. Since then he had withdrawn from many things, from the lilac-fenced house and the nagging wife inside, the church choir where he sang for ten years, and the church too; even the chess club at Pete's tobacco shop. Almost in a day Asa Bruce Harcoot, bank president, became the old Coot, living in one of the clay caves where his brick kilns used to stand against the high flank of Grandview Hill. By now the Coot was thin and straight and weathered as the old smoke-stack over the gas works, and as careless of the years that had blown through his earth-grey beard. But his eyes were bright as those of the cliff swallows nesting at his cave, and his mouth was red and alive.

Together, the two men watched the lanes of cars move on again, the town fill. Now and then the Coot scratched the mosquito bites around his ankles, bare between the city-dump shoes and the rags of his overalls, as he hummed around his pipestem, hoping for a chance to break into talk. Hamm Rufe didn't notice. He was watching the slow sun retreat from the windows of the Moorish clubhouse far out on Boulder

Heights, the vague, palish glow of evening spread like powder over the business section of the dusky city below. Out of the suburbs somewhere a long beam of light reached in to pick the white, globed dome of the capitol from the darkness. It was followed by another, and another, until the dome floated like some cold, low-hanging planet. Gradually the light crept downward, over the sculptured frieze of the People of the World and lower, until the whole tower stood out tall and white and alone against the deep blue sky of evening.

Below, in the business section, neon signs came on, a flashing of red and yellow on top of the Buffalo Hotel, steady green over the Franklin National Bank, with Hammond's, the Finest Store of the Middle West, lengthened far above the other buildings by its vertical stripes of cold, steady blue neon from street to roof.

In the duskiness of the shack wall the Coot scratched the bare chest under his beard and nudged his silent neighbor toward the brightening town below them.

"Well, there she sits, our capital city, the damned old prostitute — "

Hamm Rufe shifted his back a little uneasily against the wall. Then he relaxed, his pipe drooping towards his chest again. Seeing there would be no further encouragement, the Coot found the silence sufficient.

"Yeh," he went on. "Nothing but a damn, bloodsucking old parasite. Don't produce nothing, just living off the capitol and the university — and through them got a hand in every Goddamn pocket in the state. All taking and no giving. A prostitute — and worse — "

Finally Hamm Rufe moved the pipe from his mouth. "I suppose it might also be said that the lady is living high tonight — ?"

"Yeh, high as old Daisy Dee, back when Buffalo Bill used to drop in — " the Coot agreed, off on another telling of one of his stories that required nothing beyond silence, and left

Hamm free to consider the city below him, the city whose most quoted publicity line was taken from the oratory of the capital fight with Grandapolis, seventy years ago, pledging itself eternally to envision and disseminate the highest attributes of cultural living to all the great state of Kanewa.

"To envision and disseminate — "

But through thickening darkness and the engrossment of the two men, a fan of rainbow-colored beams spread upward from the university fieldhouse. Other nights it was a bare, barny structure that housed student rallies and pep talks, poultry shows or basketball tournaments, but tonight it became the flag-hung Palace of Coronation. Inside, the overhead steel arches would be covered with deep red sateen drapes, the cement of its balconies and the wire of the goal baskets hidden by shadowed lights and gold-corded velvet valances from the eyes of the court to congregate below. The wooden bleachers would be gone from the maple floor and down the center a strip of red carpet would lead to the gilt thrones on the stage. Here, tonight, a new emperor and empress would be crowned for the land of Kanewa.

Stiffly Old Coot got to his feet. "I rustled me a couple cans a beans today, if you're a mind to beans — "

But Hamm Rufe had eaten, and so the old man plodded away into the dark alone, his feet awkward on the rough, worn earth between the shacks and his cave, humming a song he used to sing at box socials long ago: —

> Puttin' on the agony, puttin' on the style,
> Is what so many people
> Are doing all the while.

Coronations were nothing to the Coot. He whacked bulls with his father up the old Fort Stoddard trail long before the string of stinking alkali ponds of Mud Creek Sink had been ditched and called Little Grand River. Back when outlaws painted up to look like Indians were still running off the trail station stock, old Asa Harcoot built a log station house on the slope overlooking the Sink. Not a one of that chamber of commerce bunch who cooked up this Fall Festival business had ferried the Mississippi then, no, nor their fathers either, the Coot often bragged at Old Horsemeat's. Both he and the Horse were old settlers by the time the first of those buildings down there poked a nose through the dirty sod and everybody got to turning his hogs loose along Mud Creek, only, like Horsemeat pointed out, they were branded then, and a man knew who he was keeping in sowbelly.

Working deftly in the familiar dark the Coot lit a bit of trash and broke an old orange crate into a bright fire. Punching his knife blade into the top of a can of beans, he set it on to heat while he squatted on his heels, the cave behind him a black, smoky hole. While he waited he had another pipe and wondered about his squatter neighbor as he had for the last six, seven years. Good enough geezer, Hamm Rufe was, even though he had a piece of a job and did a little writing on the side. He wasn't much on drinking or women, but he had a way of looking up at the picture of a girl over his fireplace like she was somebody important, although to the Coot it didn't even look like a photograph but only a pencil drawing of some wild-haired foreign girl. All the squatters had tried to get Hamm to talk about the picture but he was close-mouthed about that like he was about everything else, close-mouthed as a rat trap. And when he did say anything it was usually thin as a tubful of gully wash, and damn thin gully wash.

Down at Hamm's shack it was time for the Friday symphonic program, with Mozart, fitting well into the warm evening. With the radio set so a neighbor or two who liked music could hear, he settled back to the darkening stoop. Down in the smoldering city dumps a rising breeze fanned up a little blaze and out on Blue Ridge headlights began to move away from the cocktail parties and string up Boulder Heights, named for Clem Boulder, an early register of deeds. Old Clem had falsified his books and sold the hogback he didn't own to the country club. After his departure, and a painful second purchase, the clubhouse was finally built and called Grand Vista because it overlooked the unhurrying ditch through Mud Creek Sink that was called Little Grand River. The man's name stuck with the heights.

Hamm knew how it would be up there: honking, loud talk and laughing, people passing thick before the wide yellow windows into the clubhouse for the coronation dinner. Here, presided over by the outgoing emperor and empress, would be the old court and the new: six kings with their queens chosen each year from the congressional districts, the dukes and their duchesses from the larger cities, with Grandapolis, billboarded as the Metropolis of the Middle West, and the originator of the coronation idea, allowed three. Although the men were always successful and often fat and bald, they made a good showing at the dinner in their new-pressed tuxedos, with the satin ribbon of royalty across their fronts. Later was soon enough for satin britches over potbellies or legs too bowed to keep a pig in an alley. And before the night was over one of the new dukes from Grandapolis would be wearing the ermine robe of the emperor of Kanewa. The name used to be announced in the advance publicity, but since an emperor-elect landed in jail by coronation day for tricks with the paper of his bank, the ballot of the state coronation council, chamber of commerce, was secret.

The duchesses, chosen for the higher, nobler things, were always pretty girls in their teens, slim and fine in their new formals. Later they would appear in stiff, embroidered satin too, the three from the capital city in white, for one of them would be crowned empress.

It was unfortunate that the dinner, the high social event of the year, began around seven but the court had to change before the Grand Parade at nine-thirty. Years ago everybody appeared in the satins of coronation at the dinner, but the retail clothiers' association circulated a petition and now the court dressed, and no woman, not even a retiring duchess, ever dared appear in an old gown.

On the dark crest of Grandview Hill, above the shacks of Herb's Addition, stood a turreted old stone house, long empty, the windows gone, its good oak floors heaving and warped. The last few months there was talk of fleeting lights, and dark figures walking. The inquisitive boys of the neighborhood gangs who went to snoop only tried it once, and had little to say afterward. Lately the lights were plain for everyone to see, and cars openly turning off into the weedy old driveway; cars full of men in dark tan uniforms — Gold Shirts, it was said. Tonight there was early commotion at Stone House, and towards parade time half a dozen cars swung out to the pavement, driving wild and arrogant down the packed highway.

At the fork to Herb's Addition they met an open yellow roadster waiting to turn in from the city. Deliberately they crowded it off the shoulder and roared on, laughing, honking as the car lurched deep into the weedy ditch. Finally, with angry complaint of the motor it crawled out into the rough dirt trail and came bumping up to Hamm's lighted little stoop. The man stretched his cramped joints and went out. From the light of the dash he saw it was Mollie Tyndale, a veil blowing from her dark hair, the ribbon of royalty across the white satin of her young breast.

She was in a hurry. Those hateful Gold Shirts had delayed her, with the coronation parade just about to start and the traffic all jammed up. But she just had to know about Burt Parr. He hadn't called her last night, or the night before, and

now at the filling station they said he wasn't there. Maybe
he was sick somewhere, sick and alone.

Hamm Rufe shook his head. He didn't think so. The boy
had worked all day, hard, with the rush of outstate customers
in for the fair, he said, speaking cautiously as always, turning
the scarred side of his face to the darkness. But the girl wasn't
noticing. She must find Burt, had something to tell him,
wanted to say that it didn't matter about her being a duchess.
It was just to please the folks, her mother, especially. It really
didn't matter at all.

" — I'll tell him, if he comes along," Hamm Rufe offered.
"Now you better be starting back, not holding up the town's
big parade."

So with the man on the running board the girl waited at
the highway for an opening into the laned traffic. As he saw
it come Hamm leaned over the veiled mass of dark curls.
"There you are. And tonight you shall be the fairest one of
all — " he promised, stepping down and waving the girl on.

From the darkness beside the flowing road the man looked
after pretty little Mollie Tyndale, with a roadster of her own,
an expensive satin dress just for this one night. But he was
thinking of another girl, one who spent the war years of her
European youth against invasions of woman-hungry soldiers,
who was spending her American maturity against what she
knew was a far darker hunger, the hunger for money and
for power. They were very different, these two, the pretty
child with her car and the mature woman with her storm-
grey eyes steadied to a violent world, her tongue with words
that had held men in the face of riot guns, her right arm
strong and gentle, but the sight of Mollie Tyndale always
aroused the old longing for the other, for the Stephani of
the picture above his fireplace in the squatter's shack.

Hamm was well settled on his own doorstep once more,
and pounding the cold ashes from his pipe, when Burt Parr

came out of the darkness. He was young, and tall and diffident, his blue eyes night-pupiled in the light, his bright blond
hair tousled, his mouth silent.

The man moved over and the boy dropped beside him, to
sit with his wrists crossed between his knees, his hands hanging, his face shadowed.

"Mollie was up, looking for you, and very pretty too, in
her regal gown."

"Looking for me — ?" Burt asked quickly. Then he
slumped down again. "What's the good of that? By eleven
o'clock she'll be the top crust of the town, the empress — "

Hamm Rufe stretched a leg to get at his matches, struck
one, and over its flame at the pipebowl he considered the set
young profile.

"It wouldn't make much difference, not to Mollie," he said.
" — But she won't be the one selected."

"Why not? She's a duchess, and the best-looking — " the
boy defended.

The older man sucked his pipe into a redness that brought
his scar alive as with rising anger. "She could be solid platinum
set in emeralds," he finally said, "and lovely as the sunset from
this shack, which is the most beautiful thing I know, except
one — and still she wouldn't get to be empress."

But for young Burt that was no reply. "Why won't she?"
he demanded.

So Hamm Rufe had to make some justification, and lacking
words of his own for this boy, he borrowed from what the
old Coot might have said to him, but with less flavor, as
Hamm knew.

"The grandmothers of the town won't have Mollie," he
said, "not those three old women who run the capital city,
the city that our salty neighbor up in his cave retreat calls a
prostitute. They won't have an outsider, a newcomer. The
honors have to go to what they call the good old families, at
least two generations old."

A long time the boy was silent, and when he began to talk it wasn't of the city's big night and its coronation, but of himself and the Tyndale girl. He should have picked some other school, any other but Kanewa U, when Mollie's folks decided to go big bug and move into the capital city. Up at Sheffield on the Wakoon River there had been nothing but fifty years of dusty road the width of a wagon track between the rich Tyndales and the trashy Parrs. He should have known enough to go somewhere else, or to stay on the old wornout farm, where he belonged.

"Oh, no," Hamm Rufe corrected. "You couldn't do any other way, for you're from the world of action."

"Action!" the impatient boy protested. "What am I doing — ?" But he didn't get to finish before the parade bands started up in the town below them, the brasses carrying faintly across the bottoms on the night wind. Hamm went inside, ran his pocket comb through his thick hair, and slipped into his coat. "Walk as far as the bridge with me — " he suggested to Burt, as though asking a special favor.

So they went clear into town, both of them, for there was Mollie Tyndale to see, even if she was wearing the white court satin that was taking her from the playmate of her childhood spent on a river the Indians called *Wahan*, the Holy Stream. Hamm managed to get into an empty warehouse across from the capitol, where marble columns and other special portions had been stored during the time of building. They found the place already occupied by the Coot and several of his cronies who knew the Hammond watchman too.

From a high window they looked down upon Philadelphia Avenue that ran through the capital city from Boulder Heights and Blue Ridge almost to the Polish bottoms, swung around the university and the fairgrounds and then straight away past the reformatory to the penitentiary. All together it was called Horseshoe Boulevard, with one end at the ridge and the other at the prison, and the lower Franklinites liked to say that many a man had seen both of them.

Tonight all the business section of the avenue was grated with strings of lights crossing at every lamp post. Flags, the purple and gold of Kanewa and the two colors reversed for the capital city, hung from the buildings and stood all along the crowded, waiting curbs. As the music of the bands swelled, the town's four motorcycle cops moved slowly forward, followed by the university band and the long cars of the police chief and the directors of the chamber of commerce. Behind came the sage green of the state patrol escorting the car of the retiring emperor, a big soapman from Grandapolis as thick and tallowy as his product. By his side rode his empress, the nineteen-year-old daughter of Glen Doover of Franklin Mills. They were followed by the court, the outgoing members and the new, all in fine cars, ribboned, gleaming, moving in slow and pompous crawl.

"Takes a rich pile of manure to breed such fat maggots!" the old Coot called down upon them.

On both sides and behind the court were the rest of the uniformed patrol, chromium buttons and patent leather shining, their bearing protective and alert. After them came more long cars, carrying the state's representatives of outside capital, the real big shots of Kanewa, separated by the Legion drum corps, afoot, from the business executives of the capital city, the Hammonds, the Welleses, the Blacks, and their kind. Next came the important men of Grandapolis and outstate; the capitol delegation with the national guard; the Franklin High School band behind its pretty, swirl-skirted drum major, followed by the uniformed drill squads of the butter works, the flour mills, the chain stores, and the oil companies of the trade territory that was once Franklin's, with outstate high-school bands interspersed. The Consumers' Co-operative was denied representation, as Hamm Rufe, their publicity man, had expected, but a uniformed CCC camp delegation got in somehow, marching sturdily and well with their shovels over their shoulders like guns, along with several Boy Scout troops and the goose-stepping Gold Shirts, set off by bands. The fall crop of candidates came in order of rank, from congress clear on down to Dr. C. Thurston Stetbettor, the rub doctor, behind the county assessor. He was running independently for governor, with a white sound car, an astrologer for advisor, and a chalk-talk cartoonist to illustrate his harangues on America for Americans, no Indians included.

Much of the city's fire equipment rumbled along near the tail end until it was called away by radio. The half a dozen simultaneous calls sounded false but couldn't be ignored, not even the one that involved a wide swing through the head of the parade. But the marching column rejoined almost immediately and kept steadily on, the fire trucks slipping back into their places in a little while. All along the avenue the crowds stood solid to the walls, the windows on each side filled; even the roofs peopled thick as little forests against the pinkish light of the sky.

With rumble and blare the parade passed the capitol building and its statue of the seated Benjamin Franklin, weary and withdrawn, his heavy-lidded eyes looking down. It moved along raggedly towards the deeper business section, past the Kanewa Trust building and Hammond's, and the Equity Mutual, but straightening up a little as it reached the high plank reviewing stand, with its radio narrator, its news-reel man, and half a dozen other photographers, including a representative of a "leading pictorial weekly," as the capital city papers put it. They wouldn't have mentioned Jesus Christ by name, unless his sponsors paid for the space, the reporters grumbled.

Slowly the parade crept on into the earlier city, past the old Kanewa Hotel, "A woman with every dollar room," on to the chamber of commerce building, the help out on the balcony by special permission for a view of the city's magnificence. Across the intersection from the chamber was an old grey building, its high steps full of watchers too, overalled men, broad, strong, many youngish — the Labor Temple with its striking truckers. Tonight they mocked the marching police who had used billies and blackjacks on their picket lines all summer; they booed the satin-sleeved, limousine-riding court.

"Yah, yah, playing kings! Pfui!"

Without seeming to hasten, or even to notice, the paraders moved steadily on. A couple of the younger Gold Shirts did shake threatening fists towards the hecklers, and then dropped them sheepishly at a hiss from their commander, most of them not knowing why, or that the fist was the hated Communist salute. But from the sidelines the fists were answered by taunting voices lusty as the whistle of a midnight freight: "Long live Uncle Joe Stalin!" "Long live John Lewis!" and then the final insult, "Long live Samelly Finestein!"

At the mention of the secondhand dealer whose windows were broken twice the last month, a Gold Shirt or two broke step. But the band that came marching along drowned out everything, and the motorcycle escort pushed on a little faster through the poor section, where whole families lived in one room, the window looking down upon the outdoor privies unscreened. They hurried past the city mission, too, the steps full of grey, sad-faced men, past the sagging sign of a Townsend club and long rows of negro and reliefer shacks, on to the fieldhouse. The brick building looked barer than ever tonight, despite the banners, and cold as the rear of a factory under the fan of colored lights. But a strip of red carpet reached down the walk to the curb and soon sweeping-gowned women and knee-britched men were filing up between the uniforms of the road patrol, past the flashing lights of the photographers, and into the vast, steel-girded building.

With his good hand on the arm of Burt, his unscarred cheek friendly toward him, Hamm Rufe started the silent boy away through the crowd as soon as the fire department came along. Cutting down an alley they slipped into the fieldhouse from the back, past a janitor acquaintance, and up to the unreserved balcony long crowded with the waiting. Here, too far to recognize any faces, but close enough for the color and the pageantry, they waited too.

The small band just below the stage began to play, the road patrol came in at the side doors and posted themselves under the red valances of the balconies, the town's formal garb lining up slowly before them. Many of these men who stood easy enough in their dinner coats tonight walked with the long swinging step set by old plow mares, their feet still a little flexible from hours of sitting on their heels on the sunny side of the winter barn, far from the coronation palace of the capital city. Hamm knew that many with the same long gait still sat on their heels, but it was outside of re-employment bureaus, or at the relief offices. They still squatted on their heels but without the diversion of a clod's cast at an inquisitive sparrow, or the contemplation of a thick stream of tobacco juice to be rolled under with the crackling stubble of the fall plowing tomorrow.

As Hamm thought of the outsiders drawn into the capital city, used, sometimes even accepted, the CCC campers were dispersing into the watching crowd about the fieldhouse, while inside the Legionnaires, the Gold Shirts, and the high-school bands climbed the ramps to their reserved sections in the balconies. Now the three ruling grandmothers of the town led the other white-haired dignitaries of the state out upon the stage. Quietly they settled themselves on the folding chairs in a semicircle about the throne, and awaited the coming of the court.

As the band livened, the new kings with their queens came up the red carpet, the men a little unsteady in their bright satin and plumes, some of them awkward in regalia without the protection of a mask. The queens managed better, looking a little too plump, perhaps, in their rich reds, purples, and greens, but important and fine, almost as fine as the slim young duchesses following them. In couples they turned to this side or to that, lining up before the town's elite — those with evening clothes and the ten dollars apiece for floor tickets.

Last in the new court came the three dukes of Grandapolis with their duchesses, to stand stiff and waiting in their white satin at the left of the throne steps. Then the old court marched to their places along the carpet, easily, calmly, the maturity of a year's service at dedications, grand openings, and community drives upon them.

With a flourish the music stopped, those on the stage arose, the three-dollar sections of the balconies with them. Heralded by two plumed boy trumpeters, the emperor and empress entered, their ermine-edged capes sweeping out behind them as they came. Slowly, with fair dignity, the monarchs moved through the court that bowed stiff as a dry corn patch in a windstorm as they passed. The news-reel cameras whirled and the radio reporter sent a string of high-pitched superlatives out upon the midwestern air.

When they were safely seated on their thrones the state's one former Metropolitan Opera singer came out and hurled a Wagnerian aria to echo against the back balcony, the shelf of her bosom heaving. When she was done the applause spread upward, and dropped into a silence of expectation. Parkins, the energetic year-round secretary of the chamber of commerce, a lean chamberlain in black hose and britches for this night, came out with a microphone to read from the coronation scroll. At his first word the loud-speaker burst into a blaring that died as the man stumbled back before the power of his own voice. While an overalled workman tinkered, the empress smiled graciously and the emperor tried to choke down a burp that the microphone caught and echoed all over the fieldhouse. Embarrassed, he wiped a palm over his heavy face while the balconies cheered and whistled, especially the top shelfers, the fifty-centers.

Once more, and cautiously, the chamberlain started through the list of the year's court appointments "for exceptional service rendered to the land of Kanewa," each new couple moving forward as the outgoing members stepped back, passing on the left. "The left, around the left," they whispered the instructions from the *Manual of Coronation* to each other.

Then suddenly a little eddy of disturbance appeared, an uncertain stirring of heads, and much stretching to see in the balconies and from all over the floor. A duke, Colmar Welles of Franklin, seemed to be missing. He had come in all right, been there only a moment before, and in pretty good condition, too, much better than some. But an absence was no unprecedented circumstance, and so last year's duke, who knew his *Manual* thoroughly, quietly stepped back into the place he had just vacated while a page was sent to search the lounge and the washrooms. On the stage the chamberlain's dull voice droned on.

When the three dukes and duchesses in white satin, the candidates for the throne, were called forward, the silence of expectancy spread to the farthest shirt-sleeved balconies. The band started "Hail to the Chief" and the monarchs moved from their thrones to the waiting candidates, their scepters touching the shoulders of the top utilities man from Grandapolis and the blondined Helen Groves, whose grandmother, with thick braids of natural yellow down her back, had rustled steins in the old Station Hotel at sixteen. But Helen was old family, as Hamm Rufe had predicted, third-generation capital city.

Escorting their successors to the thrones, the outgoing monarchs bowed as two attendants swept the ermine robes from their shoulders to those of the new rulers, the crowns from their heads, then bent knee and fell back in relief. The band struck up the "Emperor of Kanewa" march and the grandmothers of Franklin and all those behind them on the stage settled to their seats without one chair's collapse.

Now the new court, with last year's duke still in Colmar Welles's place, marched past the throne in formal review. Hard upon the last couple two overalled workmen rolled up the red carpet, the band played a few bars of a minuet and swung into a Strauss waltz. The marching lines melted, the whole floor began to move, to dip, to swirl a little awkwardly, satin skirts flying. Through two-step, ragtime, and jazz the band leader moved into last week's hit tune, while in a telephone booth one of Colmar Welles's friends was calling the number of a pretty Polish girl, set up in an apartment several years ago. When the young woman didn't answer, nobody, not even Colmar's wife, thought much of it. He might have been more considerate this public night, of course, but Cassie Welles was of an old Vermont family by way of Kansas wheat, and not to be humiliated by any midwestern upstarts like the Welleses. Besides, she was just home from California, with a handsome young man beside her. So, without even much snickering below the balconies, the coronation ball went on.

Then a youth came slipping through the dancers to whisper to one of the men from the Franklin National Bank. He was hushed, but not soon enough. Those near were already scattering, passing on some word as they bent this way and that, like the treetops of a grove in a gathering storm. From the balcony Hamm Rufe saw this thing in the crowd, saw it spread like the smell of fire and burning hair through a corral of Arizona cattle, or the first bad word that the national guards were coming through a town of striking miners. But among the miners there had been a rallying, swift and desperate; even the corralled cattle had pawed their earth in defiance. Here there was only confusion.

By now the balcony spectators were pushing forward in a

leaning wall over the velvet valances, looking to the people below for an explanation, to the funnels of the public address system that hung grey and silent overhead. Others pushed towards the ramps to the main floor. At one of them a youth from below was whispering to the usher.

"What? What is it?" the crowd demanded, talking low, in foreboding.

"The emperor's been killed," somebody near the boys said over his shoulder.

"Killed!" a woman cried.

"Killed? Hell, no," a man answered her. "There the potgut is, still sittin' down there on the throne, his belly busting out before him."

No, no, a dozen corrected now. It wasn't the emperor, but a duke, a duke from Franklin. And he hadn't been killed, or at least there wasn't any blood, but he was dead all right, down in the men's washroom, feet sticking out from under the door of the can.

A duke from Franklin? Colmar Welles!

Cobby Welles — the news was relayed in a racing whisper all along the cement balconies. Cobby Welles found laying flat, dead, in satin britches, in a can. So? By God, that was funny, damn funny.

"What killed him?" someone wondered.

"Heart attack!" was the ready, roaring answer. "That's what big bugs always dies of — heart attack."

Yeh. A big bug had died of heart attack, in the can.

But the respectable hush-hushed. One didn't speak of Mr. Welles like that, not the president of the Franklin National Bank and Trust Company.

Now the uneasiness was spreading through the balconies too. The bank must be broke, shutting down with all their savings inside. A man like that didn't kill himself for nothing. Before this thought the laughing was suddenly gone, the balconies silent as the floor below. And motionless, too, until a woman broke past an usher and ran screaming down a zigzagging ramp, to burst out among the court.

"Crooks! Thieves!" she cried to them as she pawed in her big old handbag. The two men who started to close in on her stopped, until they saw it was no gun she wanted but only a white handkerchief to choke a burst of shaking sobs.

As the woman was led away three policemen, with plain-clothes men, reporters, and hangers-on, came in a wedge across the floor. They asked a few questions, stood around as the chief and a following went downstairs.

And when the officers were gone once more, Cassie Welles slipped out by a side door, the attentive young man at her elbow. No one else moved until the flurried leader started his band, too loud, and softened it immediately. A few couples moved automatically together, in something like dancing, and stopped uncertainly as the music wavered, the sax blaring alone a moment and then dying too.

Down the center of the floor came the three grandmothers, all in velvet, walking abreast, unhurried. Between Josina Black and Hallie Rufer Hammond was Susan Welles, the mother of Cobby, her grey, curled head held high for all those who were capital city to her, and for those of the balconies too. Behind the three followed all the court, the emperor and his empress, new and uncertain about a procedure not covered by the *Manual of Coronation,* trailing quite a ways behind.

Back on his doorstep, in Herb's Addition, its shacks like browsing animals in the darkness about him, Hamm Rufe could no longer shut out his early years in the capital city. And as he looked back over the grey waters of his life he had to admit that the best friend of his childhood, the only friend of all his early life here in Franklin, was Colmar Welles. As boys they had been inseparable, even though Cobby was older by almost four years. Small for his age and sensitive, he seemed happier with the little Hammond boy across the street than with those older. They had the same music and French teachers, one giant electric train between them in the Welleses' basement, their books together in the Hammond sun parlor.

The two boys had planned great things together, great travel, great adventures. The first step was to get out, and that meant running away from home. On the sly they dragged planks and posts to a cave on the far side of Mud Lake, hammered together a raft, and hid out canned goods for weeks. With the first June rains, they pushed off down the Little Grand, still called Mud Creek then, but quite a stream for that one week in the year. Clear to the Big Grand River they were hardy adventurers, bold and fearless. They were still in Kanewa and besides they had an old tarp for a tent and a twenty-two rifle against robbers. But the rising flood waters of the Wakoon were rougher. They were stranded for hours against one drift pile after another, teetering against this island or that, while they worked like farm hands to push themselves free. They had lost most of their provisions and the gun long before the raft hit the boiling Missouri and sank away under them. Wet, cold, hungry, the boys crawled ashore. Cobby, suddenly all of his four years older, talked grown-up and brave while they dried off in the woods before a fire built from the matches he carried in a container made of two rifle cartridges. Rubbing his chin, somehow fuzzing strong the last few days, he did a lot of planning. It was pretty smart, his carrying matches safe from the water. He could manage everything else the same way. Towards night, when folks had had their suppers, they would scout the village for left-over food. Tomorrow they'd get jobs, work themselves down to the Gulf, ship on a cattle boat. They'd see the world, see China and the Indies, maybe even dig for gold in Africa or Australia.

It was, as Hamm Rufe had to remember now, he who

sneaked away to send a telegram, collect, to his mother. He had never forgotten the cold anger in Cobby's light, black-pupiled eyes when a man pushed through the bushes to their hideout. It was cold anger and something more, something he saw once since, in the face of a young striker down on his back in the street, with the boot heel of a hired thug stamping his crotch.

"You sold me out, you Goddamn little bastard!" Cobby had cried, pulling his thin lips back from his wide teeth, boy teeth in a face that was no longer a boy's.

While Cobby Welles seemed content to stay at home after that, finish high school, go to college, and then to war from that large, friendly house across the street, he never spoke directly to his childhood friend again.

And tonight Cobby had died. A little bald-headed man in satin knee britches had died alone in a men's toilet, his feet sticking out from under the swinging door.

CHAPTER II

AT last the coronation night was done, and the slow morning on its way. Gradually the noise died from the highways and the wind over the dry cornfields quieted into the grey silence of dawn, the shallow dawn of the flatlands, with bright day striking swift as an arrow through every east window. Even the cows chewing quietly in the gullies swallowed their cuds half-finished and stood up to eat, for the sun was suddenly in their eyes.

A layering of smoke and mist hung over the city and the Little Grand and only the capitol tower rose through it, into the pale, clear sky that promised an uneventful day. A flock of pigeons swept up into the sun, circled the tower, and flew off towards the outlying fields. The west-bound mainliner passed high over the city, not stopping at the old dirt runways of the condemned airport, the drone of its engines faint on the still air. Somewhere out at the fairgrounds a calf bawled and smoke trailed blue from the pipes of the farmers loafing about the camping grounds, with nothing going on for hours, but up at dawn anyway, for the habits of a lifetime are not to be altered in a day.

The town itself wasn't asleep late this morning, not even after a night of anger, denunciation, and blame along Blue Ridge, of gossip and suspicion down in the city, of rumor that spread far out into the state. Old-timers who had seen it happen before were sure the Franklin National Bank was broke, busted, would never open again. To them the radio announcement of the death of Colmar Welles was like the smell of hail to a bunch of horses, plow horses. Before the *World's* extra hit the street somebody was telling of seeing Cobby put the Polish girl on the train yesterday, her hair doll yellow, her stockings thin as nothing, and carrying a leopard-skin jacket that talked money out loud. Of course leopard wasn't the new platinum fox for cost but other things went with the kept-woman business. Yes, Cobby Welles was probably in deep enough.

By midnight men came slipping through the dark to stand across from the solid stone of Cobby's bank, more and more of them, silent shadows clustering against an empty wall. Out on the breaks a farmer or two sneaked his car away to drive through the gloom of the avenue that had been day bright under its grille of lights just a few hours before. Perhaps he circled the bank block, or parked out in front a while, for inside there was the wheat money to go on the mortgage coming due this fall. Perhaps he was remembering that his wife or the boys had wanted to put it into postal savings. Tonight they'd all be feeling mighty good if Washington had their money.

When 'Gust, the old hunchback, came by with the final *Morning World,* they grabbed the paper from him, read it under the pale street light, holding it high for those in back to see. There was a black streamer: PROMINENT BANKER FOUND DEAD, a picture of Colmar in his duke's outfit, and the announcement of an autopsy to be performed. That meant cutting up — old Cobby was going to be cut up just like anybody. He was found with a vial in his hand, the paper said, talking like it might be a blind planted by somebody who wanted it to look like suicide.

But the hints of murder didn't take here, just across the street from the cold, dark doors of Cobby's bank, not with these watchers who knew that the officers had worked all night behind the drawn plush drapes, slipping out the back way just before dawn. . . .

Now it was Saturday, and two hours before opening time a few people gathered to wait in the marble corridors outside of the Franklin National Bank. They grew into a line that lengthened past the elevators and the stairs. Workers headed for the offices above stopped to look back uneasily upon the silent, waiting queue. Old Sarah came hobbling from behind her newsstand. "Move on, move on. Shutting off trade — " she fussed, but no one argued, no one moved, and so she went back to thumb her Hollywood magazines, one droop-lidded eye on the clock, waiting too.

By the time the staffed flags were put up at the curb for fair week, the line had reached the outside, turned the corner and stretched across the alley, silent, motionless except at the growing end, like some grey tendril reaching out. Here and there a squash-heeled Polish woman cried quietly into her headcloth, clutching at the American son or daughter standing away and pretending no acquaintance with this old countrywoman. Half a dozen widows from the Frontier Hotel clung together, their damp handkerchiefs balled tight in their palms, their whole existence in the little trust funds behind those blinded doors.

Towards opening time the fair-week traffic past the bank thickened, even some of the drivers of the newer cars coming to slip into the line, making talk of usual bank errands, papers to notarize, statements forgotten. When one of them mentioned the deposit law, guaranteeing five thousand dollars, he was answered with a loud laughing from his kind. Occasionally newcomers tried to cover their uneasiness with joking. Where were all the big bugs today, them that's usually hanging around the bank like crows in a sweetcorn patch? They must a got theirs. Yeh, got theirs and gone, leaving nothing but the cobs, ready for the box in the old backhouse.

But there was no laughing from this line of patient, silent people, small in their shabbiness, their eyes sneaking to the clock over the door, and down again, not noticing jokes, or the Grandapolis photographer setting up his camera, or even the sparrows picking boldly about their unmoving feet.

Across the street the Coot leaned against the old American Bank building that was empty and done as the cronies beside him, empty and done since right in the middle of the Coolidge prosperity. Yeh, they reminded each other, once it was them waiting in line to get the full load straight in the belly. With no J. P. Morgan to do the covering up here, crooks like that Blockert, who broke the American, beat fellows like Whitney to the pen, and beat them out too, him already riding around with a chauffeur and a blonde floogie, and the saps he'd trimmed standing along the street yelling, "Fine day, Mr. Blockert!" He'd stole his bank dry and didn't kill himself. That Cobby Welles must have got in pretty damn deep.

"Deep as hell. Them brass doors'll never open," the Coot said, spitting over his beard, and then humming again, something that sounded like Oh, Who Will Shoe Your Pretty Little Foot —

At last there was a quickening to the farthest end of the line, although not a one had moved. Inside, the bank shades flew up, the lock clicked, and the doors gave before the push of the crowd that spread in stumbling anxiety towards the teller windows. Behind the grilles stacks of banded money and naked silver waited, were handed out with no reluctance and only a word of caution as shaking old hands grabbed what had seemed gone forever.

"Now don't you go dropping all this money somewhere — " the tellers warned, making a private joke of it for each one. But there were signs of the long night and its morning on the faces of the men, and the smiles stopped well below their eyes.

Inside of fifteen minutes old Junk-yard John, iron collector, had lost his little roll, ninety-six dollars — all he had between him and the county farm, far out from his friends and even a man's eating tobacco taken away. With tears slipping through the grey bristles of his cheeks he told it all to the policeman at the door. He had forgotten the hole that got in his pocket, like they do when a man had no woman to look after him.

Others began to wonder about their money, now they had it safe in their hands, most of them just standing, looking at it. Gradually new lines formed at the receiving windows, little ones, but steadily lengthening back.

"A bank what's got money like that to hand out is O. K. by me," a big overalled man roared out as he planked down a handful of bills and fondled his bristled chin. He started an uncertain little laughing that spread over all the dark lobby, growing strong and hearty as at a very good joke. Soon the bank was almost empty and the uniformed house police had nothing to do but straighten blotters and pick up crumpled papers. The officers settled back behind the name signs at their desks, smiling to each other, but more than one hand shook on the match held to a cigar.

Hamm Rufe, part-time bookkeeper and publicity man for the Franklin Consumers' Co-operative, was busy all Saturday morning at the booth on the fairgrounds. It took several cartons of coffee from the First Christian dining hall to hold off the sleep in him and help him remember about the scarred side of his face. The grounds filled up early. There were many women with curled heads and new fall hats, only the sunburnt faces of the children at their heels suggesting that they might be from the farm. Girls strolled by in twos or more, together or with their arms about each other. Loose through the grounds ran groups of downy striplings, covering their uncertainty with bluff, horseplay, and loud talking, hoping to slip off to the midway to gawk and snicker at the pictures of the freaks and what they considered naked women on the tent marked "For Men Only."

There were farmers too, some with thirty, forty years at

the plow behind them, sunburnt, walking heavily, heads down and eyes on the ground, in the habit of men with their earth. They talked soil rehabilitation and crop control among themselves as they moved from the tractor displays to damming listers and pump irrigators, and on to the booths of sorghums, Jerusalem artichokes, and hybrid corn, their feet eventually carrying them to the cool shade of the hog barns. There was a sifting of townspeople among the visitors, too, complaining of the crowd, as though it weren't real money in their pockets, and of the heat and the dust. Usually they were with outstate relatives, or customers, the Franklinites genteelly condescending or openly amused at the hick holiday, as a gay and nimble flea might observe the clumsy gambolings of a sheep dog at the end of a heavy day.

At noon Sid Harper, the manager of the Co-op, came out and Hamm went into town to take over the filling station. After work he didn't go directly home. The Coot would be hurrying over, and probably Old Connie, too, before she started away to the mops and the floors of the Franklin National, stopping in to tell a rambling story of the bank officers pawing through Cobby's stuff all last night. Then, finally there would be young Burt Parr, back from a ride with Mollie in her yellow roadster. He seldom did that; riding around on a woman's money, he called it. But when the girl stopped for him at the station just before quitting time today he left a whole line of customers waiting, stepped casually over the air hose in the driveway and leaned his crossed arms on the car door.

"You sure looked beautiful last night — "

So Hamm hung up the hose and finished the sales. At six o'clock he cut across the Polish bottoms to old Mud Lake where he had the secret cave with Cobby. Here they hid their stuff, their raft and the provisions, more than thirty years ago. But the old lake had been drained to a grey alkali bed in the middle twenties, even staked off into lots once, although the grass never came, nor the purchasers. The city, too, without yesterday's skywriters, car-laned pavements, and special coronation runs of the streamliners, had changed. Not the dumps in the bottoms or the railroad tracks and the shrinking warehouse district but beyond that — the grey back of the university stadium, the higher huddle of the business section, and the capitol with its fine tower. And yet Cobby had found it no more endurable than the day they pushed their raft off into the spring flood. Not even with a pretty Polish girl with hair yellow as a doll's had he found it endurable.

On the way back to town Hamm stopped in at Horsemeat's for a glass of beer. The smoke-darkened place was almost empty, the old Horse free to limp over for a regular word with a friend. Usually it was of the winter campaign with Crook up in the Tongue River country of Wyoming, the Indians burning the prairie, the soldiers starved to eating their gaunted horses. But tonight he was off on Cobby Welles.

Funny, wasn't it, Old Horsemeat commented, wiping the foam from his mustache, how them big fellows was never satisfied. But it looked like Cobby'd had something else planned, with that girl from the bottoms taking the train for Kansas City yesterday, and fifty thousand dollars in negotiable paper missing. Looked like it was all his, too, and what he drew out in bills. Fifty-two thousand, and not a word about it in the papers. Disturbing to public confidence.

When the place began to fill, Hamm called Abigail Allerton, the town's new author, whose first book, *Anteroom for Kingmakers,* was to be published soon. Would she leave her work and go to the Palace with him? Greenspan, the old fuzzle-brain, had brought in a French picture for fair week, *Carnival in Flanders,* and was probably laughing himself out of his biggest week of business.

When Hamm said he was at loose ends after the town's big spree, Abigail went, as she was, in a short Indian print dress, with socks and huarachos that looked childish with her lining face, her mousy hair boxed off straight below her ears. But her eyes were quick and brown and the *Carnival* was fun, particularly for this week in the capital city, and preceded by a carefully cut news short of last night's parade and coronation.

Afterward they had beer and sausage on rye bread at Abigail's apartment with a couple of other loose-enders, Lon Rickert, the young cowboy artist, and a woman who used to gather Indian legends for the federal writers project — just happened to drift in at the unlocked door to listen to the symphony and look through Abigail's books.

It was past midnight when Hamm left, and no one had brought up Cobby Welles or the bank at all. Mostly they talked of the perennial threat of starvation to the little magazines, the need for a middle-west publishing house, and of the coming exhibit by a young Mexican track worker down near Grandapolis. Abigail had seen a canvas or two. Strong stuff that would knock some back teeth loose among the conservatives.

At the Sunday matinee of the horse show there was a subdued air about the Franklin section of the grandstand. Helen Groves, the empress, and her emperor were there, of course, but even the next box was empty, the purple bow of mourning blowing in the afternoon sun. While not even the little rodeo to follow the show could make the farmers sit through it, the stands were pretty well filled with Franklinites, who always flocked to see the Blue Ridgers and particularly after Friday night.

Hamm Rufe hated the horse-show business from way back when he had to drive a pony cart in the children's parade. Later, in Colorado, he learned to live with horses, and to despise the show stuff as a dog man despises poodle circuses. But Burt Parr, looking very fine in a new suit warm-toned as new-ground cinnamon, his hair shiny and honest as a ripe rye field in the wind, came by the booth to coax Hamm out. Mollie was riding.

She really was a fine sight, slim and straight, her dark hair brushed back under her riding hat, her skin pale with earnestness, a lovely girl on a high-headed, white-stockinged black. The next morning the paper carried a good picture of her, mostly because the important young women were related to Cobby Welles and not riding. There was also a long complaint by a Mrs. Lessing of the W.C.T.U. against the growing godlessness of the capital city and the state. Once the Sabbath meetings at the fair drew as high as two thousand worshipers. Yesterday fifty-nine came to the pavilion.

"Our young people are entering the portals of hell with a cigarette in one hand, a bottle in the other, and contraceptive devices in their pockets," she said. But her story was pulled from the nine o'clock edition. Confidence in the capital city must be maintained, the women who called for an explanation were told. Nobody mentioned the complaints from the junior chamber, or from the liquor and cigarette dealers. The story of the search for a certain young woman of Polish extraction in the Welles case was also withdrawn, and the night-desk man who let it get by was put back on the police run.

While the coronation ball was socially the high point of fair week, the little man's holiday was still Labor Day. With the capitol offices and all business except retail shut down he was free to click the turnstiles, fill the grandstand, bet his few dollars on the races, help keep the fair going. By eight o'clock the streets were crowded, quite a few pennies, even some nickels and dimes, lay among the decoy quarters in the beggar baskets. At the capitol the guides were cutting the waiting crowd into manageable groups to trail down the corridors and through the high rotunda, to be told the number of colored tile in the portrayal of man's rise from savagery and the cost per square yard, the months required to make the tapestry of The Judgment of Solomon in the supreme-court room, the height of the tower, and that the globed dome was the size of a twelve-room house, with one hundred and fifty-nine individual figures in the sculptured frieze of the Peoples of the World — the guides reeling it all off like phonograph records, leaving little time for looking.

Long before ten o'clock the steps of the Labor Temple were darkening with representatives of the local unions, the printers, railroaders, and striking truckers, the plain work-ingmen and the WPAers, with a few farmers and a sprin-kling of women. Exactly on the hour they started up the middle of Philadelphia Avenue, their cowhide shoes awkward on the streetcar tracks. There were no motorcycles and no uniformed road patrolmen to escort this parade, no long cars or bands — only uneven ranks of sun-browned workers marching four and five abreast behind an overalled flag-bearer, broad as a sandstone boulder and as unnoticing of the street-car's dingle and the traffic's honk.

Before they were barely started a photographer appeared and a red-faced contractor whipped out his little book and began to put down the names of his PWA workers in the passing parade. Here and there a man saw the face of his boss and slipped away into the crowd, to hide himself in a beer tavern over a glass. Sure, sure, this was a free country, but a married man with kids to feed — what in hell could he do?

Steadily the parade moved on, in silent, orderly files: the national flag and three blocks of the capital city's overalled workers, their shoulders back, their brown, calloused hands swinging free. Only the strike-gaunted truckers carried plac-ards. Crudely lettered on flattened pasteboard boxing, they tried to state their case: —

ANTI-PICKETING LAW IS POISON TO LABOR
MILLIONS FOR THUGS, NOTHING FOR TRUCKERS,
SAY BOSSES
KANEWA: BLACK SPOT IN TWELVE STATE REGION
PAY LABORER SO HE CAN BUY FROM FARMER

Here and there a renter raised an injudicious voice in approval as the last placard passed and then, dropping his head, escaped too, as insecure as the least of these workers marching by.

Hamm Rufe moved through the thickening crowd, keeping abreast of the parade, feeling more alive than he had since the day he lost Stephani. Today she should be out there with the marchers, her stride equal to the longest, the most defiant, the fire in her burning as none here seemed to burn, not even that of the strike representatives from Grandapolis.

As the parade reached the deeper business section Hamm and the lone photographer caught sight of something that was new to these men of Kanewa — waiting cars of police and armed deputies. With roaring engines they cut in from the alley ahead of the parade, men with clubs and guns jumping from the running boards upon the surprised, paralyzed marchers, who tried to shield their women, to fall back and keep out of trouble. But those from behind were hurrying up, the yelling crowd along the curbs pushing in to see, and the paraders were trapped, the clubs of the police chopping like axes, crunching flesh and bone, the deputies jeering, swearing, their guns ready in their hands. The big flag-bearer went down, a woman too, her voice rising to a high shriek, and as a dozen times before in his life, Hamm Rufe wanted to run, to put his arm over his scarred face and run.

Suddenly a big man came plowing through the crowd. His bushy hair, the brown of weathered wrapping paper, towered high over all the rest, his eyes dark and piercing under thick, sun-bleached brows. Pulling people aside as though parting bushes in his way, he halted between the guns of the advancing deputies and the penned-in marchers. Defiantly he threw his overall jumper down before the officers.

"Come on!" he motioned to the men and women behind him as he spit upon a hand. "Come on! This is a legal Labor Day parade and, by God, we're going to parade!"

No deputy, not a policeman, moved as the full roar of his words carried up and down the avenue. Behind the man the workers rallied. Wiping the blood from his eyes the big trucker picked up his flag and fell in beside this new leader. The officers parted, let them pass. A cheer that started back somewhere among the marchers was taken up by the crowd. Onlookers from the curb pushed in to follow this man who knew a citizen's rights and could see he got them.

While the deputies and the police hesitated someone shouted: "It's Halzer! The Bellowing Bull of Bashan!" And before the sergeant could make a decision his car was rolled out of the way, the marchers passing, the tramp of their feet regular as though there had been no stop at all.

The parade lengthened out block after block up Philadelphia Avenue to the capitol, where young Halzer had served one term in the legislature, working for the emergency farm mortgage moratorium, otherwise silent, black angry with the jockeying, the horsetrading, and the petty sellouts. But when he saw the conniving of these representatives of the people to hamstring their one hope for irrigation, to keep water from their drouth-bleached fields, and eventually to make millions for the industrialists from the swift-running streams, he pulled his furrow-wise feet from under the desk, stood up and lifted his voice to the walnut beams of the chamber, lifted it to be heard all over the state of Kanewa. That day he was named the Bellowing Bull of Bashan, but for one session the irrigation projects were saved. Afterward he went home to his farm south of Franklin, put in his corn, and refused to run again, or to come to the despised capital city at all except at fair time with his prize Berkshires.

Now the Bull was back, leading a parade of workers past the police, up around the capitol and its statue of the brooding Franklin and down through town again. With their jumpers off and hooked to their shoulders they came, singing, and the crowd following on each side too.

At the temple Lew Lewis, the big trucker with the dried blood in his hair, pushed to the top of the steps, dragging both his flag and Halzer with him. Not so many years ago Lew was center in the varsity squad and he knew what to do with a man who had pulled a lost game out of the fire. Holding up a hand for attention, he swept it over the crowd below him, this way and that, like a cheerleader.

"He's za man!" he started. And when there was no collegiate response from the crowd of laborers, he tried it again, louder. This time they caught on.

"He's za man — "

"Who's za man?"

"He's Kanewa's Labor man — "

"Halzer, *Halzer*, HALZER!" the response strengthening as they learned the name of the young farmer, booming it out on the final cheer, filling all the windows of the chamber of commerce across the intersection with faces. By the time they went through it once more, with voice enough to rock a stadium, two policemen came pushing towards the steps. Some of the men moved to stand against them, but the officers' hands were free. It was just the two big boys up there they wanted, pointing to Halzer and Lew, disturbing the peace and parading without a permit.

"That's a lie, a Goddamn lie!" the tightening crowd shouted, but Carl shook his bushy head over them, his teeth white in his sunburnt face. "It'll be O. K.," he promised. So while they let the police take their leaders to jail, a dozen or so went trailing along, not making trouble, just going down to see.

Hamm Rufe went too, hoping to stumble on information about some of the deputies that looked like Gold Shirts. Besides, he had heard about Halzer's activities in the old farm foreclosure days; he wanted to talk to that kind of farmer, one who could rally a frightened crowd in the face of armed officers. Springing the Bellowing Bull would be easy. But Carl wasn't in a hurry about bail. While he had a colt and some fine hogs out at the fair that would need attention, he was staying until Lew came free with him. "And don't make it too easy," he suggested. "Let them stew in their own juices a little."

Hamm nodded. Yes, embarrass the officers, soften them up, as Stephani used to say. She would like this man.

Once more today, Franklinites were gathering, this time the better people for the funeral of their foremost son. The papers were very vague about the arrangements and the Welleshaven telephones silent, so the curious took their pick of places to wait, some at Trinity Church, others at Memorial cemetery, a scattering even daring to stand before the empty King place opposite Cobby's house, deserted since a man broke his neck jumping from Metzie King's second-story window. BURGLAR KILLED IN ESCAPE, the papers had said. Then it turned out that the dead man was the biggest landholder in Waydon County, with twenty-three new renters the year before. Later the King divorce trial gave the bridge circles a really good week. The burglar had left his pants behind in Metzie's bedroom.

Since then, potential purchasers of the place were carefully investigated, and so today there was no one to frown upon those who came to wait opposite Welleshaven, not even upon those who came very early.

Quietly, decently, the half a dozen families who owned

most of the city gathered in the long, stone-floored living room of Welleshaven, with its curtains drawn close and careful against the street and the white tower of the state capitol. On the far side the arched doorways were opened full to the cool air of the stone court, the moist sloping lawns, and the sunken gardens below, where a black swan barely rippled the water of the little lake and the two Dalmatians Cobby brought back from a bankers' convention walked sadly back and forth along the bank.

In the cool duskiness of the long room the mourners were quietly led to their places, giving small, formal nods to acquaintances with whom perhaps not an hour before they had discussed the usual rumors of blackmail and extortion. Little gold diggers like that Polak girl do get around a fellow like Cobby, the men told each other confidentially, let him in for a lot of trouble. Then there were the marihuana stories. Nothing to them, of course, but it was queer, the old Cob taking poison that way, with no money worries; most inconsiderate too, spoiling the city's one big business week.

It was all too horrible for poor dear Cassie, the women agreed among themselves. She was holding up bravely, very bravely, but beginning to show her age a little these last three days. She had done so well, too, until now, they thought, looking towards her under their lashes.

Beyond the hushed living room was a rounded sun-nook, filled today with the silver coffin and its banks of flowers. In an arched alcove off to the right was the immediate family: Cassie Welles first, her daughter Marylin beside her. The girl had been Franklin's first empress, back before her father took up publicly with Hattie Krasinski. The last few years she drifted the calendar around from sea resorts to Arizona to Sun Valley and back again. "Marylin has such poor health — " her mother always said, with a show of regret that she had to give up her only daughter so much of the time.

On the other side was the son, Harold, twenty-one, the product of a year at a military academy and a quarter or so at five different colleges. At last Cobby made up a little job for him around the bank and hired a secretary the boy could boss. After some trouble he was given a man stenographer, and even then there was talk of peculiar goings on. But the last few months Harold had kept out of trouble, ever since he got interested in the Gold Shirts, proof that they were really a fine thing, many Franklinites thought. They were doing for the young men what boy scouting did for the sprouts.

Behind Cassie and her children sat the real mourner, Susan Colmar Welles, Cobby's mother, one of the city's three grandmothers. She was tall, patrician, and so often taken for a D.A.R. that she was asked to introduce Mrs. Dilling when she came to town to denounce the university "with a Red behind every bush of bridalwreath." Way back towards the fifties Joe Colmar started the town's first livery barn with one saddle horse, favored the right people and got the contract for hauling the stone when the capital was moved from Grandapolis to Franklin. Saturdays his saloons took back much of the day's pay envelopes and later he added a little brewery that he won in a crap game. Handsome, with dark drake tails at his neck, he married the high-headed madam to the local carriage trade. She had picked up some bank stock, cultivated a low, calm voice and a fondness for painting daisies on teacups and pillow tops. When young Susan came along she was sent east to school. At eighteen her mother let the girl marry the romantic, sideburned, forty-year-old Colonel Welles who had hunted buffalo with a visiting English lord, knew Buffalo Bill, followed the races, and was helping the railroads protect their interests in the United States senate. When the Populist uprising put him out, he turned civic-spirited and arranged the country club purchase of Boulder Heights overlooking the scummy alkali ponds of Mud

Creek. After Clem Boulder skipped the country his father-in-law, Joe Colmar, managed the second purchase of the heights for Grand Vista, as it was old Joe who got Mud Creek ditched and called Little Grand River in all the chamber of commerce literature. When Susan's ailing babies were small and the Colonel showed little taste for family life, her mother, with the calm of her wide experience, advised patience, forbearance, and a little convenient blindness in both eyes. A racing man couldn't be bothered with apron strings any more than he could be expected to forgo feminine entertainment for himself and his friends out on the circuit. But there were those in Franklin who still said it was holding her head high in those years that gave Susan Welles her patrician carriage. And when the Colonel finally came to a wheel chair, with only Cobby of his children living, Susan took over the business and ran it, was still running it, although the Colonel was dead thirty years. Her middle-aged son had escaped her twice before he was twenty, on the raft down the river with Rufer Hammond, and to marry Cassie Chase. When Kanewa's Senator Hanson sided with radicals like Norris and LaFollette against foreign entanglements of American capital, several sons of the better people joined the Canadian forces as a protest. With Cobby it was one more chance at escape.

In less than a year he was back, discharged. So Susan set him up high in her bank and built Welleshaven, the first big house on the upper Ridge, for his wife and baby. Since then there had been several passing secretaries and finally the Polish girl from the bottoms. Now he lay there before them all in a silver, flower-banked coffin.

In the deep armchair at the head of the living room sat the second of the town's grandmothers, Josina Black, born Kugler, with heaped white hair, oxford glasses, and a good throat, even now, above her full bosom. Her fine long hands that lay quietly in her lap might have done well on a piano keyboard if she hadn't been too busy rustling beer for her father's customers at the old Station Hotel. When she objected to choosing the empress of Kanewa from the beauty contestants at the fair because the prettiest girls are often so common, old-timers like the Coot recaptured a whole hour of their rooster days remembering when Seeny was pretty as a red-wheeled buggy, carrying beer and sausage and German potato salad. She even tolled some of expensive Daisy Dee's admirers from her carpeted regions down to Kugler's bare wood tables. But when the D.A.R. rage hit the town, Josina Black was the first one to get her line clear.

At her mother's command she married Wilmuth Black, quiet, a little lame, but already in control of the town's two combination hardware, vehicle, implement, and coffin stores. He got the first automobile agency in Franklin, the Pierce, with a twelve- to fourteen-mile speed and no reverse, an unnecessary expense in the open country. "It's ahead you want to be going, isn't it?" was his clinching argument to a customer the day before he dropped dead on the sunny avenue. Josina was even harder to talk down, and under her management the business grew into the seven-story Black Motor company and its loan and investment subsidiaries that took over more than two thousand farms the last fifteen years. Four of Josina's sons took orders from her, even about the property their wives brought with them. One son got away, to the staff of an unimportant little conservatory in the East, and had his picture in the Capital City *World*, handsome in frock coat and striped trousers, with his dark Kugler hair still thick. He seldom came back to Franklin and when he did he went down to Old Horsemeat's for a glass of beer with the less desirable element, as his mother complained.

One of Josina's daughters married Denny MacFarn of the telephone company MacFarns, who had started as linemen. Desk sitters, now, and working with politicians instead of wires and poles, they were the same hard-lipped outfit. But it was only Elizabeth, the eldest of her girls, with a receding chin and clumsy hands, that the mother looked upon as a deliberate affront to her own comeliness. At least she would be getting the girl out of her house.

But Denny MacFarn wasn't as easy to manage as Josina's menfolks. The Blacks and all the rest of the town's best people needn't try to give him any snoot, he told his mother-in-law before a month was up. He knew what they had been doing all these years — selling out their city and their state to anybody with fifty cents in his pocket, from the old-time land speculators to those eastern utilities that the crowd up on Blue Ridge was playing with now, the dirty-assed fat cats.

But he hadn't married the homely Black girl just for the chance to tell the high-nosed lot what he thought of them. He expected backing and when he got nothing but tears from his wife and cold silence from Josina, he used the Mac-Farn connections and got a banking department job at the statehouse. Back in the middle twenties nobody except the depositors cared much about the assets of the failing outstate banks. But after Denny had managed the receiverships awhile a nosey, ambitious legislator from Stockholm got an investigation started. Then the little Benway bank where Denny kept the papers of the closed institutions was robbed, cleaned out.

Josina Black looked into the matter herself, made a few visits to an officer or two, and when Denny MacFarn was safely exonerated she ordered Elizabeth home. Since then the daughter worked in various community drives and helped keep the Women's Democratic Club right-thinking and lined up for the anti-labor, high-tariff senator, John Bullard.

But the bank scandal didn't die. There were rumors of plane charterings to Kansas City and Chicago to bargain with gangsters and racketeers for the unnegotiable paper but nobody saw much of the results. Finally the officers picked up a burly chap called Thumbs O'Roye, also Riley and Roy-man, with prison records in Missouri and Nebraska, and convicted him of the robbery, although there was no evidence that he had ever been inside of Kanewa's boundaries. Then it got around that he was in solitary at the penitentiary, and although the depression had been on five years, things were pretty good for some of the officials. The warden's family, never farther away than Grandapolis before, went to Europe to visit a cousin and the district attorney bought up several mortgages on rooming houses that were always being raided. There was no further trouble.

But Thumbs O'Roye was an old hand at stir technique; he got religion and began whittling dolls for the chaplain's little girl, so when the national prison survey was made he was the first to get out of the hole. And while the bank case was closed, Denny MacFarn away at Grandapolis, working for the power company, it was through Thumbs that the town's petty blackmailer finally got the bill collectors off her doorstep. Grayce Adams Smith was a syrup-mouthed, grey-haired little woman, with a quiet, soft tongue and a fondness for the more expensive powdery blues to match her eyes. For years she had depended mostly on the older, the less secure capitol jobholders, particularly those with political ambitions or jealous wives. Later she added a professor or two and branched into the ambulance-chasing lot. She could get almost any older man to talk big of himself and his work, feel like a wonderful fellow, and come to her apartment for a taste of her own sweet wine. It was only sugared dago red that she bought in gallon lots from a truck farmer down the Little Grand, but most of the men knew nothing about wine or were too busy talking about themselves to notice.

Generally she managed to get in a reticent little mention of worries, money worries. Just five or ten dollars that she just had to have to settle a bit of a bill until her check came in. Her dear husband's death took all but the annuity.

Soon the little mentionings were requests and then threats to take her story wherever the man felt least secure, to his wife, his employer, or the courts. Generally the men paid for their innocent glass or two, and then paid more, as long as they could.

A complete turnover at the capitol, several petty bankruptcies, and a suicide or two reduced the woman to making her clothes over. Then a detective magazine gave her an idea. She took to attending chapel at the penitentiary and soon she was "working with the boys" as she called it. A couple of weeks after she got to Thumbs O'Roye she was wearing a chinchilla coat that she called "my poor old 'possum — " as she stroked the thick, soft fur. She had her own little car too, and made regular trips to Benway and to Grandapolis where Denny MacFarn was climbing higher in power and light. She even tried Josina Black, but left fast enough when the high-nosed woman called the police. Seeny Kugler knew about people like the soft-spoken little woman from back in the old Station Hotel days.

The youngest of the capital city's grandmothers was Hallie Rufer Hammond, and the one most intimately tied up with its history. She wouldn't sit up in the front row with the other grandmothers at Blue Ridge funerals, like three molting old crows perched on a fence croaking their triumph. A tongue like her father's, the others agreed, implying that it hadn't been too becoming even in an old radical like George Rufer. Today Hallie sat far back, only one folding chair ahead of the Tyndales, Mollie's people, who got nothing better than the last row for their six-foot floral piece standing against the side wall.

George Rufer had trailed overland to Grandapolis, still called Lasseur, a frontier river supply station and a typical outgrowth of the old Astor fur and whiskey empire that was not to the liking of this Philadelphian with a little Quaker wife waiting at home. So he pushed on up Mud Creek to the old Harcoot stockade. Here, looking ahead to a world soon short of fertile lands, young George saw the grey alkali sinks as the proper place for a city — wagon-accessible to a rich farming region, with clay deposits for brick, possibly soda and potash too, and plenty of cheap land for growing. So he unloaded his wagon, stepped off a claim, drove his stakes into the hardpan with his axe, and called the place Franklin. He considered Paine, but remembered old Ben's words on property's place in society. Like other new communities, the early Franklinites were all young, but unlike the river towns, settled by hideouts, adventurers, and the jobless, here, around George Rufer, gathered a nest of political malcontents and troublemakers who had come west not only for a better living but for a better place to live.

By 1865 he had his wife and his library with him, had started a university, and established a free, fighting Republican paper that stood out against all organized graft, whether land speculators or the later railroads with their bribery and their monopolistic rates. Almost from the start he was damned by the leaders of both parties and gradually by some of those who had come with such idealism to the new Franklin.

He defended Higgins, the head of the university, when the man turned single-taxer; he backed the Populists and Bryan, and with his daughter Hallie, who had organized the Fabians at the university, led the uproarious, hopeful torchlight parades of ninety-six. In 1900, as much opposed as old George to McKinley imperialism, she marched again, this time with her two-year-old son, Rufer, tied safely to her back like a papoose. She had married Michael Hammond, son of old Dry-goods Mike, who started business with a shoulder pack among the early settlers and died owning the best store in Franklin. From the McKinley boom Michael put up a five-story build-ing, with full basement and electric lights throughout, and treated his wife's political radicalism with silence. So old George had to look to his grandson to carry on his work.

Young Rufer started well. By the time he was eight he was

distributing handbills demanding that Debs be permitted to speak at the auditorium. When his mother turned to Theodore Roosevelt, the boy ran away with Cobby Welles. But after his return he followed her into peace work, writing the speeches for the organization, getting out their publicity. As valedictorian of his class, the thin, lanky boy spoke with passion of a world gloriously done with war. The Capital City *World* quoted him like a visiting robber baron and called him the Boy Orator of Kanewa, the more progressive *Gazette* saw in him a continuation of the great liberal tradition of the middle west. By 1917 he was going with Eloise Colmar, niece of Josina Black. She was blonde and pretty enough and it was easier just to let her mother plan things for them. Rufer was still speaking for peace, despite his younger brother's tauntings and his father's threats. For a while his mother stood by this eldest son but finally she accepted a place on the county council of defense and so young Rufer slipped away to the railroad yards and caught a freight out into the night. Almost twenty years later he returned as Hamm Rufe, to report Kanewa's farm uprising and her food riots. He came back by night, shabby, travel-stained, his face so scarred that no one would have recognized him, not Eloise, married to a Johnson now, or even his mother, had he come to her door in the fine bright sun of day.

But long before this, old George Rufer was dead, died before he had to see his old paper and even his own daughter join in the witch hunt that drove some of the finest professors from the university. But he left one mark on the town that seemed fairly permanent.

During the liquor fights of the early 1900's there was agitation to name the capital city after someone besides a drunken sot, as the dry element called Franklin. Old George, sick and shaky on his feet, went down to see his lawyer to set up an endowment for the cramped capitol grounds: fifty thousand dollars for "Expansion of the capitol site in the city of Franklin" and a thousand dollars annually for its upkeep, provided that a large statue he would order were erected and maintained in a position "permanently available to the public." The papers praised the gift, the legislature approved a twelve-inch model of Franklin seated on a stone bench, with long locks and knee britches, the plaque behind him to contain a quotation from the great man's writings. An extra two blocks was added to the grounds, the surface graded up, the rest of the money put aside for when the new capitol was built. When the statue came, it lay neglected at the depot on a flatcar until a reporter noticed the inscription in letters almost a foot tall, cut deep and well into granite: —

> Private property . . . is a creature of society and is subject to the calls of that society whenever its necessities shall require it, even to its last farthing . . .
>
> BENJAMIN FRANKLIN

There were group protests from business men, and from the D.A.R.'s, with a violent denunciation by the minister of Trinity Church of the inscription as an incitement against man's inherent property rights. But there was a clause in the contract that invalidated the entire grant and compelled full restitution if any portion of the agreement was broken. Worse, the entire fund would go to Grandapolis for its parks system. So the statue was put up at the main entrance on the south side of the capitol and unveiled with drums and oratory and no mention of the quotation. When the new building was planned, it was faced west, with a blank wall and a group of Colorado blue spruce behind the Franklin statue, a wide span of unbroken lawn between the words and the main business avenue of the capital city.

The last few years Hallie Rufer Hammond sometimes walked around the base of the new capitol to the time-ripened bronze of Franklin. His heavy-lidded eyes were lowered to the book on his knee, and his face sad, but his feet were planted firm and apart. After a moment she would slip away, perhaps to a meeting of the old symphony board, trying to revive music in the city, the Art League, the committee for the Milk Fund, or the League of Women Voters. But she never took much part in political discussions any more. In her husband's grave ten years ago she buried much of the conservatism of her maturity as she buried the last of her early liberalism in the grave of her father. About all she had now was her son Cecil, manager of the ten-story Hammond's, still the finest store in the middle west. He was slight, with the thinning Hammond hair and an elongated version of the Rufer face. He interested himself mainly in interior decoration, trying out this and that in the model suite of rooms on the eighth floor. He had a fondness for delicate tracery, liked fine laces or pale etchings of sad, leaning timberline trees in Colorado. His formal garden had been photographed for the *Homestead*, a magazine started by claim clubbers in Kansas, but now an advertising medium for building materials and home furnishing, aimed at the potential owners of large town houses, particularly those who wanted Colonial homes without research or discomfort.

Hallie encouraged Cecil and his wife Penny in this home interest, as they liked to call it, while she put in a lot of time in paternal oversight of the store's personnel and in the quiet acquisition of business buildings and locations through foreclosures by the Kanewa Investment Company, enlarged since Penny Hammond brought it into the family. But the mother was much alone since Cecil, Cees, got married. Now even Cobby Welles, almost a son these last ten, twelve years, lay in the silver coffin in the sun nook.

With a deep, solemn roll of the famous Welleshaven organ, the services commenced. There were a couple of songs by the Trinity quartet, and a long eulogy by the sweating minister, who came prepared with two extra-large handkerchiefs. Not, that the air-conditioned house was warm but his position was a delicate one. He knew of the division of opinion among the people before him. Some held that there should be no mention of the banker's unfortunate ending; others considered this a prime opportunity to cry out that a fine strong man had been hounded to his death by Washington's witch-hunting campaign against business. So he gave a memorized talk, all rolling phrases and generalities, with a little earnest praise, and the services were done.

Slowly the funeral procession moved out of the house, past the dark mass of watchers across the street and away to fashionable Franklin Memorial Park laid out by a promoter in the middle 1920's. The association was in the hands of a receiver now, the handsome promoter turning his talents to further the government's housing program these last five years, and finding the people who once co-operated most eagerly set hard against him.

There were only a few words at the grave — and a decorous bit of handshaking here and there, more than there should have been, for a few candidates did somehow slip in, their faces extra-long in their expression of sorrow.

It all seemed strangely sterile, perhaps because the two people most saddened by the death of Cobby Welles were not there. Over in Herb's Addition Hamm Rufe lay on his cot, so quiet that none of his neighbors realized he was home at all. And down in Kansas City, alone with Cobby's bags ready on the stand, was yellow-haired little Hattie Krasinski, from the Polish bottoms up in Franklin, Kanewa. Across her slim knees lay an open paper that she kept flattening with her palms, her eyes too blurred to see. If only she hadn't let Cobby talk her into going on ahead. Always before, when he felt like doing something awful, he had come to her, put his head in her lap and cried, maybe until she could feel the wet clear through to her skin. Then she'd coax him to the couch, pour him half a cup of whiskey, fill it with boiling coffee, a little sugar, and a lump of butter floating. And when the man finally slept, she would cook for him, good solid old country dishes. By the time he awoke she would be singing gay bits of song or pulling softly at her little white concertina, her hair down in a long curl over her shoulder. And he would come to her, and with his hands on her shoulders kiss her, soft and gentle, on the lips.

"Hattie, little Hattie!" he would say, as he held his head against her breast, like he'd been gone far and long from home.

CHAPTER III

COMING back from Memorial Park the string of cars moved right along, perhaps because one of the Black nephews, J. B. Groves, of wholesale groceries and liquors, and badly in need of a drink, had somehow managed to cut into the lead. Not that the rest showed any inclination to lag, now that Cobby was buried. They were right on J. B.'s bumper all the way, the back ones hitting their horns pretty hard when the line was slowed by the flagman at the new WPA sewer. But they made up for it as they swung into a through street, particularly as they passed the huge Tyndale filling station, with four others just like it on the town's best spots.

The stations were brown-stained imitation hunting lodges, with white gas pumps and uniformed attendants, backed by half a block of open market, offering milk, cheese, eggs, meats, and fresh vegetables from the large Tyndale farms, with high stacks of fruits and watermelons brought in by the Tyndale night fleet of big red trucks. In the tire section were tools for the fall yard and garden, bicycles, assorted sporting goods, with fishing tackle and piles of shotgun shells for the hunting season, and a couple new motor scooters standing outside, with price tags blowing. The whitewashed parking space was always jammed, and today the cars stretched in long queues from the double battery of gas pumps. At the little station across the corner the owner had plenty of time to observe his competitor, to curse the pushing outfit from the Wakoon River.

"Damn the radish-selling, price-slashing sons a bitches!"

he said to his attendant as the Tyndales swept past. The gun-metal town car with its chauffeur in a silver-grey uniform wasn't up close to the chief mourners yet, but already ahead of some belonging to the older families. And within an hour they'd be running out the plum-colored convertible with tan leather upholstery, Mollie's canary-yellow roadster, or maybe the buff country car with disappearing brown top.

It was showing off like this that first convinced everybody, from the Welleses, the Hammonds, and the Blacks down to the little truck farmer and filling-station man they were squeezing out that the Tyndales would go the way of all exhibitionists. But somehow they made money; worse, they indecently advertised the fact by their big talk and by openly branching out, considered very bad policy just now, with everybody else riding his brakes all they would stand to help bring the country back to right thinking and prosperity. There wasn't any particular proof where the Tyndale outfit stood, with them signing the truckers' contract over in Kansas, effective right into Franklin itself. Well, by God, J. B. Groves was holding out, and the rest of the capital city, and those wanting to haul their stuff better hold out, too.

Seven, eight years ago, when Samuel Tyndale established his first two-pump gas station at the edge of Franklin, he was welcomed as new money coming into a town that had seen it going the other way a long, long time. But lately he was branching out fresh and lively as bindweed in a clover patch, and finally some of the Franklinites began to inquire a little. They discovered that Old Samuel, the grandfather, settled up on the Wakoon River in the early sixties, one of a colonization group from Sheffield, England. He was square-faced, with a bleak, close-shaven jaw that sat hard and ruddy as a quartzite boulder in a ruff of reddish beard. His wife, small, slender, with pointed chin and dark, curly hair at her temples, was said to be some sort of cousin to a Lord Beacon-somebody. And while the old-timers along the river never

were much for the hard-drinking, wild-shooting English no-
bility that came over for outings in the early days, they saw
that the Sheffield colony was different. The newcomers brought
their families, threw up log or sod houses like the rest, followed the breaker bottoms through the tough spring prairie
and made good neighbors, especially when sickness or calamity came. Samuel Tyndale, an iron worker and handy with
tools, took over the new settlement's forge and saw and plane.
He was a good manager too, and soon he had blacksmith
shops, little implement stores, lumberyards and cream stations all up the Wakoon and was branching out towards Wild
Horse Plains and down the west fork of the Grand River.
Later he added grain elevators and turned blacksmith shops
into garages and filling stations.

It was said that Old Samuel doled out the pocket money of
his three sons until they were well in the thirties. He kept
them on the road, one running all the lumber yards, another
the implements and garages, the third the elevators. Wood or
iron or wheat was all one man could expect to learn, he said
when young Samuel asked for the Tyndale enterprises in one
community, arguing that a satchel was no fit place to live.
But the sons stayed right in competition with each other in
every community, so much on the road that only one got
married young, and he brought in a bank. It was a little one,
and not very solid, but Old Samuel took over the management and got it sound enough by the nineties so that it carried through.

The old man not only had a hard hand on the pocketbook.
By ninety-five he was foreclosing improvement and implement mortgages on hundreds of homesteads, and buying up
land on the side at sheriff sale at fifty and seventy-five dollars
a quarter section. As his holdings grew he put the pick of the
farmers back on the land, doubling their acreage, with the
tools to work it, without having to raise the interest, and
while they turned up gaunt as whippets in the fall, they made

money. When Hearst's war scare got into the papers he ordered five hundred copies and handed them out among his customers and tenants, leaning forward on his sagging old buggy seat, talking war profits from wheat and corn and hogs. Plant every acre possible.

But the end of the Spanish-American War brought a deep slump, with the banks closing, unemployed tramping the streets, wage cuts and strikes, followed by more bankruptcies, unemployment and violence. Now the old man's talk changed. He began to tell about the cutlery co-operative of his old home in Sheffield, England. And a good thing it was, he said, recalling his factory years, sixteen hours a day from the time he was ten, and even so it took the six of them at home eighteen years to save enough for the passage of one son to America. As he saw it now there were two things to be done in the modern world of machine and monopolistic controls. A man might hang onto his factories, his mines, his mills, take advantage of all his growing power to leech the masses, and thereby produce poverty, a shrinking market, and increasing unemployment until the hungry mob broke in his door. Or a man could give his employees a growing stake in his venture, increasing their purchasing power as his output increased.

"You're getting old, losing your taste for a good fight," his sons taunted.

Old Samuel blustered — looking out upon them from under the long white spear hairs over his rheumy eyes. But he held his tongue, just tightening up a little more on the pocketbook. In the meantime he put a doctor on his payroll to organize a scheme of inexpensive medical care for every employee and tenant, set up milk dispensaries and dental clinic hours. But despite the rising cost of living he gave no one, his sons least of all, a penny's increase in wages. "Teach you to use your ingenuity!" he snorted through the thin old mustaches that were supposed to cover his empty gums.

By the time the World War came along he was past ninety.

Six months before the Armistice he sold 30,000 acres of land at war prices, all but a show spot or two and his old homestead. Then he died. Within a year farm valuation dropped and never came back, and by 1933 the grandsons were foreclosing the same places, but more hurriedly than in the nineties, for a moratorium or even a revolution seemed on the way.

Then, after fifteen years of prodding by his ambitious wife, Samuel, the third, finally moved into the more cultured capital city. He knew there would be no money to interest a Tyndale loose in Franklin but what there was he would get. Besides, Mollie wasn't too content at Brillhaven. After growing up across the road from half a dozen Parr boys at Sheffield, a girls' school seemed dull. In Franklin she could try the university, and as Margaret, her mother, pointed out, she would be eligible as empress of Kanewa at the Fall Festival. So they came in, to the rise beyond Blue Ridge, and built a pseudo-Norman home with a nice row of slim-pillared arches, and floodlights to bathe the wide sweep of lawn into a bright and impressive emptiness. The building was large, purposely large enough to entertain all the visiting duchesses when Mollie became empress.

But now the Tyndales knew that time would never come. Even today, after Cobby's funeral, Margaret had to see the best people of Franklin wave her a casual hand and turn off to gather here and there along the Ridge for martinis and pink ladies. Not that they would miss anything, she and the preoccupied Samuel, just the same old cud chewed over.

Margaret was right. The talk started with the dead man and the damned government that hounded him to such an end — the regular public dish, put out in quantity, like veal loaf down to Ike's, "A full meal 25¢," although everybody knew that Cobby was in no financial difficulties, or his bank either, full to the sideboards with idle money, and his trust company taking over much of the residence section of the city since the mortgage moratorium was off. Then they moved on to the labor parade of the morning, strikers' march, as they called it. That came from encouraging the damned Reds and radicals, too. Mussolini would know how to handle such rabble, or Hitler. Yes, particularly Hitler, they told each other, speaking openly here among their own kind, with an excitement beyond that of the alcohol in their voices.

Even a strong governor willing to use the national guard would do the trick. Not old Jim Day, dying of cancer, his resignation in and to take effect the moment a new governor was elected. The Republican, Ryon, was a good party man but he had the militia out a lot back in thirty-two and -three, might be hard to elect, much harder than Dunn Powers, the old Republican who went renegade back in 1927, got up in congress and said the government was encouraging criminal speculation and heading the nation for a crash. Groves had the proof right in the *Congressional Record*. Besides, Powers had an unfortunate admiration for an old classmate named Arnold who wrote a scurrilous book about folk stories of the capitalists. This year he was letting the Democrats run him — and his father a banker, outstate, but still a banker.

Oh, that didn't always signify, Jake Black said. There were those who claimed Mother Bloor, the agitator, was a banker's daughter. Most of the Ridgers were sure she was a Russian and that her name was really something like Bloorotsky.

Glen Doover, of the Franklin Mills, and with some contact outside of the city, wondered if Ryon would make it. "You'd think he'd called in the Japs, the way some of the farmers act — "

"Well," J. B. Groves suggested, "there's always old Charley Stetbettor."

Yes, but he was so radical, so crude —

So were certain others, too — once.

By the time the electric shakers had mixed up a couple more rounds of cocktails the young folks of the Welleses, the

Hammonds, and the Blacks came trailing in from the Labor Day races, the parimutuels. They howled for drinks, griped over their losses, or explained their winning systems as they emptied their glasses and then escaped the old folks to change for the evening horse show. Frightfully stupid, of course, dusty and hot out there in riding britches, but it was for the family. Next week they'd be free again, most of them off to eastern schools, where they soon learned to mention nothing of the middle west, not their homes or anything else between the Alleghenies and California.

In the living rooms the voices came up higher as the dinner hour approached, the talk swirling back to the paraders, the dirty unAmerican strikers, each time with more heat. Here and there a woman who had disparaged the big, rough-looking truckers with the idler's fondness for personalities began to talk of the strong shoulders of Lewis and the rest, their arms like trees, particularly of the Bellowing Bull. At first their men laughed and tried a barnyard joke or two, a little uneasy under the cold eyes of the women. Finally they drifted away for a word in masculine privacy. Women shouldn't be allowed to drink, they told each other, or to see such things as the parade today. They ought to be protected, for they were never really civilized, always hankering for the brute male no matter what their cultural background, training, or intellect.

"Lusting for the Bull," fat J. B. Groves called it, his mouth red.

As always, Cees Hammond spoke up, out of his perpetual, bird-eyed alertness in defense of women. They weren't all primitive. Take his Penny, for instance. She was revolted, actually revolted, by even the faintest whiff of male perspiration. Why, after a round of digging in the garden he had to slip into the basement for a scrub so's not to offend her sensibilities. He'd finally decided on having a shower put in the garage, with closet space for clean garden clothes. No, Penny would have found the parade of laborers particularly revolting this hot day. Fortunately she wouldn't be back from the mountains for a week or so.

The others nodded, long familiar with the little-man vanities of serious-faced Cees Hammond.

The Samuel Tyndales spent the evening alone. They could have gone to the club for dinner, or had any of a hundred people in, the second-best of the town. Their business was accepted gladly enough by the biggest bank; they were asked to the very private funeral of its president; the chamber of commerce had made Mollie a duchess. But there it ended — no throne for outsiders, no getting together with the right families after a funeral.

Margaret Tyndale patted her swirl-shingled reddish hair as she sipped her benedictine. She wouldn't stay in Franklin under these circumstances, not with her Samuel able to buy and sell any two of the whole lot, and her Mollie prettier than all the rest together. That's where the trouble was, she thought as she considered her stemmed glass of green-gold liquor against the light. They weren't making the most of the girl, letting her go around with that country high-school beau of hers. Burt was a nice boy, and Samuel was fond of the Parrs from way back, but a girl married her husband's station and the Parrs were just German farmers, pauper German farmers.

It was true that Burt's great-grandfather, Jacob Pahr, was a German, a Bavarian liberal who fled the country in 1848. He came to Minnesota, took up free land, and married an American girl at the army post. During the 1870 period of Germany's aggression he went to court to change the spelling of his name to Parr, "for greater convenience and with no intention to defraud." He sent his sons to the frontier for homesteads as fast as they came of age, the youngest one to Sheffield, in the newly organized state of Kanewa. There Burt's father grew up in a family never as thrifty as their neighbors, German, Bohemian, or English; for the Parrs were given to long discussions on such things as America's foreign policy, or the modern implications of Athenian democracy over the breakfast coffee while the cows bawled and the weeds grew tall in the corn. And at night there was usually a little music, the mandolin, the guitar, the violin, and the old piano, whatever one wanted to play, and sometimes long readings from Heine or the great American, Whitman. Three generations of Parrs lived in the sprawling, grey old house on the Wakoon River and the standing pun on any loafer became: "He wasn't up to Parr." Old Samuel had a tart answer for that. No one outside of that family, no matter how smart or well-informed, was ever up to Parr.

Burt's people were little concerned with this type of community humor. They had their eyes sighted farther. They told each other, for instance, that the white flocks of sheep clouds overhead meant rain within forty-eight hours, and discussed the idea for its scientific or superstitious basis while the rain spoiled the down hay. They consulted the encyclopedia for information on remote places, like, say, New Zealand, as others looked through the mail-order catalogues for the going price of prunes. They suffered deeply over the inhumanities of the Spanish-American War and the Russo-Japanese struggle; they wept over the San Francisco earthquake. They discussed the cause and the effect of Populism, the place of Theodore Roosevelt in history, and saw the shadow of war over Europe like a hawk over a chicken yard as early as 1910. Yet, when it came, the Parrs were in no position to profit, for their land had shrunken to half a section, with much of that untillable pasture land. Even so William Parr, past forty-five, and his older brother, both able-bodied, might have hired out at wartime wages, but they were busy at home, mostly being dismayed by the methods and ends of the propagandists, sickened by the stupid destruction of livelihood and lives. One night the super-patriots splattered yellow paint over the old porch. Most of their neighborhood were a little disturbed by this but William said he was sorry the culprits carried the paint bucket away with them. An extra bucket comes in mighty handy around a place.

As the Parr boys grew up to it they went to the university, working their way, good students in philosophy and debate, but always miserably shabby, saving every bit of money they could for train fare back to the Wakoon for the holidays, back to the warmth of the Parr home, with its haphazard duskiness, its easy tolerance of every man's taste and idiosyncrasies. And when they finished school they came home to stay, perhaps clearing out the cockleburrs of the west end, or the ticklegrass along the bottom meadow, making a crop of a few hundred dollars somehow for a down payment on a near-by forty. One after another married plump-cheeked neighbor girls, to bloom into easy, happy maturity in that family.

Across the road from the Parrs were the orchards and the oak woods of the old Samuel Tyndale homestead. Here Mollie spent most of the summers of her childhood. There were no girls around near her age except old Ed Pearsons's nest of river rats, so she played with the tow-headed Parr boys, and did not think it strange that grown men read poetry aloud and bearding boys helped with the Saturday baking. She was a year behind Burt in high school, but caught up the winter his grandfather sent him to tend a co-operative filling station up in Minneapolis. Everybody said it was just like the Parrs, putting the boy out that way, getting just enough for his room and board, when he should be in school or settling to a paying job. Surprisingly, Samuel thought it was all right. So the two graduated the same year, and it mattered very little up on the Wakoon that Mollie was a Tyndale and Burt a Parr. They topped the class in scholarship and divided the valedictory between them.

That was three hard years ago, with Mollie east at school since, and better farmers than the Parrs going broke. Last fall, when the girl matriculated in Fine Arts at the capital city, Burt came down to work at the Franklin co-operative, and enrolled in the university too.

While Margaret Tyndale was laying her little plan, and most of the people along Blue Ridge were trying to talk and drink away their uneasiness at Cobby's death, Cassie Welles was all alone at Welleshaven. Of course the help was there, and the slim-hipped young man who insisted upon only one name, Dachel, to rhyme with Rachel, and called himself a surrealist poet. But she considered it alone, for the help was Cobby's, and Dachel she brought home from California herself. Neither Harold nor Marylin was with her, or even Cobby's mother. Things hadn't been good between Susan Welles and the wife of her son long before Dachel. When the mother got Cobby back from the runaway down the river with the Hammond boy, she kept him pretty well in sight, like a picketed goat, as he complained once, but he did nothing about it until the summer Susan had appendicitis. She sent him to Moosehead Rapids, up in Minnesota, a quiet place with nice people, while she was at Rochester. In the two weeks he managed to run away with sixteen-year-old Cassie Chase, the full-lipped daughter of a Kansas war wheat family. Cassie never forgave Susan Welles the annulment proceedings, even though they were dropped hot enough when the Chase family doctor pointed out that the marriage better stand. And when Cobby remained what he was, a woman's errand runner, a hired hand, Cassie blamed Susan, and later she blamed the baby Marylin that she had to stay married to him at all. From the beginning she did what she could to defy her husband's stodgy town. By the time the first prostitute in Franklin got around to it, Cassie had her hair bobbed short above her ears. She smoked everywhere when cigarettes were still illegal in public places even for men. When Cobby came back from the army Cassie plunged into Red Cross work. Somebody in the family had to win the war, she said. She hurried from bandage rolling to Liberty Bond platform to spy inquiry. She entertained the string of visiting speakers raising money for a dozen causes. The much-advertised Canadian veteran with two fingers gone stayed at Cobby's home an extra week and barely got out of town before the police were notified to pick him up. He was really an ex-convict, and lost his fingers in a safe blowing. When Harold, Cassie's son, was born just nine months later, Cobby moved down to the hotel for a while. Of course he came back to Welleshaven and the women it represented, but by then he had set his secretary up with an apartment and a grey squirrel coat. Two could play at Cassie's game.

It was almost twenty years from Cobby's gum-chewing secretary to Hattie Krasinski, the little Polish girl — from Cassie's fake war hero to Dachel, now so gracefully at ease on her lounge, with coffee and brandy at his elbow. He wasn't thinking of the woman before him, but of her daughter Marylin, so fine and long-thighed in her riding britches, her full lip rolled in contempt for what she called her mother's tame cats. It was pleasant here in Cassie's intimate little living room that overlooked the sunken garden, with the evening shadows lengthening, the little lake darkening, the Dalmatians and the swan gone, the dogs kenneled at the animal sanitarium, the swan flopping powerful wings of protest in his new home at Stoor's Park.

The day after the coronation Cassie sent her chauffeur to the university library for the files of the *American Architect*, had the maid dig up the back numbers of *Spur* and *Town and Country*. Tomorrow she had an appointment with

La Belle Rose, Charley Stetbettor's astrologer, to see if the stars were right for house remodeling and perhaps some other changes. Welleshaven was to be done over. It was really nothing but an old barn, just what was to be expected of Cobby, she told Dachel, forgetting that it was Susan who built the house, with the architect and the plans that Cassie herself selected. Her own people, the Chases from Vermont, by way of Ohio and Kansas, were really very sensitive, of fine fiber, she told Dachel over the coffee server. Then there were her mother's people from Vienna. Royal blood was royal blood, after all, even by the back stairs, and the Habsburg lip of the Austrian line the most royal badge of all.

Dachel had heard the story before. Pouring himself more brandy, he settled back to other things, to thoughts of the lacquer-haired girl who probably wouldn't consider him worth even a greeting when she came in. He knew she didn't think him much since the week Cassie brought him back with her from California. "Of course I don't suspect you, darling," she had said to her mother when Cassie accused her of it. "Not with that narcissist!" When Dachel showed a little too much interest in the daughter Cassie told him, and made him very despondent and sad that no one understood.

"It hurt him so — " the mother reported, to make her daughter feel brutal.

"Yes, he has been drooping around like a bitch that's slunk her pups," Marylin said, in her best Joe Colmar livery-barn manner that annoyed her mother so, especially since the time the girl told her: "After all, I come by Grandfather Colmar's ways honestly, or don't I — "

Alone with Dachel, Cassie, Cassandra now, because she fancied it pleased the poet, was tapping a cigarette against her thumb. Dachel lighted it gracefully and relaxed as she talked through the smoke. Against the high evening windows, curtained in pale salmon, Cassie looked young enough to be this side of forty, as she managed to suggest, by putting Marylin back to twenty-two. She was a well-restrained figure of a woman, a little over-soft about the throat perhaps, but pounded down well enough wherever there was a bone foundation.

With her hair a fixed bright brown of formal curls, set off by a new hostess gown of silver-blue velvet, Cassie talked out her ideas for a glorified Welleshaven. The balconies would become steel-grilled decks, the windows shutter-trimmed; the bricks, of the mellow tan called prairie gold, once the finest product of the clay caves where the Coot now lived, were to be painted buttermilk white. She would have the brick wall around the back painted too, and the stiff black iron grilling across the front, making it white and delicate as the shadow lace of her graduation dress.

Dachel nodded, his fine eyes moody upon the woman who was worth, according to a compromise between Dun's estimate and the local gossips, around a million, at least a million and a half with the six hundred thousand insurance that Cobby was said to have carried. Fortunately the will was not to be read for sixty days. Until then Marylin would probably stay around Franklin, and the lounge at Cassie's was comfortable even when the girl was out, though she seemed long in returning this bad day.

In Susan Welles's little upstairs reception room Marylin was having a Scotch and soda alone and planning no return to Welleshaven at all. Within easy call was her grandmother, with a glass of water and an extra sleeping tablet against the staring wakefulness of all the hours since her son was found dead, his feet sticking from under a swinging door at a coronation.

For those about Blue Ridge who could decently make a social appearance today there was the annual horse-show dinner at Grand Vista, with many who weren't riding coming in boots and britches anyway. As they gathered on the heights, the plane advertising the El Troc for dancing roared by overhead, across the bottoms the Silver City balloon dipped lightly over the Playground of the Middle West, and straight down Philadelphia Avenue the capitol tower stood dark against the last pink glow of evening.

Some of the better reservations for the dinner were canceled but because it was one of the big events of the year all the lesser people were there, those who maintain the solvency of a club. They talked of the disturbing day, called the marching laborers of the morning dirty Communists, and were pleased with the salt of bluster on their tongues. The Goddamn Reds ought to be deported, and that woman up there in Washington that's been protecting them all along ought to get the axe. The axe, that's what she had coming.

Yes, the capital city would show the country how to handle the trouble-making agitators. Throw them in jail; keep them there.

The guests away from the larger tables were almost as free with their talk of the afternoon's funeral. Some of them had gone to wait at the cemetery. Showing respect for a prominent fellow townsman, they called it, and all they got was cold looks, like they were trying to horn in on a wedding, or just scavengers waiting.

"I didn't see's he got any bigger hole than the rest of us'll have — "

"And certainly no better place to die — "

But the womenfolks and those who still had some hope of reaching the top of the Ridge hushed the loud talkers. Not that any of the relatives were there to hear, with all the reservations canceled but young Harold's. He had made none, for this was meeting night up at Stone House, with a special speaker from North Carolina stopping on his way to California and Washington state — another of those meetings never slated in the *World* no matter how short the news, although towards midnight everybody in town could see the car lights turn into the highway from Grandview Hill, the highest spot in fifty miles.

The old Stone House up there was built by Eli Jiles, who came to Franklin way back before the big prairie fire. He had smelled out the politicians' plan to get the capitol moved from Grandapolis and so he settled upon the highest hill overlooking the sprawling village along Mud Creek. On this logical place for the fashionable, the rich part of the coming city, he built a wide, turreted castle of native stone dragged in by bulls from the quarries over on the Wakoon River. But the broken slopes towards the town were bald clay banks, dun-colored and bare except for bits of old grass clinging to the edges like tufts of faded hair about the ears of a bilious old man. And through the lowest bottoms between the Jiles place and the town lay the string of stinking little ponds called Mud Creek, their grey, scummy surfaces stirred only by an occasional oarsman-bug or watersnake. Long after the drained creek was called Little Grand River and old Eli was dead, garbage was still dumped in the bottoms as it was against all the thundering words of the old man every time he pounded his buggy mare in from the Stone House to see the city commissioners.

For twenty years the Jiles heirs rented the place to a succession of starving farmers who liked the view and didn't understand the meaning of the pebbly soil spread palm-thin over the clay. Finally it just lay there, the weeds grey even in midsummer. After the war the Franklin Trust took the place over and dickered with the newly organized Wakoonian International for several years for a clubhouse site. When the market crashed and the optimistically named club retrenched, the old house was left to stand bleak-eyed and empty. Last spring the reports of lights up there became so common that a gang of boys finally went up for the hell of it. They came back with cut heads, black eyes, and fright-guarded tongues, and although one of the mothers rushed down to see Cobby Welles of the Franklin Trust about the goings on out on their property, the night lights went uninvestigated after that, particularly when it got around that some of the cars seen turning in carried numbers registered by the best families of the capital city. From the boys recognized and the tan uniform of the watchman, sometimes vaguely visible from the turnoff at night, it was decided that the ghosts of Stone House were Gold Shirts. But there was little open talk about them, with no telling who belonged.

Long before the guests at the horse-show dinner got through their roast capon, and while Margaret Tyndale was still laying her plans for Mollie, the two parade leaders were released on bail over the protests of a delegation bearing a petition of the town's important names. While no Welles was among them, for that would be sacrilege on this day, Josina Black and Hallie Rufer Hammond headed the list that charged Halzer and Lewis with incitement to violence and threatening life and property. Later, when Ellers, the climbing lawyer who had reached the slope of Blue Ridge, heard of the petition he urged its immediate withdrawal as a "too public interference" by the better people in the capital city courts, which left only the one circulated by the Gold Shirts among the business men against Communist agitators on file at the mayor's office.

But Hamm Rufe had both Lew and Halzer out before then. It was easy enough as soon as he convinced the authorities that they were really holding a former All-American center and the Bellowing Bull of Bashan. Football was big business to Franklin, and legislators, even former ones, could be damned privately but not publicly jailed, not in a town that got most of its existence from their appropriations.

Lew Lewis tried to take the others with him for a hamburger at his Nora's, but Carl was anxious about his stock, and so he and Hamm Rufe caught the rattly old fairground streetcar just outside the jail. The farmer picked an open window and with his hands on the sill looked out upon the familiar, dingy old section of Franklin as though it were one of his own fields against a bright morning of spring. After a couple of blocks he recalled where he was and flushed to red embarrassment under the brown of his skin.

"Ever been in jail — " he asked, driven to explain his unguarded face.

Hamm nodded. Yes, many times. And every time coming out was the same: the urgent need to see all of this freedom that so incredibly still existed outside the walls, the sun a shining patch over all the ground, the sky vast and open overhead, and no man to stand against you.

"It's bad to be locked up, even in a good cause — "

Yes, surely then.

As the car turned down Philadelphia Avenue at the Labor Temple the motorman was stopped by a red light. Someone from the curb spotted the farmer.

"Halzer!" he bawled out, pointing. In one rush the steps were bare and the mob was pounding at the folding door. The frightened motorman clanged his bell and jerked the old car into motion. Brakes on crosstown traffic squealed and rubber burned the pavement as the streetcar pulled forward with twenty yelling, laughing men clinging to it. Before it got any speed up, somebody knocked the trolley off and climbed over the window in upon the motorman. He jerked the handle and fled through the folded door as the overalled men crowded in and the frightened women passengers tried to slip away between them. When the truckers had Halzer out, they chased after the women, laughing and calling to them, rounding up some of the handier ones like a farm wife collecting a flock of hens panicked by the shadow of a hawk on the ground. Then they jerked the trolley back into place and motioned the motorman on. He jabbed the foot bell, missed once, found it and moved clanging away through the intersection.

"That'll make an ugly story in the papers — " Halzer warned them.

"Hell, whatta we care? If we didn't give them something they'd make it up — " the men said.

Although Hamm Rufe was not among those waiting outside of Welleshaven for a glimpse of the silver coffin or of the mourners, he put in a restless afternoon. The Labor Day races always drained the money crowd from the fairgrounds and so when he came back from his shack he wandered about the exhibits a little, looking in on Halzer's long-coupled Berkshires, and at the fine draft horses still grown on the upper reaches of the Grand. He passed the large round-roofed open pavilion used for high-school band compets between grandstand programs, and by political candidates at odd times. The time was pretty well divided between the two political parties, with the best period given to the Kanewa Taxpayers League, disturbing to some of those who wanted to believe that the organization represented the small property owner. The tag ends of time were given to the Townsendites and the independent candidates in the fall election.

Usually the audience at the pavilion was largely women tired out with dragging children past snow candy, pop, and Charlie McCarthy booths. Here, in the shade, they could sit a while, slip off their shoes and hope to get them back on later. Sometimes those in the back even catnapped a little to the drone of the voice on the far platform.

But no one was dozing when Hamm came by, for old Charley Stetbettor had taken the place over. His sound truck was drawn up alongside the stage and from the little platform on the back of it he was haranguing the crowd, mostly farmers and working people too hard up for even bleacher tickets to the horse races and the parimutuel betting beyond the walls of the grandstand.

Old Charley Stet's show was free, and through the loudspeakers of his truck everybody could hear his blaring voice as he worked his heavy face into excitement and flailed his short thick arms, until the shirt about his barrel chest popped its buttons.

Behind him, and elevated so everyone could see, was a board with a thick pad of five-foot paper clamped tight enough for any wind. And as Old Charley talked a lightning sketch artist cartooned the opponents denounced, signed the sheets, jerked them off, sailed them into the crowd. Always at the end the cartoonist finished with an American flag in color, waving in a fine, strong breeze. When he had saluted it stiffly and dramatically, Charley Stet rolled it, tied it with a bit of red ribbon, and passed it out to some pretty girl in the crowd. That always choked off any boos, brought cheers and laughs and handclaps for the flustered girl while the candidate wiped the back of his sweating bull neck and bowed to all American womanhood.

Hamm listened to Old Charley's harangue against the Communists, accented on the second syllable, and the morning's labor parade. "A Red rising on the streets of our own fair capital city!" He watched the faces of the people, listened to the applause, the comments as they scattered, and went away troubled. He was still troubled when he finally had Carl Halzer back in his tent on the fairgrounds. What did he know about the fellow with the sound truck?

There wasn't so much that was secret about him, Carl thought, except the actual names of his financers. Old Charley Stetbettor had drifted into Bordow up on the Wakoon River about thirty years ago. At first he plugged around at anything, mostly horse doctoring, carrying a madstone for snake bite, hydrophobia, or whatever came up. On the side he practiced hypnotism and healing by laying on of hands, particularly among the poorer farm women. In the twenties he went in for Klan activities, began to do a lot of public talking about God and American womanhood and got out an anti-Semitic, anti-Catholic smudge sheet. He scattered no-fund checks around and even sold a little oil stock. Never more than one jump or two ahead of the sheriff, somehow he managed to set up a radio station to advertise his cures and his prejudices, with an astrologer on the side to cast horoscopes at a dollar a shot until the government finally shut him down, four, five years ago.

By that time he was Dr. C. Thurston Stetbettor on his red, white, and blue letterheads and cards, no longer Old Charley or Charley Stet. He was bald down to the ears, his face as pink and smooth as his head, his neck thickening over the stocky body that was so short he liked his picture taken from below, like Mussolini. His voice got hoarser as he roared out vague and angry tirades against what he called unAmericanisms, including particularly the state medical regulations and the federal radio commission. From close, his protruding eyes were opaque and dull as a hoptoad's fresh out of a well. Old Charley claimed he ate only raw vegetables, nuts and fruits, drank no water or beer or coffee, not even milk, getting his liquids from huge platters of chopped-up watermelons, tomatoes, grapefruit, oranges, or whatever came to hand. He had a wife that he referred to as "the little woman," and kept out of sight, maybe because her flat voice and her chronic complaint of female weakness seemed a deliberate affront, and bad for business. Maybe there was something to the story that she had tried to poison paunchy, double-chinned La Belle Rose, the astrologer.

Charley Stet was born April tenth and La Belle got her job by telling him that he was destined to become a great ruler through his star-given power to sway the public mind. He was possessed of great organizing ability, too, she said, particularly of a social and political nature. When she said that his fifty-first year would be his lucky one, he tried to get the Republican nomination for governor and was defeated. So he was running as an independent candidate on a platform much like Winrod's over in Kansas some years ago. It was funny to some people. But others remembered that Old Charley changed, by plain push and flatfootedness, what he called the immoral French spelling of his home town, Bordeaux, to the hundred percent American version of Bordow. His secret financing, like Winrod's, wasn't funny. Whatever anybody else thought, Old Charley was so sure he would be governor he already looked through the governor's mansion for secret passages by which the Reds might attack.

"Boring from within, that's their game. But I'm ready for them!" he told the first reporter he caught. For a small sum the entire basement of the mansion could be made airtight, with a burglar alarm to set off poison gas.

"Choke 'em like rats in a trap!" he had roared hoarsely. "Like dirty rats in a trap!"

Who in Kanewa could be financing such a campaign? Hamm wondered.

Carl Halzer scratched a match on his shoe sole.

"Your guess would likely be the same as mine," he said.

Late that night there was a lot of low talking and stumbling around over tent ropes and trailer hitches in the camping ground out at the state fair, like a bunch of boys coming in from a helling around. But it kept up, and finally somebody asked out good and loud for the Halzer tent. Men crawled off their blankets about the grounds to see. Women's heads thick with metal curlers came peering out of trailers and tent flaps. It must be the police. They had no business letting a dangerous man like that loose out here among law-abiding folks without even good doors and locks to protect them.

But instead of the police it was Lew Lewis, looming huge in the pale wash of reflected light from the street. He had about a dozen men with him: a delegation of truckers from Grandapolis and a scattering of farmers from along the way. They found the Halzer tent, trooped in, making a wall of shadow about the lantern on the floor. Victor Heeley, a small, wiry chap with sharp, dark eyes, seemed to be the spokesman. He said they had the good word that was going the rounds of the state about the labor parade that morning. They had come to offer their congratulations in person to a man like Carl Halzer. It was the first public demonstration of a farm-labor solidarity in Kanewa, something that had to come soon, or it would be too late.

"Oh, I didn't do anything much, nothing except what any man who saw the paraders getting a raw deal would've done — " Halzer told them, his eyes still sleep-pupiled in the lantern light, his hair tawny and unruly as good fall pasture after a wind.

The men looked to each other, nodding over their hand-rolled cigarettes or their juicing tobacco. That's what they needed, a man with a trigger eye, and a trigger sense of justice. Yeh, and with the push and guts to do what was needed on the dot like that. They were here to ask him to run for the U. S. senate.

Why, that was a joke. He was no politician and even if he were, the primaries were past and his fall plowing was overdue. Besides he wouldn't even carry his own die-hard Republican county as a regular candidate. Every vote in Franklin would be against him, and all the moneyed interests in Grandapolis, too.

"Yeh," Heeley admitted, "the same ones that are always against the laboring man. And against every damn dirt-scratching farmer too. That's why we don't think you could do much in the statehouse, with our reactionary legislature selling themselves out without even knowing it. Washington

is the place for you. And I believe it should be in the senate
— get that son of a bitch of a Bullard out!"

Carl Halzer was silent, his head shaking hopelessly to
them. He was unknown, except unfavorably, and Bullard
could rally all the manufacturers' association influence and
money. But he could see that it was better to run for the
senate than for congress, or even his old seat in the legislature
with this district gone reactionary as a wig-wearing old
spinster.

"Say the word and we'll get you a petition the size of a
beer keg right here in your own district, right here in
Franklin — " the men about him urged.

A long time the farmer looked up at the lean jaws, the
grim mouths of these men who had been out on strike for over
four months, fighting the business men's combine, and their
gun-packing thugs, both the police and the hired press against
them. He looked into the sunburnt faces of the farmers who
had seen a lifetime of discriminatory rates and legislation,
capped by ten years of depression, drouth, hot winds, and
grasshoppers. Their eyes were narrow and unblinking in the
lantern light, narrow and unblinking from all the long
spring mornings they hopefully planted the earth into another sun.

"I'll try it — " he said.

CHAPTER IV

FIFTEEN minutes after the news of the death of Colmar Welles was on the air, people began to slip into the corridors of the Bon Tonne apartments and stand hopefully outside a closed and unmarked door. Even after it got around that Hattie Krasinski was gone, skipped out, they kept coming. At first the caretaker tried to send them away.

"No, ma'am, the apartment ain't open for no showing," he would say. "Miss Hattie ain't give us her thirty-day notice. She's a comin' back."

But he couldn't stand around at her door all day, not with twenty apartments to look after, and so slivers were split from the casing with nailfiles, the Franklin *Shopper* left at the delivery window was torn to bits for souvenirs, although there was not even Hattie's name on it, and the gas bill sold to a collector for a dollar.

Finally one woman got past the caretaker for a high-headed command and a bill folded in the palm. It was Della Loran, poor relation of Josina Black, who always thought she could have had Cobby if Susan Welles had kept her nose out of it. The mother caught the boy kissing her at a party and sent him away to the lakes the next week, where he ran into Cassie.

Della, nearing fifty, and very active in the town's censorship committees, pulled up her oxford glasses and looked carefully through Hattie's books and magazines: an old copy of Dale Carnegie, a stack of *Fortunes*, a copy of the *Banker's Digest*, and so on. Nothing sensational. Perhaps the Polish woman couldn't even read. Anyway, sin had been there. One could tell.

After considering the woman's money all afternoon, easier than finding it, the caretaker lined the crowd up at a dime a head and marched them like a chain gang through the apartment and out at the back stairs. They were mostly women and mostly from the capital city — the movie goers and the love-story-magazine readers. They were hustled through the living room, permitted a glimpse into the kitchenette, with a flour-dusted apron thrown over a hook; the bathroom, soon stripped of even the toothpaste and the blue toilet paper; the closet with its half a dozen plain dresses, and out the back. Some of them did manage to sit in a chair a second, and one woman got herself stretched voluptuously on the couch before the caretaker could stop her. "No layin' around like that in this house, lady," he told her coldly. But mostly the women and girls were awed and silent in this plain little place that so recently sheltered romance.

It wasn't much better down in the Polish bottoms, where little Hattie Krasinski had taken over the care of the younger children when she was five while her mother went out cleaning; where she grew from a serious-faced little immigrant child into a slim-legged, pretty American girl. Early the morning after the coronation cars started to creep slowly past the white-fenced little house. Some of the curious returned a second time and more, hoping for a look at a Krasinski. The mother saw them come from behind her front-room curtains and slipped away to the cellar to weep into her apron. But Marya, Hattie's eighteen-year-old sister, walked pertly down the front steps, smoothing her lipstick to the sunlight with her little finger, and tapped her black suede heels away to her office job, pretending not to see the cars slide along the curb beside her or loiter at the crossings, the men grinning hopeful teeth out upon her. And long before the girl was home in the evening the calls began, until her father tore the telephone from the wall.

"Whores they would make it of all mine girls!" he roared. But the next day he had to have the telephone repaired, for his poor business as a fixman depended upon it.

While nothing of all this got into the Franklin papers, the Grandapolis *Inquirer,* one of the Boller yellow sheets, spread the story all over its state fair edition. There was a picture of the apartment, with a woman who might be Hattie on the couch, back to the camera; a snapshot of the Krasinski family on the porch of their little white house in the bottoms and a laughing one of Hattie and Marya in bathing suits at Silver City pool. Under these was a trick photograph supposed to be Cobby as he was found in his duke's satin, his body slid forward on the floor, his head against the stool. A snapshot marked "Red Lake Lodge, March 1," showed him in hip waders holding three Canada geese by the neck. Game out of season. Fine example for a big banker to be setting the public, people would say. There was another one, captioned simply, "Waiting — " of the long line outside of the Franklin National with something so resigned about the people that it started many an old-timer talking and put a little line of customers to the savings window at the post office.

There were pictures of Welleshaven, too, in the *Inquirer,* of Cassie as queen two years ago, and Marylin as the first empress of Kanewa. Between these was an unpleasant snapshot of Cassie and Dachel sprawled on some beach, probably dug up by Boller's Los Angeles paper. Piles of the special edition were dumped on the Franklin news stands and peddled through the residence sections by youths crying in singsong: "Read all aboud it — Polish love pi-rut drives banker to soo-side! Read all aboud it — !"

The better people of Franklin were furious and threatened suit through their favorite young attorney, Harv Ellers, who was so useful about income-tax and other annoyances. The business men were rather divided on which was most damaging to the public confidence in the capital city, the *Inquirer's* sensational story of the banker suicide and his mistress or the page spread of the Labor Day parade in the Grandapolis *News*, pictures not quite explained by the story of Red violence, and vast subversive activities. But with ads from the Grandapolis Light and Power, the larger truck operatives, the packers, the automobile assembly plant, the two largest banks, and the usual blank page with only the small block letters GBMA, the business men's association, centered, — sixteen full pages all together, — the Franklin chamber of commerce knew it would be useless to protest. So the Capital City *World* followed the idea, got half a page ad each from the power company and the truck operatives and in a long editorial dismissed the parade troubles as an abortive attempt of radical agitators to lead Kanewa's labor astray, promising swift and drastic punishment in the best capital city manner.

Unfortunately, outstate visitors who would be voting for legislators in November, some who were also to send their sons and daughters to school, would be remembering what they saw of the parade, carry the papers home and talk the stories around the country. That Grandapolis photographer who took the parade fight with a movie camera, catching the police clubbing Lewis over the head, a deputy kicking a woman in the stomach, should be run out of town the next time he came in. The executives of several of the luncheon clubs met in extra session, passed resolutions, and sent them to the *News*. They didn't bother about the Cobby story; they had tried protesting to Boller's *Inquirer* before.

While all this adverse publicity on the suicide and on the labor troubles during Fall Festival week was unfortunate, it was out and done with now, and the Welles story made good reading for the town's weary mothers when they finally got their children started on a new school year. With the paper and an extra cup of coffee they could forget their uneventful lives and become for the length of a cigarette desirable and dangerous women. Perhaps the radio was right, and romance was in every woman, they told themselves, forgetting the spreading hips and fat stomachs below the dinette tables.

By Tuesday night the Grandapolis papers had dug up something more for Franklin's state fair week, sitdowners at relief headquarters, a man and wife with six small children. The father had his foot almost cut off by a homemade cornsled years back when he still owned a little farm. The doctors saved it, stiff and wooden as a hunk of oak, but the farm went for the hospital mortgage. He was a good hand with horses and machinery, and so he managed to get a little work summers, enough to get by with some relief in the coldest weather. Last spring he had to leave the county to get a job, just housing and keep, but at least they were eating. Then the June drouth came and he was out, and had lost his eligibility for aid here, or anywhere else.

"Relief depends upon residence — " the county director said.

"More than upon need?" the reporter had asked.

"Need, too, of course, but first of all upon consecutive residence."

With a picture of the anxious mother, her thin, bony little girls clinging about her, it made a fine story for the people of Grandapolis, made them forget that their own tuberculosis rate had trebled since 1929 and that food rioters in Grand County were thrown into jail without newspaper protest or even mention.

"They smear us every year, fair time," Parkins of the Franklin chamber said sourly. "Jealous that we got the coronation and Fall Festival from them — "

"And the fair, too, and way back to when we got their capitol — "

Wednesday the *Inquirer* ran a second story on Hattie Krasinski. The blonde love pirate, as they always called her, was allegedly found, but kept hidden by the authorities of Franklin for reasons best known to themselves. This sort of thing had happened at the capital city before. Thumbs O'Roye, for instance, had been kept in solitary at the prison for two years because it was feared he might spill a few things. There was Thumbs's picture, nose broken, scar lit up by prison photography, and under it: " — Still denies all connection with Benway bank robbery."

In one way the *Inquirer's* sensationalism was helping Franklin. Never before had their entry in the fair's annual beauty contest been a serious threat to the girls from the smaller towns. "Them capital city gals is horsefaced with this here culture" was one of the less bawdy explanations. But this year there was a cousin of Hattie Krasinski's in the contest.

The idea of a beauty contest at the state fair never had the approval of the better people of Franklin or of the stodgy old fair board, dominated by capital city thought. But for years the attendance had been falling. While both the Franklin papers carried daily streamers announcing the paid customers at 7000 or 8000 in two-inch letters, an agate table somewhere back about page four showed the slide downward from the high of 1927 — 25,000 in one day. Not even the coronation business, taken over from Grandapolis the year rival racketeer factions split the business men's association into temporary paralysis, could keep the attendance up, or make the fair pay. With the tickets ranging from $25 apiece to 50 cents in the back gallery, the gross receipts for the coronation were usually around $15,000, but somehow it always got away. Some said that certain prominent men of the town made more from the coronation and their percentage of the community chest than from their business. However, it was the consensus of opinion, as the Franklin chamber of commerce announced every year, that the coronation drew a better class of visitor, meaning better heeled, and was conducive to a high moral tone. To which the Grandapolis papers always replied, "High moral tone? Even the idea is a stolen one, like everything else in the lily-white city down in the Sinks of old Mud Creek." There was never any reply to this sort of thing from the capital city press, which was considered very well-bred and typical.

The fair attendance kept going down in the surrounding states, too. So several years back they began to put on beauty contests, with screen tests and all-expense trips to Atlantic City and a try at the national championship for the winner. A Franklin reporter with an electric-blue suit and Hollywood press-agent ambitions sold the idea to the fair board, under the condition that there be no bathing-suit appearances in the state, no leg-show business. So when the first winner came down the runway in the bathing-beauty parade at Atlantic City the press boys took one look at her knock-knees and labeled her Miss X from Kanewa. Since then there were private precautions to insure a more fortunate export.

By Wednesday Gerta Krasinski looked like a sure winner in the beauty contest, barring actual bowlegs or a harelip, and so half a dozen stores, including Hammond's, called up to offer her full ensembles from their choice fall stock, not to go on display until after fair week. Gerta, with her cousin Marya for counsel, spent a whole day selecting a wardrobe: formal attire at Hammond's, travel ensemble at Schendler's, luggage at Hare's, and so on, ending with a pedicure at the Beauxettes.

Thursday evening the fair turnstiles clicked busily, topping the entire week, even Labor Day with its races. The Polanders turned out in streetcar loads, including the older women in headcloths chattering across the aisles of their Gerta in a lady dress. Thousands of middle Franklinites were there too, but very few of those who lived on upper Philadelphia

Avenue or out along Blue Ridge, except, of course, the empress and the local members of her court not in mourning.

Hamm Rufe went back to the fairgrounds for the beauty contest, chiefly because the Polanders were his neighbors and somehow seemed more like the people he knew away from the capital city, virile folk, like Stephani, or the Bellowing Bull from down the Little Grand. No wonder that the Labor Day marchers had followed Carl Halzer, a complete stranger, into the face of the police, even the rifle-armed deputies, with arrogant Gold Shirts among them. No wonder that poor Cobby, sick of his world as he seemed to have been most of his life, tried to make it endurable through little Hattie, a despised Polak, a daughter of scrubwomen, gardeners, and fixmen.

The Poles of the bottoms had kept many of their foreign ways, particularly their play ways, their feast times, their three-day weddings. Those who came from among the Russians brought a stomp dance that they used to do on Saturdays, the one night free from cleaning mop and pail, until too many prohibition drunks swarmed in on them. Now the Americans did their own kicking and stomping, and showing their pants, enough to shock the old Polanders. But it left them free to have their gatherings again, usually in some empty warehouse down near the tracks, with kegs of beer, willow baskets of rye bread, and Polish sausage, and their accordions and their hammer harps for the polka and the stomp.

Well back in the seventies Nicholas Zeromski came to Franklin to find a home for a colony of his countrymen. With both freight rates and lumber prices a plain holdup in the expanding little city and its wide trade area, the clay banks where the Coot now lived had sprouted a row of kilns that grew into brick works as fast as the labor shortage permitted. Good workers would be mighty welcome, Nick was told. By the next spring a Little Warsaw was creeping along the fill-in strip of the alkali bottoms and although building slacked off soon enough, the dribble of newcomers in stout Polish boots didn't stop until after the World War.

The older Poles were industrious and adaptable. They were the first to take advantage of the FHA loans to improve their homes. They changed readily from brick hands into good green workers, sodders, planters, and yard men. They planted and nursed the lawns and gardens of the city, the finest between Denver and the Mississippi. Their energetic wives took over the office buildings when six o'clock came; they did much of the sewing and most of the fine laundry of the town. But there wasn't much opportunity for the younger ones, those who wanted to be American, with American work in stores, and offices and banks. A few of the musical boys got into dance bands, some worked around pool halls, at least a dozen were in and out of jail for bootlegging all through prohibition. One got a load of shot in the pants in a hijacking attempt and two went to the big time in Cicero. The girls preferred work in the little factories, so long as they kept open, making overalls, gloves, brooms, or dipping candy at three or four dollars a week rather than minding other people's babies or scrubbing dirty floors.

By now most of the young people in Little Warsaw went to high school a year or so, perhaps even to the university. Many of the girls were gay and pretty in their teens, danced well, had slim, vital figures made for short skirts. They became waitresses, beauty workers, clerks, and stenographers, with a teacher or two among them and one very good doctor. Here and there a Katie, a Hadwiga, or an Olga married into the better families, and although the bottoms still had many fenced yards, and women with headcloths carrying mops at night, many of the girls had fur coats, beauty-parlor curls close-clustered as sleeping caterpillars, red fingernails, and two-thread hose for their fine legs. Several even managed leopard-skin coats, the current successor to grey squirrel for kept ladies in the capital city. Some of them had, of

course, long ago moved up town, into those apartments with
trick elevators that would only scare their poor old country
mothers and make them feel strange. But all the girls went
home pretty regularly. Stopping their roadsters at the little
white-painted houses of their childhood, they ran in with
bundles and a cloud of sweet-smelling perfume. Perhaps
they had a snack of coffee and Polish baking, took a brother
or a sister riding. Then they vanished again, leaving behind them the sweet smell and much woman talk over the
back fences, lusty laughing among the older men, and much
for discussion and envy among the growing girls who had
to stay behind.

Now, tonight, one of these Polish girls might win the state
beauty contest, with an airplane trip to Atlantic City, and
a screen test, maybe even be Miss America and go to Hollywood. By eight o'clock the sponsors were sorry they hadn't
staged the contest at the fieldhouse, with a thousand more
seats. Long before the hour the steep cement cup of the
Four-H club building was filled to the roof, the later ones
left to mill around the outside.

When the band struck up, the swirl-skirted drum major
of the high school preceded the first contestant, Miss Fort
Stoddard, through the double doors, wide enough for a prize
span of mules, and down the high plank walk to the ring
usually set up for the Legion wrestling matches. But tonight
there were no ropes to climb through, no bawling referee,
just the elevated platform under the white cone of light, and
Miss Fort Stoddard, a plump little brunette in a strapless red
satin dress that jerked the row of elderly judges forward in
their seats and set some of the women of the audience to muttering over their folded arms.

When the girl had circled the ring, she giggled a little into
the loud-speaker and took her seat to a ripple of clapping
from the home-town followers. Behind her came a tall girl,
her face oval, and beautiful, but the black velvet of her dress

was too tight across her buttocks and not quite long enough
to cover her big feet. The next one was a brunette in gold
cloth, then a redhead in green, and so on, all pretty girls in
their middle teens, but walking badly, their red-nailed hands
without poise or quietness.

While each of these had some following, there was a growing impatience and neck stretching from the ringside to the
steepest balcony. "Gertie! Bring on Gertie!" the Polish boys
down in front began to chant, clapping their hands in unison
as the university students did in winter. "We want Gertie
Krasinski!" the crowd threw back to them, while the empress
and her court sat stiff and unnoticing on their folding chairs
covered with red satin throws from the coronation equipment.

Once more the double doors opened and a page boy in a
little-man suit marched out, carrying a large white card, announcing: Miss Gerta Krasinski, Travel Ensemble by Schendler's. Next came the sauciest bellhop of the Buffalo Hotel,
arms full of new luggage, and behind him blonde Gerta in a
silver-flecked travel suit of dull plum color. Hamm watched
her come: her face a little flushed at the roar of applause, but
her walk long and easy, under the surface timidity a deep
and vital poise. Yes, even from the bottoms of an American
city and after almost a week of sordid sensationalism, a nineteen-year-old Slavic girl could still walk in such calm down
the plank runway to the white glare of a beauty contest. The
man closed his eyes in the welling memory of another Slavic
woman, neither blonde nor teenishly pretty but always with
him as the memory of a lost June sun lies in the frozen heart
of January.

There was some uncertainty and bewilderment at this appearance of their Gerta in a travel outfit. What was she up
to, going high-hat on them? — throwing the contest away?
Sure, she looked like a million dollars, but the judges were
old men. Had to have everything in plain sight to get those
slack pants hot.

But as the radio interviewer motioned the girl toward him a loud-speaker somewhere off stage called out a plane flight: " — Leaving Gate Five for At-lan-tic City!" Turning, the boys ran from the arena, with Gerta behind them, stopping to wave back from the door in a fine burst from the band. In two minutes she was back in beach costume, dull yellow shirt, long grey-blue flannel slacks, bright fishnet about her waist and her head, an eager wire-haired terrier pulling at a leash. Preceding her, the two boys carried the credit card and an armful of sun-tan oil, beach umbrellas, magazines, and thermos jug.

Next Gerta came out with her blonde hair loose over her shoulders, a long white bathing cape caught close about her, and carrying a red hat big as a cartwheel in her hand. Her bare legs, sun dark and smooth as polished wood, showed well to the knees as she walked around the ring, completely unconcerned now by the yelling crowd, the staring judges, or the boos of those backing other candidates. The last time she came out in soft, voluminous black, with a prim little bouquet in her hand, the cluster of pale curls at the nape of her neck tied with a bit of blue ribbon, the hair drawn back from her face bringing out her wide cheekbones, her long eyes, and the delicate taper of her chin.

Hamm Rufe had to remind himself that this smoky cup of faces was the Four-H club building where prizes were annually awarded to young Herefords, where every week all winter crowds hissed and booed the grunts, grimaces, and heavy foul play of the Legion wrestling card, and that slap outside the walls lay the cornlands of Kanewa. True, Polish Gerta was an art student, taking costume design and dancing, and it was very possible that with the judges five old men from a farming state, she might have lost herself the prize. But when she spoke into the little microphone the sloping walls of the cup about her crumbled into moving, roaring humanity. Even the empress and her court circle applauded, held to their seats only by long habit of inaction while the rest of the crowd swept down upon the ring.

The reporters got a statement for the papers. Yes, Gerta thought, it would be nice to be a moving-picture actress, but what she really hoped for was a career as a designer. The reporters improved on that, put some zip and go into it, and got a couple leg photographs of her climbing into the shuttle plane that would meet the mainliner at a more modern, a safer airport.

When the girl was finally on her way to Atlantic City, the crowd moved on to make a night of it, scattering to the few public places in town, the dance halls at the edge, like Silver City and the El Troc. Gus Pilton, of the Troc, was a descendant of one of the old Franklin families, but one never in good economic standing. He had been in what he called the amusement game all his life, beginning back in the Orpheum circuit days as a hoofer, before, as he used to say, his hair and his belt started coming out simultaneously. After the war he leased a little second-story place on Fifth Street that he called the Pilton School of the Dance in the afternoons, the Pilton Party House at night. It just got by, until the night a big fellow threw his wife out the window. By then the house on Twentieth Street that the country club had built temporarily while they bought Boulder Heights a second time was empty again. Never more than a sort of two-story barracks, the Klan had it until the fiery cross disappeared from the capital city for a while, then Gus ran the place until it burned to the ground in one bright hour of flame.

In the market speculation days the new Grand Vista clubhouse looked so magnificently down upon the lesser folk of the city that two more country clubs were organized, and plans accepted for buildings and financing, one in semi-Algerian, the other Southwest Spanish. One, the Skyline, was completed during the fading promises of the 1920's — a low rambling structure of whitish stucco, with steps to the flat roof and porches of iron desert props and striped awnings along the sides. But the market went before they got the cracks in the swimming pool tarred, and so Gus Pilton took it over for a party house, and still just barely got by until Chamberlain's war scare gave him an idea. He covered the old pool with railroad ties for beams, equipped the orchestra with imitation gas masks, and called it the Bomb Shelter. When Munich was forgotten, the candle duskiness of the booths held its customers. The clubhouse had been worked over a little too, the partitions cleared out, a red neon sign, readable at half a mile, strung across the roof outside: EL TROC.

While part of the customers were usually the high-school age crowd, boys who had to keep an eye on both the check and the juvenile officers, there were many older men too, men who came out to relive the days when they could swing deals like the old Skyline, and yet not be reminded that they hadn't quite made it. Often they had young women, really girls, with them, girls who called them Mister and listened to their past exploits without reflecting the sterile present in their faces.

Here at the El Troc the young Poles ended up the celebration of their Gerta's victory, a lot of Franklin's gayer set trailing them tonight, for there was no telling how far that girl might go, Hollywood, even stardom, they told each other. Besides, there was something exciting about these people from the bottoms. The Troc was pretty full when the new crowd came but by making disturbance enough the Poles got a stein of beer apiece and promises of places as soon as somebody left. Hamm, Carl Halzer, and Burt Parr were with them, Hamm and Carl because the Poles wouldn't let them go home, Burt because he could not face an evening of remembering that Mollie had broken her date. Now here she was, in this place, with fat-necked Milo Groves, of the groceries and liquor

Groveses. But after her first startled acknowledgment she didn't look up to meet the stricken blue eyes that kept returning to her bowed head.

There were other representatives of Franklin's best families at the long center table of the Bomb Shelter. Eloise Johnson, Hamm's old girl, a little drunk, her flesh looking softer than ever, was calling to the Polanders from the far end. Hamm knew she probably would keep right on, so he sent Burt over with a couple of the younger boys to have a taste from her beer mug. He kept back among the others, quietly waiting for a table, the scarred side of his face turned to the girl of his youth, who would be content enough with the three young men about her.

Not until the unaccustomed beer drove Cassie Welles's Dachel from his shadowy booth to seek the gentlemen's retreat did Hamm notice him or her daughter, Marylin. Alone the girl lit a cigarette, her face standing out clear and well-molded in the match fire. As she put it out she considered the waiting group, particularly the tall man with the strong uprush of fall-tawny hair, and for the first time she noticed Mollie Tyndale publicly, asked her to her booth, and why not bring her waiting friends along? No need of them standing, with all the room in her booth. Hamm went with Halzer, curious, now that he had been drinking beer with the hilarious Poles, to meet this daughter of Cobby's. It was Carl Halzer the girl motioned to sit beside her, where the light struck direct. She looked him over frankly, her eyes dark in her shaded face.

"I would have known you anywhere, from your picture in the *News*," she told him. "Your hair — "

The man blushed and ran his palm up over the wiry mass that wouldn't smooth down, but when the manicured Dachel returned, he hid his farmer hands under the table. Still, he seemed to be enjoying himself and so Hamm rescued Burt and took the next bus back to town. They had it to themselves except for some girl along in the back seat, crying softly into her handkerchief.

By Thursday evening the stock judging was finished, and most of the farmers were ready to pull their tent pickets at daylight, hook up to the trailer with the young bull or the colt looking through the crate, and hit for home. But Friday was thrill-spill day, with the daredeviltry billboarded all over town, and because children had more to say about such things than when their parents were young many got to stay. Some of the townspeople came out too, the sensation seekers, as the others called them, hoping to see somebody get killed. The high-wire acrobats all landed in the net but the daredevil driver who jumped his racer off a ramp and over four pairs of cars hit the ground rolling, turning over and over while women screamed and children whooped. Eventually, of course, he crawled out smiling, unfurling a little American flag. A few minutes later they were silent when the old engine of the stunt pilot didn't pull him out of a nose dive. But by the time the fire department got there everyone was convinced it wasn't just a trick, for there was the smell of burning flesh all over the grandstand. The parade advertising the circus showing that night was hurried out and soon the clowns had everybody laughing again, going away happy.

Next day the Grandapolis *News* had its annual fun over the art exhibit at the fair. Under a cut of last year's prize winner, a copy of a tourist folder photograph of the Lower Falls of the Yellowstone, was the story of this year's award. All week the fair judging had gone quietly, from prize baby beef to angel cake and tomato preserves, only to hit a snag in the Art corner. A woman from outstate who got second prize for her painting of a jar of tulips protested loudly to the judges that Mrs. Milltner of Franklin, first prize, had copied her Girl with Cat from a painting in the Fine Arts building at the university. The fuss gathered a crowd comparable to that of the ribbon dancer at the Midway. "It was high time," the unnamed outstate woman said, "that someone with an art background were appointed to the judging committee, in addition to a retired minister, an anti-saloon worker, and a patent-medicine salesman." Finally, the judges had gone across the quadrangle to the Fine Arts collection. They came back and pronounced their decision: Mrs. Milltner was awarded first prize because her picture, a copy of Girl with Cat, was an artistic improvement on the original. Many of the readers of the News agreed when they compared the vacant, blue-eyed stare and wooden but normal-sized arm of the copy with the intense, burning eyes, the enlarged and fiercely possessive arm of the original.

Now the state fair was over, the last couple of girls had started out, with new curls and best dresses, to the fairgrounds or to Silver City to pick up dates. "We'll tell them we won't split up. It's together or nothing," they still promised each other. That was the way girls met fellows in stories and movies, not only at fairs but even right on the street or on the highways, sometimes even the good-spending son of the boss. Of course, they knew it didn't always work out that way, and so there was usually a quarter in the back of the dorine or in the puff bag down inside the brassière, mad money, enough to get home on, if they didn't get too far away. And they wouldn't have the men parking, either, at least not out away from everybody.

Yes, they'd stick together, they promised as they ran for the bus, but there was less conviction behind the promise tonight. Of course there would be other times, Fourth of July next summer, and another fair, but there seemed to be fewer men every time, with almost 2000 extra women in the capital city.

Still it might be safer to stick together.

With the fair done there were Rooms for Rent signs to

come down all through the middle residence section, many that might as well never have gone up, although most of the householders long ago stopped telling lone women that no men were allowed in the rooms, didn't even seem to notice the frayed, middle-aged customers they sometimes dragged in, or complain if they forgot to flush the hen skins down the toilet. Every year more of the wide porches were empty all week.

Once more Kanewa's state fair ended in the red, despite the coronation, the beauty contest, and the parimutuel betting. Maybe it was because the farmer no longer felt it was his show and stayed away. The Buffalo Hotel did what it could to make him feel important, even built a little corral of velvet ropes in the lobby for the prize baby beef, had a colored boy around handy with pan and broom to clean up behind the cud-chewing young Hereford. But the people who stopped to look at the clean, curly hide of the white face were dinner-dressed city folks.

Not that the fair would stop, at least not so long as the legislature financed the deficit, and the Franklinites would see they did so long as it put one dollar into capital city pockets. But it was admittedly harder to get out the better element, meaning by that the spending element, to anything except the coronation ball and the horse show. The outstaters had discovered that fair week was a poor time for shopping, with the stores crowded and the good merchandise put carefully away. Even at Hammond's the shelves were full of leftovers the last few years.

Usually the better Franklinites put off their fall return until after the noisy, dusty week. Those who once went to Okoboji or Madeline Island were usually at Colorado Springs or Central City or perhaps even Alaska now. Those who used to go to Florence, later to Salzburg, went to Sweden and then Mexico if they termed themselves liberals; if not they went to Germany, so long as they could, bringing back the opinions dispensed by the foreign representatives of American capital; still rolled them on their fat tongues, no matter where they were this year. Hitler put labor in its place, kept it hungry enough to work —

Of course, the best families including the few whose ancestors had founded the capital city as a good place in which to live were always well represented in town fair week, for patriotism springs up rank as weeds about a down tree where virility and courage are dying. But their presence at the coronation did not make a fair.

Someone suggested that the university opening might be moved up, bringing in the 5000 students, and compelling the return of the professors who, even though still under a fifteen percent pay cut, eked out their freedom from the capital city to the last hour. But since neither the students nor the faculty could spend what they didn't have, the idea of early opening was dropped.

Out at the fairgrounds the last bit of trash left by the campers had been pawed over by Coot and his fellows, the midway swept clean by a grey wind that rolled every cigarette butt from under the seats of the grandstand and lifted the last curl of loose dust from the race track. Even the hog barns smelled dry; it was time for the big annual dinner at Grandapolis. Usually the guests were owners of strategic newspapers, business men from key towns along the Grand and the Wakoon rivers, and some of the right men of Franklin. Never any legislators, who merited other, solider approach. There were always invitations out among the administrators of the university, but not to the regent who was a director of the Grandapolis Power Company, or to the dean who wrote for the press service of the Associated Manufacturers. The justices of the state supreme court were passed over too. Fine men, the justices, mostly fine, right-thinking men, but by position above the horseplay that would creep into a big stag dinner. Even those of the university who received invitations were never exposed to the raucous crowd of the annual blow-out. They met in small, pleasant groups of two or three with handsome, greying, well-groomed Cole Dringer from the east somewhere, and obviously a man who got around, who could do things for them. In the end they did things for him but later in the fall four or five new cars always appeared in the administration parking, always the same make, good, but not ostentatious, and never alike, or delivered at the same time.

For the regular run of guests less finesse was required. An entire floor at the new Rio Grand Hotel was reserved for the party, with a dinner of trout, pheasant, duck, and venison, a jolly bartender in the refreshment room, and entertainers enough to go around for as long as the guests wished. A couple years ago a story got out about an old newspaper man from up in the Grand-Stoddard Reservoir region. The thick-lensed old Scotsman had been pretty set on favoring the government irrigation projects. "We need the water," he replied doggedly to all persuasion.

So he was invited to the Grandapolis dinner. He came, stuffed his old hat in his pocket, and accepted a bit of whiskey and ate a little pheasant. But when the women entertainers came on and a cute little brunette picked him for herself, he looked at her a long time through his thick glasses. "Madam," he said, "I am a married man!" and pulling out the hat, he went home.

The story got all over Kanewa, and perhaps it was true, for while a staunch Republican, old Duncan never deviated from his sponsorship of water for this drouth-stricken region, fought hard against the utilities' attempt to hamstring the irrigation projects in Kanewa's legislature as in other states, nor did he run any of the press matter that came to him as promised, no matter how dressed up it was or how free. But usually the guests were more pliant than old Duncan, and the invitations to the dinner were anticipated for months.

It was always a gay, noisy gathering and through it strolled

Cole Dringer, with a pleasant little smile under his neat mustache. Tanned and easy-mannered, he always had a new story or two to tell, just good enough to make those around him feel like telling theirs, never new enough to make any guest feel like a plow poke and out-of-date. He led the men to drink freely and to talk as freely. Later he saw some of the more likely ones alone. Until then there was no proof that he and not the Grandapolis Business Men's Association was their host, and sometimes in these private conferences he managed to convey the idea that the big shots from the metropolis were no more than the rest of them, than, say, the editor of the Hill City *Echo*.

Over the cigars Cole Dringer expressed deepest regret that his good friend Colmar Welles couldn't be with them, and sighed. There were probably many others who felt like Cobby did about life today, with the nation so uncertain, he said, making an expressive gesture with his well-padded, persuasive hands. The men about him nodded, very serious, and seeing his restraint and his gentleness raised their voices to furnish the extremes, the violences.

"But are you sure he's O. K.?" a newcomer to Franklin asked, one accustomed to much more beef and bile from any sound right-thinker.

Oh, yes, it was understood he had added a nice bit to the war chest against the truck strike, and put the operatives in touch with a dandy spy and incident maker, an ex-Communist, to worm into the local organization, one who knew how to stir up dissension and to aim at the front page on the days when news was scarce. He was usually good for a Monday headline like: —

REDS LEAD STRIKING TRUCKERS

Best of all, he wasn't connected with any strikebreaking organization the Labor Board could track down.

Yes, there was no doubting that Cole Dringer was a good picker of men. Even before Kanewa's Hoover Republican senator conceded his defeat by John Bullard, an unknown from Benway running as a mildly liberal Democrat, Cole Dringer wired his congratulations, and arranged a smoker for the new senator, treating the small-town politician like a man of ballast, a man of power and parts. He spoke a little sadly and fatalistically of the senator's unfortunate tie-up. One month in Washington and Kanewa's new man was already talking high tariff, anti-farm and labor legislation.

"Don't he understand that it's the small consumer, the farmer and industry's hired man that we got to have for prosperity?" some of his home-town business men asked each other, privately, of course.

"Old Johnny, he's a talkin' like some dumb kid that's been told what to say, a kid that ain't even got sense enough to get out of the questions what he ain't been give answers for — " the old farmers told each other in back of the hardware store.

"He's shore sold us out — "

"Yeh."

Friday of fair week Bullard was scheduled to speak to the Kiwanians. At what was characterized as an overwhelming flood of requests, the talk was moved out to the fair, where all could hear. When John Bullard got up, he was given no opportunity to ride his regular pony to applause: a ranting against dictatorship, and a praising of its ends if the means were a little drastic. It was hot and under the lights the senator looked particularly plump and pink and so someone from the back howled out, "Hi, lookit! Hitler's girl friend!" Even those who were much annoyed saw it was funny, for somehow, in his deep blushing, the toss of his embarrassed head, Bullard did look like a plump, sweating blonde fresh from the kitchen, but one who could carry malice behind the thin, mean mouth.

Even the Tory Franklinites found it easier to praise his quiet, unassuming wife than the senator. There were, however, some hopefuls who saw him as potential dictator material. He was a little man, with a little man's gnawing ambition for power. He was unscrupulous about promises and had a good, sound loyalty to folding money — just what the country needed.

Saturday evening of fair week the papers carried an agate line among the building permits, announcing the proposed remodeling of a brick dwelling, owner, Cassandra Chase Welles, estimated cost $30,000. There was also a small unheaded item in the local columns announcing the dismissal of all charges against the men held in the Labor Day troubles, without any indication that the parade had really been scheduled with the mayor's office, according to law. Confronted with the signed permission the interference was finally passed off as due to a clerical error. The next day there were fifty applications for the clerk's job. So someone had to be fired. Fortunately there was a member of the Consumers' Co-operative on the staff. That he had nothing to do with streets or parade permits made no difference. He was out.

The Sunday paper carried another bit of news. Saturday night the El Troc was raided, and among such names usually suppressed by the local papers these last thirty years were those of Marylin Welles and a youth who insisted that Dachle was all the name he had and would they please not misspell it? They did. Among the things that didn't get into the papers was the report that a new lot of strikebreakers had been imported and put in with the scabs in the trucks — rifle-armed toughs, and knife-carrying negro giants. This time, evidently, the operatives intended to get their trucks through.

CHAPTER V

THE new week began under a low, wet sky, the morning tower of the capitol a grey pillar in the fog as the early workers hurried out to start the day. Waitresses yawned themselves awake as they pushed coffee across the counters to the truckers dragging in, stiff and hollow-eyed, from a night behind the wheel. Most of them were over-the-road men from other states, where the strike was long settled. In at Ike's coffee shop a big fellow lifted a leg over a stool and winked to a girl he knew. But there was no devil in her blue eyes for the customers today, and her pretty little mouth was naked and miserable.

"You don't look so good this morning, Nora," he said, when he got his hands around his hot coffee. "No break for the boys yet?" The girl shook her head, then suddenly threw her arm up over her face and ran through the swinging doors toward the kitchen, leaving the trucker to stare after her, his cup halfway to his open mouth.

"Lew got shot last night — trying to keep the finks out a their cabs," the other waitress explained.

"The hell you say?" So it really was hired gunmen — like they'd heard. After twenty weeks of no pay a man gets lead in the guts. They had a bad layout here in Kanewa all right, with the anti-picketing law and all.

Inside of an hour the fog settled down into a drizzle that promised long and patient raining, good for the farmers whose wheat plowing was overdue, but bad for the merchants with fall opening Wednesday and university rush week Friday, the stores full of new clothes for the coeds and their ambitious mothers. Sunday the *World* had carried a double page of photographs of prominent outstate freshman girls to come in, a sort of sorority shopping guide, with the fathers conveniently listed by name and business, and representing a little more money. Here and there a store manager who had called the weather bureau came down to the curb to look at the dripping sky for himself. Unsettled, and general rain, the meteorologist predicted for Wednesday night's opening, with all the windows newly decorated to draw the crowds out, Schendler's even going back to their living models, like in the old days of the twenties. The worried men took the early edition of the *World* from the newsboys, read the headline: PICKETING STRIKER SHOT IN GUN BATTLE, and forgot the weather. Crumpling the paper in their soft hands and without troubling to discover that this shooting was not even by their police and deputies they hurried in to dictate protests to their Senator Bullard against this interference with business in the peaceful city.

Out in Herb's Addition two men came for Hamm. Serious-faced at their report, he called Carl Halzer and then hurried down to the jail and found what he had learned to expect in his twenty years as reporter of labor troubles. On a bare cell cot lay Lew Lewis, his face empty in semi-consciousness, on the floor beside him stood a tin bucket of bloody water, the wound in his shoulder packed with a wet, bloodstained towel, the round hole under it seeping a persistent string of red.

At the desk Hamm was told that they could not be chasing their prisoners around to hospitals and things. Anyway, that big bruiser'd be all right where he was. The city physician had come in around four, gave him a shot and left some little white pills for when he got to raising hell. He'd had a couple and was sleeping pretty, with his wound all washed and dressed.

The wound dressed — with a folding of wet towel? And what about the bullet?

Still in there, if it didn't come out on the other side, they said, staring at Hamm's scar as it reddened. Hell, lots of people was walking around good as anybody with bullets in them — no worse than knifings, the officers said, laughing.

For one minute he wanted to throw his name into the faces around him, to watch these men fall on their fat bellies before the big sound of the name of Hammond. But before he could bring himself to any action there was a roar at the outer door of the jail, a clatter and a banging in the corridor. Carl Halzer had arrived. In twenty minutes he had Lew in the hospital. Dr. Russ Snell gave the man one good look and hurried away to the office. "Call the papers," he ordered, "all of them. Have them send reporters and photographers out immediately!"

Before Lew was ready for the operating room, the Franklin men were there, listening sourly to the doctor's denunciation, looking uneasily towards the Grandapolis representatives as they photographed the trucker with the wet towel dressing, took notes. They'd cook up a pretty stink on the capital city. Hamm watched the whole procedure with impatience but knew that Dr. Snell didn't intend to have the case covered up as an unavoidable injury to a lawbreaker. This was one citizen shooting another, shooting to kill, and with the criminal negligence at the city jail, it might very well succeed. He would force an investigation if he could.

For the second time on this rainy day, business men along the avenue thumped their newspapers and talked loud to their secretaries. Now it was the Grandapolis *Inquirer,* carrying a picture of the injured trucker on the front page, playing up the inhumanity of the capital city, and reporting that one of the more popular police officers, a former varsity end, had resigned that morning in protest against the Lewis affair. But they called the fight a gun battle, too, with both Lew and his spell partner, the only witnesses, swearing it was their fists against two strikebreakers with rifles — "unidentified men" as the police kept calling them, even though both of the strikers reported the number of the car the gunmen used, a Red Line Conveyer number. The Franklin papers said almost nothing except that the man injured in last night's outbreak of violence had been removed to Samaritan Hospital for observation by Dr. Russ Snell, pointing him out by name as a warning against mixing in.

Hamm knew the doctor well, often went out to his home in the evenings. The capital city called him lacking in ambition because he was content with the small practice his wife's father left him. But it assured Doctor Russ, as everyone called him, a moderately secure existence, with time enough for the crippled children across the street from the old home. He was an immense, homely man, with a face like weathered sandstone. His hands, with the fingers usually curled in upon themselves like a baby's or a monkey's, were the heavy burr-ends to the hanging oak of his arms. But at the hospital the children waited hours for his step and when the doors closed upon him and he was gone from the walk below, their watching for the next call had already begun. He never talked of his work, but out as far as Wild Horse Plains and far beyond the state were strong and straight young people who wrote him grateful letters each year on their birthdays like the cramped little note from a Swedish boy in Stockholm: "To-day my father and I run together clear to the west forty and back for a present on my birthday for you"; or the one from the little girl at Walden: "We have a sparrow nest in my old brace hanging up in the grainery. Mother says to let them use it for my birthday present to you. She thinks maybe the old harness gets lonesome, now that it don't have to hold me up any more."

Letters like these Doctor Russ laid away to the memory of the crippled sister he had to see trampled to her death under the hoofs of a mad bull because she could not run and he was too small to help. As he grew up the memory remained a hard and green thing within him, so he turned to the study of medicine. By the time he was done, redheaded Ona Shelley had married him, given him her father's practice. During the last few years Russ Snell had calls to far and fine positions but he preferred to stay in Franklin, near the little cripples, with his books, his small daughter, and his energetic, laughing wife. Ona Snell arranged the programs for the League of Women Voters, and fought the conservative membership almost singlehanded to give the younger candidates of every party a good hearing. She got herself appointed to the city library board and helped clean up the paralysis brought on by inbred management and ten years of shrinking appropriation much as her husband fought the same trouble in his little charges. Then one day, two years ago, there was a letter from an old classmate in medical college who was with an ambulance in Republican Spain. He wrote of a friend, a Spanish doctor who died in Franco's prison pens, leaving an orphaned son of ten, sensitive and brilliant and fine as his father. The Snells were reading the letter together. They looked at each other, and then grinned a little under their moist eyes, for they had said the same words exactly together: "Let's take him!" So they carried their baby bonds down to the post office and after a long wait the boy came, with a tag on his coat. He was incredibly thin-legged and had a shock of gleaming rye straw hair that fell into his eyes, deep, and night-dark with what they had seen. He had two prides. He could speak the English, and he was no longer like falling walls inside when he heard the airplane come.

They had taken him home by way of Stoor's Park, to see the lone buffalo whose picture his countrymen had first given to the world. But it was the slim white deer behind the high fence that made the boy cry out his first word of Spanish,

and then blush with shame and correct himself. He was
sorry. It had made him think of his father — and the fences
with the prisoners inside. "I promise I will remember it that
I am the American now," he said, speaking very formally,
as though repeating a ritual.

So, somebody had been at the boy. Quietly Ona Snell
put her arm about the thin shoulder. "No," she told him,
"here, too, you will be what you are, a fine young son of
Spain, come to live with us in America."

Gravely the boy thanked her, his dark eyes upon her,
without understanding. " — Son of Spain?" he asked finally,
with embarrassment. Could one here perhaps be José — like
his father?

But of course. José was a beautiful name.

Ona Snell was an officer of the Consumers' Co-operative
and because neither she nor the doctor had ever seen Hamm
Rufe when he was still of the Hammonds of the capital city,
he felt free to go there, to sit easily among them with the
sound, the whole side of his face turned towards the light.
Sometimes on Sunday afternoons little Onie crawled up on
his knee to see his sick cheek, perhaps even asking to touch it.

"Ouu! Hurty-hurt!" she always cried, shuddering within
herself, making the boy José come once more to see, calling
upon her dad to make it well.

Here, at the Snells', Hamm met the liberals of the university campus, in one of the few places where they felt secure
to speak out. Sometimes they turned upon themselves as
teachers, castigating their craven hiding of honest opinions.
But a man with a family — what was he to do? — speaking
just like the renters out over the breaks of the Little Grand,
and many a man beyond.

One of these was Elvin Ford, a dark little man who specialized in frontier history and spoke heatedly of the wasted
vision of Jefferson. "He could see that if the tremendous re-

sources of the Louisiana Purchase were not kept out of private hands nothing short of a revolution would ever make their full benefits available to society or save us from the tyranny of their power."

Sometimes Walford, teaching the Continental Novel, and his wife who sponsored the little theater, were there too. Till Walford had deliberately chosen to live in the middle west, in whose streams he saw man's one hope for escape from the trap into which the industrial revolution had thrust him. Here, with so much fertile soil, and with its unlimited waterpower regulated for cheap and competitive use, he saw scattered factory units grow up in small, semi-rural communities, each man a farmer and a worker. Here the family of the future would grow up free of the menace of hot winds and the devastating drouths, of slum disease, layoffs — grow up healthy and strong in body and in spirit.

It was fine to hear the Walfords talk of Till's vision, and of the place of the arts among the people of this newer world, this better world to come. They had taken a refugee too, a Jewish boy from Leipzig, where Till studied. He was eleven now, black-thatched, with fingers fine as carved ivory and eyes that searched out every face. He was the son of a small publisher killed by the Nazis. He and José were inseparable.

It was the evenings with these people that made the old shack out at Herb's Addition such an empty place to Hamm, made him sit long on his couch with the picture of Stephani in his hands. Deliberately, it seemed he had chosen this place for a retreat from life, and now out there in the hospital, under the hand of Dr. Snell, lay a strong young trucker with a bullet deep in his body.

By Monday there was no one in Franklin, unless it was the collector of White House stories, who hadn't heard of the spontaneous gathering at the El Troc the night after the beauty contest. Those from the foot of Blue Ridge found it most amusing, the clerks and office workers screamingly funny — that high-hat Marylin Welles and the Polanders drinking beer together. Yes, but Marylin Welles with her mother's Dachel, that was even better, and getting caught in the Saturday night raid, with both their names right out in the paper.

"Like old times," the Coot said as he warmed his wet feet at the stove of the shelterhouse out in Herb's Addition. "Like back when the sons of the carriage trade was listed in all the round-ups of old Sixth Street."

Yes, the sons got in the papers in the old days, Hamm thought as he watched the Coot's shoes steam, the sons, but never the daughters, or with their mothers' boy friends. That was new, and planned.

All day Sunday Cassie's telephone had been busy, and Monday too, with sweet voices offering sympathy, saying "Poor, poor dear Cassie," to each other. By evening others besides Hamm remembered that the Welles family owned stock in both the Franklin papers. Then there was talk that Cassie engineered the raid herself, like school authorities getting rid of a teacher that couldn't be fired because of his following.

"Well, by God, the old gal may be a little butt-sprung but she's got a head on her," the Coot told his cronies as he shook his pants down over his dry shoes and started home, humming.

Yes, she was up and coming all right, and old Cobby just barely cold out on the hill, they said to each other, their faces turning towards Blue Ridge across the dark town.

By Monday Cassie Welles began to be a little sorry she had reported the El Troc for raiding. It was making Marylin more popular than she ever was, even as the town's first empress. Still, it fitted her notion of a smart young society matron with a rival daughter. Like in *Harper's Bazaar*. So she commanded Marylin's appearance at lunch, with martinis. Over her glass she considered the girl, the first time in her mother's house since Cobby's death, and really a little self-conscious.

"You will, of course, be immediately off to wherever it is you are planning to go — " Cassie announced.

But at the open attack the daughter was instantly at ease, smiling a little, curling her short upper lip from her scalloped teeth, exactly as she did ten years ago when her mother warned her about petting for little girls of sixteen. She emptied the glass, picked out the olive and chewed around it, with her lips drawn back.

"Oh, I'm not planning on going anywhere just yet — " she finally said, pounding her cigarette twice, hard, a habit she picked up from a black-bearded young writer down in Arizona. "No — not just yet."

Color crept up Cassie's softening neck. "Then I shall be compelled to take Dachel away — "

The girl laughed over her match. That lazy lap dog! He wouldn't mind where he was so long as he had a soft nest, and certainly his comings and goings could be of no interest to her.

"No — ?"

No. It was a man that was keeping her here. A man whose shoulders were like a stone beaming above her head, a man with hair like sun on a fall hillside, and eyes like a winter stream, dark and deep and swift.

"My, aren't we poetic?" the mother exclaimed. "And who may this superman be?"

It was a man called the Bellowing Bull of Bashan — a farm boy from down yonder.

Cassie Welles laughed, liked the sound of it from a mother to her romantic daughter, and laughed again.

"I know," Marylin told her, from full, curled lip. "My low tastes, like my father's — "

That stopped the posing. Yes, Cassie Welles admitted to herself, she might have said that, if she hadn't been too relieved to think of it. But perhaps there was no real point in antagonizing the girl. Recalling the dozens of men who had passed through her fuchsia-nailed fingers during the last ten years, bankers' sons, cowboys, poets, even a fake Russian nobleman, and all with no particular after-effect, the mother couldn't very well balk at a farmer. In fact he might help fill in the interval between Cobby's funeral and Arizona or Sun Valley, or wherever one would be going this fall if one were twenty-six.

This man, Cassie Welles inquired — he had won some prizes at the fair, perhaps grew something special, pumpkins or something? He probably did; otherwise he wouldn't be coming to the fairs. She'd have Dora look it up. They would need some of whatever it was, for those dreary farms Cobby had accumulated along the Wakoon River. She would write him to call.

Pleased, Marylin did stay for lunch, with Dachel up but sulking in his room, refusing to appear until she was gone. It seemed she had called him a pansy pants when the police took them down to the jail Saturday. He had been so humiliated and didn't have a handkerchief with him. That could happen to anyone, couldn't it? — anyone sensitive enough.

All Herb's Addition knew about tow-headed young Burt's hard turn-down by the Tyndale girl. They wondered what he had expected from big bugs like them. But they felt sorry for the kid, Hamm having to fetch him home late Sunday night, still drunk and sick as a calf. Early the next morning the old Coot slushed down through the wet to offer advice.

"What you'd oughta been made to do was drink a bottle

of milk before you was put to bed — An' next time you better take up with one a them pretty Polak girls. They won't do you like that Tyndale outfit."

Burt only pillowed the misery of his first real hangover in his palms and wished he could poke the old Coot in the face. But that wouldn't dispose of Margaret Tyndale's determination to make something of Mollie, as the girl told Burt Sunday. He needn't think she liked fat-necked Milo Groves any better than he did.

Hamm knew what was in the mother's mind. Milo was the nephew of Josina Black, and the grandson of Jacob Stoor, donor of the capital city's only ambitious park. It lay on the breaks southeast of town, with curving drives that wound through the formal entrance, past the golf links and out over rougher knolls dotted with clumps of new-planted juniper, like tufts of unruly hair in a wind. The shaggy sod of the breaks had been torn up long ago, its earth-nested little clumps of Easter daisies, fragrant wallflowers, purple sweet peas, and June roses; its midsummer clumps of flaming Indian paint root; and its autumn pussytoes and purple wand that used to fill the winter vases of the town — all these were gone. In their place thousands of peonies were arranged in orderly patterns of red and pink and white on smoothed slopes and terraces. Below, on the artificial lakes and ponds, clip-winged wild ducks and Canada geese swam slowly or pulled at their feathers along the bank when no far-bound flocks were passing overhead.

On Sunday afternoons hundreds of middle Franklinites pushed themselves back reluctantly from their dinner tables and drove the two miles to the park, telling any visitors the story of the city's one big land feud, back before the railroad days. It was a feud between two men, wild-haired Eli Jiles, who picked on the far, high ridge west of the river and built the old Stone House, while Jacob Stoor settled close in and bought up a pre-emption of rolling land on this side. They were like opposite forces, Stoor on the side of the righteous, a member of the Red Ribbon club for temperance, and a prudent and saving man, while old Eli smoked, drank, whored a little, and kept race horses, even laid out a track on the tableland beyond his house. At first it seemed that the fashionable district would follow the horses and the devil but the forces of thrift and morality won, as was inevitable, particularly after Jacob got the garbage dumps in the bottoms between the town and Jiles's land legalized over old Eli's loudest protests. From the foresight and prudence of Jacob Stoor the city received this beautiful park with nice picnic grounds, far enough out to eliminate the baby-buggy trade and the messier and more destructive element that did so much damage to the formal rose gardens at old City Park. Besides, the distance saved everyone in town the smell of the deer, the elk, and the one lone buffalo, morose and shaggy as an old man living too far beyond his generation.

On the highest point there was a graveled parking where one might stop to look over the wide bottoms of the Little Grand. In the foreground were the old stockyards and the deserted packing plant, then the smoke of the switchyards and the vague clustering of the business section beyond. On the far side Little Warsaw, the smoking dumps, and Herb's Addition were lost against the blue hogback of Grandview Hill. Only the capitol tower rose high and clean through the smoke and haze that clung like dusty cobwebs to the city on the Little Grand.

Perhaps a flock of swift-winged teal would sweep by, to settle on the ponds among their ground-fast kind, or a string of riding-academy horses come along the bridle path, pushed into a canter by much offside kicking, the riders trying hard to hold position on the flat saddles, to make a showing, for a dollar and a half an hour from a stenographer's pay is a dollar and a half.

Old Jacob Stoor started his grocery business with a pushcart in Grandapolis when the mud of its streets was still churned by the feet of freight oxen and frontier cavalry. At the first homestead opening he moved up to file on a quarter of free land on Mud Creek, taking the cart along. Soon he had a little store, and then a bigger one, finally a wholesale outfit, and, as his son-in-law always said, fortunately died before he had to compete with chain stores and bootleg truckers. His wife had died over ten years ago. But long before then the Stoor house that proved up the homestead was squeezed in by taller, newer dwellings. Even with the maples in the back cut out, only a few petunias could bloom where she used to have clumps of magnificent peonies, a bed of cross-bred zinnias, two snowball bushes, and a plot of old country painted daisies on one hundred sixty acres of land. So she died, squeezed on all sides while her man still owned two thousand acres of land almost within sight of her bed. One thousand of this he left to the town for Stoor's Park, with money for its development, and a bronze plaque for the red sandstone gate pillars: —

IN BLESSED MEMORY

OF

ELIZA ECHERT STOOR

ERECTED BY HER

SORROWING HUSBAND

JACOB ALBERT JOHANN STOOR

The wholesale business was managed by J. B. Groves, under the eyes of the three Stoor girls, as Jacob's daughters were still called, J. B.'s wife as spinsterish as the other two. They were directors of a trust company too, and still owned the old retail grocery, not really much any more except a cause for complaint and calamity. Eliza, the eldest, was the senior member of the library board, her face set sharp against all dangerous innovations, such as adding experimental magazines like *Esquire* or radical ones like the *Nation* to the reading rooms, or installing modern stools in the toilets.

Eli Jiles left a park too. Because his protests against the garbage dumping went ignored and the city moved east from the Mud Creek to Jacob Stoor's holdings, Eli left the whole clay slope from Stone House almost to the Polish bottoms to the Knights of the Road, as he called them in his will. He left plans and money for the building and upkeep of a shelter-house, with heat, water, and toilet facilities, and a penny coffee and doughnut corner. Within this forty-acre park outside the city limits no one should ever be questioned or disturbed except for a criminal offense. It was long a barren spot, with only a few temporary campers on the grounds, but the shelterhouse always had a handful of guests who didn't mind the scrubdowns. During harvest migrations and hard times hundreds of the far-homed stopped here for a night or two. If it was cold they took the required shower and slept indoors, if not it was a newspaper under a clay bank and penny coffee and sinkers at Joe's next morning, even if there were no pennies. Bums' Rest, Jiles Park was called, and it seemed symbolic of the man who left it. But after 1929 the slope began to fill up with the huts and shacks and dugouts of the homeless. A transient got a piece of an old walnut bed from the dumps and carved the professional-looking signboard at the entrance: —

HERB'S ADDITION

And while there were protesting letters to the papers, and denunciatory editorials about the festering sore at the gateway of the noble city of Franklin, there was less trouble here, unpoliced and almost unlighted, than on the far slope of Blue Ridge where the best people lived. And what there was usually came from the jallopy trade, as the Coot called it; dispossessed families on wheels stopping on their way south before the winds of November or headed west toward the golden land of opportunity, California.

The shelterhouse, set on a little knoll, was on a foundation of the Coot's old bricks, with log walls and porches. Joe Miller, a bald little bachelor, ran the place. He was one of the bonus marchers who stopped in on the way back from Washington after Hoover broke up their encampment on the Potomac. "With steel hats and Tommy guns," Joe always ended his story the few times he could be urged to say anything about it. By now only the newer comers referred to it. To the rest it was as taboo in Joe's presence as a public jilting, or the public elopement of a wife. He was an army cook, was clean as an old-maid aunt, and hated the town across the bottoms — just the man Eli Jiles would have picked.

Scattered around the shelterhouse were over thirty shacks, including Townsend Club No. 6, sixteen feet square, co-operatively built and owned, and the half a dozen dugouts and caves besides the one the Coot lived in, which was on his own land.

The squatters were mostly lone men, with a woman or two among them, and even a few families, like the Dillards, who housed four small children in a seven-by-ten shack of boards and rusty sheet tin, with a sagging old screen door on leather hinges. Fortunately one of the WPA privies was put up right handy to the young Dillards, and was immediately their special pride, with its roominess and clean white paint.

It was then that Herb's Addition made its one appearance in the Sunday society section of the *World*: —

West Franklin Civic Improvement Club meets Monday for official opening of their new community house, 260 Jiles Road. Music by Wind Sisters, paper by Mr. M. Ward.

It never happened again, for the telephone began ringing as soon as the paper hit the street Saturday night and the managing editor came swearing up through the newsroom to fire the green girl who let the item past while the society editor was out to supper.

The early settler among the squatters in the Addition was Old Connie, who scrubbed offices in the Franklin National building at night, and by day looked after her bedridden Henry, that some people said wasn't even her husband. But she stuck to him, in a shack with floor cracks big enough for rabbits to crawl through. Every fall Hamm and Dillard patched the tar-paper siding and banked it up high all around to keep the wind out from underfoot.

Only one youngish woman lived alone in Herb's Addition. She was known as Sophie, and seldom came out in the daytime unless her little, striped red kitten got away. Several times a week it would come creeping through the grass like some wild tiger, springing out upon Hamm Rufe's foot, to nibble delicately at the strings, to rub against his pants, making a rumble like distant thunder. Nobody knew anything much about Sophie. She showed up in Old Scotty's shack last spring, about a week after he died. She fixed it up nice, hunting the dumps with more diligence than any of the others. The women went over to talk, to find out about her, and then the men, making various excuses. Even Hamm showed up at her door one evening, the red kitten asleep across his arm. But he got no encouragement either, not even for a moment's visiting. She spoke well and calmly the few things she found it necessary to say to these neighbors, and it was plain she wasn't like the last young woman in the Addition, the one whose place got to smelling Lysol clear out to the road.

Hamm's favorite neighbor was lean old Cash Overtill who came in six, seven years ago. He borrowed a saw somewhere and built himself and his wife a fine hooverville with a bit of kitchenette in the far end and padded wall benches under the windows. With the drop boards raised, the benches made a narrow bed on each side of the seven-foot room. Under them

Cash stored his sacks of seeds, a bushel of good fall wheat, a bit of Turkistan alfalfa, and some corn he'd been developing, hoping that sometime there'd be a plot of land again, like his father did, when he was foreclosed off his place in Ohio in the seventies. He had come west in a wagon with a sack of seed corn for a pillow. Only now the free land was gone and a man who'd been put off a Kanewa Investment place couldn't get on any company-owned land. Although he was a good farmer, he was permanently blacklisted because he marched on the capitol back in 1933 with the rest.

"Sometimes it's a relief not to have to make up cash rent, with the drouth an' all," he told Hamm once. But he did wish he had a spot of ground that wasn't like a bucket of lye soap when it rained and nothing but brick when it dried. He had some good corn he was developing.

Monday's rain brought down an early darkness, and Carl Halzer, going to Wallgrin for a campaign talk, dropped Hamm off at the fork to the Addition, the wet clay trail inside too slick for any wheel. Even the cinder paths they had built up with the wheelbarrow from the shelterhouse were soft underfoot.

Hamm found his shack empty, Burt Parr gone. In the shaded glow of his wall lamp the little room was very pleasant, the old bricks of the fireplace blending softly into the rose-flecked building paper of the walls. The horizontal windows above the bookcases were covered with dull blue denim curtains and at the head of the daybed was Hamm's only luxury, a good radio that brought him symphonies from all over America, and from London and Paris, even from Salzburg back before *Anschluss*. Over the fireplace was the picture that puzzled the Coot so, a sketch of a young woman with the hair rising loosely on each side of her high-winged temples, wide cheekbones slanting to a firm chin, eyes long and deep-set under tilted brows — Stephani.

Hamm had been to the hospital again. Lew's fever was high, his shoulder swollen tight and round, Russ Snell and his friend Dr. Klech, refugee German army surgeon, watching, talking over man's age-old struggle for freedom and the right to a decent existence. Out in Herb's Addition Hamm tried to remind himself that this was only one more incident in the long years, but for over twelve of them he had Stephani beside him, and this dreary night it was as though he had lost her yesterday, yesterday, instead of almost eight years ago.

He met her in 1919, after he had put in two years of life on the road, in hobo jungles, and with the Wobblies in at least a dozen strikes. He had been in jail as many times, too, chiefly because he was blacklisted as a sympathetic reporter. The first time they got him only a tricky heart saved him from an army training camp or jail as a slacker and draft evader. After that he was usually just pounded up and kicked out of town. It was during the police strike at Boston that he really got hurt, and that a fifteen-year-old girl dragged him away. He remembered the soldiers rushing the crowds along the street, and that he tripped on something, probably one of the bricks torn from an alley. Before he could get up a uniformed man brought a rifle down two-handed, like a woodchopper's axe, across his face and the wrist.

When he came to, someone had him under the arms and was half-carrying, half-pulling him down an alley. As his head cleared he discovered that it was a girl, young evidently, but strong as a boy and whispering urgent silence upon him in broken English. It turned out that this girl knew something of men, particularly of armed forces loose among civilians.

"Come, come, make quick!" she kept urging. "What they do not find they cannot kill — " And so with his head pounding with pain, an arm hanging limp, and warm blood, fresh and salty, in his mouth, he tried to help the girl get him through a little basement doorway into a lamplit room that he didn't leave for a month.

The girl turned out to be Stephani Kolhoff, the daughter of a village printer from Poland, who had fled to America in 1912, hoping to send for his family soon. But the war came, and the girl had to see many things. The hardest of them was to stand by while her crippled brother of sixteen was shot down for hiding wounded soldiers of the enemy. Enemy! — What was the word to them? To her father no needy man was an enemy, whether of their own oppressors or of an invader. A month later she and her mother were beaten for the same offense by the other side, their home burned, their last goat driven away, and much of the time she had to hide for now she would do as well as a woman for soldiers who had made war for a long, long time.

Then by Christmas, 1918, they were in what seemed this so safe a land of America with Anton, the printer. Almost at once they learned that man is much the same here, and becomes oppressor whenever he can, and so this immigrant girl who was no stranger to treachery and to violence was afraid to have a doctor in, caring for the man she rescued as well as she could with her mother's fearful help. Yes, yes, truly, this was America, but here too were beatings on the streets; might it not only give more beatings and worse also when they were discovered?

A month later, still pale and weak, a shocking red scar across his cheek and nose, Hamm came out into the sunlight of Boston Common for the first time. He sat under the bright October leaves that were falling so quietly upon the row of benches full of the poor, the homeless, and the lost. But he was not of them, for if he watched carefully he might see Stephani's red tam rise out of the roaring hole of the subway that would bring her back from work, bring her to him. And as she approached he recalled the sweet wildness of her lips that was like the sun-ripened plums in the thickets at

home, and like spring thunder over the greening fields of
Kanewa.

That was over twenty years ago, and many things had come
since, and gone. At first he tried to get a job but the violent
scar was against him, and the fact that he had neither
the muscle to compete with the immigrant and the returning
doughboy, nor the training for anything else. So he kept on
writing about the workingman, the growing unemployment
that brought wage cuts, strikes, organized strikebreaking, and
violence. He went from one strife region to another; from one
social ulcer to another, the outspoken Stephani called it. She
went with him, always a part of the nation-wide, world-wide
struggle; he never more than an observer, a bystander.

They saw much violence and many things besides in those
years together, sad things, and amusing ones, like the old sod
house with Venetian blinds and two painted lawn chairs before it out on the sagebrush plains of middle Wyoming.

Then there were fine things, like the slim green-black trees
standing aloof from the highway down towards Santa Fe,
or the miles of pink rambler roses spilling over the railroad
cuts around Providence, in Rhode Island. And there were
mutilations, like the once lovely countryside of Indiana and
Illinois now cut into gingham crossbars by roads; the woods
gone, the lakes and ponds drained, even the streams laid out
by compass through knoll and hill to carry the water quickly
away; to dry out the uplands, flood the lower river regions,
and do violence to all the beauty of nature's curving lines.
They saw dead things too, like Central City, just beginning
to be overrun by the arty revival folks, gaudy as the fireweed
that crept over the old mine tailings; and the dry-rot of lower
Manhattan, a diseased potato that looked good enough on the
outside, and still firm, perhaps a little too firm to the touch —
black and empty inside.

There were disturbing things, like the grey and tired figure
of 'Gene Debs the day he came out of Atlanta, broken in

health, sheared of his civil rights, the old convicts blubbering to see the man who was their brother go. Five years later Hamm stood beside Stephani over the casket of the great man, and knew the world would see few more sincerely mourned. He went to all these places with Stephani, for long ago she had openly become the leader, as she really was from the moment she dragged him into her basement home. He was like those others born in Franklin, mere followers, his brother and all the others here, content with the feel of money flowing under their hands, their mothers' money, or their grandmothers', or someone much farther removed; even exhilarated by the movement, as though it were their own making, like the blanket of green plantlets rising and falling with the pulse of a turgid stream.

All content but Cobby. He got away, and somehow it was good to think of that. He, Rufer Hammond, born to indecision and to inaction, was only good for following, or like river scum, for dipping on the surface of a slow stream.

In those years with Stephani he wrote a great many items and articles as Hamm Rufe, the only name the girl knew, the one he decided upon the night he caught the freight out of Franklin, forever a slacker and yellow coward to the Hammonds and all the capital city.

More and more his inability to identify himself actively with his fellow man, to be anything but an outside observer, irked the energetic, vital, partisan Stephani. Yet between times she tried to excuse him to them both.

"Maybe we all have to see somebody we love smashed down and killed before we can get mad enough to do anything," she said once. "When you see that, you will fight too, my beloved. And perhaps it will not be too late."

Sometimes he thought he felt a community of interest, a brotherhood with his fellows, even an identification with their struggles. But since he came back to Franklin he went through the old files of George Rufer's *World* and saw the difference

between the men who built the capital city and their grandsons, as different as the liberal, fighting *World* of the seventies
and eighties was from its cautious, reactionary descendant today. For instance, there was the editorial his grandfather
wrote after the Haymarket massacre, when the courts, unable
to find the bomb thrower, and compelled to condemn someone to death, sent seven unquestionably innocent men to
execution.

"If agitating for a decent standard of living in this glorious
land of the free is treason then let us all ready ourselves
for the firing squad — and it is well that Washington and
Franklin and Lincoln are safely buried," he roared out in his
paper and on the street, too, and in the town's smoky checker
parlor.

But already the Franklin that George Rufer had founded,
and that was "to envision and disseminate the highest attributes of cultural living to all the state," was turning to
lawless force. The night after his editorial appeared, the windows of his office were broken, his desk spattered with rotten
eggs, the shop upset by toughs from down in the lumberyard
and warehouse district, ordered to a task made much pleasanter by the gift of a brown-topped jug of whiskey.

Hamm could remember his grandfather telling of those
years, when it got so he never walked into a group of business men that the words didn't die out. Either they were giving him hell, or talking of some crooked deal they hoped
to keep from him and his newspaper. Once Hamm tried to
tell Stephani of this grandfather, along towards the last, when
the impatience with him had already grown heavy within her.
Must America then go down to destruction, she demanded,
while those who should be saving her spent all their time turning their eyes from the unpleasant realities of the present back
to the courage and the bravery of their pioneer ancestors?

After the Oklahoma food riots Hamm had come northward through Kansas and Nebraska and Minnesota to report

the Farm Holiday Association activities. He ran from train to bus, and plowed muddy side roads in topless Model T's, perhaps to see a gaunt old man behind barbed-wire entanglements holding off the law with a squirrel gun or to watch the protesters of a forced farm sale scatter before tear gas, the water streaming from their eyes not all from the chemical. He marched upon the capital with the distressed farmers in one trans-Mississippi state after another, and finally in Kanewa, too. They were lucky here with Eli Jiles's old park a free camping place. Safe, for a while, behind the sign advertising Herb's Addition, they rested and looked down upon the new Hammond building, the finest in the city, and the scaffolding already standing where a capitol tower, straight and tall, was to rise within the year. And when the marchers scattered, to what spring plowing they would get to do, Hamm Rufe remained behind to write a special series on the farm rebellion, he told himself, for here he was free to stay as long as he liked, here where he knew something of the background, something of the capital city and its domination of the state. But the first few days in Franklin he had found himself searching the crowds for someone who might be Hallie Rufer Hammond. As he should have suspected, no one of Blue Ridge exposed himself to so depressing a sight as the patched, sunburnt, gaunt-bellied farmers from outstate, and so the evening before Hamm settled down to writing in Herb's Addition he went up past his mother's home. The slim, bare poplars along the back were much taller, two of them gone, and the blue spruce he liked so well and space for the flower beds on the front lawn too. Everything else was the same as when he left, that early spring evening. Finally he saw his mother come out to her coupé, a fine grey-haired woman in smart blue tweed. Turning the scarred side of his face towards her, he passed along the walk, not three feet away. She looked up at his step, and he thought he caught a start of pity for the horrible, clumsy disfigurement.

But there was nothing more, and he knew that he was safe, and that sixteen years under a scar and a threadbare coat are a long time.

So Hamm Rufe stayed in Franklin, partly because without Stephani the struggle of the underdog seemed so empty of hope, and partly because the larger insurance companies seemed about ready for a mortgage moratorium, pretending a magnanimous humanity to cover up their defeat by the organizing farmers. That meant his farm reporting was done, with no Stephani to furnish initiative and the courage for a new venture.

Of course he could have written up the swift mortality among the banks, full of farm paper all suddenly frozen, and closing like village doors slamming before a rising storm. But even now those months of complete paralysis of the intellect, of the initiative and the vaunted ingenuity of the American, were appalling to look back upon, a glance through the papers of early 1933, with their mass panic and their helplessness still frightening.

By the time of Roosevelt's dramatic inauguration Hamm was settled in the shack vacated by the jobless little teacher who found the ridge plank really high enough to keep her feet off the floor the night she tried to hang herself.

Hamm still heard from Stephani every week or so. For a while she operated a relief kitchen in Harlan County, had her food truck dynamited out from under her, and was barely scratched. Gradually her letters began to speak of a dynamic organizer from the dark, the depressed regions of England. When he spoke to the American miners in the light of a lantern swinging from a tree he filled their empty stomachs, not with food but with daring. When he said "Grab a rock!" the rocks became weapons equal to the rifles of the company deputies and the militia. Later Hamm heard again. They were up in Williamson among the marching strikers, twenty-five thousand, it was said, who were met by carloads of deputies armed with riot and machine guns. Buckshot was fired point-blank into them as they fell upon their faces. The militia ordered even the mayor of the city off the street. Stephani stayed with the dead and wounded and was jailed. From there they went into steel, the workers unorganized and starving, ready enough for unionization, now that their jobs were gone, Stephani wrote.

Perhaps that was why Hamm took the little half-time book-keeping and publicity job at the quiet and orderly Consumers' Co-op, just starting up in Franklin, the only new thing that had come into the capital city of Kanewa since the Non-Partisan league organizers were jailed here, over fifteen years ago.

But he had not escaped the conflicts, the violences of life, for in the hospital was a man with a strikebreaker's bullet in his shoulder, too infected for operation, and under the door of his shack appeared the first issue of the *Christian Challenger*, a mimeographed sheet of denunciation, with the hysteria and the poison of the old *Menace*, but it was Jews and Reds this time who were the antichrists instead of the Catholics, and among them Hamm found his name and Carl Halzer's.

CHAPTER VI

FALL ripened swift towards October, the days rich and warm and blue, with silken cobwebs floating and the smell of frost-burnt leaves. From the capitol tower the city was a blur of soft, yellowing mounds that were autumn maple and elm and ash and walnut. Only the oaks about the steeple of Trinity Church, where Blue Ridge worshiped Easter morning and on Thanksgivings, were still dark and green, as though the frost that followed the week of rain had hesitated to approach. Beyond the city the fall-bred covering of weeds on the bare spots was browned by the frost, the cornstalks greyed by the rain, but between them long fields stretched dark as spring with new plowing.

Most of the Franklinites were glad to see September go. It had started so well, with the finest of Kanewa weather for the coronation night that ended in the death of Cobby Welles. Since then there had been little reason for joy, except by the Safety Council and the road patrol. Serious highway accidents in the capital city region had dropped well below the five-year average. Franklin was celebrating its seventy-eighth consecutive day free from automobile fatality, with only three more days to go to top the nation for the year in its class. Already congratulatory editorials were set in type, waiting. But they went into the hell-box, for the night of the first junior high party at Longfellow School two boys were killed by a hit-and-run driver.

Hamm heard the first announcement over his radio, a bare news flash that interrupted the violin of Spalding. In five minutes there was more. The dead were the capital city's two refugee children, the Spanish boy, José, of Dr. Russ Snell's family, and the twelve-year-old Isaac from Germany, with the Professor Walfords. Hamm knew their stories of lone survival in the midst of violence, only to come here to die in the security of a midwestern capital town. He knew from Ona Snell that the boys were seldom in the street, perhaps because of the tauntings of the rest: —

and

> Ikey, kikey
> Kill a Christy —
> Drink a baby's blood!
>
> Red! Red!
> A dirty Red!
> P-p-p your pants
> An' s-s-s your bed —

the boys and even some of the girls saying the words right out if no teacher was near. It had happened more often when they first came, among the younger children, although lately those who had Klansmen or Gold Shirts in the family got worse. But perhaps what really stood between the boys and others of their age were the things their dark eyes had looked upon, things that made all the life of this new America seem a little childish to them, a sort of game to be played even with the grown-ups, and one that must inevitably end in the restoration of grim reality.

The boys had been a problem to their teachers — especially José, the Spanish boy, called Whitey because of the blond hair that fell over his dark skin and somber eyes. In Current Events especially he was always jumping up, crying passionately, "They lie!" at this or that account. But otherwise he was an exceptional student, on the school paper and already, after only two years in America, writing English well enough to get a sketch called "From My Childhood" printed in the university's literary magazine, speaking of his first nine years as though they were a whole generation away.

Isaac was dark-thatched, with fine, sensitive hands for the violin in the school orchestra. His lips were sensitive too, quivering easily, and then firming as though an inner maturity had suddenly asserted itself, for Ikey too had seen the blood of his people on the pavements, had watched his father come creeping home, a hand over the hole in his pants where his own war bayonet from the office wall went through, thrust deep by a brown shirter. So he came, the blood streaking the walk, and collapsed on the sill. Two days later they found Isaac sitting against the door, guarding the dead and swelling body of his father. His mother, at the market that same horrible day, was never heard from again.

There had been considerable letter writing to the papers when the boys came to the capital city, more over Ikey than José, perhaps because Isaac was Jewish and because Till Walford, on the university staff, was more vulnerable. "Flooding the country with undesirable aliens and taking the bread out of the mouths of white men!" they said, and "Bringing in Reds and Jews to cut the throats of our sons and rape our daughters!"

There was a long defense of the boys, with quotations from Voltaire, Swift, Heine, Ben Franklin, and Whitman, ending: "Lift your eyes to the pure and noble pinnacle that stands unsullied above you, and recall that the globe that surmounts it rests equally upon the shoulders of all the peoples of the earth." Many thought they recognized the style of Dr. Steele, head of the English department, but with half his faculty plotting for his job, his defense of any underdog in Franklin had better remain anonymous.

Then there was the trouble about a month ago, when a speaker came through looking for homes for refugee children. The woman was given written warning to leave town by both the Gold Shirts and a rising organization among the jobless youth called the Christian Crusaders. She talked, but frankly said she could not recommend Franklin as a fitting home for children to her board. The papers commented particularly upon her straight hair and what they called her ungracious manner.

Fortunately José and Ikey were settled before the Gold Shirts became so arrogant and although the boys were always drawn closer to each other than to their classmates, they seemed really well liked under the little persecutions that so easily become habitual. Tonight they had a good time at the school party and were hurrying out to Dr. Snell, who waited to take them home. As they ran across the street, arms about each other's necks, a car shot through the stop button, upon them. A hundred of their classmates coming down the steps cried out in warning, rushed forward in an avalanche to where the boys lay, like rag figures thrown by the vanishing car.

Russ Snell saw it happen but by the time he could reach them little Ikey's face was already staring blankly into the dark sky. José was alive and moaned softly as the doctor straightened the twisted little body. He died in the ambulance, his fingers tight upon the hand of his American mother.

The *World* gave the boys a six-column streamer and headed its lead editorial FATED TO A VIOLENT DEATH, making of the hit-and-run car an engine of destiny. In the last paragraph there was a hint of complaint against the rumors that the driver's identity was known, merely because some people thought they recognized the car. Red convertibles were made by the thousand, and although there was only one licensed in Franklin, no one was certain of the number. It might be from outside, even another state. The police were competent to carry on any investigation required. That part was read and reread in the pool halls, the garages, and on street corners. Investigation? Then why weren't they detecting the death car like in the magazines, by scratched fenders, particles of hair or clothing clinging to it, or bits of paint on the victims?

"Hell, everybody knows who owns that red convertible," others said. "And ain't nothing going to be done about it. The police, they got their orders."

The funeral of the two little refugees was the largest ever seen in the capital city, larger than the public memorial for the first Franklin boy killed in action in the World War. Even high-up Gold Shirts like Joe Willper, said to be commander, and Harold Welles, were there. "To kill the talk," it was whispered, for by then people were openly saying that Frankie Doover, son of Glen of the Franklin Mills, owned the red car. He was away, left for California the day before the funeral, driving his aunt out. There was talk, too, that he was to be promoted at Stone House, but maybe that was just villagey gossip.

The services were serious and impressive, with the Lutheran minister of the Walfords officiating. "Two innocent children came here among us," he said, "fleeing a vengeance they did not arouse and could not appease; they were greeted with the cry of 'Red!' and 'Jew!'; shamed in the schools and in the public press. May our great city sleep in peace and in safety tonight, now that they are gone."

Hamm stopped in at the Snells' for a minute that evening. It was a stricken home, empty without the bright hair of the studious José bent over his books at the living-room table. Little Ona cried for the boy almost constantly. "You find him, please go find him," she begged of Hamm as she crept into his lap. With her face buried in the crook of his arm she quieted a little, but even in her sleep she sobbed: "Hosey, Hosey — "

To some of the Franklinites there were more important things than car accidents to little foreigners. Several of the outstate operatives, from places like Benway and Stoddard, were signing the Twelve State agreement with the striking truckers. Much of the over-the-road traffic was being rerouted to avoid both Grandapolis and the capital city, where there was bound to be trouble on the highways between the hired gunmen and the pickets. The Lew Lewis affair was too much for the outstaters — a fine varsity center like that, All-American, and a damn nice fellow.

The Franklin chamber of commerce objected to what they termed the boycott but the operatives had the arguments of shorter mileage and less road congestion on their side. So another strike parley was announced by the operatives with the hope of saving this last business. There was no optimism left among the wives of the strikers, with winter coming on and relief cut off weeks ago. Of course there was a little help from the union but with the men to defend in court, and hospital bills, too, it didn't go far. The children weren't so hungry any more, not crying much, just dragging around.

Then there was the terrible accident out beyond Weld City, four of five people killed in a car as a big truck lurched out of the dark on a curve and threw them over the steel fence into a deep canyon. The trucker was accused of sleeping at the wheel and he admitted that he must have, but he had been driving sixteen hours steady and two-thirty in the morning was a damn treacherous time for a tired man. When the officers tried to break down his story he got proof enough from stations along the way, Franklin, Walden, Carstairs, Minerva, and back as far as the accident, all in one stretch. But a man alone couldn't drive more than twelve hours at the wheel of a commercial truck, the officers told him. It was against the law.

"Whose law?" the trucker asked. "Not no law that'll feed my wife and kids when the boss says go and I don't go — " So he was held for manslaughter and the next noon a pretty girl walked up and down Philadelphia Avenue in a sandwich board.

> Your LIFE is in the hands
> of one doctor
> and in the hands of every
> TRUCKER
> on the highways.
> Help him keep it SAFE by
> giving him a decent
> WAGE
> for decent HOURS

It was Lew's Nora, happy with the first good news from the hospital. All the smaller people of the capital city stopped to look back at her passing, feeling it was almost like New York, seeing such a thing on their own streets. A mighty pretty girl too, with maybe some sense to the stuff on that board. J. B. Groves didn't think so. He rushed into a drugstore and called the police station to tear hell out of the chief, as he called it, for permitting the outrage. But it seemed there was no ordinance covering the case, and it being a woman, maybe they'd just be making a martyr out of her, instead of a joke, like now. "Joke, hell!" roared J. B., and got in touch with the mayor.

The old roosters along the American Bank wall enjoyed the girl's passing. "I be damned," said the Coot, spitting, but it wasn't the pretty legs he was noticing this time, just the sandwich board, that he had seen Hamm and Dillard strap together the night before.

In addition to the truck troubles, particularly the treason of the outstate operatives, there was the death of Colonel Frank Edwards, head of the Trans-Mississippi Life, just dropped on the street, and the week-long rain with a cloudburst fall opening night to depress the business men of Franklin. Instead of ten thousand potential customers passing every window, the whole avenue was a grey wall of water thick as the upper falls of the Grand. Even old Hayden, who had lived dry in a cave off the First Street sewer since back in Coolidge prosperity, was flooded out. And when the sky finally cleared, the morning brought a frost that cooked the gardens like live steam, the first killing frost in September since the World War.

Now La Belle Rose, Charley Stetbettor's astrologer, came forward to say that she had predicted a bad September for Franklin way back in August, the supposed prophecies appearing in the evening paper in an inky half-page ad marked "Paid for by the Friends of Good Government," no individuals named. Although only old Charley seemed to recall these predictions, they made good talking, these calamities she had foreseen, including even the Red labor disturbances and the killing frost. For October she promised that men would become wiser, see the wickedness in high places, and prepare to vote for a man born under Aries to leadership.

"Yeh, vote themselves into the little Hitler fists of old Charley Stet and his 'America for Americans' crowd!" the old-timers told each other over their beer down at Horsemeat's. Even if that La Belle had really predicted a September swing far away from the officeholders no old politicians would have been impressed.

"It don't take no stargazing to see every incumbent's licked in September," they said, "but it's October that tells the story. And election day."

Many Franklinites, publicly pretending amusement, were privately doing what they could to scratch together the ten dollars for a complete horoscope including the "Intimate Guide to Success in Love and Business," as the fine-print footnote to the advertisement promised. The next evening the papers carried the professional cards of six other capital city astrologers, under pressure, because they had carried the one. When the Coot came by to look through Hamm's paper he thumped the page with his pipe. "A bunch of buzzards sure gather quick when they see one a gorgin' himself — "

"Yes," Hamm agreed. "There's something about insecurity that draws fortune-tellers — hard times and election years."

"And particularly capital cities," the Coot finished. "I bet they're thick as roaches at the City Mission around Washington — "

There obviously was a growing courage among the reactionaries of Franklin, perhaps because Senator Bullard had spent two days in the city delivering addresses at such varying places as a beer hall down in the Polish bottoms, Josina Black's Norman living room, and the fieldhouse at the university.

The newspapers had done a little predicting too, prophesying that no one would sign the petitions for Carl Halzer's candidacy for the United States Senate, but although the petitions grew big as syrup buckets, almost no one would admit that his name was on them, until the *World* printed the whole lot, to encourage withdrawal. Even with his name on the ballot the Franklin papers ridiculed the new candidate, running pictures of the farmer-labor delegation that brought the petitions to the capitol, calling them "aliens and red-necked bums, like that scarfaced Ham from the clay banks." That week the papers were swamped with letters, mostly from out of town. Some said they thought strikers were still citizens, even in Kanewa, and if it was the farmers who kept the state going that they were calling red-necked bums, it was getting to be too good a joke, since the money boys of the capital city had made bums out of so many farmers. Others wondered if the editors knew that "Scarfaced Ham" from the clay banks was a writer for several magazines, including the *Nation?* The editor telephoned around and got several letters from good Franklin names, like Black, Welles, and Doover, to print with the less literate ones for Halzer. The one from Glen Doover was pulled after the first edition

— stirred up too much talk about his son's connection with
the hit-and-run business. Editorially the papers tried to discuss the candidacy as a joke. The Bull of Bashan, like others
of his kind, must have his season of bellowing, and then he
would quietly return to his pasture, as the Bull had before.
Then it got around that Marylin Welles's blue roadster had
been standing in the Halzer farm twice in one week, and a
neighbor even told of seeing the girl out at the hog lot with
Carl, looking at his Berkshires. It took some of the edge off
the letter in the *World* by her brother, and made a good story
for cocktails and tea. It got action, too, from the easy-going
Billie Bamper, who ran a little sporting-goods store for the
country-club trade, the university executives, and a few of
the higher-ups at the capitol. Sometimes people wondered how
he lived, and managed to keep his civic interests going, char-
tering planes with Cobby Welles to follow the football team,
putting in whole months of time out with Senator Bullard
on campaign, and going with the Kanewa delegation to the
meetings of the associated manufacturers. When Billie heard
about Marylin's car in the Halzer yard he rubbed the top of
his pink head with his palm, pulled at his fat lip, and decided
to drive out to Susan Welles. He found Marylin in the sun-
room, in overalls, a Scotch and soda before her, looking
through back numbers of the *Swinebreeder*. Billie picked one
up, pointed out Halzer's name on the address slip.

"Doing your fishing in mighty shallow water, don't you
think?" he demanded.

She handed the man a glass. "Have a drink and remember
that you're fishing clear out of your depth, Billie Bamper,
trying that tone on me. Besides, maybe I'm really interested
in stock improvement."

"Then you better put it off till after election."

"How do you know I'll be here then?" she asked, without
looking up from her magazine. Of course she couldn't be
meaning Washington, but there was no use putting ideas into

women's heads, so Billie hunted up Cassie, who had moved into another house and was fighting with the architects and with Cees Hammond and his decorator over the rebuilding of Welleshaven. Not that Billie expected to get anywhere much with her either. Somehow poor Cobby never did learn to manage his womenfolks, and went and died, leaving them to run loose and raise hell for other people.

"I'm only Marylin's mother, you know — " Cassie reminded Billie. "Anyway you're not worried by a hog farmer. His leading the strikers Labor Day will defeat him with all right-thinking people — "

Silver City was closed for the season, the stands boarded up, the swimming pool drained. The fairgrounds, too, were deserted, except the parking space for the weekly wrestling match. But the university was open; five thousand students in town. There would be another seven, eight hundred as soon as the capital city got the agricultural college moved in from Benway, and more than that when they killed the four teachers' colleges scattered over the state.

While half the students plodded up and down looking for a little work, the rest were welcomed as guests, with special windows along Philadelphia Avenue featuring photographs of last year's school celebrities: the honorary colonel of the R.O.T.C. in her white uniform with purple-faced cape; the prom girl with gardenias in her hair, the May queen, and the sleek-lined Buffalo goddess. The football team was used everywhere, from the twelve-foot photograph of the squad in Hammond's main avenue window to the crumb cookie men iced in purple and gold in the bakeries of the Polish bottoms. Greek-letter motives were popular all through rush week; even Samelly Finestein, the secondhand man, had a Sig plaque in his dusty window and wouldn't say who hocked it, certain there would be no broken glass to disturb this week. When Harold Welles and half a dozen of his fellow shirt wearers went down afterward it was gone, a hair wreath in its place, and a smile of welcome on Samelly's face. "What can I do for you gentlemen today — ?"

Every fall it was the same; the ambitious, the impressionable, the idealistic youth of the state swarming into the capital city. Many were from the remotest homes and got their first glimpse of the magnificence of man from his handiwork on the campus, the fieldhouse, the huge grey football stadium, the Greek-letter castles on the terraced Row, and from the capitol building that overlooked all the city. If they made a frat, the local sponsor had them out to tea or a smoker on Blue Ridge, talked to them of his kind of success, of ways to get ahead in the world. By Christmas many couldn't bear to go home.

"Fat ticks down there is what makes thin sheep here," a father out on Wild Horse Plains told his complaining son. But that didn't make the thin sheep any more attractive.

If the student turned out to be exceptional at all he was soon headed away east; if original at all he was driven out; if studious, he went away on a fellowship to Harvard or Yale, or even Oxford, perhaps to an interneship in one of the large medical centers; if ambitious, to bigger business opportunities or to the staff of corporation lawyers. Those who stayed in Franklin or had to return to their home communities disseminated the ideals — economic, political, and cultural — of the capital city.

With the castles along the Row heavily mortgaged there was always competition for the more likely freshmen, with illegal pre-rush groups gathering for midafternoon caking and cards in the dusky booths of the Buffalo coffee shop. Rush week was a milling of dinners, teas, and evening parties with high laughter and much gushy talk among the sisters, hardboiled big-shot blowing among the brothers — all to impress the confused rushees, usually away from home for the first time. Then suddenly one morning the newcomers awoke to find themselves pledges whose business it was to answer the door, the telephone, and fetch and carry for everyone — the new house slaves. If they were really too unprepossessing or not long enough on financial backing, they found themselves living in a dormitory or rooming house with the poor and the studious who came here to work.

Mollie Tyndale had, of course, gone Kay Dee, with the newest, the finest house on the Row, its buttermilk-white front flood-lit, reminding Hamm Rufe of the Kress building on Fifth Avenue. It wasn't paid for, and so a nice donation from Samuel Tyndale was acceptable. But Mollie was never initiated. After a week of school she drove down past the Co-op. Burt saw her coming and slipped into the men's toilet and so Hamm went out before the manager noticed. She had stopped by to see how Lew Lewis was getting along, she said, but when Hamm started to tell her, she couldn't keep up the pretense. "He's here, isn't he?" she whispered.

The man nodded, wiping at her shining windshield.

"Tell him," she said finally, "tell Burt I've got to go away. To England."

"England?" Hamm asked, afraid for the boy.

"Yes." She started the engine, released the clutch. "Alone," she said low, and slipped out of the driveway.

At the hospital Lew Lewis was slowly pulling out of his long infection. He probably owed his life to the same stuff that had killed half a dozen young fellows trying to cure themselves of a dose of something besides lead poisoning, two, three years ago right around Franklin. The striker was pulling through, his big frame, once the fulcrum of the varsity line, bare as the scaffolding of a barn. But with her Lew eating again, the little waitress on the morning shift smiled on the truckers once more even with no investigation at all of the shooting, and with the anti-picketing law probably coming up before the state supreme court this week, and Lew stewing that he couldn't be flag-bearer for the protest parade through the capitol — couldn't even get himself to the can without a woman helping.

He had other worries. Twice a sweet-mouthed, grey-haired little lady came in to sit with him. She never said who she was but he thought she'd get around to the God business pretty soon. Instead, she led Lew to talk of himself and the trucking situation, gently prodding his resentment to get him to name the company whose hired gunmen shot him. Finally he rang for the nurse, but before the girl came she was gone. And every week the mimeographed *Christian Challenger* was thrown over the screen upon his bed, reporting his progress as a menace to the city.

When Lew got well enough for visitors, the striking truckers came trooping in, to stand awkwardly around the bed, whispering at first, and finally roaring their laughs right out loud, forgetting the three other patients in the room. But Lew could see they were worried. He got the story out of Nora when she came. There was talk of the national guards, more hired thugs, too, but on top of that the guards.

He had to get out of here, he told Dr. Snell. Oh, sure, but how about the hospital bill? Until it was paid he was in hock. That was the hell of it, Lew complained. The doctor didn't agree. He was eating, wasn't he?

With Halzer a candidate, Hamm Rufe had to think over the state situation. Not that there was any chance of losing the big farmer to Washington, but a good protest vote would do more than merely jar the back teeth of the Capital City *World* and its Ridge customers. There were, of course, many stratifications in the city of sixty thousand between those who sat in the cool duskiness of Welleshaven before Cobby's coffin and the squatters of Herb's Addition. About two hundred families in Franklin were comfortably fixed, with good security of business and, excluding the football coach at the university, the chancellor, and the governor of the state, with some security of job — the backbone of Hammond and Schendler customers. Below these were the twenty-five hundred or so who got along pretty well, but with no security of the future: the small business men, the upper half of the university staff, and the departmental executives of the capitol. About five thousand families were just managing, the breadwinner subject to layoff any time, with no security of bed or breakfast. Any day these people might find themselves seriously answering civil service institute ads, trying to write for the confession magazines, wearing out the library dictionaries making three-letter words from commercial slogans, and writing testimonials to go with box tops, especially right after Franklin's quota of prize money was doled out. Between these spurts of hope they would consider mushroom culture, chain letters, addressing envelopes at home, and finally door-to-door peddling. In the end they could try to join the two thousand eligible for government projects if the money was ever voted. Until then there was the six dollars a month direct relief, which would drop to four and perhaps three dollars when the seven thousand on the list climbed to twelve thousand in February, or more, if there was another WPA layoff or if the little tannery followed the other factories that shut down the last fifteen years: the broom, the glove, the overall and shirt factories, and the little packing house. Or they might join the two hundred or so, mostly lone men and women, who looked to the city dumps and the garbage cans as more generous and reliable than the county relief agency.

Yes, there should be a healthy protest vote right here, if Halzer could bring it out.

Franklin, however, was still better off than the rest of the state, or the usual industrial center. Through all the depression the state government expenditures in the capital city increased much more than the fifteen percent cut of the university faculty or the reduction in student money. The administrative expenditures of the statewide federal programs went into circulation here, and much of the eight million put into the capitol building since 1928. In addition, the Kanewa branches of eastern investment companies were here, to be close to the legislature.

"Just followin' our money," the dispossessed explained as they pulled into the capital city, forty-three families the last week in September, and more to come by cold weather, many more.

With September done things did look up, the conservative candidates gaining ground, football spirit running high at bonfire rallies, with the stadium white-birds collecting an average of five bushels of empty bottles after each game. That meant a spending crowd, so far, at least. But the coach had better be whipping the boys up. Kanewa wasn't used to losing games.

There was literary news too, as the *World* called it. A book about the town's own Frontier House was chosen for October distribution by one of the book clubs, giving the capital city some fine national publicity.

"Abigail Allerton has told the very human story of a hotel with flavor and character, and, through it, the story of a city, a state and an era. A witty piece of writing, and profound too," the paper quoted from the advance folders. They were well gotten up, with an etching of the old hotel as it looked in its good days, before the front balcony was pulled down, the grilling used to fence the Gilson lot at the cemetery. W. J. Bryan stood on the balcony, his long hair blowing, the flaring torches of a mid-ninety parade massed in the street below.

The Wakoonian Internationals moved fast, almost as fast as the insurance agents and the reporters. Would Miss Allerton honor them with her presence at a special dinner? The

Waks were the newest of the luncheon clubs, still pretty local for all the optimism of their name, but not yet muscle-bound. It was well that they weren't. When the evening pink with Abigail's picture and the announcement of the book's acceptance was out, everybody seemed anxious to honor the new author. Billings, the manager of the old hotel, looked around the faded red plush of his lobby and planned to re-model a bit, with a grand opening and the author as honor guest. There'd be a revival in business sure now. He'd take it up with the receivers tomorrow. A landmark, that's what the Frontier was — a national landmark, and he'd billboard it so for a hundred miles each way.

That evening there were a dozen telegrams and special deliveries at Abigail's door, and a box of flowers, purple and white chrysanthemums, from Hamm, with a note: "For the town's new glammer gal." There were strangers at the door, too, lone men, drawn to a single woman with a little prospec-tive cash like old mules to a bag of oats on a passing truck. The next day the postman brought a bundle of mail clear up to Abigail's door, ten times too much for the box. Among the lot were half a dozen manuscripts from Franklinites, people she had never heard of. They wanted her to correct them, to get them published — and keep the matter strictly confidential, please. Towards noon Cassie Welles called, with congratulations. She was so glad for Miss Allerton's good fortune, and would she come to dinner that night? The driver would pick her up at seven.

When Abigail refused, saying she didn't go out much, Cassie got down to business. She had a young friend who wrote, not history books, like hers, but poetry, things that were beautiful.

Abigail was pleased to know it.

But he was having a little difficulty, Cassie went on. He was so adorably impractical. "I thought perhaps you might have your editor buy them.". . .

Despite the boycotting of the Wakoonian dinner by Cassie Welles and her group, the reservations piled up so they moved to the main dining room of the chamber, hired a string trio for five dollars, added two more speakers, and got radio time. They decided to send Abigail a corsage of orchids and a chauffeur to pick her up, and were disturbed and embarrassed by her unprepossessing appearance, straight boxed hair, and plain navy street dress, but they saw almost at once that it really magnified the generosity of their gesture.

Abigail was uneasy. With the prepublication copies of the book out she had expected resentment, Franklin being what it was, and could see nothing beyond a little disappointment as she walked into the high plaster and gold room with long tables narrow as the double planks set up for threshers at home. The place seemed full of older women, some with artificial flowers on top of their heads, their shoulders bare with the indecent, plucked look of skin seldom exposed. Half a dozen professional book reviewers were set up close to get personal bits for their circles. "She makes you just *see* things, much better than reading the books," Mrs. Beal's group always said of her. Somehow she managed to get at least one slip with a writer's autograph for each member of her group during the year. The bookstores objected to her particularly, for she had all their better charge customers.

When the food came the chicken-fried steak was cold, but the ice cream had a chocolate center in the shape of a book, and the coffee was strong and plentiful, as men like it. While the speaker introduced Abigail he held a copy of the *Anteroom* in his hand for everyone to see, praising it fulsomely, using the publisher's blurb as his own words, and heating Abigail's uncomfortable ears to a steady, burning red.

He told of this woman who had come in from one of the small outstate colleges to a history assistantship at the university for work on her doctorate: "The Inception, Growth and Culmination of the Movement for Popular Election of

United States Senators in the Trans-Mississippi Middle West,"
stumbling over the difficult title as he read it from a card in
his hand. The audience was undisturbed, laughing freely as
he explained that from such a slow-freight title Miss Allerton
had "elaborated" a book the publishers were calling *Anteroom for Kingmakers*. The title left them a little doubtful,
although it had appeared correctly in some of the newspaper
stories. Several requests brought a repetition, followed by a
dead silence. But the speaker, a pushing young attorney with
political hopes and a charter membership in the Wakoonians,
knew what to do — snow them under with words.

"We have then with us tonight," he said grandly, "a lady
who has caught a vision of the glory and the romance of our
fair city of Franklin as typified by the Frontier House. Studying our immortal townsmen, our politicians and our statesmen, this lady has carved through their deeds and personalities
an everlasting niche for herself as the recorder of their great
service to the glory of our fair city and our great nation.
Here you will find such picturesque great ones as the vener-
able Colonel Welles with his long flowing locks and his Prince
Albert, United States senator and friend of Buffalo Bill; Jacob
Stoor; Drygoods Mike Hammond, the farseeing builder of
Hammond's; the handsome Joseph Colmar; T. S. Shuler, long
majority leader of the house, and so on" — apparently not to
give any mention to the founder of the city, the old radical,
thought Abigail. But the man was far beyond George Rufer,
to "our distinguished junior senator, the Honorable John
Bullard, who as a stripling learned sound politics at the feet
of these statesmen. You will see Blaine, the Plumed Knight,
address an enthusiastic rally from the old Frontier balcony,
and from the same place McKinley turn our fair city back
into the true path of sound Republicanism from which it has
wavered only once since, and, God willing, shall never do so
again!"

A full hour later the man was finally whipping his hoarsened voice into a climax: "Here you will see," he roared out, "our nation at her most gloriously American, when every man was still a free individual, and growing prosperity walked with her hand on every shoulder. Business grew big, land values skyrocketed, labor was free from disturbing outside influence to work or not, as it preferred; and every man was free to climb the ladder of success without let or hindrance. As the biographer of the greatest period of American Individualism, I give you Dr. Abigail Allerton."

Abigail was struck dumb. She could barely rise and because there was nothing else to say, she told them they were most kind, and that she hoped they would not be too disappointed in her book.

"Indeed, I think I can say without hesitation that we will not be disappointed. I think I am safe in saying that Franklin has added a lustrous star to the great literary names of all times and all nations!" the young attorney generously replied for them.

It was a long, long evening, and when Abigail finally escaped, she ran up her stairs, tears of anger and humiliation burning her fine eyes. How could she have been so stupid, expose herself to such inanities?

Hamm Rufe was waiting in her apartment, the radio still on, a dance band blaring instead of the voice of the fulsome young Wakoonian.

"Is the book really as putrid as they suggest?" he asked. "I can't conceive your doing anything so bad." He had beer and pretzels sent up and when Abigail had talked herself into a little calmness he got her to bring out her copy, let him read from it.

There was a preface, and a short introductory chapter on the region, covering the fur-trader period, the Indian wars, with a cut of the old Harcoot trail station, the first place of lodging in the Franklin vicinity.

The story of the hotel itself was headed with a line drawing of the first unit of Frontier House, built the year before Franklin wangled the capitol from Grandapolis. Almost immediately, Abigail showed, the hotel became the rallying place for the Stoors, Colmars, Kuglers, and the Jileses of the early city, with a fringe of smaller real-estate boosters and outstate politicians who wanted the capital away from the entrenched Grandapolis crowd. For fifty years after they succeeded the legislative caucuses were called at Frontier House, and much of the legislation formalized in the capitol was arranged in the hotel bedrooms over cigar butts and whiskey bottles. Here all the major sell-outs of Kanewa prior to the period of utility expansion took place. In those days the powers of the state were the two main railroads, in a perennial struggle for control of the state supreme court, later the railway commission and always to name the legislatively appointed United States senators, for it was in Washington, then as now, that the big killings were made. When appointment time came around the railroads set up rival headquarters at the Frontier Hotel, a floor apiece, and ribald stories were still told of the outstate legislators who wandered into the wrong camp for their entertainment and stipend. Not that the big-town lawmakers were more honest, as George Rufer's *World* pointed out, only more conversant with the hotel, since they were usually full-time railroad tools. Gradually the practice of milking both sides became so common that the president of the C. G. & W. moved his headquarters over into the governor's office in the capitol, away from bad influence. To this President Herrald of the North Line replied by roaring that an honest legislator, like an honest senator, was one who stayed bought. The stench over the railroad's actual footprints in the governor's office got the incumbent impeached and once more the Frontier housed both sides. This time the back stairs were blocked and the boys running the newly installed elevators memorized the names of each floor's consignment, as the legislators were called.

The entertainment at the Frontier during session time was always lavish and lusty, with a guest bar, a resident gambler, and plenty of women. When the time came for a senate appointment each railroad brought in a special host, Judge or Colonel somebody or other, with a florid face, a Prince Albert, and a hearty palm. He set up a free bar on his backer's floor for the key legislators. They drank what they wanted for a starter and received a pictorial booklet of the railroad that they always tucked carefully into an inside pocket, for between the pages somewhere was a bill, sometimes as high as five hundred dollars, and once it was a round thousand. Then the guests were eased into the gambling rooms, where imported big-time card sharpers worked for a two-way cut with the railroad, the hotel getting either half of each gambler's take or a full third of the total. For those so inclined there were good friends of the Judge or the Colonel, girls from Omaha, or Kansas City, Des Moines or St. Louis.

Few of the men refused to play, none squawked when the easy money was gone. The Frontier's take, even with the crookedest gamblers, was usually five to fifteen thousand dollars a night like this, and of course the hotel paid no freight charges all the fifty years.

"Greatest period of American Individualism!" Hamm snorted, and by now the evening was funny to Abigail too, perhaps because of the beer.

Several trials of midwestern railroad senators for bribery hastened the shift to popular election, the final chapter pointed out. Then the Franklin House was built up the avenue beyond the noisy business zone, and later the Buffalo Hotel, up-to-date, and within four blocks of the statehouse. The empty red plush of the Frontier began to fade and by the time lobbyists were legalized, they registered elsewhere.

But even before the town went dry in 1914 salesmen were planning their route sheets with only daytime stops in Franklin. Too damn many women wearing high collars, even for a capital city, one complained to his boss.

Long ago the old Frontier became a stopping place for those of small expense accounts, and teachers and Sunday School groups. There was a register of regular guests, too, older men and women living on annuities, or pensions, a retired petty politician or two, an ex-preacher, and always about thirty widows. There were still plenty of set-ups ordered football time, but the rest of the year the excitement was usually limited to a mouse behind a dresser, a stray Saturday-night drunk in the halls, or the roaring of the third-rate wrestler who had to have hot milk toast and absolute silence as soon as he came in.

Hamm Rufe was pleased with the book, amazed to see so much that he vaguely knew brought to such reality by an outsider. Abigail had made a sound protagonist of the hotel and its three main employees: Boswell Dillings, the manager with the glass eye, called Crock behind his back; Spider, the wiry little pastry cook whose fingers were as clumsily deft with a deck of cards as with the icing bag; and Mrs. Miller, the housekeeper, named Dewlaps by a cowman from out on Wild Horse Plains. Dew didn't mind, for she had never seen a cow from close and thought it meant something fresh and morning-sweet. She also thought every young woman stranded at the hotel an innocent maiden betrayed. Not even succoring the girl from Daisy Dee's, planted by the town's jokers, cured her.

Through the story of the hotel ran the change that had come upon the town and the state, the change from the open and direct bribery of a legislature through a little good whiskey, a few thousand dollars, and a set of bedmates to the vast and usually indirect and unrecognized business it had become today. Now there were millions at the command of representatives of eastern interests for the purchase of crucial newspapers, for free propaganda to the press, the schools, and the churches, and for outright bribery, when this crudity was necessary. And there were always high-salaried jobs for any young men smart enough to become dangerous; entertainment, flattery, new cars and further advantages, so-called, for anyone in a strategic position.

"Enter our mysterious Grandapolis party giver, Cole Dringer," Hamm said.

Yes, Cole Dringer and all his poor dupes in Kanewa, in Franklin particularly, with the responsibility of the capital upon them, living off the state and selling it out, selling out their fellow men, and themselves.

Why?

It seemed that even the sons of old independents like George Rufer had become so dubious of their ability to stand alone that they would reach out for any dangling liana that could only bring them down. Worse, perhaps they were not great trees with errant branches at all but only poor little roadside weeds swaying towards the dodder that would suck their blood and move over them to the next.

To this Hamm had nothing at all to say and as the three o'clock streamliner, the *President Coolidge,* was whistling in, he left. Outside, leaning against the wall, was a very sleepy young man with an autograph book.

"You're my first author," he confided to Abigail Allerton.

Early the next morning a professor's wife called. She was to review the *Anteroom* for the Faculty Club on publication day, and no copies were available. She would consider a loan a great favor.

But the book was back before breakfast the next day, without an explanation or a thank you, and at the review the woman said, "I found *Anteroom for Kingmakers* so sordid

that I took the liberty to change to *Sun on the Window Sill*
as more appropriate. When the other — the other thing has
been read you will understand."

The book was on sale an hour when the landlady came
lumbering up to Abigail's apartment. "It's a lady by my
telephone, a very mat lady. She say you do not answer when
she ring you — "

The next few days there were dozens of mad people, with
threats of libel, and of direct bodily violence, like, say, a fist
in the snoot. There were angry denunciations in the papers
that had been so immoderate with praise less than a week ago,
and loud demands that Abigail be asked to resign her job at
the university. People fell away before her on the street, even
old acquaintances, and then sought her out privately to get at
an enemy through further exposures. They could really give
her the inside dirt, the real stuff —

Some of the people who called hoped to avoid future exposure through pretended friendliness, for there was no telling
what that woman might dig into next. When it was discovered she had been looking through the records of the Benway
bank robbery, Johnson Black, nephew of Josina, and the
town's perennial bachelor, offered himself as a public sacrifice
by asking her to take his good, sound capital city name. He
got pretty abusive when she said she wouldn't care to, but
quieted down fast enough when she asked him about the
paresis in his family. Yes, he admitted, his father died of it,
in a sanitarium in Switzerland. Abigail was ashamed now,
sorry for the man as he went slowly down the stairs, his hat
in his hands.

Of course, he didn't have sense enough to keep it, told it
in purpling anger around the city club. It went through the
town like water poured on gravel, particularly through the
second-best people, and on lower. But even some of those
most pleased at this take-down for a Black couldn't forgive
such talk in a woman.

Abigail's most violent denunciator was Della Loran, the poor-relation cousin of Josina Black who got into Hattie Krasinski's apartment for a folded bill. Since nothing came of the one kiss she had from Cobby Welles she seemed to have turned against men, and anyone contaminated. She liked movies of the *Girl of the Limberlost* type, read *Freckles* and tried *Black Oxen* too, but decided it was slow. Instead she hunted up a woman doctor who might know about the transplantations. Yes, the doctor knew of the various Steinachs, but she suggested that nature be left alone.

Della finally gave up taking casual acquaintances to strange towns after a girl called the house detective to get her out of the woman's room. While the story was kept from the papers it made fine talk over the bridge tables when contract was losing its edge. It was Della who denounced the Monastery, the old rooming house full of men, an ex-convict, a renegade priest, and a dozen others, including several university students. The place was raided at her insistence but the capital city police felt mighty foolish taking half a dozen young fellows to the station just because they wore silk panties. So they turned the lot loose, without any publicity, but a woman picked up for soliciting on the post-office steps told the story around among her customers. "I tells 'em, 'Boys, you oughta go to Kansas City. That's the market for lemon suckers.' "

The last few years Della was stalking out of moving pictures, snooping over news stands and through the stacks at the city and the university libraries, copying out passages to take up with the right people. As soon as she got around to the *Anteroom* she hurried with her page of excerpts to the mayor. But he was having trouble enough with a co-operative packing house that somehow got a building permit, three traffic deaths at the First Street crossing, and, of course, the strike. So Della made the rounds of the town, even to her relatives, who did what they could to keep her out of their affairs. But she had good luck this time. When the church notices came in Friday there was scarcely a one that failed to list a Sunday sermon against Abigail — one opportunity for contemporary comment that would enrage no organized group. Several of the sermons were listed by the book's name; one was on "Realism versus Godliness in Current Books," and one on "The Viper in Our Bosom." With these went a lead editorial in the Sunday *World* headed: —

RENEGADE FOLLOWERS OF IDA TARBELL

recalling that at the turn of the century there was a muck-raking woman loose in America, a certain Ida Tarbell. But the successful business ventures that she attacked were so solidly conceived and grounded in the American Way that they were today stronger than ever, while who remembered Ida Tarbell?

"So will it be with the recent scurrilous attack upon the fair name of our capital city and the people who built her greatness."

Hamm Rufe was ashamed. This was the same paper in which his grandfather once wrote so eloquent a defense of the exposé of the Standard Oil. He copied it out, with page and date, added a review of Miss Tarbell's autobiography, and sent it to the editor, wishing he might sign it Rufer Hammond, part owner of the Capital City *World*. That would put maggots into the man's belly, as the Coot would say.

There was no acknowledgment, but the paper got together a long symposium made up of local opinions of the book, some of the authorities quoted frankly admitting that they had not seen it but knew the contents. Only the head of American history at the university and the local Y.W.C.A. secretary were for the author. The professor said he had read the book in manuscript. All the material was from Miss Allerton's published dissertation, completely documented and available at the library to anyone. There was more the author might have told.

But the man was reminded that he had a good position for these times and a big family to keep. After a trip to the chancellor's office he made another public statement. The Allerton book, upon second reading, did seem needlessly sensational and in bad taste. Factual material proper to the specialized use of the historian was not necessarily proper for public consumption.

Dora Stilwell, from the Y, stood fast. Sidestepping unpleasant facts never remedied them. Miss Allerton's book was on the whole well-written and completely convincing, as the storm of protests should indicate. It also seemed, Miss Stilwell said, after her ten years of residence in the capital city, exceptionally moderate in tone. That got her name into the *Christian Challenger* as a Red, and when it was called to her attention she was undisturbed. Oh, the Y's were often labeled Red. She, herself, was more frequently accused of anarchism. Dr. Snell and Till Walford wanted to enter the fight but Hamm and Abigail talked them out of it. Why sacrifice themselves for a victory that time would win if it was worth the winning?

For two weeks the witch-burning went merrily on. Here and there a woman pitied the writer her plainness, but seeing so many men turn to look after her on the street, then straighten themselves a little and walk on with unFranklinish jauntiness, the women hated her more than they pitied.

By this time the university was involved far beyond the history department. Two men who had lost their powerful positions in the purchasing department after the old chancellor died, for commission taking, came forward to charge the present administration with encouraging subversive activities and all-around laxness — Abigail Allerton and her book, based on a doctorate, their Exhibit A. Senator Bullard joined their demand for a legislative investigation, and Charley Stet came to town to thunder against the immorality of the students and "the devilish plans of the International Jew bankers and Jew Reds, aided and abetted by the Scarlet Woman of the campus!"

By this time Hallie Rufer Hammond got around to reading the book and wrote Abigail a long letter. She must apologize for the stupidity of her townsmen and say how sorry she was that her father, George Rufer, could not have lived to see the fine job Miss Allerton had made of the old Frontier House story. She was right to quote him, for he was always open and free in his denunciations of all the things in the *Anteroom.*

Abigail thanked her, saying she was pleased that the capital city's most vigorous founder left something of his strength and courage behind. That night Hamm was in, laughing a little over the letters about the book with Abigail. When he came across the Hammond one with the carbon of the reply attached, Abigail noticed that his face sobered, bleakened like the clay slope above his shack, especially when he came to the end: "For the good of the history department, I am resigning my position — "

He stood up, letting all the letters in his lap slip to the floor, and without even a good-bye escaped to the street, leaving Abigail to look after him in concern.

CHAPTER VII

FOR two days, ever since he saw that the town had driven Abigail to resign her position with the university, Hamm Rufe sat hard and bitter as an osage orange within himself. At work or on his chilling stoop in the evening it was the same, and one after another his visiting neighbors got up and went away. But the Coot stayed. He wanted to talk about the city's protestations against *Anteroom for Kingmakers*.

"Ain't that just like a hysterical old chippie — flying into a tear just because somebody's dug up a chunk of her past?" he asked several times, so finally Hamm had to reply, Well, if the capital city really was a chippie, would the advertisement of her past whip up a failing business for her too?

The Coot nodded, pulling his pipe out of his beard to spit. Yeh, it seemed to, down to the city library, anyhow. Hamm knew about that. They told Abigail that if the reserves for the *Anteroom* kept accumulating, they ought to double the record set by *The President's Daughter*, years ago, and so far the all-time high for capital city reading.

But suddenly Franklin was faced with a scandal not so conveniently in the past as the purple days of the old Frontier House, and much more disturbing to outstate parents of girls at the university. The abortion mill on lower Philadelphia Avenue got into the paper.

The whole thing was started by a small item about a student from Walden who died in a local hospital, "after a brief illness." Such death notices were common enough in Franklin, but the girl's fiancé was the nephew of Dr. Luden of Zena, who had moved out of the capital city after fighting ten years for a liberalized attitude towards sex education and the establishment of a birth-control clinic, even if it had to masquerade as a maternity center.

One evening in late September the boy came running blindly across lawns and flower beds to his uncle, the paper with the little item held out before him. It was Nellie, his Nellie. She had been acting queer the last month or so, sent his movie camera back and wouldn't even let him go down to take her to Franklin to school. Then the letter he mailed to the dormitory where she stayed last year came back, marked "Not here."

The doctor drove straight to the capital city to talk to some of his medical friends. A few days later the story of an abortion mill in Franklin broke in a streamer across the Grandapolis pinks, with a picture of Eddie Chimmer, former vacuum-cleaner salesman, who called himself Doctor of Electro-Adjustication, and several of his office and consultation rooms taken from peepholes in the ceiling. Two officers had watched the place at night, saw fifteen women receive treatment and almost as many go away because they didn't have the fifty-dollar fee. Eddie Chimmer was a gaunt, stoop-shouldered man, with a sloping forehead and deep eye sockets that he fancied resembled Lincoln's. "Like the great Emancipator — " he told the reporters. But his mouth was a thin inverted U and his receding chin disappeared into a loose fold of skin like a lizard's.

There was a picture of a book, too, that the doctor, a native of the city and an autograph collector on the side, required his patients to sign. Of course the women used fictitious names but in the back, by key number, he entered the right ones. This book work, the investigators said, he did after the place was empty, sometimes pretty late, for business was best when the alley door to the stairs was in thick darkness. With the office finally locked Eddie sat at his old desk, his thin back bent over the book, his bony fingers creeping through the pages that held some of the best names of the town. Finally he locked it away in his old safe and went out to his supper at a chili joint near by, where nobody ever seemed to take the stool next to him.

At the first smell of the story the Franklin business men scurried around to kill it, but with the Grandapolis *Inquirer* scattering the details over the state like goatsbeard seed on the wind, they had to let the local papers use it too, toned down, of course, implying doubt of the practitioner's guilt, and hinting at personal animosity on the part of unnamed individuals — perhaps certain outstate physicians whose patients were coming in for electric adjustments.

"I got enemies who'd go to hell to get me," the prisoner said in the *World*.

Right to the last the capital city officials tried to stop the autopsy of the dead girl. Why break the mother's heart? they asked, not saying anything about implicating the doctor who signed the death warrant. But by this time both the father and mother of the girl were in town, demanding a complete investigation, their determination strong.

In the city's loud indignation Abigail and her book were forgotten. "Such things going on, and right among our own young people!" Then, remembering the source of much of the city's income, added, "And all those lovely young girls at the university, scarcely more than children, and far away from their mothers — "

Naturally the case would drag on forever, but in the meantime stories got around, stories about the hundreds of entries in the back of the brown autograph book. Mostly the names were common enough: young married women of the town's working people, and waitresses, clerks, office workers, and students, none of them very interesting for, of course, the men were not listed, although some of the best names were suspected. Those who wondered if Cobby's Hattie was on the list got snickers. There was no evidence that she had been exposed to what could be called fire, not with Marylin born too soon to be a Welles, and Harold blamed on that fake Canadian war hero — not unless little Hattie had been stepping out on her Cobby.

Anyway, wasn't there some sort of saying about specialists for the mistress, the family doctor for the wife, and the quack for the party girl? Not that Eddie Chimmer wasn't a specialist, in his way. And he did get some good names, mostly girls who were afraid of their mothers, and women who thought they were fooling their husbands and the family doctor. Even this year's empress was mentioned, her name almost the last in the book. After that got around there was a great deal of neck-stretching over the booth walls at the Buffalo coffee shop when she came in. She did look peaked, didn't everybody think? they asked each other. Yes, gaunt as a new mother cat.

Not that anything Franklin said mattered much to Helen Groves. Next week she would be away east to college, with photographs to prove she was the empress of Kanewa. Besides, her father had considerable money in American Electric. So she strode, long-legged and confident, among the booths, greeting her acquaintances with her usual little gasps of delight.

Lew Lewis was better, putting a little meat back on his bones, anxious to get out, with trucks upset every night or so at the county line, and a striker's head grooved by a bullet. Then there was the supreme court decision, so long overdue — He just had to get home.

The last trip out to the hospital Hamm took the bus around by way of Welleshaven for a look. Cassie had the curb solid with cars, the house lit up bright, working double shift, evidently. Half the front of the house was out and the center of the second story cut back, probably putting in one of those deck things everybody wanted just now. Probably with grillwork, too, like around the grounds, painted white as valentine lace, with lavender or baby-blue shutters.

Hamm knew that Cassie and Dachel were established down at the old Culbert place, Harold probably lounging around the Sig house most of the time, although he wasn't going to classes this semester, too many incompletes, Burt said. There were rumors that Dachel's lack of interest in Gold Shirt activities set hard as green apples with the son. At least he'd been talking pretty free around the Siggery about that scheming, self-loving bastard sucking around his mother. It seemed strange to Hamm that he and Cobby used to loaf around the same fraternity, up in the old Black dwelling, then, of honest Harcoot brick, with a round tower and high stained-glass windows. Now the Siggery was a big grey stone rectangle on the Row, with side panels of glass brick and an $80,000 mortgage. He and Cobby got to hanging out at the frat way back in their high school days, already against the rules — Cobby smoking and drinking with the peg-top pants and coonskin coaters, Hamm arguing politics with the cellar gang, where the ideas seemed to have settled.

Cassie Welles made her first really public appearance since Cobby's death by taking her poet to the Kanewa Authors' Club. Dachel made a fine showing, slim and handsome in his new leaf-brown suit and sand-colored shirt, his tie the mottled hazel green his eyes were in the sun. When he was introduced among the guests, he acted modest, had nothing much to say, and so gave everyone the impression that he was probably a great poet, as well as quite a lover. Sensitive too, Cassie Welles whispered to those about her, for while he wrote sheafs and sheafs of poetry, he couldn't bear to expose it to the eyes of strangers, not even to editors. Dachel seemed not to be listening, or to notice all the older women turning their faces toward him. He nibbled a radish daintily, and patted his pretty lips with his napkin.

Hamm watched them from a side table where he had taken Ona Snell, who preferred the less conspicuous place herself because the staring over little José's death was not yet done. She could understand something of the man's need to turn his scarred side from the room. But there was little chance of recognition here, either of face or voice; unlikely that those of twenty years ago would be among the writers. Even the capital city's Sunday School versifiers were imports, and anyone beyond that usually spent his first check for bus fare to New York and then on to Connecticut.

The president of the Authors' Club, a teacher in the social sciences at the little Congregational College in Weld City, had tried his best to get Abigail to speak, even made a special trip down. All he got was a lot of encouragement to do something with the story of his pioneer aunt who came out to teach the Bible to the Indians and married a French trader instead. While this really pleased him more, he had hoped to honor the debunker of Franklin publicly. He did manage a promise that she would be at the dinner after Hamm agreed to go; he even got her name into the *World* as an honor guest, back into the runover on page eight. Naturally the first-page space went to the main speaker, Wesley Brown Lowe, script director of eight daytime radio serials, all with villains who had Russian or Spanish names and thought up such devilish schemes as sending rattlesnakes in candy boxes to virtuous heroines.

Since her resignation, Abigail found herself becoming the persecuted underdog to an increasing number of middle Franklinites, who had the parasite's contempt for the institutions that kept the city alive. "Always making the little fellow the goat — " they told each other. Hoping that Abigail might be coaxed to speak after all, a large crowd of the town's more curious turned out for the dinner, with many more coming in later. They got to see Dachel, anyway, with his thick auburn hair waving back from his pale temples. They stared upon the leisurely grace and the fresh youth of him with envy and nudged each other at Cassie, whispering: "He's living with her — and the ground not yet settled in on old Cobby — "

Because Cassie demanded that at least one of her children attend the dinner with her, Marylin came. The mother would have preferred Harold. Two handsome young men were so becoming to a mature woman, she always thought. But the son had an important meeting on, and Cassie called Carl Halzer instead. He would be her guest, hers and Marylin's, she said. He made a previous engagement in the best Blue Ridge manner, but when he wondered about her purpose at Hamm's, the Coot said he'd ought to go.

"They's a free meal in it and while Cassie's outfit won't vote for you anyhow, hundreds a people in this one-horse town will, just on the strength of you showing up there with them."

"And hundreds won't for that very reason, and a smart decision — " Carl said.

The Coot was right, Hamm thought. Truckers and farmers didn't usually go to the writers' dinner, and besides most of them were pretty solid for Carl anyway. He thought it might pay to go — besides being pretty funny.

The farmer complained that he preferred growing corn and Berkshires for a living to politics and fun like that.

"Well, you'll probably have to go right on growing Berkshires after election, but you owe a little something to the signers of your petitions, if only a sincere effort — "

The back of Carl's neck was red enough from the sun and wind without the extra embarrassment that the airs of the Welleses caused him. But he managed to get through the dinner by looking over to the speakers' table where Abigail was struggling with the big-shot talk of the script director, or off to the corner where he could see Hamm's straight back.

Before the coffee came the guild president arose to introduce the honor guests, Abigail, as the state's one writer of significance, and then the surprised Carl — the most promising new timber of the election year. He was thankful, he said, to be living in Kanewa, and have the privilege of voting for a man like the Bellowing Bull of Bashan.

"It is to young men like you, Carl, boys from the farm and the small town, uncontaminated by the parasitism of our midwestern capital cities, and to the young liberals from the industrial centers of the east, that we must look for the preservation of our democracy, for the America Franklin and Jefferson hoped to build."

Carl's face burned dark under the words of approval and the public smiling of Marylin Welles. Cassie managed a polite little nod too, and because the script writer's talk was pretty dull the young reporter covering the dinner wrote an enthusiastic personality paragraph about the farmer, but Halzer had already become one of the unmentionables in the *World,* along with the words *lousy, swell, suicide,* and all forms of *to seduce.*

When the radio man's wise-cracking talk was done at last, and people were moving about to sit at this or that table for a moment of visiting, Hamm suddenly found his mother at his side, although he had not seen her come in at all. So for the first time in twenty years he rose for her presence, awkwardly unable, without turning entirely around, to hide himself behind his scar. But Hallie Rufer Hammond paid no attention to him. She had been to the Patricians' dinner, and just ran over for a glimpse of Wesley Brown Lowe, who once spent a summer in stock here — played the lead in *Lightnin'* — and very well. Seeing Mrs. Snell, she recalled a talk she heard at the League of Women Voters last week, on co-operatives. She was asked to give the independent dealer's side, although Hammond's, of course, wasn't in competition with gas stations. However, it was only fair that she familiarize herself with the arguments for co-operatives too, she said, smiling. They put out some literature, she supposed.

Oh, yes, of course, Ona Snell said pleasantly, and she would see that it reached Mrs. Hammond. "Perhaps Mr. Rufe here could answer your questions," she suggested. "In addition to keeping our books he handles our publicity."

Indeed? Hallie Rufer Hammond acknowledged the silent bow of the man at her side. She might avail herself of the opportunity, she said, politely. And about the literature — could it be left at Hammond's — at her own office, please. Their employees were really so busy, and she was always careful not to make extra work.

Hamm looked after his mother, tall and handsome in her smoke-blue velvet dress under the sweep of a burgundy cape as she moved between the tables towards Cassie and the script director beyond. He saw her give a gracious hand to the young farmer from down the Little Grand, heard her tell him, "We are very interested in you as a rising young leader for the agricultural groups," and then pass on to an exchange of compliments with Wesley Brown Lowe. A story that his grandfather often told came back to Hamm: the story of a young woman carrying her first-born son on her back in a torchlight parade down Philadelphia Avenue. It seemed well that old George Rufer was long dead.

While the local papers refused to mention Carl Halzer in any connection where "the wild-haired farmer from down the river" didn't fit, the Grandapolis *Inquirer* found praise of him good baiting for the capital city. They quoted the words of the president of the Authors' Club and ran Carl's picture, a good one, with his hair upstanding and strong, his mouth uncompromising, with the line ". . . Called Preserver of Democracy" under it. Charley Stetbettor denounced both Halzer and the professor as Communists, offering to prove that at least the professor was listed in *The Red Network*.

Hamm Rufe told Carl, and they laughed a little over old Charley, and grew very serious. It wasn't Stet's saying these things that mattered but that people believed such a man.

Somehow Carl was drawing better crowds lately, in spite of Marylin's roadster so often parked around close. She generally brought someone, not Harold, or any other man, but some girl or woman; once it was Josina Black's daughter Elizabeth, and several times Hallie Rufer Hammond, who really did seem interested. In the old days, in normal times, the farmer from the Little Grand might have become the outstanding young candidate of the campaign, made a good start towards a future victory. His background, as Hamm Rufe pointed out, was exactly right: a poor boy, with his mother either the only parent or at least the one who carries the load. There was Nebraska's Senator Norris, whose father died when young George was four, Old Fighting Bob LaFollette, whose mother seemed to have kept the family going, and Kanewa's own Senator Hanson, whose father was killed by a claim jumper before Gunnar's eyes when the boy was twelve. Perhaps Norris and Hanson were not really the last of the great midwest liberals. Perhaps Carl Halzer was the first of a new vintage. Certainly he had the uncompromising honesty and the courage. Could he capture the popular imagination sufficiently to be elected once? After that it was up to him.

It was true that Carl Halzer seemed headed for liberalism early. In the eighth grade he memorized that portion of the Constitution called the Bill of Rights, and most of Goldsmith's *Deserted Village* because his overworked teacher had been too busy with the primary folks to give him much time. He still remembered the portion beginning "Ill fares the land, to hastening ills a prey, Where wealth accumulates, and men decay." Sometimes the teacher, not much older than Carl, had let him walk part way home with her evenings, and talk to her of these things, and of his great-grandfather, who, when only a boy, had followed Andreas Hofer, and then fled to America when the Tirolese patriot was captured and taken to Mantua. Once Carl sang a song for her, in a young, strong voice: —

Zu Mantua in Banden Andreas Hofer ging

* * *

Mit ruhig festen Shritten
Ihm shien der Tod gering . . .

So it would always be with patriots, didn't she think? To them life without liberty was a death ignoble, to be despised. But his tongue wasn't so ready around anybody else, and when he had to give a talk at the Farmers Union children's day, it puffed like snake bitten and choked him down before them all, shaming his mother so he could scarcely come in for the milk pails that night.

Years later when he was out helping to hold up farm fore-closures during the depression and saw the whole program collapsing for want of a spokesman, he found himself on his feet, and talking hard before he could be scared. He wished his mother were alive, then, to see, for she was of rebel stock, too, one ancestor a follower of Shays, in the great rebellion against debt and foreclosure. "You come by it natural," she would have said to him.

Each time after that words came easier to his tongue, as they did to others who were so driven, until the movement spread into every county of the state, even in the face of armed deputies, militia, and tear gas, and the papers denouncing them with the same old names of Red and Communist. But the insurance companies weren't wasting time name-calling. They saw this for what it was, a rising farm rebellion, and consented to a moratorium just in time.

So with foreclosings done, Carl went home to put in his corn and that fall he found himself elected state representative by a margin of twelve votes that survived a recount. He had gone out once more, as the Bellowing Bull, to talk for a try-out of the federal farm program. This time his lean-faced neighbors stood away from him, their mouths snapped shut. They had been burned once by listening to a Washington outfit, Hoover's Farm Board. Millions of dollars had been handed out, but did the farmers ever see a red cent of it? No, by God. "If you want to help a tree grow you got to get the water to the roots," they shouted to him from the back seats.

And when a heckler pointed out that the Halzer place was clear enough of debt, the young farmer stopped his talk, stood silent, as though confused. Then, his voice low as any other man's there, he answered: "Yes, I got the land, every acre clear — because my mother knew it was cheaper to have her son with old Lizzie Updike to help than to get a doctor from town. And my father figured it was cheaper to die than to go to the hospital for a pain in his side. They were right, for the east never let the land pay us enough for a decent birth and dying, and a decent living too."

Hamm was disturbed about Marylin Welles's interest in Carl Halzer from the start. There was no telling how far a pretty, tricky girl like that could get with a serious, honest man, particularly an idealist like the farmer from down on the Little Grand. He was more disturbed the evening she drove right up before his shack in Herb's Addition, stopping her car beside Carl's and laying her palm upon the horn. The young farmer went out into the evening, his tawny hair red as fall meadow grass in the late sun. An hour later Marylin brought Carl back to the turnoff and he came to the dark shack and sat in silence on the chilly step beside Hamm. After a while he began to talk, not about the girl from Welleshaven but about his teacher, back in the eighth grade. She had urged him to put in an extra acre of corn every year, even if it meant plowing clear up into the very fence corners, one extra acre for books, magazines, and phonograph records. She even made out lists for him, and he still liked the "Spinning Song" that she gave him from her own records the day she went away. A laughing young man in a pink shirt had come for her in a new Model T, and Carl never saw her again.

"But sometimes I remember a little how she looked," the man said slowly, picking at a calloused palm in the dark. "On nice days she used to come over the ridge on a short-cut to the schoolhouse. I never missed looking for her there. Did you ever notice how a woman looks on a ridge against an empty sky? — "

Somehow the chamber of commerce almost forgot the seventy-eighth anniversary of Franklin, what with election coming on and the papers full of sensational exposures and denunciations. But at last someone looked ahead in the calendar of events put out by the Federal Writers' project — more of their good money thrown away.

Ten days wasn't long to get ready, but probably enough, with times not picking up as they had expected. Two years from now, for the eightieth anniversary, they would really put on a show, with whiskers and crinoline clubs, and the old-timers, like Horsemeat and the Coot, all rigged out with oxteams and old Springfields for the parade down the avenue. With right-thinking men back in office they'd all have more time and heart for the job. But they could manage a little parade for this year, too, with the school bands to get a crowd downtown, help the merchants. Then Parkins recalled that it was annual Franklin day on Kanewa's football schedule, with Vincent Lopez playing for the All-City dance at the fieldhouse. Looked like somebody down at the stadium had been foresighted.

There was foresightedness in the newspaper offices too, with proofs of the annual editions already considerably thicker than relief mattresses and still fattening.

Each year the Capital City *World* set aside five or six pages
in the *Annual* for greetings from famous gone-aways. Those
who didn't reply in time got in anyway, with a listing of
their affiliations, their wanderings, and their high positions in
the world, generally without too much concern over accuracy.
Many of the more famous names were borrowed. Lady Loper,
for example, wasn't from Franklin at all, but grew up Celia
Stodding out on the Wakoon. She went to college in the east,
and came back to finish up at the university, where her
mother received the first law degree issued to a woman in
Kanewa. But Celia was dismissed two weeks before commencement for admitting her connection with the outlawed
Torch. The handout sheet was started on the campus by
Hallie Rufer's Fabians back in the Populist nineties, revived
by the pacifists during the World War, but driven under-
ground almost immediately as pro-German. It reappeared
during the Sacco-Vanzetti trial, with a reprint of Edna St.
Vincent Millay's eloquent defense of the condemned men.
The newspapers raised the cry of subversive activities on the
campus, and the university authorities hired a Pinkerton detective. But he looked so much like the moving-picture
correspondence school flatfoot — short neck, mean gash of
a mouth, knife-edged hat drawn down to his nose — that the
students spotted him at sight, and made much mysterious
business for his attention. He had them rounded up in squads,
grilled them for hours in Administration Hall, and got nowhere. Heckled by the whole country the administration
decided there must be results and so a starved-looking little
chap from outstate was dismissed from school. The boy was
paying for his education and trying to help his family too
by working eight hours a day in addition to his classes. It
was spring, with lilacs outside the windows, and because the
authorities kept him waiting ten minutes, he was asleep when
they got around to him. Even after the detective slapped
water in his face the boy couldn't wake up entirely, and so

that evening his picture appeared under a streamer, "*Torch Man Discovered!*" But before they got him hustled out of town another issue of the *Torch* appeared in huge stacks at the street corners. The language, pungent as the wet mimeograph ink, denounced the faculty as waterlogged jellyfish, the administration as malicious and stupid jackasses, the detective as well-fitted for clubbing striking garment workers over the head. And at the bottom of the one sheet was the editor's name: Celia Stodding, with her address and phone number and an offer of a personal escort for the detective if the administration feared he couldn't find the location, "Naturally on an obscure street." It turned out to be the Kay Dee house on Sorority row, and the alums, including Hammonds, Blacks, and Welleses, called a meeting to decide upon measures to protect the good name of the sisterhood from this flapper generation. They voted to drop Celia cold.

The boy had to be released, after listening to a free lecture on the evils of shielding wrongdoers, particularly attractive women. Uncomprehending, the boy kept saying yes, yes, and finally got away, to plunge desperately into his studies. "You just can't afford to get far behind if you're fixed like I am," he explained.

So Celia Stodding loaned the boy two hundred dollars she was to spend on her graduation, and took her dismissal. The administration had suggested voluntary withdrawal, and Celia considered it, because it would be less humiliating to her parents. "Make them throw you out!" the angry mother telephoned. "Make them put themselves on record as the jackasses you said they were!"

There was considerable moralizing from the pulpits, and hot denunciation of this wayward and dangerous daughter of Kanewa by the American Legion, the D.A.R., and the Colonial Dames. But even so the Franklinites suffered no discernible embarrassment, only surprise and envy when, three years ago, Celia Stodding married Lord Loper.

"I'd like to know how *she* got to him," the ambitious mothers of the town demanded. It seemed that despite his title he was a liberal. While Blue Ridge refused to believe that, it seemed that he met the girl while in America investigating the federal resettlement projects. Celia, it was said, had been editing bulletins on the government setup.

"Ah," everybody said, knowingly, "then she really was a Red!"

This summer she ignored the invitation of the chamber of commerce to attend the Kanewa Fall Festival and coronation ball, and the offer of an honorary degree by the university, too. The *World* wasn't balked so easily. Somebody rooted her picture out of the Buffalo yearbook files. So Lady Loper in a mannish 1927 haircut topped all the gone-aways in the *Annual*, the account of her triumphs unmarred by any mention of her outstate origin, or that she didn't bother to acknowledge honors from the capital city.

Like many another countrywoman of hers, and one particularly familiar to us all as Wally Simpson, Celia Stodding has won the love of a man of high title in our sister democracy. But with what a difference! She is on intimate terms with Queen Elizabeth and her entire household!

The story was pure luck for Margaret Tyndale, still angry that her Mollie was so deliberately passed over for a skinny, store-made blonde at the coronation. Poor Samuel had done what he could; closed up his account with Groves for wholesale groceries entirely, trucking in everything for his stations. In addition he bought up the mortgages on the Acme Lumber and Grain Company and started a little price war with Franklin Mills and Doover's lumberyard. But back in early September, when they decided that Mollie should change Burt for escorts of more importance, they had schemed farther — towards a visit with a distant relative in England, including court presentation, if that could be managed these times.

Finally one Saturday morning, early enough to make the Sunday papers, the cablegram came. It was an invitation from Lady Pyle to her dear kinswoman in America to be her guest for the winter and the court season. Samuel Tyndale waylaid the chamber of commerce reporter, spoke casually of Mollie's invitation, quite casually, but managed to show him the cablegram and told him something of a possible Presentation dinner before their daughter sailed. Yes, they might decide to humor Lady Pyle, and let her present Mollie at court. Not that it was important but womenfolks liked that sort of thing.

Now there were suddenly many luncheons and parties for the girl, and by people who barely spoke to the Tyndales two weeks, even one week ago. No one dared risk omission from the Presentation dinner guest list. Eloise Johnson was the first with a cocktail at home, the day after the announcement, "For friends of Mollie Tyndale who wish to congratulate her," the paper said. No one missed it.

Burt Parr, too, felt the results of the coming trip. He was offered a night job at one of the Tyndale stations, and at much better pay. He didn't like losing all his evenings but he couldn't afford to refuse the money, even from Mollie's father.

Of course it was to keep him away from the girl, since fat-necked Milo Groves didn't please her. Lately old Chester Esthler's son was taking her around, usually with Milo and his girl. Hamm was surprised. Old Chester was always considered pretty queer, even though he was of an early family, earlier than the Blacks, and related to them, too, through his invalid mother. Peedie, the son, was a clear-skinned, mild young man, who was brought up by his cold-eyed grandfather, a minister, with no sparing of the whip and spoiling the colt.

All except newcomers like Mollie seemed to keep away from Peedie. The rest had probably been told that he used to take little girls up to see his father and that old Chester would scare them so they ran home crying. But that was before the boy went away to a military academy and Chester was taken to the asylum.

Sometimes Hamm wondered if Mollie shouldn't be told about the boy's father, but the women in his life, from Hallie Rufer on, even friends like Abigail, all seemed so solidly able to look after themselves. Perhaps a man should grow up with at least one sister, younger and a little dependent, or better still with a lot of sisters and brothers, too.

Hamm didn't see much of Mollie while the plans for the Presentation dinner grew. She drove out past Herb's Addition alone several times, looking very smart in a new hematite red suit, furred deep and rich with pale blue-grey fox that set off the velvet of her eyes and the blackness of her hair. But she didn't stop in, and Burt Parr didn't come any more either.

The seventy-eighth anniversary of the capital city was almost lost in the excitement over the Tyndale dinner and the Franklin day rush of the football crowd. But the parade finally came, not too long after the earliest of the fans had started down towards the stadium. Somehow the coach let the football squad take part, leading off down the avenue behind the band, their cars whipping with purple and gold streamers, the crowd singing for them as they passed, enough for a losing team. Behind them came the cheer groups of the school, in color, too, followed by the important cars of the capital city, with pretty girls everywhere wearing golden chrysanthemums chenilled in purple *K*'s. There was one unfortunate incident, which the *World* played down and the Grandapolis papers broadcast to all the state: at the first gap in the parade a bunch of placard-bearing truckers poured out of an alley into the street, fell in and marched along, five abreast. In the center of the group half a dozen men carried a long white sign at least ten feet high between them, giving the shrinking income of the state since the World War, the shrinking production of Franklin, and the sharply rising amount of tax money spent in the city. And under it, in flaming red letters, was the line: BLOODSUCKING CAPITAL CITY! Here and there a shout or a little laughing broke out, spread along as the marchers passed.

But this was a college town on a holiday, and so when the band began to play, the crowd all took it up singing "Kanewa, We love you, Fairest state of all," to echo against the buildings as they marched down the walks of Philadelphia Avenue to the football game.

The farmers in for their Saturday trading didn't follow. They gathered as always around the old Union Market, the boys with an eye out for a girl that might be satisfied with a bottle of pop or a dime picture show, the women still trading a few eggs and poultry, making the warm feeling of money to spend last as long as possible. Outside the men hung around to meet other renters, not saying much, although there was a lot to talk over this fall, if they had a mind to.

Yeh, a hell of a lot, the younger ones admitted openly. Company men been around, making poor mouths, saying times was hard, taxes sky-high, no profit.

Retrenchment talk, the farmers agreed, moving their slitted eyes cautiously over the others, trying to single out the spy always among them, drive him from them with their private ways.

Finally it came out. They were all holding back the same thing, as they had figured. The company reps were saying that if men like Powers won the election they were shutting down the tenant farms.

"Shutting down all the places?" a lean, stooped man asked, not believing.

That's what they heard.

"Why, that'd put five thousand, maybe ten thousand of us on the road, like them Okies going through — "

Yeh. Yeh, it would; twice, three times as many as that, maybe; if all the companies got together.

Evidently fall was really well started, with the final softball tournament done and with Saint Thomas parish slating its annual fair and Bingo evening for next week, first prize a trip to Hollywood. The other church women contented themselves with bridge benefits, bake and rummage sales, or Swedish and Chinese suppers, with their prettiest girls in costume ready to serve the men they hoped would come.

Fall was always a time of celebrating in Franklin, a time for definite and conspicuous looking-back-with-pleasure by special groups and by the city as a whole. As the future became less promising, the past increased in importance, particularly the farther, the more distant past. So while the Kanewa Historical Society managed no increase in its membership in Grandapolis or most of the smaller towns, in Franklin both the membership and the interest grew stronger every year.

This fall the town was taking special interest in the Society's annual meeting, for the long-projected Coolidge Room at the Historical Building was to be opened to the public and formally dedicated. It was really the capital city room, for the display of such items as the first land patent, the first church roster, the first organ brought to Franklin. But the space, much of the display and its upkeep too, was made possible by a grant from Mrs. Patton, a prominent W.C.T.U. and Woman's Club worker. Quite naturally, she dictated the name.

It started back in the prohibition days, when, in a book on education, somebody ran across Franklin's advice to a young man upon taking a mistress. The good women of the town, without any special crusade under way, were free to be shocked and horrified to find their fair city named for such a lewd and lecherous man. Mrs. Patton and two others went straight up to the local legislators. They wanted the name of the capital changed from Franklin to Coolidge, in honor of that noble American, Mr. Coolidge.

One of the politicians hesitated, pulling at his lip. It would be hard to manage, would run up against natural inertia, and all the natural opposition to change.

But it was most important, the women argued. They would give a good deal to have it done.

"What backing," he wanted to know.

"The Woman's Christian Temperance Union," Mrs. Patton said, and when he seemed unimpressed, she added the State Federation of Woman's Clubs. She, herself, would stump the state, see that appropriate resolutions were passed, the legislative desks flooded with letters and telegrams.

"Who will finance this?" the practical Franklinite inquired.

The women of the state would raise hundreds, even thousands of dollars if necessary.

"Any trading stock?"

Oh yes, of course, the W.C.T.U. politician agreed.

Well, that being the case, there might be a way. What were they prepared to offer?

"Anything!" Mrs. Patton said firmly, the others nodding.

"Anything? . . . Um-m . . . m," he said. So they got the bill through, although it cost them the Child Labor amendment, the anti-gambling bill, and the repeal of the anti-picketing law. There were a few unpleasant editorials from such remote papers as the Minerva *Thunderbolt*, which the women bore with Christian fortitude, as they did the surprising amount of criticism from their fellow townswomen, even from such a civic leader as Hallie Rufer Hammond. They found her peculiarly unreasonable, perhaps because none of them bothered to ask who named the town. But hardest to bear was the governor's veto. They finally took the matter up with Jim Farley himself, Mrs. Patton going all the way to Washington to see him, and a pleasant-spoken man he was, she reported, talking to her as one politician to another.

"You are a woman of great influence, Mrs. Patton," he told her, "and I'll give your request every possible consideration." Not slangy at all, as she had expected. But he didn't change the name of the postoffice, and by now almost everybody had slipped back into calling the town Franklin, even the chamber of commerce. But Mrs. Patton and her followers never did, and when she died she left the money and her early Franklin collection to the Historical Society for a Coolidge Room.

So there was a formal dedication of the gift at the annual meeting of the Society, with Susan Welles in charge, assisted by Della Loran, and the Empress of Kanewa, off to school the next day, but looking mighty good, if the story about her name being in old Ed Chimmer's book was really true. Someone hurried to make the first contribution to the room, a copy of William Allen White's biography of Coolidge, not *A Puritan in Babylon,* which the ladies considered in very bad taste, but the earlier one, the campaign book.

While Hamm knew that the city's grandmothers would all be there, he decided to go to the Historical Society banquet anyway, and take Abigail. They went late, slipped into a back table, and beyond a little pointing out, they were almost immediately lost in the large crowd out to hear the well-publicized speaker of the evening, an old Indian warrior, Little Bull, one of the last of the old buffalo-hunting Sioux. As the papers said, he had known Crazy Horse, Spotted Tail, and Red Cloud, and was sixteen at the time of the Custer battle. But he never joined Wild West shows, spoke little English, and at the dinner he spoiled the high-flown introduction that was interpreted for him by a great-grandson,

John Little Bull, by interrupting with a very loud and un-mistakable "No!"

No, he was no great chief, not now or any time, the old Indian insisted earnestly, his face like wrinkled brown kid leather, his braids thin and dust grey. But his lean figure was straight and noble in the snow-white, fringed and beaded buckskin, his hand proud on the long eagle-feather head-dress he did not wear but held up high, the ends trailing to the floor.

No, he was no great chief, only the leader of one band of the Oglala, nor was he among the first Indians to cross the Little Big Horn to attack Reno. He was a boy then, with his uncle, the band historian, and was making pictures of the Indians gathering for the Sundance on the Greasy Grass, to help with the story telling for the campfires of the winters ahead. But when the column of dust that was like smoke on the hills showed the Indians the many soldier enemies that were coming to steal their lands, to kill their women and chil-dren, the duty of camp protection from attack came before history keeping and so he rode out, too, and shot some soldiers. He did not know how many, because the battle was thick and fast, and the dust hot and stinging in the eyes. Afterwards he rode back to find his sister and his mother and help gather the frightened people at a new place for the mourning time and the victory dance that would come afterward. He took no part in this dancing because while the warriors told their stories he had to make the pictures of the battle for the book that his sister always carried safe under her dress. He had to listen to the coup-counting, the challenging or acceptance, and put it all down. Then the Lakotah, the Indian people the white man called the Sioux, scattered for the summer hunt, many going to the Milk River country away from the white man, for the Indian wanted only to be free and to keep his women and children safe.

But what Little Bull had come to tell the white man was

not the story of himself but of their river, the *Wakan,* the Holy Stream, that runs to the land from where the summer comes. It was named for the great black robe who had spent a winter with the Lakotah on this river when Little Bull's own blood father was a small boy, many, many winters gone by. He was a very good and holy man, this black robe, and given great power of healing. When the stinking disease of the white man was cutting the Mandan down like hail on the new green grass of June, the holy one held their band back from going to the trader for one whole moon of praying to the Great Spirit. And when the time of fasting and songs was done the grass was hidden, the snow too deep for the pony drags, and by spring no one of them was dead of the stinking disease but many of their brothers up at Soldier fort were gone as the snows before the Chinook. It was good work and holy by the black robe and so it was said that the river must be called *Wakan* the Holy Stream, so long as its water shall flow.

That was all, and when the people saw that the old Indian was really done, the applause was very long, for there were few unmoved by the man's simple, earnest tale. All this time Little Bull was calm before the staring faces, before the whispered word, and the hands of these people reaching out to finger the fringe of his buckskin, pretending that he did not notice these very great discourtesies to a guest among them.

When there was silence once more the white men rose with many rapid questions: "How many scalps did you take?" "Did you steal horses?" "Did you see Custer killed?"

To the interpretation of these questions the old man smiled a little and said "Hou!" meaning only that he understood, and then set to answering them, carefully and patiently, as they came. But at last he spoke sharply to the youth, who said, "Great-grandfather, he is very old and very tired, and will go now." So they both sat down. Many were cross at this abruptness, thought the old Indian was rude, still a savage, despite all the money the government had spent on him and his kind. But he seemed gentle enough as they crowded around him to examine his costume once more, to tug at the precious eagle feathers of his headdress. It wasn't until afterwards, when the youth led his great-grandfather out, that many discovered that the old Indian was totally blind, blind from the white man's trachoma.

CHAPTER VIII

THE sky of early October lay bright as naked steel on the clear flowing streams of Kanewa, the timber along their breaks golden, the sweeping uplands browning to belie the pale spring green of sprouting wheat. Sumac blazed red as Indian blood on the crests along the highways and dusty clumps of seeding goldenrod and white asters leaned in ragged confusion against the ditches and cuts, while out in the pastures bunches of purple wand stood like sticks thrust into buried pots.

It was picnic time for middle Franklin, with a great hurrying around after work to change into slacks and flying shirt tails; early honkings on Sunday mornings, and weary evening returns with armfuls of bittersweet for house baskets, and sumac and cattails for the old umbrella stands dragged down from the attic to the living room.

The society columns were full of engagements and marriage plans under the standing head "October Weddings." There were half a dozen from the homes along Blue Ridge and the slope this side — nice young people, mostly girls marrying out of town, Dallas, say, or Denver or perhaps Washington, D. C. Appropriate positions would be made for the local boys in the family interests of the capital city; Felton's, Fine Stationery, was very busy, and the price of white chrysanthemums was mounting.

Yeh, the love business sure was picking up, the gas-station manager told Burt Parr. The fine, warm, moonlit nights of early October were topping any spring week in rubber-goods sales at the station, three for a quarter, old and rotten and a lot of the damn fool kids getting themselves on fire, but his business was to keep the Tyndale stock moving.

"Quite a sideline they've worked up over there for you — " Hamm told Burt.

The boy looked down upon his hands, his chin line getting lean the last few weeks. Yes, it was pretty bad, he admitted. Sometimes a girl tried to remind the man, poke him, or say something low, and maybe all she'd get would be a "What the hell! You can take stuff afterwards — "

No, hopping cars for Samuel Tyndale wasn't like working at the Co-op. Burt had never worked for a private concern much, and he guessed it was up to a man to do what he was paid for, but sometimes things around there certainly made his home up on the Wakoon seem like a fine place to be. Hamm nodded. It must be a mighty fine place to be, but there were always considerations beyond the moment.

Yes — well, Burt couldn't remember that Old Samuel and the others were like this, up the river there. Maybe living here, with the capital city folks, made them so different. The people stopping at the station were always hurrying to get away, always acting trapped, like the old grey wolf up in Stoor's Park that even runs around his little pen between chews at a fresh bone. Here they all seemed to be tearing out every free minute, even if only for a swing around Horseshoe Boulevard. Those that could, got way out into the country. Even if they had to turn right around and come back they'd go as far up as the cabins on the Narrows of the Grand, where the water runs swift and clear over the rock, and the oaks begin to thin to elm and ash, and maybe farther on, to the cottonwoods, and the cedar bluffs, way up the river towards Wild Horse Plains. Out there ducks were swarming thick over the sweetwater lakes, they told Burt, and geese came honking in at dusk, or gabbled soft in the cornfields, the pheasants running with heads out like spear points through the Russian thistles of the stubblefields.

Yes, Hamm knew how they talked about it. And weeks before the hunting season everybody in Franklin seemed to be oiling up a gun and letting out last year's hunting pants another notch, maybe even leaving the top button open for extra spread under the belt. They seemed to be laying in a little more whiskey than last year, too, and a little less ammunition, for, privately, of course, times were better, with a real building boom on in town, much of it federal money, but still the biggest year since 1928 and the second biggest since 1900, not counting the capitol, of course, which was public.

Fall was really here, with haze thick as prairie fire hanging over the ridges just outside of town as though waiting to move in. On the capitol grounds the wide sprayers were still turning over the lawn that had greened up dense and soft as a new rug since the frost, but most of the town lawns were deep in browning leaves waiting for a wind. Down on the avenue the better windows were cold with artificial snow for the skating and ski-suit displays, only Hammond's giving space to a southern cruise window. Sheepskin coats, rubber boots, and fleece-lined overshoes were neatly pyramided at Montgomery Ward's, piled in stacks three feet deep at the Army and Navy store. The first cold morning would bring hurry-up calls to storage for the fur coats. It would come with a sudden thickening of the ice in the bird baths, the sky greying, and the wind sweeping chill along the streets, banging the loose signs and awnings of summer. Out at the rendering works the old coyote would howl late at night and the next morning there would be snow. Already the root-beer stands were deserted, the neon signs down, the windows boarded over, like the eyes of a weary toad closing to await another spring.

Then suddenly there was something besides elections, picnics, hunting, and winter coming soon to think about in the capital city — another death on Blue Ridge. It was no duke in satin britches in a toilet this time, but quiet little Penny Hammond, found dead on her chaise longue in a new maroon velvet house gown, dead of an overdose of sleeping tablets. The maid couldn't wake her, or Cecil Hammond either. Two doctors came; she was dead. She hadn't been very well the last week, must have suffered a lapse of memory, and kept taking the tablets until the bottle was empty.

Slowly Hamm Rufe dropped to his step to look through the story in the evening paper, stopping several times to look at the picture of this woman who had married his brother Cecil, the mother's baby, his father's favorite son. Penelope had evidently been an attractive woman, and quiet, with wide-set eyes, a broad forehead, and a sadness about the far corner of her mouth, as though she, too, had a side she must turn away. Hamm looked down over the city, with its capitol tower high and remote, and beyond, to the dwellings of Blue Ridge, with their lawns that were the dark fall green of generous sprinkling and long, chilly nights. And all around that tight little world overlooking old Mud Creek Valley, wide, rolling plains reached far out towards the headwaters of the Grand, the Lasseur, and the Wakoon, plains tawny as the antelope that once roamed their slopes, the air moving as free. It was from out there that Penny came, and it must have been hard for her to die here, when the sky was the knife blue of October over all the earth of Kanewa. Hard for little Penny to die so.

He thought of Cecil, Cees, as everybody called him, the son that remained with Hallie Rufer Hammond, to peter away towards chicken-skinned middle age in the capital city. Since he married, ten, twelve years ago, he was secretary-treasurer and manager of Hammond's, once a hardheaded concern that made no compromises at all on quality. But under Cees, an arty, modern air had entered the business, particularly when the new building was added along in the late twenties, with two floors of interior decoration, including a model suite of rooms that he did over every few months. He took an interest in the private lives of his help, too, knew the marital troubles of his window dresser and the latest complaint of the bedfast mother-in-law of the head shipping clerk. He arranged employee savings accounts for small stock purchases in the company, and initiated bonuses. Of course there were those, even among the Blue Ridgers, who pointed out that the bonus idea came to him when the undistributed profits tax was put on. Still, other concerns in the capital city seemed to get around it. Few doubted that Cees did try to be completely honest with himself and the whole world. Hallie left him pretty free so long as the dividends came in regularly.

In his own pale, yellow-grey eyes, Cecil Hammond was a great home body. When he married Penelope Shelton from outstate, he built a large, loose sort of home on the Ridge, the whole structure planned about a living room easy with islands of chairs and low tables and books within reach of either hand. In the alcove was a built-in pipe organ for the lessons both he and Penny were taking. They had many informal evenings with comfortable people in; a congenial professor or two, or a writer or painter or musician, not to be lionized, definitely not, but to mix casually with a few of their own set. There were always extra men to help things along, and the new book out and open, to start the talk going, or something especially appropriate, as the biography of Pilsudski during the siege of Warsaw, a Zaharoff biography when the talk turned to Chamberlain's holdings in munition firms. The Hammond dinners were the pleasantest in town. Cees carved well, knew enough about wines, and had a working series of host signals with his wife. He was the solitary male of a very feminine establishment, as he called it, consisting of a saddle mare, a Great Dane bitch, a maltese tabby, and his Penny. At his office he kept track of their seasons by x's on the calendar, his wife delicately, discreetly, in an almost invisible marking down in the corners of the dates, the cat's frankly under the figure, the mare's covering the entire square, for he liked to ride and must keep those days clearly in mind.

With Penny he read a great deal of modern psychology,

particularly on the more intimate human relations; he specialized in civilized understanding and dissected every attitude, every emotion, calmly and scientifically. Certain characteristics in himself he labeled dominant maleness, in his wife as female possessiveness — not for purposes of praise or condemnation but strictly for greater appreciation, sympathy, and understanding.

Because Penny never seemed very strong it was agreed that they take Cecil's vacation in the winter together, and in the summer she should go to the mountains alone. These months of retreat in the pines did her no end of good and contributed much, Cees was certain, to their exceptional compatibility. He maintained, however, that the real key to their happiness was their scientific approach to the physical aspects of the problem. To acquaintances who seemed in need of advice he explained that woman was a delicate and sensitive mechanism. Fortunately a doctor had done a rather good book on the subject, and because he couldn't discuss such intimate details, he was always glad to help by writing the title down on a sheet of his pale blue scratch paper.

"There — and you'll find this perfectly reliable — and conducive to the — ah — the greatest happiness in your marital relations, as Penny and I can attest," he would say, looking up through his desk glasses as he held out the little blue slip.

This fall Penelope had come back from the mountains a little later than generally, and on her off week, too. They talked over her decision to return then, and agreed that it was really because of the unseasonable heat in Franklin and not from any subconscious desire to avoid her husband. That was a month ago, and now she was dead. Dr. Carlson had been most sympathetic. Pregnancy sometimes affected delicate, sensitive women that way the first few months, a temporary depression which passed when the endocrines adjusted themselves.

"She should have been in for an examination and advice long ago — "

Cees, dazed and appalled by the suggestion of pregnancy, his head bowed over numb hands, hadn't been very attentive. The charge of neglect roused him to some defense of his Penny.

"But Mrs. Hammond couldn't have guessed more than a few days, at the most!" he objected.

"Oh, more than that," the doctor said reasonably, seeing how confused the man was. "I should say a good two months and over — "

Cees Hammond looked up blankly and finally nodded, his habit of automatic polite agreement saving him. "Yes, yes, of course — I'm so confused — the shock — " he apologized. Known over two months — he calculated as clearly as he could. That put it back to July. He had been up to see her the Fourth, which was to have worked out well with the calendar, but the last day a wire had come from Penny saying that she was unavoidably indisposed. He knew what that meant, but he went anyway, and found her nervous and cross with herself for disappointing her husband. The altitude had never affected her so before. He had acted the kind and understanding pal, and was touched by her good-bye at the station.

"You do love me a great deal, Cees," she had said.

Now all that week-end looked so different. When he could slip away from the house without it seeming strange, he went down to the store, to his private files to look through his letters from Penny, one every day, all summer. From the earliest he searched them, trying to read significance into every line now. But there was not one name he could single out, not one circumstance. And so at last he had to go home, to the house suddenly much too large and too loose about him, as though he had shrunken so much.

The city below the Ridge rolled the death of Penny Hammond on its tongue, although still a little jaded by the stronger meat of Cobby Welles's ending. Casual acquaintances remembered the everlasting talk Cees was always putting on about Penny's sensitiveness and decided that perhaps he was right. Many of those who knew something of Penny's condition remembered the advice he was always offering, particularly to newly married couples.

"I didn't think old Cees had it in him," Freddy Black admitted in the lockers out at Grand Vista. "Josephine and I fell for his song and dance about his system, and found ourselves parents in nine months flat. Since then I'd had a suspicion that maybe Cees wasn't so inflammatory — "

Long before this there was talk of another man.

Confused, miserable, Cees Hammond sought out Penny's older sister Marian, married to a poorly paid professor of Greek up at Walden. When she saw how aged, how broken and lost Cees was, she could only go on as his wife had all those years, comforting him by letting him talk it all over and over, until the last bit of flavor was chewed from it, until only bare, tasteless shreds remained. Time after time that long night he returned to Penny's delicate condition, as he called it. Why hadn't she confided in him? Of course he was proud of their system of, ah, control, but to die for its failure — he couldn't get over such a thing.

Towards two in the morning he finally broke down. He had to know the truth.

Marian looked through the grey water of her tears upon the man who had married her beloved baby sister. Little Penelope came trailing along several years after the other girls. Without a playmate her own age she grew up pretty self-reliant, mothering every alley kitten, buttoning the pants of every crying youngster of the small town that Grandfather Peter Shelton had built. And somehow it had come to this.

But there was no shirking the need of Cecil now, or he

would be a man bedeviled to the end. So Marian admitted that there was more to it than just Penny's fear of disappointing him, wounding his pride in a vulnerable spot; she was afraid of hurting him mortally. Penelope, their little Penny, had fallen in love this summer, and with her natural honesty, she could make no pretense to herself or to the man. They talked it over between them a hundred unhappy times, and finally decided to come to Cees, tell him as well as they could, and go away together. But it seemed too brutal, and when the man said he must come, Penny forbade him. She would tell Cees herself. She had tried to tell him when he was up the Fourth, and couldn't; she tried the first day she was home, and the second. But it wasn't easy for Penny to hurt anyone, not a man who had put his whole thought and dependence upon their life together as Cees had, and all his deep affection.

Marian spoke slowly, in a monotone, as impersonally as possible, trying to save the man she had to wound. But now for the first time she saw the Cecil Hammond that was the son of Hallie, his mother, and something more that she couldn't know, something of old George Rufer, the Pennsylvania grandfather. Dry-eyed, controlled, he stopped before her chair. Only the thin, sensitive hands hung too straight at his side.

"Would you have taken this way out?" he asked at last, and the woman had to admit that she thought not.

"No — " he said slowly, with his habitual preciseness. "No, nor would Penny, ten years ago. It seems — yes, I fear it means that I have done my most beloved a very great wrong."

Tuesday Penelope Hammond was taken away to Memorial Park on the hill, the second of those small, private processions from Blue Ridge within little more than a month. Burt Parr watched the cars come back past the Tyndale filling station, Old Samuel's car sweep imposingly by, right up behind the oldest families now. Mollie must be on the far side, probably sat there deliberately, he thought, looking for her under the visor of his brown cap, and letting the tank he was filling run over.

Out in Herb's Addition Hamm Rufe thought of the day Stephani left him with only a picture to hang over the fireplace and he found it hard not to go to his brother, to stand without clutter of words beside him in this bad time. But nothing would be mended so, no pain made easier, and so he walked out northward, as far as the breaks of the Grand River, a clear, swift stream that gleamed in the late sun like the hot new metal he once saw flowing from a furnace up in Leadville. But the Grand was no blight upon the landscape; no blackened skeletons stood along the bottoms, but trees golden with autumn; the farm homes broad and clean-painted, for here there was water, and good soil, and hope for the spring.

Hamm came back tired as from a day at rock crushing and slept, but the next evening he had to see his brother. It was night when he walked from the bus stop to the wide terraces of the Hammond home. The row of windows across the front stood undraped and tall, their light stretching far down the sloping lawn. Hamm kept close to the high side fence of brick until he could see into the living room. There was only Cees, sitting on a low bench, bowed forward over something on his knees, a book or a picture probably, something that took him back to a time when Penny was still there.

When Hamm finally started away he walked far out around the town to his shack, keeping to the deep darkness that gathers just beyond a field of lights.

Ever since the coronation ball the capital city had been stirring and restless, with sit-downers at the relief offices, strikers parading and fighting back against finks and gunmen, fiery crosses burning on the capitol lawn, Gold Shirts accused of hit-and-run driving, bricks flying through old

Samelly's poor window, and people up on Blue Ridge swallowing bottles of poison.

"They's actin' like a string a green pack horses in lion country, mountain lion country," Old Horsemeat said.

"Hell, any herd a green horses has got more sense than this outfit here," the Coot snorted. "This here town's been acting like the frost-chilled cockroaches in that old rusty bake stove outside of my cave when the sun hits it direct — scurrying around, scart crazy at anything, even if it's only the sun warming up their freezing butts a little — "

Over a cup of coffee Hamm Rufe listened to the old-timers already chewing the winter fat, although it was not yet middle October. Last year it had been the power fight in the legislature but mostly the disappearance of small nations in Europe, with old Joe Srb and Nick Zeromski sitting among them reading letters from the old country and blowing their noses hard into their colored handkerchiefs. A pack of hungry grey wolves, eating up the weak ones, the Coot had called it. No, Old Horsemeat insisted, those foreign countries were acting just like human critters, like that Donner party did, fooling along all summer and then having to eat each other up in the winter to get across the mountains to California.

Hamm Rufe listened to the old-timers, a little smile on the good side of his face as they compared his city to a string of green horses in lion country, or cockroaches scrabbling in terror at a little warmth on their rears. But perhaps there was something to it. For twenty years he had followed what at first seemed sporadic outcroppings of stress and violence but later saw as great waves breaking over America like the lines of a weather map. Perhaps these old-timers who had spent most of their lives in the capital city as outsiders saw something in her uneasiness that neither he, the politicians, nor the business men could yet suspect.

The last month Hamm had been occupied with his shock over Cobby, his grief over his brother's bereavement, the difficulties of his acquaintances. Now trouble had suddenly moved in at the Co-op. From the start Franklin was even less friendly to the co-operative idea than other towns. It was expected that the advertisers' combine would close the papers to all news of the venture and even to their ads, but from the first the police kept pecking at them like chickens at a sprouting lettuce bed, beginning with the builders, accusing them with alley blocking. Since then it was one petty charge of public nuisance or another. Now, apparently the junior chamber of commerce, Milo Groves, president, had settled upon the final destruction as a sort of graduation exercise.

It wasn't the first organized attempt to put the Co-op out of business. Almost before the gas pump was up, the private oil companies began to cut prices to run the new competition out of town. The manager met the cuts until they reached delivery costs, and when the private concerns went farther, he called a meeting. Along towards midnight, after the two old Socialist members had exhausted their fondness for dialectics, Ada Jims and her husband had their usual public quarrel, and everyone had ridden his pet hobby, Ona Snell and Professor Ford of the history department took the initiative. The purpose of the co-operative was not to undercut private concerns but to save, through dividends to the shareholding consumer, the profits between tank car and automobile. At the present low price no such profit existed, and with it their reason for running. The station's closing was described by the *World* in an obituary editorial as "another Communistic venture that started optimistically into the air, has nosedived, and like a ragged kite of spring, has been left to flutter its tatters into winter on the solid wires of private endeavor." Two weeks later, when gas came up again, the station reopened. The shrewd Samuel Tyndale, new to the city then, had seen the importance of even a fraction of a penny saving per gallon to a city of small-salaried white-collar workers. He lagged behind on the price rise, dropping periodically to half a cent under the low of the private companies, and thereby built up enough trade for his five big stations. But it didn't help Mollie become empress of Kanewa.

Since then the Co-op had faced a rezoning order, suits over their fine corner location, and delayed and inadequate deliveries, an old complaint that compelled the co-operatives of the upper Mississippi region to set up their own wholesalers in Minneapolis, where Burt Parr had spent a year. The purchase of an oil-blending plant at North Kansas City and their own truck lines insured the Franklin supply, but no Franklin affection. In addition, as Milo Groves told the chamber, they were siding with the strikers, some of their employees taking an active part, particularly that scar-faced tough called Hamm Rufe who lived out at Bums' Roost and wrote dirty articles about the employers for the labor papers and the *Nation.*

Now that the local co-operative was trying out a sort of sample line of groceries, orders filled in three days, the planned attack was hurried. With the station's most pleasing young attendant, Burt Parr, already hired away by the Tyndales, Milo didn't have to hand advancement to a man he still believed was a rival, no matter what Margaret Tyndale planned. But he offered Hamm Rufe a job, full time, at Groves, Wholesale Groceries. Hamm refused, and at once the young politician dropped all his air of flattery, his talk of their need of an extra-good bookkeeper.

"You may find it expedient to change your mind — "

Hamm Rufe rubbed the burning scar of his cheek, his usually mild eyes suddenly a dense grey. Fat-necked Milo, junior member of Groves, with a large block of Hammond-owned stock, coming to threaten him — Milo, with the broad, tallowy face that spread to jowls sitting flat on his shoulders, threatening.

"Have you ever seen a liver worm, Mr. Groves?" Hamm asked, conversationally. "It is a leech-like creature that grows in the liver of sheep, and kills its host. It breeds along small, stagnant streams, and it, too, has no neck."

For a few days there was nothing more, not until somebody remembered that Sid Harper, the manager of the Co-op, was also head of one of the agencies on the Community Chest list. He received his orders: "Get out of that collectivistic set-up or you're off our payroll."

He was a young family man with a future before him, as they pointed out, and so he took the job offered by Smith and Batton, Real Estate, a job with a desk but no buzzer. Smith put him on but didn't pretend to like it.

"Why I always got to give all your crippled ducks a swimming pond I don't see — " he complained. But he knew there were people in Franklin who could put him inside of stone walls for a nice stretch, no matter how big a Klansman he was.

So Harper went into the basement offices, and Hamm refused the Co-op managership, telling the board that he lacked the initiative and drive. Reverend Ausberg grinned broadly, and in his outspoken manner admitted that they had discussed these shortcomings and decided upon him anyway. Perhaps Hamm would accept an acting managership until they found someone?

Yes, that he couldn't refuse.

Next the energy boys from the junior chamber tried to get at the members from the university staff through the regents, demanding their withdrawal from the Co-op or their resignation from the public payroll. It looked easy, until they were shown the list, over forty, some with powerful outstate followings, like Erickson, the Engineers College's expert in irrigation and water power, and Dr. Reynolds, Kanewa's most popular high-school commencement orator. A delegation was sent to appeal to their pride in the American way, to stress the importance of the university taking a strong stand against Communistic enterprises, but the members stood fast, asking some disconcerting questions of the platitude boys, as Professor Ford called them. The regents, so far as the public could discover, took no action.

But the better people were determined that Milo Groves make a showing to get him to the legislature next election, congress later, since he was no good in the grocery business anyway, and the Ridge needed representation. So one evening along about seven Hamm Rufe heard the Dillard boys calling out, "Yeh, there it is — the one with the screen door — !"

A small, fussy, bespectacled man came up on the stoop to knock and stand. Hamm turned down the Beethoven and went to the door.

The man said he was Purdy Gilson from the Vigilant Taxpayers and would like to come in a minute. He had some ideas that might interest a voter of Mr. Rufe's caliber.

So he came in, took the one chair, and looked around. No, he didn't smoke, as though impatient at the interruption. Mighty snug and comfortable spot Mr. Rufe had here. And books, too. Any rare ones in the lot? He bent over, raked one out, one of the backless *Godey's* that Coot had found on the dumps before Franklin started to collect old things. He looked at the date, 1858, and peered silently over his glasses to Hamm Rufe, his mouth puckering as he laid the book down.

"Ah, a music lover, too," he said, turning up the radio and whirling the dial through screaming stations. Hamm nodded over his pipe.

Yes, indeed, a *very* comfortable place, under the circumstances, Purdy Gilson thought, and went away without saying anything about his ideas, but leaving the Taxpayers League card, the platform on the reverse, with two black-face lines across the bottom: Rigid Economy in Government and Immediate Return to the Principles of the Founding Fathers.

Another crank, Hamm thought, and went back to his music.

But the next day the *World* carried a front-page story of government waste: single men living in luxury on relief, with fine radios, collecting art works and rare books. With typical anonymity the paper gave no names and only along in the second paragraph Hamm Rufe began to realize he was the example used. There was no mistaking the photographs of his shack and its interior, with a close-up of his radio and fireplace, a volume of *Godey* set up conspicuously under the picture of Stephani. For the first time it seemed necessary to put a lock on anything out in Herb's Addition.

Within an hour after the paper hit the front porches of the town Jo Davis, a case worker delegated to investigation, came out. The county relief office was swamped with protests about a man living in luxury out here, living in indolent luxury by the sweat of the taxpayer's brow.

"Although they've got my shack in the paper it couldn't be me — " Hamm laughed. "You know who's on relief."

Of course, but people are up to tricks, sometimes. There had been considerable trouble the last two months, with several deliberate plants and so on, to make scandal before election, and the office wasn't taking any chances. Too bad, too, with so much real work to be done.

Hamm nodded. He understood about those things, was wondering if the trouble wasn't started by Purdy Gilson, the nosey little ferret out from the Vigilant Taxpayers. Of course the case worker couldn't say where the complaint originated, but he did know the man when Hamm showed him the card. Gilson was investigator for the two, three thousand farms that the Kanewa Investment Company had taken over the last ten years.

So — ? Hamm smiled a little as he rubbed his scar. So Old Purdy was working for the K.I.C., for Hallie Rufer Hammond, president; he, Hamm Rufe, a big stockholder. He fancied the shake of Gilson's slack pants if he were to walk in there with his identification tomorrow, say about ten-thirty, and the place full of poor devils waiting on the straight-back benches.

Yes, the case worker was saying, a town like this made a lot of trouble for a conscientious relief administrator. Took so much time to scare the eye-picking buzzards away there wasn't much left to help the old mare to her feet. Besides, there were two families getting help out here. Hamm knew them, the Overtills and the Dillards. And there would be more if it weren't for the rule that single people had to go to the poor farm. Hamm had heard a lot of talk about that rule around the shelterhouse on cold nights last winter. The poor farm was ten miles out, with no chances to come in at all to pick up a loose penny. Old Hayden, flooded out of his cave in the sewer early in September, was already writing complaining postcards to his friends; the social contacts out there were most restricted.

Hamm still couldn't see what they hoped to gain by making him out a relief case, beyond embarrassing the Co-op, but after that first professional call the tall, serious young Jo Davis often stopped in on his rounds for a cigarette and a bit of talk. He was of a middle Franklin family, graduate of K. U., with a double major in history and sociology, the sociology because the history had led him to suspect that perhaps everything was not for the best, even in the *laissez-faire* days that the Franklinites admired so. With his degree, and with a doctor in the family, he thought he knew about poor and hungry people, even though he was distantly related to the Hammonds. "You know — of the store and finance Hammonds, filthy with money," the young man said. Hamm refilled his pipe and gave silent acknowledgment. Yes, he knew of the Hammonds.

Almost at once the youth discovered that his knowledge of poverty was like that of most of his associates, knowledge of the intellect only. When the food riots brought federal relief, with a shortage of trained case workers, he was taken on, sent out with an old hand. He came back dark with bitterness against his parents who had brought him up to speak of a pauper class, to say "People are like that because they want to be." So he got a transfer to Grandapolis and took over the unemployables in the squatter section on the Wakoon River bottoms, nothing like Herb's Addition, on this high ground, its shacks dry, even the Coot's cave a decent home compared to the Canned Heat Flats. Hamm agreed. He had seen the moldering dumps on the Wakoon bottoms twenty years ago, and the same thing in California and in Louisiana and along the Shore Line back when Hoover was still the great engineer who had fed millions of starving people somewhere across the sea.

Jo Davis from middle Franklin was shocked by the habitations, some built way back in the hard times of 1907 and '08, or before, in the packing-house walkouts, with the strikers blackballed in every plant in the country. Three of these were still there, their families scattered thirty years ago, the men old now and crippled from the damp, but still unwilling to go to the county farm. A man's house was his castle, even a moldy old hole of tin and driftwood on fill-in land was his castle.

Since his father died Jo Davis came back here, and saw what a few years under the slow starvation of county administration did: children slipping into tuberculosis all around him, grown men and women grey-skinned and listless from chronic malnutrition. Those who plumpened in a puffy sort of way were dragged up before protest hearings to prove that the reliefers were well fed, living on the fat of the land. If anybody made too big a rumpus he lost his $6.00-a-month food allowance, stood to lose it anyway if the reactionaries won the election. Not that there was much trouble; a couple of years living like that and the kick was gone out of a man. Once in a while somebody got excitable, asking, "Why don't they take my kids out and shoot them, or drown 'em like too many kittens? Better than let them starve right before my face!" If he said it so the town heard, the Workers' Alliance was blamed — agitating among the clients.

Jo Davis came to Hamm's shack once more on business. He smoked a cigarette and talked a little about the latest protest against work relief by business men, the very fellows who'd be howling the minute the flow of money was cut off. Election stuff. But on his way out the young man stopped, tall and serious in the doorway. Hesitating, he finally came back in, stood with his back against the boards. "I'm taking a chance on losing my job — " he said. "But I've got to warn you, Mr. Rufe. You ought to keep a gun handy."

"A gun?" Hamm asked.

"Yes, a revolver. It might be best to carry one a while. The Gold Shirts may be taking in a little night work any time — "

"Because I'm on the Co-op?"

"Well — I'd carry a revolver — "

The Eddie Chimmer case came to trial the Monday before the World Series started, with the district meeting of the P.T.A. and the fall's first big Dollar Day coming towards the week-end. Maybe the first, the juiciest part of the trial would be over by then. But picking the jury, seven women and five men, took until Thursday. At dawn Friday the courthouse steps were covered with early risers and long before opening time the line, mostly women, reached around the block to the town's blacksmith shop, reminding the whittlers squatting in the sun of the old hustling days in the district. Many of the late comers took one look at the line and went home to their radios and their telephones, calling for the drug company that hoped to sponsor the trial on the air, like the Lindbergh case. But the judge dumped the requests into the wastebasket, spit on top of them, and called court.

The first day furnished the Grandapolis papers with another capital city banner. The Chimmer autograph book, presumably in the hands of the authorities and safe for the trial, had disappeared. There was a little editorializing about negligence and much talk about who probably managed the disappearance — who was being shielded. Not that it would make much difference in the case, but it was just one more instance of the corruption of justice by money and influence. Several girls and women were finally called as witnesses, nobody important, only waitresses, maids, or clerks, but even so a mother or two slipped quietly into the back of the room, sitting with her bowed face behind her hand, waiting to take her girl away.

Townswomen took their knitting and their needlepoint to the courtroom, even their lunches. Della Loran, in high righteousness, headed a delegation to the front row, and missed no session. Some of the better people sent their maids, or their husband's secretaries. Old Charley Stetbettor made a special trip to town from outstate and tried to get the fieldhouse for a roaring clean-up talk. At first the authorities refused but he used the pull that he seemed to have acquired lately. Hamm went down alone to the top tier of seats, banked with young men in their early twenties, regular lower and middle Franklin, most of them with high school, or even college behind them — not the crowd Old Charley used to draw. But they were shabby, jobless, without future. And a scattering of them already wore the small enamel cross and sword buttons of the Christian Crusaders. Below Hamm sat a few women, mostly middle-aged, a couple of garrulous ones showing off their inside information by pointing out the higher-ups among the town's Klansmen, Gold Shirts, Crusaders, and American Liberty party members.

"When we get to working together we'll have the whole caboodle in the palm of our hands, right in the palm — " one of them bragged.

The audience was receptive, whooping and stamping as Old Charley Stet rehashed in lurid detail the testimony of the investigators who had looked through the hole in the ceiling upon Ed Chimmer's operating table. That night a young woman was dragged into the bushes not a block from the fieldhouse, and the next few days there were dirty words on walks and fences, peeping Toms in the residence sections, a whole flood of obscene letters and postcards in the mails, and a dozen complaints of men trying to coax little girls into alleys. The rest of the Chimmer trial was behind closed doors. The trial judge, a long-boned Swede, born near the forks of the Grand River, denounced the hysterical interest of the town, "Unconcerned with the evils of society, these people gorge themselves on the morbid details like buzzards after a hard winter." The Methodist bishop backed the judge, saying it did little good to preach against the Charley Stet-bettors or to punish the Eddie Chimmers, "without an honest attempt to diagnose and cure the sick and corrupt society that breeds them." Another churchman took to his pulpit against the bishop, accusing him of loose and sensational talk designed to shake the faith of the people. For weeks the papers were full of angry letters on both sides. In the meantime, Eddie Chimmer drew a hung jury.

There seemed to be about as many visitors at Abigail's apartment as ever, townspeople coming as before, but looking up and down the street before they slipped in at the apartment-house door. She still had to carry much of her work to the researchers' alcove of the university library, or the newspaper basement in the Historical Society building. But there were few public invitations to turn down and when Erich Hagge, the poet of the Montana wheatlands, came through on Town Hall he had to insist that she be asked to the dinner given for him.

"Miss Allerton has written a good book. She has made a living record of your city — " he told the committee. Yes, yes — of course, but she was, well, not the social type. Perhaps one must permit a writer certain peculiarities — So he called Abigail himself. Diffidently she came down to tea with him, a little shy because he was known as a great poet of the folk and a great liberal.

Erich Hagge turned out to be a large, quiet, and friendly man, his face strong as weathered hickory under a thatch of mouse-grey hair, his eyes wrinkle-nested, his brows wide and steady. While Abigail was wishing that Hamm were there, Erich Hagge said there was a man in this region whom she should know. He had written some fighting articles for the liberal press the last twenty years, a recent one on the strike-breaking tactics of the trucking operatives in Kanewa. Hamm Rufe was the name. Abigail nodded. Yes, she knew him, and his writing, but very little beyond that. He never talked about himself.

"I have been told he's from an old midwestern family, liberal once, well-to-do now and reactionary, like so many. It seems he left home over his objection to the World War — " Yes, that might be true, Abigail admitted. Anyway he was living in a hooverville shack out across the bottoms now, and working for the Consumers' Co-operative.

At that the poet laughed deep. So it was the same here too, the interesting people living in hoovervilles! Was she from out there? No, but Abigail had to admit that she wasn't liked any better by the city. Yes, oh yes, he saw what faces they made when he would have her called. He knew the look well; for years it was directed toward him.

Of course. Track layers and harvest hands were not always considered fit subjects for poetry here.

"Exactly, nor camp cooks, or labor orators, or WPAers." Those still weren't, not here, Abigail reminded him.

"No, for these people feel the instinctive fear of the parasite for the man who produces. But they seem no longer afraid of me — " he said, a little amusement about the corners of his wide mouth, and a little sadness too. He was only a speaker now. Still, they had treated him generously out on the Ridge, piled on cocktails, food, and flattery; had taken him through the capitol. He found it a fine building, but they made him listen to the cost of every pillar, almost every tile —

Abigail nodded. She knew how it would seem to this man who spoke so directly, who looked so straight and steadily into her face, as a stranger might look upon a new country, appraising its contours, its soil, and its sky.

"You are to come to the dinner, you know — " he said, "and sit beside me so someone within hearing will find me intelligible — "

"Not when they don't want me — "

"Then I do not go."

Knowing that he probably meant it, she went, and didn't mind so much, because he told them all that she was there as his special guest, "one of the capital city's distinguished citizens," he said, making her ears burn. After the speech she went to the depot with him. Over coffee they talked about their growing years on the farm, plowing time, and threshing with its grain scooping, its band cutting, the dust of the strawpile, with beards thick down the sweating neck. Yes, yes, and then there was that trick of walking around on the old horsepower to keep from getting dizzy and sick.

It was good fun, this talking over old times, as though they had grown up across the two ruts of wagon wheels from each other instead of two states and twenty years apart.

"Today I have found a friend — " he told her as the train pulled out.

Just when things had quieted down Hattie, Cobby's little Hattie, as everybody called her, decided to come back home for Pulaski Day. Not that the Poles of the bottoms made a great fuss over this holiday here, but it was a time of sitting around together, of recounting tales of the old country, with food all day and drink; and in the evening their own dances. Even when those in the old homeland were bombed and shattered and dying they danced, for was that not the greatness of their people, that they could be killed but never defeated? Then the next morning they always hung their flags once more, for the Columbus Day of their new homeland, America. This year was not all badness, for one who was away would return. After the first word from the letter in Mother Krasinski's hands there was a chattering and a moving from one back fence to another to tell that Hattie, the Krasinskis' Hattie, was coming home. While some stood away at the news, it was only a short time before there was knocking on front door and back at the little white house for a word, and a taste of Anton's bottle, brought up out of the cellar, as is proper when a wandering one returns.

Somehow the papers heard about it and had reporters and photographers at the train. But the Love Pirate line didn't seem just the right one to use any more, particularly since the talk over Penny Hammond's affair. Nor did the title fit Hattie very well, in spite of a little retouching on her picture, a shortening of her skirts, and the addition of a lift to its flare as though by a gust of wind or a saucy flip. She still looked a lot like any pretty, warmhearted little Polish girl. Her apartment, stripped of everything that could be carried away, was waiting for her, but she went down to the white house in the Polish bottoms. The mustached old Polak father took up his yard rake against the reporters.

"Go'dam chicken hawks!" he roared. "Always hangin' roun'!"

The authorities wanted to know about a few things, like Cobby's fifty thousand dollars in negotiable paper missing from the bank.

Oh, she had it; all signed over to her.

But she knew it would all have to be returned?

"Why?" she wondered. "Didn't it belong to Mr. Welles?" That was as far as they got, and while Hamm was a little uneasy about the Gold Shirts, afraid they might threaten Hattie, there was nothing that he could see to do.

When the girl tried to get her old job as stenographer back she was told that no married man would dare hire her, so she took up beauty-parlor work, and was sought out almost the first day of her apprenticeship, for it must be that she had some strange and vital secret.

There was another juicy bit for the gossips of the town, too, another bit of Wellesiana. The globe-trotter, Colonel Richard, stopped off at Grandapolis to talk on "Unsettled Estates in the British Isles" to a woman's club, and drew a very good crowd, including every hopeful contributor to the recurring Drake swindles. Cassie had him up to Franklin to look at an old parchment will that hung in Cobby's office, framed and conspicuous. In its more decipherable portions an early Welles had left most of his wife's clothing to her, with instruction that she display proper gratitude. Cobby often showed it to visiting bankers, saying that in those days women weren't getting their clutches on everything, were they?

The Colonel made something of the more obscure passages of the darkened old parchment, explained the pendent seals, estimated the probable value at a nice high figure, and became Cassie's guest for a whole week, until Dachel, in an angry pout, moved down to the Buffalo Hotel. After the Colonel's sudden departure it got around town that he had made pretty close inquiries about Cassie's financial standing, which was around a snug million all right, but unfortunately it was mostly in investments controlled by old Susan or in trust funds, with only the income available. So she was left free to go down to the hotel to bring Dachel back. He was such a help with painters and decorators out at the house, she explained, and anybody who ever had any work done would know what that meant.

Hamm Rufe had other things on his mind. A note was slipped under his door, signed by the Committee for American Liberty, warning him to get out of town in forty-eight hours. And Stephani wrote she was driving through next week on her way back from California, stopping off to look into Kanewa's Midwest Farmers' Association.

CHAPTER IX

FEATHERS came drifting down along the lighted front of the Buffalo Hotel like the first flurries of a snowstorm, then thicker, settling softly upon the passers-by, who looked quickly up into the warm clear night and then more closely at their dark sleeves. Pillow feathers.

High above the walk a row of hotel windows were open, with young heads hanging out and arms shaking ticking squares into the night, showering feathers downward. They shrieked with laughing as the people below brushed impatiently at their clothes and hurried past. "Hoodlums!" the women told each other angrily, trying to cover their hair with their hands. "Young hoodlums that ought to be in the reform school — !"

But many of the people stopped to look up at the windows and call out words that were lost in the traffic noises, or to tell each other that it was only those school kids, celebrating Coolidge High's victory over Alexander Hamilton School from Grandapolis. The coffee-colored doorman, student at Baptist College, held his dignified pose until the flying down got into his little mustache. Then, his sneezings echoing through the lobby, he hurried his long coattails around to find the manager. Before he got back to his station it was water in paper bags the students were dropping to burst on the pavement among the passers-by, splattering their feet, wetting down the drift of feathers along the walk. One bag hit a man in a tuxedo squarely on his bald spot and sent him, wet and swearing, into the hotel, while up in the windows the laughing of the girls soared over the breaking voices of the boys.

Suddenly there was a high, thin scream from among them, a plopping thud, a squeaking of metal above the street, and a girl's frightened crying. All the crowded avenue stopped to look to a third-floor awning that moved and bellied against the red brick wall, while somebody up at the windows wailed "Sadie, Sadie! Sadie Cooper's fell out!" and then was silent with the rest.

The street below was still now, too, watching the struggle in the folded awning that might flatten down any moment or split open and drop the girl to the pavement. The house detective and then the manager appeared in the window below the girl, sticking their heads out cautiously, their faces turned upward, calling to her to keep quiet or she'd fall through, break her fool neck. The fire department was on the way; be here in just a minute now, just a minute. On the pavement below them the doorman and a waiter came tearing out through the crowd with a big tablecloth. One at each end they stopped under the awning, looking up; a dozen men caught the edges of the thin cloth too, and waited.

With sirens going the fire department crept through the jammed traffic, grazing fenders, pushing on to the hotel. The ladder was swung up and a fireman came back with the girl, kicking and crying all the way. On the ground he set her on her feet and retreated, leaving fourteen-year-old Sadie Cooper to blink about at the crowd and stagger when she tried to move, drunk, and smelling like a prohibition still. For a moment everybody stood away from her, only the doorman thinking to help the girl inside; then, remembering his color, he dropped his dark hands from her arm and stood helpless too.

Inside, the hotel was full of people, with half a dozen Friday-night parties. By the time the police matron and the officers arrived the sixth floor was jammed. They cleared the spectators out, but they couldn't keep them from carrying away stories of furniture broken, beds torn up, piles of empty bottles, and couples of students in rooms together, some completely naked and too drunk to dress with the law banging outside their very doors. The stories were good, and lost nothing in the swift retelling as they spread over the town.

When the officers got the children sobered up a little it came out that no one was guilty of selling the minors anything to drink. They had come prepared with a crowbar to force a hotel liquor closet that Jimmy Ellers spotted long ago. It was his party; he brought all the equipment, and a room passkey. When they got tired of the dancing down on third floor they went foraging. That's all there was to it. Nobody knew how Sadie got through the window. Sadie had no idea.

It caused a nice stench, with investigations and accusations of all kinds. By the time Jimmy Ellers's father, the ambitious attorney from the slope of Blue Ridge, got to the hotel the boy's whole story was out. And just when Harv Ellers was hoping to move in on the Ridge itself by buying the old King place, across from Welleshaven, through Kanewa Investments. This mess would cook him with the Ridge folks, he told his wife angrily, this mess that her worthless son had stirred up. And wasn't Jimmy his son also, she demanded, and wasn't it to further him with the right people that the party had been planned in the first place?

This time the papers couldn't sidestep the matter, not after that fool of a Sadie Cooper went and fell publicly out of a window, before a Friday-night crowd in football season. So the *World* puffed itself up with the pompous wrath of a Chautauqua Park camp meeting evangelist. Were these young high-school students who destroyed property so wantonly and disported themselves in such a sinful manner typical of the city and the nation — even granting the excitement of a great athletic victory well won, were they typical? Representing the best section of the capital city as they did, must they be considered worse than those of poorer environment in this city or in others offering fewer advantages? Most certainly not. What, then, was the younger generation coming to and where did they learn these things?

The Eddie Chimmer case, breaking so early in the fall, had already disrupted the usual campaign program of the capital city politicians. This always included a clean-up attack on the taverns and dance halls outside the city limits just before election, to get the people interested and make votes for the Franklin candidates. Sometimes the fight got hot enough to shift votes as high up as the governorship, and carrying Kanewa's second city was important in any election.

The regular plan was to wait until the university and the Baptist College students were safely settled, and then catch a country tavern selling liquor to some minor from the town. Because it meant unfortunate publicity, the decoy was usually a boy from some family indebted to a politician, perhaps saved from the reformatory for this very purpose, or his sister from the industrial school. Afterward, the story was always rushed into print under approximately the same head: COUNTY TAVERNS PITFALLS FOR YOUTH. It came with such dull regularity that the assignment was shuffled off on the newest reporter, who was then called Pitfalls until the next campaign.

At the time of Eddie Chimmer's arrest he had a lot to say about venereal quacks and about jealous doctors who were afraid he would undercut them on fees for inspecting and treating the prostitutes.

"But they got no call to be scared of me," he had said, stroking his dewlap. "I wouldn't dirty my hands — "

Whatever the public thought about Eddie's hands, they wanted to know more about this prostitute trade he talked about. Where did it come from? Surely not from within the city limits. While the *World* suppressed the story, the Franklin *Gazette* pointed out that the growth in venereal quacks in

Franklin, as elsewhere, was not necessarily evidence of more infection but probably a growing demand for treatment that the public couldn't get. The next day the *World* carried a symposium by the local doctors, calling the surprised little *Gazette* a nest of Reds who were advocating socialized medicine. After all this the edge of surprise was certainly off any clean-up for this fall.

Now the women were aroused, a delegation headed by Hallie Rufer Hammond and several prominent P.T.A.'s plowing through the halls of the rickety old courthouse to demand the prosecution of the country tavernkeepers as demoralizers of the city's youth. It was a windy day; Hallie's grey hair was flying, her eyes defiant, once more the daughter of old George Rufer. She got the wholesale roundup, swiftly, too, although not without a tip-off over the telephone: "Big party coming in for spring fries," and the click of the receiver.

Because the proprietors always knew the date of the regular raid, they decided this must be an extra shakedown for campaign funds, and pretty hard to take, with twice too many places licensed. Hell, they were family men and didn't want to keep fries around, skinny girls barely out of grade school, but they drew the older bucks. Even when a man got so he couldn't do anything but look he liked a hard little butt beside his chair. So they sent a few of the younger girls home for a night or two, shifted the older ones to front service, turned the scrawniest of the high-school trade away, and scratched up what money they could, hoping the collection percentage wouldn't be too high.

Evening brought a cold drizzle, little business, and no officers. The next night was the same, although the full moon was spilling silver over all the country parking lots, full to the gates. Maybe the telephone calls were a joke, and so to business as usual. Then Hallie Hammond got her roundup, from the proprietor of the newly opened Treasure Cave, the El Troc under another neon sign, down to the curb-service girls at hot-dog stands far out along the highways. There were half a dozen bookings for liquor sales to minors, several dope charges, a candy box full of marihuana cigarettes in envelopes with the details of each purchase, and another one of aphrodisiacs picked up around the places where the older men, some of them already smelling like wet matches, hung out. Two dozen girls were charged with soliciting, half of them under eighteen. For the first time since the government got the boy tramps off the road the Franklin County jail was filled.

Before sunup it was half empty. The first one out was a marihuana peddler with a Christian Crusader button. He told the sheriff that he'd better be taken care of or he'd talk, and talk plenty, snarling from the corner of his mouth like in the movies. Five minutes after they let him get to a telephone the sheriff had his orders from Billie Bamper. Harold Welles's name was one of those suppressed from the list of the detained, his arrest considered a mistake. All he did was jump into a car and tear away when the officers came to Treasure Cave. Not recognizing the roaring machine, they shot the tires out. He claimed no knowledge of the boxes of rubber goods in the locked trunk, and denied that he was a reefer. Just had a little too much gin, got excited when he saw the officers, and jumped in the wrong car, he said.

There were plenty of names that could be used, with several Polish girls from down on the bottoms among the waitresses and some WPA workers picked up as frequenters of the beer joints.

Hamm was at the Snells' the next night. The doctor was pretty cynical over his pipe.

"You notice that it's only the Polish girls they label by nationality, and the WPA workers by employer — "

"Yes, too bad there were none they could call Jew in the catch," Ona Snell added. "And yet those women, including

Hallie Hammond, are honestly trying to protect the morals of the youth of the community."

"They'll have to catch themselves a new crop of youth — " Hamm said, and was as surprised at the words as the doctor and his wife.

"A fine political display of dirty linen," the Grandapolis papers called the roundup.

"Yeh," the Coot agreed, "but not one breechclout of it'll get a washing." Hamm sat empty-handed, silent, and after a while the old man got up and went humming off to the shelterhouse. Not so much brains up there, but no mooding around like a moulting shitepoke either.

It was true that even Hallie Hammond cooled a little when she saw the clean-up reach towards the Ridge. Her Rufer blood had thinned considerably in her sixty-five years of life in the capital city.

Of course there was some showing for the papers; a couple of tavernkeepers fined, their licenses revoked, and eight girls sent to the industrial school. Russ Snell told Hamm that the examining doctors found two of the girls still virgins but the officials ignored that and sent them anyway. The papers didn't say that one of the men went on relief when his place was closed or that Jamie, son of Eloise Johnson, Hamm's old girl, was put on probation to Hallie Rufer Hammond. He had been in trouble since he was eight, got kicked out of the Franklin schools with an uncle on the board of education, then out of military academy, was arrested for speeding, and finally lost his driver's license on a hit-and-run charge. The court had tried probation to his mother and his father, and then to the judge, who was pretty sick of him. Let one of these women who thought something could be done with juvenile delinquents try a hand. In the raids seventeen-year-old Jamie was caught drunk in the back seat of a stolen car, the keys and a supply of marihuana in his pocket, and a half-dressed woman with him.

The woman went to jail and Jamie got one more chance. He was to move into the large, old Hammond house with Aunt

Hallie, as the children of the Ridge called her. He was to tutor
for prep school, and work outdoors two hours a day. As Hallie
brought the boy home, the wind was moving brown leaves in
waves across the Hammond lawn. He could begin at once.

"First she drives my lover from me," the platinum Eloise
cried to her hairdresser, "and now she takes my son — "

"Yeh, you gotta protect yourself from them good
women — " the girl said through a mouthful of invisibles.

But by the time her hair was set in a wealth of smooth
little curls about her softening neck, and her face was out of its
pack, Eloise was glad. The boy really was a problem. Took
after his father's people. The Johnsons lacked emotional stabil-
ity, she said. Let Aunt Hallie look after him; it was her
fault he wasn't a meek, quiet little Hammond.

By this time Hamm had another letter from Stephani, im-
personal as always, but good to receive. She would be detained
a little, stopping on her way through Texas to look into the
Farmers' Association there. It seemed to be the same sort of
setup as in California, and as in Kanewa too, probably. But
she really was coming to see Hamm. She must know how it
had been with him all these years. There was an enclosure,
a letter from an acquaintance about the strike articles. "Good
stuff," the writer said. "That man Rufe is a shrewd observer,
but leans too much toward the intellectual liberal, who must
find good on both sides. My God! The employers of Kanewa
don't need him to state their case. They've got their Senator
Bullard, and the public press."

Hamm asked Abigail and Carl Halzer to look into the
Kanewa Farmers' Association for Stephani's coming. This time
it was certain.

The crested invitations to the Tyndale Presentation dinner
were out, three hundred of them, including even a few to
people from the university, the chancellor, and the deans of
bizad and law. The governor was invited too, the only outstate

capitol official. But he would be too sick to attend. There were some who thought he'd never live until his successor was elected, when his resignation became effective.

Big stories of the Tyndale blowout got around. Evidently Samuel had given Margaret a blank check with the world the limit. There was talk of big fights with the social director at the Buffalo Hotel, the steward and the head chef, too, and even with the manager himself, although this was obviously his biggest chance for free advertising. Every day the Tyndales wanted something more, until he was afraid to look into a paper. No telling what screwy idea Elsa Maxwell or somebody off in Hollywood would get into print and then Margaret Tyndale would be wanting that.

There was talk of roast pig, and strolling minstrels, and food from gold plates, golden china, of course, and a velvet hanging twenty feet wide with the Tyndale crest, made special for the dinner. Everybody that knew about coats-of-arms laughed. Old Sam from Sheffield? He must have had his made along in twenty-eight, too, they told each other, when that man came through the country doing them for a thousand dollars each, on a fine velvet banner for the living-room wall. He left eight or a dozen behind in Franklin, better looking than most and without the bother of getting a line through, as Prudence Bamper pointed out. She knew; she tried to get traced for the D.A.R.'s, at a thousand dollars, flat rate, and had court costs on top of that because she refused to pay the professional researcher, who wanted her money whether the line went through or not. With the coat-of-arms man there was something to show, a banner with whatever the client wanted, fleur-de-lis, plumes, armor, or anything else antique that he fancied, all combined artistically in any color scheme. But when Josina Black, the town's genealogy expert, looked the Tyndales up, there was old Sam's family, all right, coat-of-arms and all.

In the meantime Mollie was tearing from hair stylist to

luncheon and from fitter to cocktails. She was interviewed over the radio, and news photographers snapped her calling on the governor for the first contribution in the Community Chest drive, greeting the Town Hall speaker, catching a plane to New York for a little shopping. Through all this Burt Parr stopped by the Co-op a time or two before his morning classes, but he never mentioned Mollie any more. Hamm couldn't really say that he mentioned anything much, just sat a while, the October sun bright on his hair, and went away, his notebook rolled under his arm, his cigarette half-smoked in his fingers.

Serious matters must be coming up in the capital city, for the *World* was running its Culture, its C line, as the newsroom called it, this week over its editorials: —

To envision and disseminate the highest attributes
of cultural living to all the great state of Kanewa

It wasn't the usual agitation for the revival of the symphony, allowed to die over a WPA fight, or the complaint that music lovers had to go to Walden to hear Stokowski, where the chamber of commerce sponsored the arts as though they were money in the bank. This time it was the Allerton woman backing an exhibit of oils in the chamber lounge.

Not that Abigail got any credit for the show put on for National Art Week until after the trouble started. The better Franklinites always thought of themselves as patrons of the arts. Along in the 1860's they started the old Culture Society, which broke up into reading-circle groups and the Franklin Art Association, still sponsoring exhibits of flower pictures and still-lifes. Since the war they usually bought a picture or two a year, usually cheaper ones, often by unknown artists, and some turned out good investments even in the eyes of the banker members of the association. Unfortunately they were lost in the sentimental stuff and the hundreds of bad copies they accepted to get the endowments the gifts carried. Every year the committee brought in an outside speaker, usually well-investigated. Somehow it hadn't seemed necessary with the nationally famed artist son of an American first family, last year. He came, a fine bold figure of a man standing there before the dollar-a-seat audience and accepting their applause. Modestly, and almost before the last white-gloved hand was silent, he was talking of the WPA artists and the Treasury art projects that grew out of their work. The federal government had nurtured the first really creative period in American art, and one probably unequaled since the days of Athens, he said, speaking so plainly no one could help hearing every word, and understanding it all. By this time muttering grey-haired men and women both were stalking out, for these doors, like so many in Franklin, always opened outward, and readily.

The committee sent a formal note of apology to the public columns of the *World*, promising a more careful investigation of all speakers in the future, and pledged their opposition to any government murals in Franklin, either by the WPA or the Treasury department. There were communities in Kanewa less vigilant, Stockholm and Sheffield, for instance, and even little Minerva, far out on Wild Horse Plains, with some foreign element that praised its postoffice mural, but the walls of the capital city would remain free and uncontaminated.

Not that Franklin frowned upon good art. Local exhibits, properly sponsored, were always encouraged by both the university and the chamber of commerce. Before her boycotting Abigail had arranged one for the chamber lounge, and by the time the date arrived her connection with the exhibit was easily overlooked, Parkins, the secretary, gladly accepting the responsibility.

Although Lon Rickert was claimed as a local boy, he was really born in a trapper's shack on the Powder River somewhere, and grew up drawing pictures all over the buildings of the cow ranch where his mother ran the cookhouse. While he studied painting at K.U. in Franklin, he worked as night chef at the Station House, humming old cowboy songs between closed lips to hold off homesickness for the open country. Finally he made it as far as New York, still painting, frying steaks, and humming. About a year ago he came back to his grills at the station long enough to work up a one-man show for Harkoff's, on New York's East 57th Street.

Lon was still as lanky as an old cowhand, and as close-mouthed about talking when Hamm Rufe met him at Abigail's. He liked the artist and went out with him on a few sittings, once to the home of a colored maid from the Grand Vista Country Club. They found her in a second-floor, west-side room of one of the old shacky places owned by the Kanewa Investment south of the avenue. The low ceiling was the under side of the flat rubberoid roof; the air quivering heat; the unscreened window sill speckled with crawling flies from the garbage cans and the open privies in the yard below. The woman was just up from a mishap, as she called it, her dark face clay-pale and glistening with sweat, her eyes set in deep secret hollows, her lips brownish soft. With her faded blue kimono held about her, she seemed somehow remote and holy, like the primitive figures Hamm saw in old Mexican churches. The artist said nothing at all, but his hands shook as he put up his easel and set the woman at the window, the junky yard and the dirty yellow walls of a creamery beyond as a background. Hamm moved the other chair to the hallway door to catch any bit of breeze, and settled down. After a while a big negro came to squat silently on his heels, watching too. That would be Bo, the woman's husband, out of work for six years.

"We can't afford us no children," the woman had said mildly, but as though explaining something too.

Word got around of doings up at Bo's. The audience grew. A couple of Negro women came to sit on the gaunt bed, two hound-ribbed little yellow boys brought a crippled baby in a goods box and leaned her against the wall to see, dropping down too, one on each side of her, motionless as rough ground metal figures. Several small white children came to stand shyly against the wall, followed later by a naked baby, his soiled diaper dragging between his creeping feet. There were soft sounds of awe and interest, even little talkings, but Lon noticed nothing now. With a stick of charcoal he stroked in a swift, loose sketch and then daubed it with little patches of color for later guidance, painting in only the face now, the grey skin, the quiet, sad Madonna look, and one of the hands in her lap, the palm pink and empty. Not until they were walking through the dusk of evening, the wet canvas held away from him in a double frame, did the man part his lips from their humming.

"I'll call it Bereaved Madonna," he said.

When the show opened the *World* gave the picture front-page space, with the title in quotations. There was a rush downtown to see this sacrilegious painting of the black woman, and a morning-long protest by telephone and in person to the papers, the chamber of commerce, and to Lon Rickert. It was all right if the painter wanted to choose unpleasant subject matter when portraying foreign scenes, as in his Powder River Cook, that no one knew was Lon's own, hard-working mother, or Union Square Harangue, of a painted-up old tart standing on a box, wrapping herself in the American flag before the disinterested pretzel women, pitchmen, and the flowing street beyond. Even the portrait of old Zeromski, of the Polish bottoms, with a grey stubble over his knob of a chin, his eyes still fierce and blue, was all right, too, for it was not the capital city. But calling a Negro woman, with Glen Doover's Franklin Creamery plainly recognizable in the background, a Madonna, that was sacrilege. But it was the picture called Capitol Vista that the town really wouldn't tolerate. In the background stood the white tower, touched by the evening sun, and in the foreground was one of the old brick apartments on Seventh Street, with two thin, dirty children sitting on the back step, behind them a cluttered hallway and an open indoor toilet. To the protests the artist pointed out that this picture was not only true, it was factual — sketched from life. The chairman of the Art Association, who was a photography hobbyist, came forward to answer that. Under normal lighting the inside fixtures wouldn't show.

"But they are there, you know, and help make the composition — " the artist said.

It was all really quite polite and pleasant, a matter of artistic preference, of course. Unfortunately the house committee of the chamber had decided that the lounge must be redecorated immediately, so the pictures were taken down the next day instead of hanging the full two weeks. For days afterward old Poles from the bottoms came puffing up the stairs, repeating each time, "I see it by the paper, is pictures here. I want see — "

Lon Rickert was disappointed, too. He had hoped to sell a few paintings, small ones, of course, not of Negro Madonnas, or of capitol vistas, but some of the pleasanter ones, to help get his show to New York. He wished now he had shown the other picture he had, the one called The Defender, of the Labor Day parade: the police and the deputies advancing with drawn revolvers and rifles, the foot of a deputy on the flag of the down bearer, three other men on the pavement, and a woman crawling away towards the paraders, who were thrown back like wheat at the first big blow of a storm. Between them and the officers, towering over all as he pulled off his blue jumper, was the defender, his hair standing like a flame and his face lightning terrible.

Lon talked his troubles out with Abigail and through a newspaper man she knew in Grandapolis, he managed a show there. This time he put up all the smaller things he could get together, with a dozen or so hasty water colors done in Grandapolis, deliberately quaint and stylized. These he framed as quaintly: one with a dark grey sky touched to morning red over the flour mills he finished off in faded denim and the rough-sawed, wine-colored heart of a red willow tree. Some of the others he framed in burlap or cornhusks shellacked flat on old boards. "The stuff is enough to make you heave up," Lon told Abigail, "but I'm afraid that's what people here want."

The show was up ten days, and almost sold itself out, a dozen of the pictures finding their way into Franklin homes, now that it was evident that the artist's bad showing in the capital city was all the fault of that horrible Allerton woman.

Anyway, Lon had his Bereaved Madonna, Capitol Vista, and his Defender safe for his New York Show.

At last the week of the Tyndale Presentation dinner came. The Sunday before there was a big barbecue and picnic out on the family homestead along the Wakoon. All the old-time friends from around Sheffield were invited, and business associates out over the state, including a dozen or so from Franklin — those not quite important enough for the dinner. The barbecue fires were started at daylight for the fat baby beef, half a hog, and a sheep. The park was a hundred and sixty acres of golden October trees, with the original log house of Old Samuel restored and a public address system put in for community sings. Samuel made a speech and presented Mollie to their old friends, blushing and very pretty, in a sage-green suit with red fox. It was a fine day, with every Parr but Burt there, and all the other old-timers who knew Mollie from her diaper days.

The Co-op kept Hamm so busy he saw nothing of Burt Parr or anyone else much. Then along about two o'clock one morning when the sky had cleared from a fog and drizzling, he was awakened by a light, timid rattling at his door, like a field mouse trying to get in from the cold. It seemed higher up, and was so persistent that at last Hamm put on his robe and went to see. It was Mollie Tyndale, holding up her long velvet cloak in both hands, her hair flying, her face blood-streaked and dirty, her pretty sandals clay-caked. She had to get to Burt. No, no, she was all right, but she had to find Burt.

Hamm saw that her face was bruised, her eyes frightened, and so he coaxed her inside and called a student who knew of Burt's hours and places. Then he built up a good fire and while the girl shivered before it he cleaned her little satin sandals, making a great fuss over the job to give her time for calm. At last the girl began to talk, slowly, and what she omitted Hamm could well fit in from the shock of her girl face.

The evening had started like any other cold, damp fall night. After the dinner for her at the Buffalo a dozen of them made the rounds of the town, ending up at the Country Club for a dance or two, from there to Milo Groves's apartment for another drink and then home. Somehow Harold Welles got her away from her crowd and into the Doover car with Frankie's new girl, Sadie. Frankie's girls were usually just Sadie or Zella or LaVerne, nothing else, but generally good fun and all right. Harold suggested they do something different tonight, not go home yet. He had heard of a place a couple of blocks off the campus that he thought he could get into. Oh, a lowdown place all right, but O.K. for an after-hour beer, and a look at the crumby people. The rest thought the idea grand, so Mollie went, not objecting too much. She never liked Frankie and Harold's whitish eyes gave her chills, especially lately. But one couldn't be a mudball all the time.

Leaving the car half a block away, they went stumbling over the sunken walk to a dark old frame house on an empty, unlighted street. On the porch Mollie really tried to hold back but Harold kept on knocking a complicated tattoo on the thin door. Finally there was a commotion far away, a shuffling as of slippers, a yawning, and a man's voice asking "What-you-want — ?" running the words all together, like some foreigner.

"Friends of J. W.'s," Harold said low, his mouth against the door crack. Mollie wondered about the J. W., afraid it was for Joe Willper, the leader of the Gold Shirts, a convict and blackmailer, some people said.

After a little rattling the door opened and Mollie was pushed ahead into the darkness. None of the rest hesitated at all, Sadie giggling a little as the door closed behind her and a small flashlight clicked on, swept over their faces, and was shut off.

"O.K.," the man said like any American, and they followed his steps over a long bare floor into an inside room, lit by a smoky lamp and smelling of an oil heater. The room was dark to their eyes, even after the blackness of the hallway; the walls water-streaked and dirty. Four or five people, men and women, sat around a wet old dining table drinking canned beer. They looked up at the newcomers, their mouths open a little, keeping their hands on the grey cans as though they were rocks, ready for defense. One of the women laughed out loud at Mollie's face. "My God, lookit the bundle a new goods!"

"Shut up, Belle," the man beside her snapped, drawing his thick arm back with the can in his fist, and winking heavily to Mollie. The girl looked swiftly about her, but neither of the boys, not even Sadie, seemed surprised at the dirty room or the loose-faced drinkers. They pushed her on at the heels of the thin, stooped man beckoning from another dark hall. "Right this way, Buddy," he said, businesslike, switching the flashlight on again, and leading the way down a chicken ladder of steps into a long narrow hallway, wet and stale with a queer, sickly, sweetishness smell. Mollie pulled back again. "Let's go, please, Harold, let's go home!" she begged. "Sh — sh," he ordered, and nudging her, pointing out the necking couple on a narrow bench at the end of the hall. "Waiting for another round — " he whispered, laughing a little, his voice going up like a silly girl's. Now Mollie noticed dark openings along the left side of the hall, half a dozen of them, with the man stopping at one after another to listen. At a silent one, he flashed his light inside and she saw a bare space hardly a foot wider than the iron bed, with an old grey blanket bunched on the dirty mattress.

"There ya are, payment in advance, fifty cents fer fifteen minutes — " the man said, waving Harold in.

At that Mollie got very sick. Clapping her hand over her mouth, she jerked free, and ran back into the darkness towards the stairs, the man behind her whispering loudly, "Catch her! You damn fools, bringin' a runnin' drunk in here — Catch the broad!"

Just as the man's flashlight found her Mollie stumbled against a door. It shot open at her weight. Probably for use in raids, she guessed. Hamm nodded.

Well, she fell through it, out into cold, fresh air. Feeling her way she scrambled up some broken steps to the ground level and began to run down the middle of the dark street. Almost at once she knew that this wouldn't do, not now that her face seemed to be bleeding and her knees skinned. So she slowed down, walking along the muddy curb as though coming home from a girl friend's. She had no mad money with her; the buses had long stopped; no taxis cruised the streets, not even a car. She was alone in the silent, sleeping town. So she came here.

By the time Burt Parr roared up to the shack in a borrowed car, Mollie was quieter, her bruised forehead washed, her skinned knee taped. When she saw the boy in the doorway, his tousled hair shining in the light, his eyes deep and black, she ran sobbing into his arms. . . .

Early the next morning Hamm had a call for Burt Parr.
Where was the young fellow and the car he borrowed the
night before? Hamm didn't know. He thought about little
Mollie all day and about the miserable son Cobby Welles had
fathered, Cobby, the friend of his boyhood. Perhaps there
was something to the story the Coot told around the shelterhouse, about the fake Canadian war hero. Maybe there was
more than gossip to these stories about the woman Cobby had
married.

Hamm thought of Burt Parr, with his hair bright as any
Polish girl's from the bottoms, his shoulders broad and fine
as the walnut beams old Jacob cut in the early timber of the
Wakoon, and he wondered how Margaret Tyndale would take
the jolt her fine plans might get today.

In the evening he found the boy waiting for him in the
shack, hunched over his knees on the edge of the couch, his
face in his palms. Hamm put the coffeepot on and spread a
thick round of ham in the frying pan. Finally Burt began
to talk. They had gone across the state line to Parson Sam,
the Marryin' Man. It had seemed so right last night to both
of them, right and beautiful.

For a long time the boy was silent, his hands working, his
eyes tight closed against his cheeks. Then slowly he started
to talk again. This morning, when they got back, it was all
different, with Mollie's mother crying that he had spoiled
everything, their lives, the trip to England, the Presentation
dinner. Yes, Hamm thought, angrily, she would put it so,
the dinner the climax, the most important of all.

So now it was all done, like the fine tall trees standing over
the Wakoon and suddenly undermined by the river. Nothing
left but Mollie looking back over her mother's shoulder as
they took her away. They were beginning annulment proceedings. Samuel had hurried down to the little inland town
to suppress the publication of the marriage.

Chartered a plane, Hamm supposed.

No, Mollie's father had intended to, but Burt convinced him that the publicity would make suppression impossible. Now he wished he'd let the old show-off fly down there; but almost at once the boy's loyalty to an old friend made him ashamed.

"Samuel Tyndale wasn't like this down home," he said through his fingers. "I don't know. Something's happened — "

Yes, things do happen to people, Hamm admitted. And all this was quite a complication, with the Presentation dinner only a couple of days away. So he pulled his bed up, got the boy's shoes off, and stretched him out. When Halzer came by on the way to Abigail's for a cup of coffee, Hamm went out to send him on alone. He couldn't leave the boy, not tonight, to wake up to an empty shack.

The next day the paper had a half column of further plans for the Tyndale dinner, with a solid paragraph of out-of-town guests, in agate for the first edition but hastily reset in larger type for the city. Nothing else. Hamm looked over to Burt, hunched at the foot of the couch, as though he had been so all day.

"Well," he comforted, "you still seem to be a married man. And every day of delay means just that much more chance of the family getting used to the idea — " But seeing the boy's face he fell silent, and when Burt finally got into his coat to go to his room, Hamm made an errand to walk at his side. At the door he put his arm across the young shoulder. "Mollie is the one you must think of," he said. The boy nodded, and slowly went inside.

The Presentation dinner made three columns in both local papers, with a ten-inch cut of Mollie in a white satin gown, her second in two months, the office girls and the clerks of the town told each other. In her soft black curls stood the three white plumes of presentation, and at her heels swept the court train. The floral piece, eight feet high, was three curled plumes, too, made of white chrysanthemums on gold and blue, small ones for corsages at each lady's place. The food was brought in by a long string of costumed viand bearers led by a plump, red-faced man carrying the roast pig on a mammoth pewter platter. They marched around the entire room singing. Some doubt had arisen at the university over the authentic songs for such an occasion, and in impatience Margaret had the bearers learn one she remembered from old Samuel of Sheffield: —

> Then round the board,
> And fill the cup
> And pile the viands high!

There was some arguing over these words, too, and over the tune, but it really went very well, with enough applause to take a second round, the bearer of the pig getting noticeably weary in the arms. But it was something to see in Franklin, in all of Kanewa.

Finally, the minstrel had sung his last song, the dancers, the tumblers, and the jester were gone, and the ink was dry on the last signature of the guest book. When the door closed behind the Tyndales, the hotel people dropped wherever they happened to stand.

Yet it had gone well. Even the town's three grandmothers, who were seated on the only scheme of ranking they never resented, by age, thought so. Everybody, literally everybody, except Harold Welles and a few of his lot, was there. When somebody teased Mollie, asking about Harold's absence from her big party, she answered, "Oh, he had more important business on tonight." She said it lightly enough, everybody knowing his important business, usually up on the hill in Stone House, and yet there was something about her face that brought a look or two among the older guests and a wondering to Hallie Hammond. There was something special behind Harold's absence, she thought, from the look those who were Gold Shirts gave each other. Could it be that they were stirring up the old story she heard years ago about Old Samuel, the first, the settler from England? It was said he or his wife was Jewish, a quarter or something, by people who couldn't stand up against his competition. Perhaps it was only used in the frontier sense, meaning a close trader. Certainly there was nothing to suggest it in the Samuel before them here, with his blunt nose and thin sandy hair. It was true that Mollie's dark hair lay in fine, soft curls, obviously natural, compared to those of Marylin or Helen Groves, or the others about her.

But before the Presentation dinner was done, the ineffectual Harold Welles and his Gold Shirts took on more importance in Hallie Hammond's eyes, and perhaps in the eyes of the lesser people there, too, especially those who felt the pinch of Samuel's competition, although no word of all this was made for anyone to hear.

Almost immediately those who had been to the Presentation dinner found their stories so much weak tea compared to one that was going the rounds of the town. It seemed that a finger waver named Sadie who considered herself Frankie Doover's girl friend was telling her following that Mollie ran out on Harold Welles at a cat house last week. Right from the first she found it better than any White House story to keep her customers patient under the drier. And each time she improved it, adding the explanations and details the previous customer demanded, until it was a lengthy, hilarious narrative, with women from the other booths slipping up to the lavender curtain to hear.

"I thought I'd spring a leak right there in public — laughing!" Sadie always ended, holding her sides. "I mean," she corrected, "when Frankie told me about Mollie seeing the crib Harold was takin' her to — !"

Even those who considered the Tyndales pushing outsiders

and their scandals of secondary importance were interested in the story because it included a Welles. First that Cobby, who'd been keeping a Polak girl in an apartment for years, taking poison; Cassie openly bringing a gigolo home from California; and Marylin chasing around over the state after a red-necked farmer who had been in jail for disturbance and rioting. Now it was Harold too. That business of running with the Gold Shirts was just high spirits, like sowing wild oats, they thought, only not so harmful, maybe a little more like boy scouting for older fellows. But nobody from the Ridge should go sneaking off to places that could be so exaggerated by a girl like that Sadie from the beauty parlor. And her claiming it was right here in town; everybody knew that was a lie. Such talk should be hushed, forcibly, if necessary. It broke down respect for their class and for their city.

Anybody who wondered how Margaret Tyndale was taking all this could see for herself. In a flippant new hat that reared up from her head like a double swallow's wing she was out every day, to club meetings, bridge parties, taking her exercises. Not even when the whisperers about her got careless did she take an extra drink or seem to smoke one more cigarette. She made one friend that bad week — Hallie Rufer Hammond, who remembered when these same people were whispering so about her first-born son, still called a slacker and a coward among them.

It was harder for young Mollie. She couldn't stand to see her mother adjust the calm of her face as she would a hat to go out and know that she, herself, was to blame for it all. Once the girl tried to go downtown and came running back to escape the coyote eyes of the people on the street, and maybe all of them knowing how it was with Burt, all except she. But when Mollie tried to talk of these things to her mother, Margaret kissed her daughter and told her she must run, positively run, for that fitting.

So finally the girl drove down to the Tyndale parking lot

and slipped into her father's office by the back way. Somewhere in the man behind the heavy, hand-hewn walnut desk from the Wakoon was the father who used to make willow whistles for her and Burt, so long ago — whistles that had holes along the sides for their small fingers. Then he would hold one to the side of his mouth and pipe out a merry little ditty as he tapped his shoe on the soft wet earth of spring.

But today it was the Samuel Tyndale of big conferences, of important man-business. He gave his daughter another signed blank check and sent her away. There must be some things to finish up her wardrobe for England.

"Oh, Dad — " the girl cried. But he took her through his waiting room and held the outside door for her, very grand. "Amuse yourself, my dear!" he called gaily after her. So she waved back and gathering her coat about her ran through the big outer office, the eyes of all the clerks lifted to her face, although the heads seemed bowed in diligence.

Not that the day had been an easy one for Samuel. Mollie was the second woman he had sent away this afternoon. Half an hour earlier Grayce Adams Smith had talked her way into his office, with her lady ways, her soft grey hair. But when she asked Samuel Tyndale for hush money he rose, short, solid, and stocky against her.

"Dirty buzzard! That's what all you people of this town are — buzzards! Tell it that Mollie is secretly married. Yell it up and down the streets. She is one you can't touch, for she is alive."

It wasn't long before Hamm heard about Sadie's business-getting story. An old Polander whose daughter worked at the beauty shop came up to tell him. Maybe it be better for American young fellow to know.

"The Welles is a no-good people for girls — " the old carpenter added thoughtfully over his pipe.

Yes, it looked that way, Hamm admitted.

"Anyhow, your friend Burt, he can feel happy. His girl, she get away."

Hamm found the boy's room empty, no one in it since the day before, the fat landlady said. They didn't know anything at the filling station either, and the manager didn't like it. Tyndale employees are dependable and reliable, he said. Hamm agreed, and let the man talk on while he called up everyone he could think of but Mollie. No one had seen anything of the boy.

The next morning there was news on the radio and in the paper. Young Burt Parr had been found in Dakers woods, beyond the old Chautauqua grounds. He was tied to a tree, a gag in his mouth, his back blood-crusted and swollen from a clubbing, with three teeth knocked out and his jawbone broken from a kick in the face.

The Franklin papers minimized the incident as student hazing, a little extreme, to be sure, as hazings sometimes were. But the Grandapolis *Inquirer* gave it front-page coverage as one more blot of violence upon the honor of the capital city. They ran the photograph of Burt, face down on a hospital bed, his jaw strapped tight, his back scarred and dark, writing his story on a scratch pad under his hand.

Night before last when he was coming home to his room a man in a car drew up alongside and asked for a direction. When young Parr turned to give it, he was hit over the head, a cloth stuffed in his mouth, and dumped into the car. The boot kick in the mouth he got out in the woods when he put up a fight. But there were five against him and so they tied him to a tree, his arms around the trunk, and took turns pounding his back with any clubs they could find until they were played out. One of them came back and struck a match to his hair, but it was so wet with sweat it only made a stench.

At the question of a reason the injured man had hesitated, then wrote his reply on the scratch pad: "One told me it was to teach me to keep away from other people's women."

"Had you ever heard the voice before?"

"Yes."

"Anyone connected with campus affairs?"

"No."

"So," the crusading reporter wrote, "tied and gagged, and suffering from the brutal beating and from exposure, young Parr was found two days later by the barking dog of some small boys."

Not even the Grandapolis *Inquirer* used the name of the man Burt accused, although it was known from Blue Ridge to Herb's Addition. It was omitted from the records at the courthouse, too, for of course Burt Parr was not himself today, after the exposure and all.

It was not until late in the afternoon that anyone seemed to get past the story of the whipping far enough to discover that on page four a Wolfgang B. Parr figured in a Margaret Beaconsfield Tyndale marriage annulment suit, filed late the day before. Even then it didn't mean much until the telephoning got started, and the talk over the cocktails. Wasn't that Mollie the sly one? So slim and cool and poised under her plumes at the Presentation dinner, and secretly married to a filling-station attendant all the time. That he was also a childhood playmate, and the grandson of an old friend of the first Tyndale of Sheffield, wasn't mentioned. He was a pauper and the marriage was secret, and that generally meant something, the Franklinites reminded each other. Maybe Mollie Tyndale's name would be in Eddie Chimmer's book too, if he wasn't having to step pretty careful just now.

Still, somebody must have helped her, or they wouldn't be annulling it, the older woman said, remembering Cassie when she was young.

Then there was the story about her going to that place with Harold Welles. Was that supposed to be before or after she was married? And what about Burt Parr being tied to a tree?

Hamm went to see the boy as soon as he could get away. The nurse was doubtful about visitors, but Burt heard his voice at the door and banged against the iron of the bed until she let him in. A long time Hamm Rufe stood over his young friend, on his stomach on a sort of slide, the fine young body awkward and wooden in its swollen bandages, his free eye dark and angry, the thick blond hair clipped off close. To Hamm it was as though this injured boy were his son, and something swift and blinding rose up before his eyes, a dark violence from some far-back Rufer throbbing under his jaw. With his uncalloused hands he could have crushed the throats of those from the Stone House. But in a moment it was gone and he was empty, his hands slack weight against his thighs.

He must make some words for Burt, careful words, letting out nothing of the annulment. So he asked of the night in the woods, pulling the slips off the pad as Burt filled them. But finally the boy wrote Mollie's name, and Hamm promised him he'd see her if he could. Then he nodded to the nurse hovering about the door and went away.

Back at Herb's Addition he pulled out his typewriter and set to work with the small sheaf of notes from the boy's pad. It was the Gold Shirts, of course, with Milo Groves and Harold, the two he would recognize, mostly standing off outside the light from the car that was turned on him and the tree. Neither of them talked much until the baldening Harold Welles set the match to the boy's hair. Hamm suspected that there must have been some good scratches and bites left from the tussle at the foot of the old cottonwood, some nice dun-colored shirts torn to rags, evidence enough for the officers, if any was wanted.

Sheet after sheet he ripped from his typewriter and towards morning he set the alarm and went to bed, the final draft of "The Ripening Fascism of the Corn Belt" ready for the mail.

While the papers saw nothing serious in the attack on Burt Parr it was too good material for the politicians to pass by. In less than twenty-four hours Charley Stetbettor had come blaring down Philadelphia Avenue in his sound truck, damning the university for its refusal to let him use the fieldhouse, and calling on everyone to attend his meeting in the old auditorium. People stopped along the street to listen, in cars and afoot, or turned in behind him, to follow.

In the dingy old grey building where Bryan once addressed the hopeful and cheering Populists, where a young man who later became the pacifistic Senator Hanson denounced bribe-making railroads, Charley Stetbettor plunged into his incoherent tirade. He attacked the morality of the city, the state, and the nation. With Communists in the government and Jews running the country, young men were openly taking under-age girls across the state line for immoral purposes. In these times there was a crying need for more strong young defenders of the flag and sacred American womanhood!

When a heckler pointed out that Burt Parr had married the girl he took across the state line, three husky young fellows came swinging down from the front rows. They grabbed the man and rushed him to the door amid cheers and stomps and boos. When the three had returned to their seats old Charley Stet went on, his hoarse voice rising and falling in short, staccato rhythms, ending up by calling upon God and all the lovers of the flag to preserve America for Americans, Amen.

The next evening Senator Bullard spoke from the same platform, asking a return to the good old days of Harding and Coolidge.

Yes — America for big business, the scattering of workingmen and farmers in the back told each other.

Senator Hanson passed through town on his way to Washington and was asked to speak, too, by a few hopefuls. They'd get the fieldhouse for him. No, he said, his wide, slow smile breaking up his craggy face; he wouldn't need anything bigger than a telephone booth to hold his audience in Franklin. The things happening here couldn't happen if that were not true. So the papers wrote editorials against him, calling him "Kanewa's Senior Senator, who has no time for anyone from his home state except every sixth year, and this isn't the year."

But they were wrong, for he had asked Hamm Rufe to meet his train and come as far as Grandapolis to tell him something of the situation in Franklin. He knew a great deal about Hamm's writing, said he had a fairly complete scrap-book of his articles on Kanewa's Co-operatives, and the state's labor and farm problems. At Kohl Carl Halzer got on, also a guest of the senator. The farmer was diffident before the sharp, wrinkle-nested eyes of the old Scandinavian liberal. But when they had considered him a disconcerting minute, the brown skin about them crinkled.

"Sit down, young man," he said, "and let us hear the Bull of Bashan bellow!"

CHAPTER X

THE fall was a long, dry taste of ragweed to the tongue. For weeks dust lay like fog over the highways, the goldenrod alongside weighed down with its powdering, the sun setting as through smoke. Then two days of a leaning wind cleared the air, swept the scattered trees naked as dead November, and cracked the earth around the new wheat. In the cornfields the shucking teams moved at a steady walk, with now and then a nubbin clattering desolately against the bangboard.

Down in the capital city the shadows were lengthening early across Philadelphia Avenue, and a small grey wind collected bits of paper into deserted doorways, many empty since the Harding days. A stray corn leaf zigzagged along the walk of the business section, the sparrows flying before its unfamiliar rattle, and then turned to pursue it, pecking.

The men who had hung along the empty buildings all day began to move, stiffly at first, their backs bent in protection upon themselves, then hurried away as evening deepened. Along the curb the gold and purple banners of the city of Franklin came down, the office workers thinned on the streets, only the retail clerks staying behind to get the unsold stock back on the shelves. Another Fall Dollar Day was done. Tomorrow the nation's chiropractors would begin to drift in, and next Thursday the bankers for their state convention. It was fortunate that the half a dozen business buildings had new fronts or the old sandblasted, that the excavation for the Schendler annex, seven stories, was well started. A big hole in the ground always draws a crowd, makes things look good, Parkins, the secretary of the chamber of commerce, was supposed to have said. Yes, good for those who won't get beyond bankers' row on the avenue, the Workers' Alliance replied.

The Franklin papers had disposed of the attack on Burt Parr as a student hazing, but outstate, in the rawer regions, papers like the Minerva *Thunderbolt* took a serious view, as did many as far away as Des Moines and Denver. Even in the capital city some of the more thoughtful were disturbed, particularly around the university. But with one dean writing for the giveaway insides that Cole Dringer was distributing to the country press, and the son of another a known Gold Shirt, talk among the best of friends became a little formal and constrained, even the oldest cronies fearing the solvent action of the secret glass of beer, secret though legal, because out-of-job Ph.D.'s were thick as rabbits in a brush pile.

Some of the League of Women Voters, like Hallie Rufer Hammond and Ona Snell, who tried to get up an organized demand for an investigation found themselves labeled Reds by the local patriots. One whole issue of the *Christian Challenger* was devoted to the Dupes of the Red Agents of Stalin as they were called. Ona was for pushing on, but the chamber delegated Cees to intercede with his mother, and so the matter was dropped as bad for business, with the market down just now anyway.

Through all this Hamm remembered the injured boy's parents at the hospital the night after he was found. They were a quiet, shabby pair, soft and well-spoken. There had been no tears, no anger while they were with Burt. The only complaint at all was outside, on the walk, when the two had thanked Hamm for his friendship to their son in the capital city.

"Our people fled to America from oppression," the father said slowly. "But now there is nowhere to go."

Hamm shook his head. No, there was nowhere to go. Great-grandfather Joseph Pahr had fought tyranny in his homeland at the risk of his life and not until the very last hope was gone did he flee to America. Now, if no land of refuge remained, there was certainly no taste for battle in these descendants of Old Joseph. Yet freedom had still seemed worth a fight in Madrid, Warsaw, in China, and in the industrial regions of America, where men died readily enough for such a matter-of-fact thing as the right to a decent way of work. Freedom had been worth a struggle in this trans-Mississippi region in the Populist days, even in 1917, to the western liberals who faced an ostracism less merciful than a swift shot between the shoulder blades. But those men were dying off, for even such virility is mortal, and none were coming up to take their places. Perhaps it was as the Coot always said, and worse; perhaps the midwestern capital cities were not only parasites, but poisonous parasites, insinuating their paralysis into the bodies of their states to affect the sons of the Joseph Pahrs out on the far rivers as well as those of the George Rufers within their limits.

The Gold Shirts weren't out around town much for a few days after the tree affair, probably been tipped off to let the matter die. "Got word from above that the time wasn't ripe for the revolution," Al Jackson, Franklin's one Communist, told his chair neighbors at the city library, where he spent all his evenings. Some recalled that it was the exact expression used by the town's Tories against Al when he backed the movement for a non-political unicameral legislature several years ago, because old Ben Franklin had favored a one-house congress. Of course, the idea got nowhere in Kanewa, even with Stalin backing it, as Franklinites pretended to believe.

Now there was talk that Willper, the commander of the Gold Shirts, had busted Harold Welles for unauthorized action, put a young German import into his place, and that

Harold was pretty sore — a Welles being disciplined by that ex-convict. In the meantime the dark-suited young men with the enameled cross and sword of the Christian Crusaders in their lapels suddenly seemed to be everywhere, on the street, in church, at football games and political gatherings. They were probably trying to justify the money spent on them, too, Abigail Allerton said, not wanting the boys from the Stone House to get all the publicity. Flaming crosses had been appearing on the capitol and the courthouse lawns, burning into the morning. Only this time the town's Catholics and its scattering of Negroes were told it was the Samelly Finesteins and the strikers that the night riders were after.

"Just so much American hokey-pokey," an old cowman in to buy up ranch mortgage bonds said. "An' won't last no longer than it did back when we used to sneak a little of the stuff on an old crow bait to make 'er buck — "

Others dismissed it as so much American joinerism, an infantile fondness for secret lodges and regalia. But there were some, even in the city club, like Mona Stone, who couldn't pass it off so easily. She had spent many weeks of the last two years at her radio, dialing the short-wave stations, sometimes her lovely, angular face strained to gauntness, a desperation in her black-lashed blue eyes as her Jewish mother fled from Austria, then Prague, then Warsaw. Even when her mother wrote so cheerfully as she had before *Anschluss*, before Munich and before Danzig. Now, she was in America at last and the same thing was coming here, even in the quiet little midwestern capital city, which did seem to disseminate the cultural standards for the state, as it so proudly claimed.

But at the fall opening of the city club Mona was slim and calm as ever in silver lamé and larkspur-blue velvet beside her husband, John Stone, who was capital city attorney for the Grandapolis Power. Often she wondered about the company and its campaign contributions, assessed by the eastern directors — were these really only for the anti-labor, anti-public power fight, or was it going farther, deeper? Twice she had asked John to return to his little practice in Baltimore, but he refused. Perhaps she wouldn't mind living small again, but he was determined to climb, he told her bluntly, alone if necessary. So Mona Stone played bridge with Cassie Welles and others of importance from the Ridge, and smiled with friendly detachment when Jewish stories made the rounds of the tables.

One day two men in brownish drill uniforms, polished black belts shining, came to Abigail's door. They said they were from outstate and had come up to talk about her book. The moment they were in her place they started off with what they called the inside dope on the great Jew conspiracy to deliver America into the hands of the Communists. It was horrible to listen to them — like living in the world of her George, who came back from war forever bedeviled by conspiring enemies, the only refuge from them the cabbage patch at the mental hospital. Yet here were two men who talked just like George, but free to gallop in excitement up and down her rug, through its bright patch of Kanewa sunshine. The taller, darker of the two tried to thrust mimeographed diagrams into her hands, pointing to this and that statement as proof of the financial domination of the country by Jew bankers. And when she asked them to give her the names of two Semitic banking firms, the short, round-bellied one got loud, his mouth opening wide and red. "We're again Jew lovers just as much as the damn Jew himself!" he roared out in warning.

A moment Abigail looked the two men over, from their puttees to the campaign hats, dented, flat-brimmed, still on their heads, setting far back. She opened her door wide, stood beside it, waiting. The taller man started out, protesting a little. "Hell, lady, my buddy don't mean you no harm — we was just getting signers for a boycott of the Jews in this town, the big fellows, like Greenspan and Plaska and them, them that you ain't got no more cause to love than we got — " pulling a thick, folded petition from his pocket, opening it.

"Hasn't anyone told you — " Abigail demanded, "that I'm an American citizen, and believe in the Bill of Rights?"

"We ain't holdin' no truck with that there radical stuff. We're a standin' solid on the Constitution an' we're against them Reds and Jews."

Abigail had to laugh at that. "You should read the Constitution some time — " Then her anger rose. "Get out — get out!"

They went, the fat one sullenly, turning back at the landing. "You're a goin' to be damn sorry about this some day!"

"Yeh, gonna be in a bad spot — " the other added. Then they fell into conspicuous step and marched down the stairs, their boots clumping as one heavy pair. Out on the walk they looked up at her windows, as though marking it in their minds, and then went on to the next house, where Abigail had often seen the caretaker and his friends slip out through the dusk of the alley with their arms full of white stuff, like bundled-up sheets, or perhaps regalia.

When the men were finally gone Abigail was limp. It seemed inconceivable that this was what her America might come to accept, the America whose winning had been the long, long struggle since the first brown-skinned hunter crossed the Bering region and set his foot southward; doubly inconceivable in this capital city, built by such seekers after freedom and the good life as old George Rufer, the city that still held itself up as the model of culture to all the state of Kanewa.

The next day Abigail saw the two men again. She was coming down the postoffice steps, across from the side entrance to the old American Bank building. Together the two turned in and she wondered, for the building had been empty since the Blockert scandal, years ago. But when she got around to the front a wide sign was going up over the door: —

DR. C. THURSTON STETBETTOR
FOR GOVERNOR

Whatever the builders of the town might say to it if they were here now, at least this fall the capital city wasn't dull, really almost as exciting as back before the World War, when the suffragettes were getting themselves clubbed and jailed, and the disapproving W.C.T.U. finally outdid them to get the saloons closed.

With all the Tyndale-Welles-Parr talk, a two-day stream of women not invited to the Presentation dinner had passed through the Buffalo Hotel to see the floral piece, set up in the lobby in the moisture of a salad stand sprayer from one of the Tyndale stations. It made the lobby clammy as a bath house and brought complaints from eastern traveling men, but it drew local trade.

Even those who didn't get down to the hotel had seen Mollie's picture in the papers, fine in her long sweeping train and plumes, a girl born on a dirt road, outside of a small town, just like anybody.

Then there was the annulment suit, and Burt Parr found tied to a tree. To be sure the radio newscaster who made the story as exciting as a scene from Gang Busters was suspended, not for that, but because he said the culprit was "a vengeful enemy of the more favored suitor of a local duchess of Kanewa." That made it plain enough, even before the Grandapolis papers came out with the story Sadie had been telling at the beauty parlor, and Harold Welles not at the Presentation dinner that night.

The International Contract Club, experts in bridge and on court etiquette, were divided on the presentation matter. A married woman couldn't be presented at court, the cousin of a state-department clerk said very definitely.

"Why not?" the others demanded.

"Well, she can't. Look at the Duchess of Windsor — "

"But that isn't the same at all. It was the H.R.H. that Davie demanded for Wallie, something much different — " a woman who once saw Queen Victoria corrected. Unfortunately everyone had heard about that, and so the conversation jumped on to middle Franklin's notion of the attitude of the Church of England on annulments, before and after it changed on divorce.

But the woman who had lived in England raised her voice, as was her right. Hadn't she seen the Prince of Wales ride in the park, she asked, and been patted on the head by a maharaja? She didn't mention seeing Queen Victoria because it was making her seem old lately. About the church attitude she was firm. Yes, it had changed on both annulments and divorce. But the cousin of the state-department clerk was still against married women. Anyway, court wasn't much, these days.

By the time Burt was out of the hospital, the interest in the Tyndale stories had passed on like a patch of shadow from a brick wall. The collector of White House stories could get a hearing again, and middle Franklin was playing bridge for drinks and points once more.

Weeks before the hunting season opened there was always a lot of big outdoor man talk all over the capital city, at the clubs, the pool halls, and clear down to Old Horsemeat's. Enough ammunition for a little war was ordered, and all the season's new gadgets and hunting clothes, including dozens of pairs of hip waders to smell up the hot attics of summer for years and probably never get wet unless the roof leaked. Fine shotguns were dragged down to Old Steve's, across from the police station, to have the grease taken out that he put in a year ago. Arrangements were made around the hay country for the prairie oyster fries at the ranches up north of the Grand. Liquor purchases were approached like hydroelectric deals. Those from Blue Ridge stocked their hunting shacks with hard liquor by the case and beer the dozen cases through Groves, Wholesale Groceries; many of those above just picking up a little on the way out into the country dickered with Al "Better-than-Wholesale" Faber. The serious hunter who really wanted to fill out a bag of pheasants, or mallards, or maybe get a Canada goose or two, had to plan carefully. Hunting fatalities often ran as high as six or eight on opening day in Kanewa, and before a week the game, never too plentiful, was shy as any lone antelope that had had his tail clipped by a bullet.

Every year Horsemeat got to tell his customers that the fool who'd pull a gun barrel first out of a car or through a fence ought to be killed before he gets somebody else. With each hunting license he sold he threw in a little advice: "Keep your gun pointed in the ground, and never depend on that Goddamn safety. Better file it off. It ain't never on nohow except when you got to make a quick shot."

This year opening day brought its usual casualties to the capital city. Before noon a shoe clerk out his first time stumbled over some down sunflowers and shot his girl in the heel. Around four o'clock there was a more serious radio news flash. Archie Greenspan, manager of four of Franklin's moving-picture theaters, was found dead, shot in the back. He never drank, always went out with little Pete Mario, running a west-end pool hall, and while rough enough, a teetotaler too. This afternoon Pete came roaring up to a filling station out at Liberty well ahead of his dust, but when he got his car jammed to a stop, he just sat there. "Call the sheriff," he said finally, mumbling so he had to say it twice. "Archie Greenspan's been shot."

The row of Sunday loafers along the stucco station let their chair legs drop, pushed their hats back. By God, the little runt was a crying.

So the sheriff, with a dozen loafers following along, went out with the man. "I knowed I didn't dare move him, so I leaves him, but he's dead all right — dead — "

Twice Pete looked from the road to the sheriff sitting beside him. "You ain't thinkin' I done it, are you? I wouldn't kill him, not my buddy in the War — " But even way out here on Long Grass Creek the sheriff knew that Pete was an ex-convict and before that fact his twenty-five years of peaceful citizenship and his war medal were nothing.

When the story first got on the radio it was called a hunting accident. Next time it was murder. "Prominent movie house manager hit in back with a load of heavy shot. Pete Mario, hunting companion, held."

Here, at last, the Franklin papers could let go. Pete was the son of an Italian immigrant from the Colorado beet fields. He had been in the penitentiary as an accomplice in a holdup. He always denied any connection with it. "I was just killing time at the drugstore; slack season and nothing to do. How I can know two fellows from little Italy gonna come in and shoot up the place?"

The authorities comforted him with the reminder that he got the shortest sentence of the three. When war broke out he was paroled in time to enlist, and came back to Franklin with Archie Greenspan, from the same company, and friends ever since. Pete was rough in his talk, but no more than the rest of the boys when they came back. The unfortunate company they were thrown with, everybody said, toughs from the city slums and the ranch country, and immigrant laborers. Pete never got over it, but his little pool hall was orderly enough, a sort of club for the quieter ex-service men, with a bowling alley that the women's teams liked. Pete always looked in on them during the evenings, making friendly comments, remembered what everybody rolled the last time and even the time before that.

He was a bachelor, and whenever some new acquaintance

asked kiddingly why he never got married he rubbed his thick palm over his bald head in embarrassment. If he was pushed for a reply he would say, "Marry; me? Can you ask a decent woman to marry a convict?" Then usually he'd walk away to the back somewhere and the kidder would feel pretty mean. Now little Pete was down in jail, for shooting his hunting partner, his war buddy.

"The dirty Jew had it comin' — " Willper from Stone House was reported to have said, and it was no secret that the manager of the other two theaters thought so too. Archie Greenspan had been hard competition. He had a good racket getting important people out to midnight previews of pictures he thought might be slow starting — as *Winterset, Night Must Fall,* and *As You Like It.* He was the one who had brought *Carnival in Flanders* to the little show-house off the avenue, fair time. He managed to make something from them all, even the *Flanders,* because he could talk people, doctors, professors, even Abigail Allerton, into saying something about them. "Your recommendation will mean much to the people who don't frequent ordinary pictures and might otherwise miss this," he always told them. His competitor tried the system, asked the Dr. Snells and Abigail to a preview of *Made for Each Other,* and was furious when they told him their opinion. It must be that damn oily Jew way of Greenspan that got around people. Well, now he was shot to hell and gone.

There were people who wondered what Pete's story would be. It came, thin as wet cigarette paper and about as strong. He said they hadn't scared up more than a mangy rabbit all day and so they tried their usual trick when game seemed scarce, they separated. One or the other would be sure to run into a flock of pheasants tearing off through the grass in every direction, and only one gun.

Pete hadn't found anything when he heard a shot boom mighty hollow off in Archie's direction, so he went over. He didn't see anything of him at first, not until he almost fell over the man, face down in the weed patch below the Johnson field, where they'd got many a bag before.

The sheriff reported that he found Pete's gun clean as chromium inside, but he always carried a felt-tipped ramrod with him. Said he was choicy of his gun, learned to be in the army. Even cleaned it after trying out those new high-power shells at a target on the way out that morning. Oh, there was no doubt about it, Pete was guilty, all right.

So they took him away to the Franklin jail, more room there, and Joe Manders, a young deputy from Liberty with FBI notions, got a couple of fellows to hold the sightseers away until he had looked the ground over. From the tracks, Manders decided that the dead man was knocked forward as though he'd been hit with a doubletree in the back of the neck. So he started in a straight line, down the shot, looking the ground over carefully at every step. Far back, in the moist earth of a patch of tall horseweeds, he found two heavy tracks with some fainter ones leading off across the sod towards the graveled road; nothing else, not even the empty shell.

When the crowd was gone, the deputy made casts of the footprints, one clear, the other with the heel lost on the grass. They were of broad, flat shoes, like those he used to wear when a boy — Sears, Roebuck's cheapest split cowhide, ninety-eight cents a pair and hard as boiler plate. The tracks showed a little slip, particularly the right one, as though the man in the shoes had been pushed backward, perhaps by a shove against his rigid body, or more probably by the kick of a shotgun inexpertly held. Greenspan had been hit dead center, all right, but the tracks and the slip in them convinced the deputy that the murderer wasn't Pete. A workingman, from the size of the tracks, but shooting like a woman or a green-horn.

The next day Manders appeared in Franklin and got his first taste of capital city opposition, even in the county sheriff's office. They wouldn't let him see the hunting boots Pete wore that day. "Got anything comes under the head of new evidence?" they demanded, not moving off their hunkers for the outside man.

Not sure of his rights, Manders started off towards the state sheriff's office at the capitol. On the way he passed a WPA crew tearing out an old streetcar track. There he saw what he had been searching for, the oldtime split cowhide shoes. So he went back downtown, to the Farmers Outfitting company, the Army and Navy store, and finally, with little hope, to the Consumers' Co-op.

Hamm Rufe was there. No, they carried no shoes, not yet. And when they did, it wouldn't be split cowhides. Some Co-ops did, but here the trade was with white-collar and university people. Franklin had almost no laboring people with enough security to go into a co-operative venture. It was live from day to day as best you may with them, all their lives. In fact, the only split cowhides that Hamm had seen around town for a long time were some distributed to the relief cases a while ago, probably elsewhere too, and booming the corn-plaster business something grand.

So the deputy went away, to look in at Mario's pool hall. All the talk was about Pete's going haywire like that.

"That's the way with them quiet, easy-going fellers — " one of the men at the spittoon said.

"Yeh, and him pretending to be a friend of the Jew's all the time — "

"You think it got anything to do with him getting that chunk of shrapnel in the head?" a friend of Pete's asked, trying to justify this thing the little man seemed to have done.

Franklin, jaded with two good Blue Ridge suicides this fall, lost interest in little Pete by the middle of the week. He was the same as out in the Big Walls right now, and it'd be the chair for him sure if he didn't have that service medal.

As it was any shyster lawyer would know enough to make a lot of that brave savior-of-his-country stuff, and it'd go over too, big enough to keep him out of the chair.

With so little to read in the papers, mostly just election and foreign stuff, the townspeople looked through the item about a little domestic trouble among the reliefers. It seemed that a woman called Ada Smith came to the police station with her three children, saying she was afraid to stay at home because her husband was threatening her with a gun, a big old shotgun he'd borrowed somewhere to go hunting Sunday.

And why did he threaten her?

Accusing her of planning to leave him. And she was, she admitted. He couldn't work, and with relief what it'd got to be in Franklin she could do better for herself. Anyway, they'd lost that, way back when she got her job, which wasn't much, even with Jim cooking and looking after the children. She'd been making eight dollars a week taking cash at a movie house; been doing that ever since she was picked for that *Pygmalion* moving picture.

The judge remembered the publicity story. Ada Smith was the woman made over, a permanent in her shaggy hair, a whole new outfit, with hat, veil, and purse in exchange for the loose, shapeless dress and flat shoes she had from the Salvation Army. Some good girdling, too, around the hips, as he recalled the pictures now.

By this time Ada was laughing heartily. Yes, quite a little girdling — and brassièring too, Judge, upping them four, five inches.

At her explanatory gesture the judge frowned. What was this about her husband, he demanded.

Well, she was leaving him, she admitted freely now, going into a little place a friend had set up for her. But she couldn't take the children along, and there was no need to, with Jim such a good hand and able to get relief as soon as she filed her divorce. It was all fixed except that now he'd taken to waving the gun around, and she was afraid to leave the children. Seemed like he'd gone outright crazy, saying there'd be others like Greenspan, getting buckshot in the back — meaning her new boy friend, she guessed.

Because it was a particularly dull Monday, the police reporter gave her story some time and got most of it into the paper, with a picture of Ada in her *Pygmalion* clothes last spring over the caption: Remember Her? Then there was one of her little girls in old reliefer dresses and Jim, with a gun awkwardly in his hand, standing in front of the old basement house they occupied for six years, since he hurt his back helping a friend lift the engine from a jallopy.

Once more Deputy Manders came to Franklin, and this time he got the authorities to listen to him, to let him see the boots of Peter Mario, take a look at the reliefer shoes of Jim Smith. When Jim's fit the plaster casts of the tracks in the horseweeds, he didn't deny anything. Yes, he'd been hanging around Pete's for years. It was handy to a lot of reliefers in that row of Franklin Trust shacks they all had to live in or lose county aid. So he knew where Pete and Greenspan always went hunting. He borrowed an old ten-gauge gun and two shells and hooked a ride out that way. The son-of-a-bitch had busted up his home.

But he had named another man yesterday, Jim was reminded.

Oh, yeh, the one who was taking his wife — but that bastard wouldn't a looked at her a second if Greenspan hadn't spent $12.75 on her for beauty treatments and maybe fifty dollars more on an outfit for publicity for a Goddamn moving picture.

"Well, there you have it," the better Franklinites told each other. "You can't do anything for such people. Give one of those reliefers a permanent and a manicure and you are shot in the back by her husband."

However, the incident had its good side, too, for it got

a murderer behind the Big Walls, and rid the town of a man who showed disturbing pictures like those government ones on housing and such crap. Besides that, all Jews, even those who weren't pushing and greasy, were an embarrassment to a town nowadays, especially a capital city with a university.

Saturday there was more good news. The Italian had sold his pool hall, was leaving. One of the women bowlers collected nickels from among the old customers and at the depot they gave him a ring with the insignia of his company, and engraved around the inside: *To a Good Soldier*. Frightened in his surprise, little Pete looked into the faces of the men and women before him and tried to give them some word of thanks. But nothing came, and so, his eyes pouring, he fled to the train, while many of those left behind wondered who would loan them a dollar now when the relief check was late, or something unforeseen came up.

"Cities of lost dogs," an ex-legislator from over in Nebraska called the state capitals of the middle west. "Out-of-jobbers from governor to capitol janitor just keep hanging around, can't seem to get away from their little taste of soup meat."

Then there were the thousands of students turned out by the university the last fifteen years, most of them just waiting around too. "The outstate kids come in in style but mostly they'll have to hitch-hike home," the Coot said last spring from his stand on top of a fire hydrant where he watched the cap-and-gown parade gather for the march to the diplomas. "Yeh, mostly they'll thumb out, those that get away."

Many never would get away, Abigail knew. Like calves that have followed a noseful of clover up against a fence, they would stand there bawling, unwilling to return to their own grass pasture.

"Just waiting at the corner of Schendler's for fifteen minutes depresses me for days," Abigail once told Hamm. "The uneasiness, the fear in the faces passing — naked, the trouble of

shuttering them somehow become too great. Not only entirely
too many old women with soft ropes of veins inside their cotton stockings, and middle-aged men with rolls around the
backs of their necks, the warp of their suits dark at the knees
and elbows. There are the many, many younger people, young
men in shabby pants slipping along close to the walls so their
failure won't be noticed, those of thirty with their backs carefully straight, the women hiding a little behind their masks
of curls, arched eyebrows and waxed lips. But in the privacy
of the crowd all the mouths are thin and weary, the hope of
their eyes already burned out — all caught, just so many figures in the census returns of a city of lost production and vanishing trade."

Perhaps that feeling of insecurity and inadequacy ac-
counted not only for the city's toryism but also for the fortune-tellers flocking like crows to a wind-stripped cornpatch.
Every trans-Mississippi capital was thick with them, from
teacup readers to trance mediums and astrologers, at least a
dozen to every one in all the rest of the state. This fall the
business boomed in Franklin, even for such poor beginners as
Goldie Dunn, who had to take her first customers to the hall
bathroom for privacy. From Old Connie out in Herb's Addition who still hoped that the wife of her bedfast Henry might
die so he could marry her, Goldie worked up as high as Cassie
Welles of Blue Ridge. Bursting through the tight chiffons
she learned to like in an earlier profession, she still used much
the same technique.

"Oh, it's too bad, darling, that you, so beautiful, must have
so much trouble," she told Cassie sympathetically. "It is
others, always others with you, your soft heart torn between
love and loyalty. But you will win out, and everything will
come right, for you are psychic too, of the Chosen Ones — "

Soon Goldie Dunn was setting herself up in an apartment
with burgundy-colored rayon hangings, a handsome black cat,

and an appointment book, with the names of most of the
women of the Ridge. And she really was wonderful, Eloise
Johnson told Elizabeth Black. "Makes you feel so desirable — "

Of course, Goldie had no time for Old Connie any more
now, or for any of the long list of employables on relief who
wanted to know if the WPA quota might be raised to include
them this winter.

Most of the bridge-playing wives, the divorcees, and the stenographers still went to the velvet-hung quarters of Charley
Stet's La Belle Rose in the old Fox theater. She had tried to get
into the Equity building, with marble corridors and Venetian
blinds, but the doctors officing there wouldn't have her. Anyway, the Fox was handy to the board of trade and the side en-
trances helped the business men avoid their wives and stenographers, or anyone else, if they paid La Belle to arrange it
so. Not that this business was new to them. Glen Doover of
the Franklin Mills had a long telephone bill each month for
tips on wheat from a New York astrologer; and in his office,
beside the picture of a sailfish he once caught, was the horoscope cast by Evangeline Adams.

"I made fifty thousand that year on her advice — " he
would say, a little nostalgically. "And plenty are doing the
same right now, only in millions, with the right tips."

For those of shorter pocketbook there were dozens of un-
licensed numerologists, palmists, card layers, and trance readers scattered over the town. The spiritualists had a large following that split into factions over Dr. Robert Maxell, whose
business card labeled him The World's Greatest Astro-Psychol-
ogist and Former Associate of the Great William Dudley
Pelley, that some knew was the head of the Silver Shirts. To
one group Bob Maxell was only a crude and vulgar eater of
raw meat, with a fake Indian control. The others believed him.
Both groups had Sunday evening services, with prayer, song,
and reading services after the silver collection. The readings

were either from some article, as a string of beads or a pencil brought up from the audience, or by simply closing the eyes, and beginning, in a deep, flat voice: "Someone comes to me here, comes for the lady in back, on the aisle. You — " pointing a finger out ahead. "He brings a message for you. It is of a private nature. I cannot speak it here. — Do you understand?" So the lady in back, on the aisle, usually stayed for a special twenty-five-cent reading and perhaps even came for a five-dollar one next day.

While the chiropractors kept pretty well to the aspects of their calling, with only a minor tirade against regulatory state legislatures, and a recommendation that each bathroom have two scales, one for each foot, for inbalance, the bankers did a good bit of government baiting during convention hours. Outside of that, it was mostly heavy drinking and bragging, bragging about big-game hunting, women, and of farms and buildings foreclosed. One more bad year for the farmer who still imagined that war profits might soak down to him and the last of the good places would begin to break loose, like an ice jam in the spring. Yes, but already there was talk of special taxes for absentee landlords in Kanewa, like in Alabama.

It looked like that was the only way to keep the rural schools up, Gilley from the Carstairs National pointed out, with the tenants either not daring to vote enough taxes or losing the places to those who saw the light. His associates laughed good-naturedly. Should the schools really be kept up? Wasn't a great percentage of the public spoiled by a literacy beyond their understanding, which only served to make them victims of propaganda and too big for their britches?

When the convention was over it was pronounced a success, with only two discordant notes: an argument whether Blockert, out of the penitentiary six months now, should be welcomed back among them so soon, and the invocation by a minister up at Stockholm. From the text: "Money is the root of all evil," the old Swede lectured the gathering for twenty uncomfortable minutes on their responsibility as handlers of the world's greatest degrader of individuals and of government, the cause of almost all crime and misery and of all poverty, the prostitutor of the arts and of the very church itself.

"Christ drove the money changers from the temple once!" he roared over them. "May he appear among us again in this hour of our need — Amen."

The date for Mollie's sailing passed and she was still in Franklin, though none could say she had seen the girl. When the annulment trial didn't come up, Della Loran went to the courthouse and was told the suit had been withdrawn, withdrawn until it was decided whether Parson Sam, the Marryin' Man, had a legal right to marry anybody. So she hurried up to the club, just in time for the tea hour, and ladies' day, too. There was news. Maybe Mollie Tyndale had gone off for a whole night with a man without even being married to him.

"Pride goes before a fall," many an older woman told her neighbors, reminding them of the white satin duchess dress back in September and that Presentation dinner. And maybe the Gold Shirts were right to take that Burt Parr out and whip him good — protecting the good women of the capital city.

Every time Hamm went to the hospital he was afraid the boy would ask about Mollie, but as his back healed and the swelling left his jaw, Burt became very quiet, almost never using his scratch pad any more. Usually he just nodded soberly as Hamm came in, his eyes glad for a friend to sit there at his shoulder, and then turned his hospital face away.

Hamm was a little worried about the quietness down at the Labor Temple with the truckers either starved into their cabs again or the armed strikebreakers taking over the wheels. No, neither one, Lewis told him, although the finks were all over the state, and the men uneasy as horses at butchering time. Negotiations were still on, the strikers asking federal arbitration, with Kanewa the last hold-out against the Twelve State agreement, and with plenty of evidence that most of the operatives were ready to sign at the start. But they had been threatened with the loss of their hauling by organized business if they did, and now it was a freeze-out, with the strikers refused relief, and all working members of their families fired. Around Grandapolis the picketing must be keeping the roads pretty clear; every week or so another delegation of business men came roaring up to the governor. When he pointed out that he had no power in county enforcement of the anti-picketing law, they wanted the sheriff removed and the national guards called out. With Walnut County controlled by the strikers, the bridges over the Grand and through them the main river roads were closed to hold-out operatives, the business all going to the few signed-up outfits in Kanewa and the out-of-state companies. The governor was sitting tight until his resignation was effective, right after election. He was a sick man, he said, and felt no call to mar his last month in office with an illegal action or with civil war.

Around town the pitying expression "sick man" became an angry "weak man" but beyond that there wasn't much they could do. Unfortunately, the lieutenant governor, a right-thinking Franklinite, was under indictment for accepting a bribe from the Grandapolis Power company to vote off a tie.

"That's what he gets for straying off the reservation and trying to cut out the middleman's profit. The capital city boys take care of their own," was the comment around the chamber. Stone, resident attorney for the company, only laughed.

The supreme-court decision on the constitutionality of the anti-picketing law was still expected every Monday. Each time the strikers gathered early at the temple, ready to pick up their flag and their placards and to march quietly through the stone corridors of the capitol past the supreme court. "We're no hoodlums and rowdies making trouble. We're good American citizens, only asking what's our rights — " Lew Lewis tried to tell a reporter, who only shook his head regretfully and walked on. And each Monday noon, when Lew came to Ike's for a hamburger, Nora welcomed him with grateful eyes. Not this week; the trouble hadn't come this week.

Yet each delay only made a clash with the police or the superpatriots seem more likely. Some thought that was why the decision was held up. Others said it was to give Judge Golden time to get sick. He was from the irrigation country up on the Grand, the one liberal justice, and said to be a quarter Jew. Ill health would be an easy out for him, with his gaunt, pale face, and that look of pain. Not that he'd missed a day in fourteen years, but he'd better be taking time off now, and the right time, the louder patriots around the City Club told each other over their drinks. With him out the decision was in the bag.

Along towards the middle of October the business men's general viewing of the future with alarm took on more specific aspects. All PWA grants were postponed.

"Mebby the howling around here won't be quite so loud as over government spending, but this time it shure will come from away down under the pants buttons," Old Horsemeat told Hamm. Nor was the howling only from the capital city and Kanewa. Several other states had been allotted their full share of money for the year, it seemed.

Now suddenly the chambers of commerce were anxious that the government spend as much money as possible. They were solicitous, too, in their long telegrams and telephone calls to Washington, about the probable effects of this curtailment in public works just before election. In addition, a hurry-up protest meeting was called in the main ballroom of the Buffalo Hotel. Abigail went down to see what line the talk would take, knowing through Carl Halzer and from her own investigations how hard the winter without this work would be.

The bald barrel of a man at the door seemed doubtful about letting a woman in, but she got past him to a place in the back; folding chairs creaking all through the room, and heads craning to see as her name was whispered along. To amuse herself, she sketched the doorman, his head a swollen red, and completely bare. Franklin grew none so full-blooded as this; he must be one of the Grandapolis politicians, perhaps a favorite. They did have a mayor with hair once, she remembered, but he wasn't re-elected.

Among the disappointed contractors and labor representatives, Abigail noticed the city dads from all over Kanewa. Of course the Grandapolis delegation got the floor first, windy as March on the farthest stretches of Wild Horse Plains. They showed great concern for the workingman and anger with the government for breaking faith with the needy. Even the president of the Business Men's Association, which furnished the armed thugs and strikebreakers, stood up to bewail the plight of the poor workingman who had put up a heroic struggle against unemployment, with winter just around the corner, and his government going back on him.

"I'll tell you," the big soapman said, his voice rising to fill all the room, "it's hard for a man willing and able to work to sit around idle while his wife and children starve!"

The labor leaders were called upon to say a few words, and even the head of the striking truckers received loud applause from the fink-protecting mayors of Grandapolis and Franklin. But the real push of the meeting came from the contractors, mostly lean, sun-browned, serious men who had somehow pulled through the ten years of depression. While they hated the government supervision of PWA money that cut so deeply into their profits, they were in productive work, realists. They joked a little about this sudden concern over the workingman; admitted that hungry and barefooted women and children were the best argument with the Secretary of the Interior and the President, but thought the plea should come from someone not aligned and armed against them.

"There's no sense in fighting labor," Bill Colder, for fifty years a bridge builder in Kanewa, often told the rest. "When you once get your eyes open so you can see your nose before your face you'll know that a well-paid workingman is your best guarantee of a steady customer. His money is the circulating kind."

And while the city politicians kept interrupting with campaign oratory, the contractors moved firmly towards a resolution stressing the seven years of drouth and the long, pre-depression hard times of the farmer and the stockgrower of the state, with its subsequent chronic unemployment, and insisted that the first signers be the labor representatives. When this carried, Abigail slipped out the back way for lunch with Hamm Rufe and talk of the meeting. Perhaps Carl Halzer would make it too. He was due in town; had been outstate since before the Presentation dinner, although Marylin Welles saw that he got an invitation.

"You might convert some of your table neighbors — " she had tried to tell him, but really hoped he would notice her new blue suit, a blue he once said he liked on her; soft, green-cast.

But the farmer had other things on his mind than fall clothes, and better things to do than sit through the folderol of the dinner. He was going out into the state to talk for a thinking farm vote, and to look into the growth and backing of the Midwest Farmers' Association instead of campaigning for himself. Marylin Welles had some urgent visiting to do among her outstate sorority sisters. Her persistence worried Hamm Rufe. At first her fancy for the shock-headed farmer with his hard, broken-nailed hands, his eyes dark and unwarming as a glacial stream, had seemed just another version of her chase from Atlantic City to Arizona to Sun Valley. Later Hamm began to wonder if she might not be like her father, grasping at the one honest thing she saw in a decadent, parasitic world. But with the rise of the new Farmers' Association, probably with the same backing as Willper's Gold Shirts and old Charley Stet, Hamm was getting pretty uneasy about a Welles's interest in Carl.

The farmer came in around one o'clock, gaunt-eyed and tired under the bush of hair no more subdued than before he ever saw Marylin, although his hands were softening and slimming down considerably in their escape from the grain scoop and the husking hook.

He had made two talks last night, and afterward started the four-hundred-mile drive to Franklin, with a stop for a short one at Dix this morning, because he was disturbed about the Burt business. Still, he had rather been expecting it, with things going as they were in the capital city. Parasites were natural-born fascist. The hope of Kanewa was in the outstate voter, he thought. But a high-pressure membership crew for the Midwest Farmers was sweeping the state like a hot wind in corn-tasseling time, clear out over Wild Horse Plains. They pretended it was a non-partisan organization whose business was looking out for the farmer at the capital and in Washington, all for the fifty-cent membership fee. Some of the organizers were the same as for the Farmers' Non-partisan Association in 1936, when they got themselves investigated by a senate committee and their pictures in the paper. But the speakers sent out were honey-voiced boys who come high and all the writers of Cole Dringer's patent insides for the country papers appeared in the *Midwest Farmer*, which was violently anti-administration, anti-labor, and anti-Semitic, too. Every man with a plot of ground big as the seat of his pants found a copy in his mailbox Saturdays, free. The subscrip-

tion list was supposed to be over a million. Even at half that
it ran into money.

Yes, that was serious, Hamm admitted over his cold pipe.
He wished Stephani would come. She would know how wide-
spread this was.

Mollie Tyndale could do nothing for Burt, not even come
to see him, but every day there was a little unsigned note and
when he was ready to go home, and wondering where the
hospital money was to come from, he was told the bill was
settled, settled in full. He knew then that there was still
the old neighborliness between the Tyndales and the Parrs
of Sheffield and it made the loss of Mollie no easier.

Hamm brought the boy out to his cabin. Burt let himself
slowly to the edge of the couch, to sit, saying nothing, while
the fire burnt up high. Several of the squatters hurried over
to see him, Old Connie shaking her scrub-reddened fist
towards the Stone House. "Them feisty loafers — !" she cried.
She knew all about them, tramping over her clean floors at
all hours at the bank. They'd be robbing the vaults next. She
wouldn't put it past them. And what she could tell about
their goings on! The Coot came in too, standing awkwardly
against the closed door, his grey head sooted and smoky from
the winter fire already laid in his cave, for the nights were
getting pretty cold and the slopes white-frosted twice the
last week. As he filled his pipe from Hamm's tobacco he
looked over his busy hands to Burt.

"Carry knucks, brass, with warts on 'em," he advised.
"That way you can fix the bastards — "

Inside of an hour it was all over the bottoms that Burt was
out. After dark, when the place was finally empty of visitors,
there was another knock at Hamm's door. It was Cobby's
little Hattie, in a short, gay-striped house dress, a red kettle
in her hand, steam creeping out under the lid. Chicken and
Polish dumplings for them both. That would give the young

man strength. Well, yes, she would come in a minute, just a minute. On the couch beside Burt she accepted a cigarette, and drew the smoke in deep.

"It's pretty bad for you," she said at last to the boy. "But it would be much worse to have a son like that — like Harold!"

Hamm nodded, thinking once more of the Cobby who had been his best friend so long ago. Then he noticed something in her voice he hadn't noticed before, and wondered if the Gold Shirts might be after Hattie; or, worse, Harold himself. Hamm looked at the small, blonde girl sitting so quietly beside Burt. Pretty, but with something beyond that, something that was a refuge, as in Stephani. He got up to put more wood on the fire and then returned to the silence of the others.

When Hattie left she stopped in the doorway. "He better not come around me again, that Harold," she said, as though in a warning, "or he will not drag girls like Mollie Tyndale into that house or tie people to trees any more. If he bothers me I think maybe I shall kill him myself."

CHAPTER XI

THE blue skies of October were streaking, greying rapidly towards a bleak November. On the windier days the Coot and his cronies left the dumps early and went into town for the noon rush, to lean against the buildings and watch the girls go by. Not that they really cared much about seeing what was under the wind-swung skirts but they liked the pretending. They could feel like old hellers, poking each other, laughing, making the passing girls prance a little, and switch their butts like pretty young mares out on spring pasture.

None of them went around Hamm much the last week. His dump was gloomier than an old clay cave, the Coot complained. Why, he might as well be living over on the other side of town, where they were taking turns swallowing poison. That's where he belonged.

Hamm lifted his head but the Coot was already humming softly at one of his old songs, probably "Polly-Wolly-Doodle," from the beat of his shoe on the floor. Evidently he meant nothing special. But Hamm really was worried. Nothing had been done about a manager for the Co-op, and last week two strange women came in to hang around the lending shelf of books and pamphlets on co-operatives. They looked like snoopers, and when they refused Hamm's advice about reading matter, he went away to restock the candy case. Watching through the glass he saw them thumb everything over, and slip a couple of books and several pamphlets into their long oilcloth bags.

When they were gone Hamm called the police and was told that books were hard to locate. "They's a mighty lot of them, mister." So he reported the loss to the board, *Sweden, the Middle Way*, the Fowler, and five pamphlets. They looked concerned, Ona Snell particularly, and told Hamm they would consider the wisest action. Saturday the *Christian Challenger* came out with a special Co-op issue, giving excerpts from both Child and Fowler to illustrate their dangerous un-American beliefs, with an open boast of the raid on the station's books, as though the shelves were steel-barred and guarded with machine guns. Several paragraphs from Hamm's articles during the past year in the *Nation* convinced him that there was more than local talent behind this. He was right; the attack on the Co-ops for distributing subversive literature was a general one throughout the middle west, and most heated in Kansas and Minnesota, perhaps a gauge of co-op success.

The Franklin organization needed a manager, a strong one, Hamm argued, but the board gave him even more evasive answers and he went away wondering if the long pressure wasn't softening them up, particularly those on the university staff who hoped for advancement; wondered whether the only new thing to sprout and grow in the capital city in the last forty years might not already have its taproot cut.

The night after Burt left the hospital Carl Halzer stopped in from a talk at a suburban schoolhouse. He was depressed, heavy as the worn fall earth of a tenant farm. He sat unmoving beside the radio through the end of the Toscanini program, not even knowing that the music was done. The other two seemed to have little better than sitting to do either, their heads bowed, their wrists hanging. Ten o'clock; Stephani not arrived, and young Burt still up.

At last Hamm called Abigail. Was she busy; were all the writing boys and gals gone, and was it too late to have them over a little while?

Of course it was not too late. Everyone was gone but Smith Bridges, the son of the old Populist Tod Bridges and really not too violent a tory, Abigail told them, laughing, although he did waste his time collecting such things as Dwight Fiske records, and recited, at almost no provocation, one about a Mrs. Pettibone. He also could reproduce an unorthodox version of the Adam and Eve story.

Oh, they were not to be scared out by any admirer of Mrs. Pettibone's, not this night, Hamm warned.

Of course not, and they were to hurry, please, for she could smell the doughnuts Smith was frying in her kitchen.

So they went over, stretched Burt flat and easy on the couch, and brought out the coffee and Abigail's big green mixing bowl piled high with golden doughnuts. Already they were feeling a little more human. Nor was Smith Bridges so bad. He was a small, thinnish man, with a humorous cut down the center of his full lower lip, and a slight cast in one eye that made the English call him Blinky. He didn't offer to recite anything, but did tell them a little about himself. He got out of town once, as far as England on a Rhodes scholarship, and picked up infantile paralysis. While he pulled out of that pretty well, with very little crippling, it brought him back here for the long cure. "Not that I wasn't grateful to have a place to come — you understand — " he said. But he had a newspaper job lined up with the *Times* in Paris and just being ad man for a Franklin paper somehow wasn't enough, even though it was the *World* with the tradition of George Rufer behind it. "Much, much too far behind it," he said, with rueful lip.

Hamm looked at the little man with new interest. Carl, too, evidently, for when Bridges asked how things seemed out in the state, he frankly admitted that he didn't like the situation. The region around Franklin he always considered especially blighted by the capital city. But now it was as bad outstate. People told of the fine orchards and shade trees of the early settlers where only weeds stood dusty and grey now. Even the occupied houses seemed to squat lower into the earth every year, as though they had to brace themselves to hold up the lean-to kitchens and the sagging back porches, usually crowded with a stinking old separator, maybe a tub of dirty wash, a kerosene can, a sack of boiling potatoes, and even a bitch and her pups. And usually the poddy pot, sitting out plain all day next to the baskets of corncobs fresh from the hog lot. Off in the capital city the owner, or more often the local representative of the eastern owner, laid cherry-wood sticks from the old orchard on his open fire, or just turned on an electric log, the world's cleanest heat, as the page ads of the utilities claimed, while the renter's wife fed her fire with stinking pigpen corncobs.

Something of the old Populist father stirred in the son. He got up, walked around with a saucer in one hand, the coffee cup in the other, waving them both. Yes, that was all true, and it would get worse. It made a man sick to know that all this might have been prevented if his dad and the Pops had won.

And they would have, too, he believed, if there hadn't been the Spanish American War, which was a shot in the arm, for finance, if not the little fellow, with more shots every so often since. But the last twenty years at least one patient, the capital city, hasn't been reacting so well, with more and more empty fronts along Philadelphia Avenue like sagging pockets under the eyes. When Wall Street started paying high interest on security loans along in the twenties, business concerns way out here in Franklin became investment and banking institutions, with fellows like Glen Doover, J. B. Groves, even Cees Hammond actually squeezing every loose penny out of their business for speculation.

Hamm looked up at that. So it even got cautious old Cees, and their mother, at least enough to let Cees do it —

"When the end came they wouldn't believe it. They kept

trying to prove that where you lose 'em's where you find 'em. And, well," Smith said, finally gulping the coffee to hide his embarrassment and setting the cup in its saucer — "they still think they can do it, here."

"How does it happen that you see these things?" Abigail asked curiously.

"It isn't perception that the parasite loses first, you know; it's the courage to face the reality he sees, and the will and power to act — " the son of old Tod Bridges told them.

"Sounds just like the Coot over on Grandview Hill, only a little more elegantly phrased," Hamm said.

Well, the Coot was often right, if a little dirty. Franklin business men thought they could make more loaning their money in the call market or trading in securities themselves than in their own companies here.

"But they did make some money — " Abigail pointed out.

"Well, they drained their companies of everything except the red ink and made what they thought was big money on paper. Then when it all blew up they went into tantrums like the foolish wife who finds that the lover she left her husband for has decamped."

Abigail laughed. "Yes, when I was investigating for the book I found that the money in the capital city was made from the rise of Kanewa's real estate, mostly from free land, the country's hundred fifty year long WPA project for the unemployed. You were sent west to camp on a chunk of the public domain for a certain time, and it was yours, without even bothering with a shovel to lean on. Just so you kept your embarrassing carcass off the doorstep of the east, and, incidentally, helped open new regions for exploitation by capital."

"Yes, and when the system broke down in the nineties, you could buy up the country if you had fifty cents ahead, or an uncle had died," Smith Bridges admitted. "That's how the Franklin National got going — and the rest of the town.

Even those who didn't get their money off the land direct got it from the settlers, or," nodding towards Abigail, "from the sell-outs over at the old Frontier Hotel — "

"Yes, and that all came out of the soil, not only the fields, but the pastures, too, all the earth of the state," Carl added. Even the beauty of the country was drained out, the bittersweet vanished from the creek lines, the harebells were dug up, and who remembered that columbines were once wild and as common as dogtooth violets in the oak woods of the Wakoon and the Grand? All that was left of the oak woods were the stubborn old stumps in the weedy pastures, and the redbud that once bloomed in rosy smoke along the breaks were only a few scrawny bushes beside the garages in Franklin and in Grandapolis.

"Our whole country, hills, valleys, creek-bottoms, all skinned down like a bald man's head, and holding no more water — "

Abigail looked up at the wild bush on the farmer's head. "You're still saving about all that falls — " she laughed.

But Carl was not to be turned from his theme. He'd seen a lot of the government's work out in the state. Under all the dog-howling in the papers about the shelter belt and the poison-ivy gardens, the men had been going quietly ahead with their job and were bringing the farmer back to the tree-planting of his grandfathers. Even the highway engineers were setting out little clumps of juniper and evergreens to relieve long, monotonous stretches — with such native stuff as buffaloberry and wild plum and redbud set against the scars of the deeper cuts. In time this generation, too, would learn by what labor you got these things, and value them accordingly.

It was fine talk to hear, and Hamm looked in admiration upon the farmer from down the Little Grand. The courage of the man he had seen that day when he threw his jumper down before the rifle-armed deputies in the street and called the terrorized marchers to follow him. And now Carl was learning to make words for his thoughtfulness; good words.

Abigail heard the milkman at her door with the cream and slipped out to put another pot of coffee on. Everyone had forgotten Burt, but it didn't matter. He slept right through all their talking, deep in the first security he had known since the night in Dakers woods. At the hospital the doors were open to anyone, with at least one Gold Shirt on the staff. No wonder he was a dead log here on the friendly couch.

About these things Smith Bridges had less to say, trying to pass the beating off as kid stuff, too.

"Kid stuff? — You mean that with a few lessons these kids will learn that cute little trick of stomping the boot heel where it'll do the most good — !" Hamm said bitterly, the scar of his face burning purple-red.

When Smith Bridges was gone, they drained the coffeepot and talked over his point of view. To Abigail his words, not about the Gold Shirts but about the other things, were a rebellion, a pale one, but still a rebellion against life in a community that had nothing at all for the young but to think the thoughts of the old, the entrenched, to think their thoughts and trot around at their fussy orders.

In his shack, Hamm hunched over his knees, his thoughts grey as the day-long fog. Yesterday Burt had gone away to his room. Sitting on the windy stoop for several days had brought back some of the tawny look to his skin, naturally the high tan of a magazine-cover bathing-suit blonde. Now the boy was trying to make up his school work with a dogged sort of plodding, probably inherited from the mountaineer stock of old Jacob Pahr. A little money came from the father at Sheffield, for of course Burt couldn't go back to the Tyndale station, even with the annulment resting until the trial of Parson Sam was over.

Although Hamm did not see it, outside his window the evening sky was breaking, the sun setting towards the promise of a clear, cold night, and at the highway an old coupé was turning in. Under the direction of a small boy and the supervision of a dozen curious squatters, it drew up at Hamm's shack. Not minding the friendly stares at all, a woman got out, shook the dust from her weary skirt, and went up the little path to the stoop.

At her knock Hamm opened the door, squinting his eyes into the sun, for a moment seeing only the dark silhouette. But even so it was enough. He knew that strong, free bearing, the calm poise of the head.

"Stephani," he said, before she could speak, saying the word awkwardly, as though it were still foreign to his tongue, and not the silent habit of every hour.

Later, in a dusky booth at King's coffee shop, Hamm found his hands no more quiet on his pipe than Burt Parr's would be if Mollie were to come to him today. Yet Hamm could look into the face of the woman before him without turning his scar away, directly and unembarrassed as though it were her picture. She was just as he remembered, unchanged to him since the night she helped an injured man into an alley in Boston. The high, brown forehead seemed as smooth, the hair darkening but still rising in the same free wings from the temples, her eyes the same serious, troubled grey of a November sky. Even her cheekbones were as sharp-cut, the mouth almost as full and gay over the pointed chin. Yes, she was the same as always, slim and dark as the rushes growing along the Little Grand when he was a boy, the rushes that he found lost their color almost as soon as he cut them, and went limp as rope before he got them home to show to his mother.

Hamm tried to listen to her investigations into the farmer associations of California, and New Mexico and Kansas, but somehow irrelevant things kept creeping in: the first high spray bringing a storm wind in from the Atlantic; a whiff of fragrance from a Kanewa plum thicket in Maybloom, the sweetness aching his temples as it did when he was a boy. Then the food came and over their steaks Stephani spoke of the things at home: her mother's diabetes that was much the same, her father's pleasure in his new work. He was setting the type for two books of folk songs, one from upper Pennsylvania, one of the Poles of Hamtramck, in Detroit, the same songs that he knew in the old village at home.

And as Hamm listened to Stephani speak with such warmth of her home, he wondered if his inheritance could matter to her, if she could permit him to build a place for her on Blue Ridge. Perhaps she was tired of wandering too. But instantly he knew that he could not ask her to become one of a city that he, born to, never brought himself to acknowledge, not even to this woman who was so much of his life.

But he might take his heritage away, not to her Boston, for too much of the Franklin of these later years was of a piece with the genealogy pages of the old *Transcript*, but to some other city, to St. Louis, perhaps. Of course, there also were the things Stephani hated: injustice, stupidity, graft and commercialism, but he remembered the people for their *Gemütlichkeit,* with a fondness for music and a frank warmth for their fellow men. Yet as Hamm looked under his dark brows to Stephani he could see no hope that she would go to St. Louis, or anywhere at all with him, and before he could bring himself to make words for his question Carl Halzer was beside them, shouting "Hello!" in his big, man voice, and stopping, embarrassed. "Oh, excuse me, I thought it was Abigail with you — "

Stephani glanced up from her dessert to the tall man, sun-browned, hard and smooth and strong-grained, his hair standing as though from a strong wind fresh out of rain. She smiled, and to Carl her woman teeth were the warm flash of milk in a winter morning pail as she held out her hand. So the two were introduced. This was Stephani, the girl above the fireplace. Carl nodded; he saw it now. And this was the Bellowing Bull of Bashan, the only honest man in politics here who wasn't too stupid to be worth a bribe. Ah, yes, Stephani knew of him, too, and how he rallied the Labor Day parade. That took something special, here where the common man was so in awe of the police, of his own hirelings; here where he knew so little of his rights.

Almost at once they were in talk of the farm associations. Silent, but attentive over his folded arms, his scar pinkish, Hamm listened, pleased that these two he loved so well would be friends.

Despite her weariness, Stephani asked to see this Abigail, this woman who seemed to know so much of this region. Why not take her over for a minute, before dropping her off at the old Frontier Hotel? Yes, Hamm agreed, and she must have a copy of Abigail's book, to read while she was living in the shabby old hen-roost that was once an anteroom for kingmakers.

Abigail met them at the door. "We have heard so much of you — " she said, and drew Stephani to her as an old, old friend. Then, in surprise at their impulsive greeting, particularly the plain, quiet little American of Yankee stock, they examined each other. "But you are grand!" Stephani cried to Abigail's embarrassment at her familiarity. It was very warming to find these friends of Hamm's so kind, so unlike strangers. In a midwestern capital city she had expected it otherwise. Yet her father had once said it must be good to live out in these newer lands, where the earth was not bitter with the hatred of old, old quarrels, and every foot of sod heavy with the bodies of the murdered. Here there must be great patches where no one at all had been buried since the stone was laid down by the receding sea. Perhaps this capital city that Hamm had chosen for a refuge was then really a warm, a living place after all? Perhaps that was why he had come here?

Hamm grinned from the good side of his face. "You haven't seen anything of the Franklinites, Stephani," he said. "Neither Abigail nor Carl belongs here, nor is very popular in our capital city — "

They talked late of many things. Stephani started it by asking what their greatest resource here was.

"We have only two resources," Carl answered her, "the soil and our water-power — "

And there had of course been difficulties about the power? Yes. When the TVA fuss didn't end in the hoped-for discrediting in the public eye, there was the attack on the Little TVA in the Nebraska legislature and the GVA, on the Grand River, in Kanewa. It was said the utilities spent a million in each state, and it almost did the trick. Nobody here seemed to realize that the large industrial centers are probably done; that in the future most of the factories will be in semi-rural setups, in small units, using electricity as power, the workers living on acreages and small farms; no more soot and slums, no more starvation from crop failure. The key to this future is in the middle west, with its still fertile soil and its cheap water power. But the industrialists will control it if possible, and the fight will have to be won and rewon, next legislature, even this election. New England senators are asking for an investigation; anything to detain the growth of public control, to sell it out; break it.

Yes, control the means to freedom or to slavery, Stephani agreed. Was there no bright young crusader here with a reputation to make? No young La Follette, Norris, or Hanson coming up to expose these things to the voters?

Nobody with a chance. The last thirty years the bright young men have been going away, or getting in with the corporations and utilities here, hoping to get fat-pillowed jobs in the eastern offices. Even some of those who get to the legislature work toward that end, particularly the capital city members. The occasional young radical in the university is kicked out or is bought off by a good job. The bright young law students go to Harvard on fellowships, and are warned not to take courses under Hicks.

Abigail verified Hamm's conclusions. In the future the country's liberal leaders would have to come from the industrial east, with some hope for the west coast. The great midwest liberals were dying off without political progeny.

It was a good evening, but finally the long hours at the wheel weighed impossibly upon Stephani. Her head kept dropping forward, and Carl looked sleepy, too, his hair bushier and wilder from all the pulling it got when words for his ideas wouldn't come. But they must get together again, Stephani insisted. They had information she needed — the true history of the region and the underlying local forces, both difficult for the outsider in these flying investigations through the country. The national tie-ups, political and economic — these she hoped to ferret out.

"I don't believe anyone can discover it all, until long after, for no one seems to know or understand much of what is being done, the men behind the Cole Dringers no more than the Welleses and Hammonds here — " Abigail said.

Stephani nodded, but she must know, if possible, why states like Kanewa were headed deep into tenancy long before the depression, as the census reports show, and why the energetic young people all went east. These were things to consider before she could hope to understand the Farmers' Association and its backing, and why a state so close to the frontier was already slipping into decadence.

"That'll be a large order for even you, Miss Stephi,"

Carl Halzer told her, using the nickname he learned among the Bohemians down towards Kohl, and pleasing her immensely by it. Her mother, half Czech, sometimes called her Stephi.

Watching the dawn come from his stoop, Hamm went back over the whole rich evening. It was fleeting as a spot of sunlight on a stone floor, or a cardinal feather drifting on the wind, but it had been fine. Of course Stephani would run into trouble with her investigations, particularly the minute she was traced to Abigail, to Carl, or to him. Tomorrow, perhaps, or the day after, her errand would be out. But in the strife and conflict of this fall it was good to have had this one evening with her; even shared with his friends it was fine to have Stephani.

When the alarm rang he shaved, looking long at the good side of his face, smoothing out the new depths in the folds at his mouth. His hair, too, was greying out of its tarnished silver to whitish triangles at his temples. Not until he remembered that this fall in Franklin had not been an easy one did he think of Burt. He hadn't seen the boy yesterday or called, and the Gold Shirts were working in the open again. The *Christian Challenger* was on his stoop, poor old Samelly's windows were broken and the Co-op's glass door smashed, the shelf of books and the candy case cleaned out. The *World* called it the work of petty thieves, but the *Gazette* reported that a pile of burnt books, apparently from the Co-op, was found on the slope behind Stone House, where Willper's new drillmaster paraded his boys, and the Klan was said to meet.

The morning after her arrival Stephani was ready for work. First she would get all she could about the Midwest Farmers' Association tie-up in the town, and then out in the state. She talked several hours with Abigail, went through whole sections of her files, and got the names of some of the university people suspected of liberal tendencies. It would be difficult to get them to talk now, Abigail warned. They had to think of their families.

Then there were those known or suspected to be tied up with Cole Dringer or writing for his news service — the gift-car-every-fall crowd, as they were privately called. Stephani got a list of likely business men of the town too, and started out with Parkins, the secretary of the chamber of commerce, telling him what her purpose was: a survey of the farm organizations of the middle west, their history, aims and purposes, their progress, and any plans for the future. On him she used only the letter from her publishers, eminently successful ones, with four books among the year's big moving pictures. Even Parkins knew of their importance and asked for no more. Nor did the presidents of banks, land and insurance companies, or the local heads of the power company and the railroads. They agreed, too, in their attitude towards the farmer — considering him not a stupid dolt any more but a recalcitrant servant who was increasingly inefficient and ungrateful. While they all started with the same expression: "If the farmer has no crops we have no business," they implied that his failure was one of incompetence, with a great deal of deliberate malice towards his betters.

Stephani went about with an impressive brief case and simple hat that men would like. She always wore blue glasses until the interview was well started so the strangeness of her wide-winged cheekbones and the directness of her eyes would be less disturbing. She wore sensible shoes and the Oxford-grey suit of a serious worker, with a fluffy blouse the color of a mountain jay that warmed her eyes to the same elusive smoky blue when she unbuttoned her coat.

For the interviewing Stephani carried a dreary list of questions beginning with the Grange and ending up with the Midwest Farmers, if necessary, but she preferred that these men bring the Association up themselves. They usually did. Then she could say that she had heard of it, but considered it rather too new and without permanence for her study.

"Let me tell you something, young woman. This is the real farmers' organization," Parkins, the chamber secretary, interrupted in the voice he generally reserved for announcements on coronation night. Pawing about among his papers, he finally brought out a clipsheet that she recognized as one of the many services of the *Midwest Farmer*. But he kept it in his own hands, adjusted his glasses on his thin nose and read her the elaborate program for the M.F.A., including all the usual professional Americanisms except outright racial discrimination, and that was implied. Stephani made a flattering number of notes, laying the sheets in an orderly pile upon the man's desk. He gave her more and more time, sending his secretary away at each interruption. In the end he referred her to Purdy Gilson as the man who could tell her about the officers, the personnel in each region, the membership campaign, and the invaluable services of the organization. See him of an evening. He was with the Vigilant Taxpayers, and well posted.

Not trusting the hotel switchboard, Stephani called Hamm from a pay station to ask about Purdy, found out that he was farm rep for the Kanewa Investment Company and that he was the one who reported Hamm as living in sinful luxury on relief. They had a good laugh together over it, but Hamm was disturbed with this further evidence that his money was being used for the M.F.A. Anxious as he was to see Stephani he had to tell her they were poison to her work here, particularly Abigail and he. She must not be seen with him, not until she had all Franklin would give her.

"Sounds just like a company town — " Stephani said, and Hamm found himself without defense. Perhaps it was he and Abigail who were to blame, rather than the town. Anyway she'd be under suspicion soon enough.

It took Willper of the Gold Shirts three days to discover Stephani Kolhoff and denounce her as a Red. Hamm looked at her picture in the evening *World* under the head: "Woman Communist Quizzing Business Men," and laughed to himself as he tried to imagine the face of the fat, bald city editor of the *World* if he knew Stephani Kolhoff was the lawful wife of one of the bigger stockholders of his paper. Or the face of the whole town, for that matter.

The next day there was a letter in both of the Franklin papers from Al Jackson, the town's one Communist, the quiet, fussy, bookish fellow who was always appearing at the Workers' Alliance meetings but never getting to say anything because he was an independent printer, if a little one, and not a worker. Stephani Kolhoff was no Communist at all. If she were, he, as a good party member, would know of her and her errand and be prepared to offer every aid. She was not even a Trotskyist but a *New Republic,* a *Nation* liberal, probably voted for Al Smith, having written an article, clipping enclosed, against the anti-Catholic propaganda of the 1928 campaign. By this time the Grandapolis papers were ready with a story, and the managing editor of the *World* got another one together himself, for he had heard of the excellent publishing connections and there was an old novel manuscript in the bottom drawer of his desk. So Stephani's picture was in the *World* again, a better one this time, beside her battered coupé, the Massachusetts license showing plain, and a long story of her investigations, with no mention of Communism or of the Midwest Farmers.

Now that she could go about openly Stephani spent a whole afternoon with Abigail. On her screened balcony, over coffee and cigarettes, they talked about the fall-hazed town in three directions below them. Westward was Grandview Hill, with the Stone House of the Gold Shirts on top, Herb's Addition on the slope, and below that the Polish bottoms and the old warehouse district, where gradually one factory after another had closed down, partly because of the general centralization of the last forty years. Yet many in smaller

towns around kept going, even expanded. Perhaps the Franklinites found it easier just to live off the state through the
capitol. Something like two thirds of Kanewa's annual budget of around twenty million dollars was spent here.

"So much — ?"

Yes, around twelve million was the estimate, with what
went to the university, all in Franklin but Ag college. Then
there was all the student money. No wonder the dispossessed
farmers, teachers, and jobless college graduates all flocked
here like hungry crows. One hundred and eighty unemployed
families moved in the last three weeks, mostly following
the money they laid out in taxes and farm-mortgage pay-
ments. Of course much of that flowed right through to the
east, swift as the Grand River cutting its way down from
Wild Horse Plains.

Off northward from Abigail's window lay middle Franklin, the houses close-set among the naked trees, a few oaks
still brown splotches. Most of the stained roofs, dark blue,
white, or moss green, belonged to the three grandmothers
and their investment companies. The others, particularly the
grey, weathered ones, were still eluding their direct control,
helped a bit by the federal loans. Now it would be the government foreclosing, the *World* told its readers.

The scattering of church steeples above the trees were
the accusing fingers lifted over empty pews. The half block
of yellow brick walls was the start of the town's associated
church and community house, never roofed, the windows
empty holes because Blockert's American Bank closed on the
funds along in the middle twenties. Of course he was out of
the penitentiary now, and working for the Kanewa Investment Company, along with Purdy Gilson. "As the Coot says,
the public will kiss the ass of any scoundrel if his pants are
pressed."

Yes, it was true, and funny, Stephani said, but not for
laughing — this city too, so much like a village, as the middle

of any city is, except that here, without industry or commerce, there must be little for the sons or the sons-in-law; no future, nothing but the poor importance of being a Gold Shirt, something perhaps a little like a grown-up Boy Scout to most.

Abigail believed that the poorer ones were joining Stetbettor's Crusaders, no expensive uniform and equipment to buy, no Blue Ridgers running things there too — a sort of club for the boys like the Klan seems to many of their fathers. It was here, in this section, that Franklin's excess of women lived, either members of the family or outstate girls rooming. They worked or hoped to work in offices and stores, lunched at the horseshoe counters of drugstores on maybe an olive sandwich and a malted milk, finishing up with a litter of cigarette butts, twisted and bleeding red at the end, while they talked of ways to get Joe to propose or Steve closer to the church steps or the courthouse. Perhaps it was less serious talk, of the new metallic hats for Thanksgiving, Mickey Rooney's new picture, or their current pretty-boy crush. Few of them liked Henry Fonda much. "He looks like he was ready to sit down alongside a cow any minute," they said, condemning their origins, as they exposed them.

The householders out there kept the installment business going, the insurance companies and the town's lodges. They played bridge, listened to Ma Perkins, hillbilly singers, Gang Busters, and Charlie McCarthy. They bought oil stock, or, if containing any English blood at all, put five or ten dollars into the Sir Francis Drake estate swindle, and were always about to break Wall Street and inherit the United States. They read *Liberty* and the *Saturday Evening Post,* the women's magazines, and the confessions. Most of them grew up on Kathleen Norris and Helen and Warren, many invested a little on Brisbane's advice. Almost all got their economic and political notions from either Father Coughlin or Mark Sullivan. They flew into long-winded defense of the Constitution with a vague notion that it was written by Washington and dug up somewhere the last ten years by Senator Ham Fish. They were suspicious of advertisements, but bought every kind of mouth wash and believed what they saw in the news columns, the editorials, too, if they read them. They were against WPA and relief or old-age pensions except for their relatives, and all hoped for security for their children and for their own old age.

"Notice the trees," Abigail suggested, and now Stephani could see that many of them either had their branches lopped down, or grew up around dead, bleaching tops. "Deciduous trees, mostly short-lived, planted by the city's grandfathers, and not a whip put out since to grow up into their places," Abigail said. One of Hamm's friends, a Dr. Snell, who worked with crippled children, once told the Professional Men's Club that a city was like its trees. Unless the old wood was cut out to make room for good young stock, the seedlings grew warped or disappeared. All you'd have would be dying trees, white and bleaching at the top.

"They look a little like a Grosz painting, don't they, the branches cut off so?" Stephani said thoughtfully.

Eastward was, of course, the capitol, with its frieze of the Peoples of the World supporting the stone globe. Stephani peered up at it. "A fine idea. Why isn't that given more publicity?" she asked.

"With the shoulders, the hands of Negroes and Japanese and Jews bearing an equal share — ?" Abigail asked.

But there was something else there. On the south side was a statue of Benjamin Franklin, looking down on a book, and behind him was carved: —

> Private property . . . is a creature of society and is subject to the calls of that society whenever its necessities shall require it, even to its last farthing . . .
> BENJAMIN FRANKLIN

"Those words, there on your capitol grounds — !" Stephani said in surprise. "And yet you have such things as the Farmers' Association — "

Ah, but the donor, the city founder and an old liberal to the end, was dead, and the new capitol was planned so no one would read the dangerous words by simply omitting the walk. Only the grounds men ever get near to Old Ben.

Beyond the capitol, on the slope towards the foot of Blue Ridge, lived those who must have a good address, seem successful — university department heads, business men who deal in public confidence, lawyers, and doctors. There were over fifty doctors in less than a square mile, some existing there by precarious dodges. All of them used the "thorough examination" racket, making it almost impossible to get a cut finger tied up without one, and of course calculated to reduce the patient's self-respect and thereby his resistance to the minimum. Then there was the change-of-life bogey. Abigail had scarcely a woman acquaintance past thirty who wasn't scared into taking shots to hold off premature change of life. And two thirds of Franklin getting almost no medical attention at all.

That would be expected in an industrial city, Stephani said, but not here. Was there no group movement of any kind?

In Grandapolis, yes, and with hard sledding; nothing here. A health survey showed Franklin's facilities far below the average, despite all the doctors with good addresses, and the dozens of specialists with even better ones, five of them out on top of Blue Ridge.

Stephani was less interested in the Ridge and its people. They were the same everywhere, as nearly the same as possible. Yes, Abigail admitted, but here three grandmothers not only ruled the town in a larger sense, but they passed any job worth a man's salt on to their own kin. Others had to be flunkies, and many of the university's brightest graduates left the state because they couldn't even get flunkying to do.

Well, that left the Farmers' Association, Stephani said. There was probably a financial tie-up between the Gold Shirts, even with Ridge representation, and Old Stet, the rising rub doctor — at least a similar source of funds, but proof was imperative.

Yes, Abigail as a historian understood that. She knew too that there were fascist ramifications far beyond the few crack-brains the Dies committee seemed able to dig up. Among the Allertons were a retired navy man and an old West Pointer, and both of them wished to see the country run by a good military dictatorship, firm and orderly, as Hitler, but nothing messy. Some of their friends weren't so interested in limiting the messiness. Along in September, with her book accepted but not yet out, Abigail, as a literary relative of old Colonel Allerton, was asked to cocktails at the Major Steeleys'. It was a sort of get-together of the older officers from seven states, some retired, and their flattery seemed a little heavy to Abigail, knowing that the military likes its women handsome. But they carried it off well enough, the women too, her hostess even asking her to the party arranged for Saturday so their football visitors could meet Abigail. When the talk became general, someone brought up Charley Stet, passing him off casually, as unimportant and without money. Abigail dared express an opinion on an unwomanly subject, predicting that old Charley Stet could get financial backing, all he wanted. There was Winrod down in Kansas, running for governor some time back. Apparently he managed.

"Oh, Preacher Winrod's all right, you know," one of the men said a little thickly. "He's radical, a bit too radical, maybe, but his principles are good Americanism — "

It came when no one else was talking, the words dropping like stones into a silence. The women stirred a little, but the disciplined men preserved the pleasant vacantness of their faces. The host recovered first.

"Ah — but we didn't bring Miss Allerton here to listen to dreary Kansas politics," he managed, offering Abigail a smile and the cigarettes. "She is here to talk of herself and her literary achievements."

Almost at once the man from Kansas was gone, and when Abigail left, her host apologized for him at the door. "The major has been permitted little drinking since his retirement. He gets out to celebrate so seldom — He'll be very contrite for his rudeness tomorrow — "

The next day the Steeley secretary called. Unfortunately the Saturday party had to be postponed. Mrs. Steeley was ordered to bed by her doctor. "She regrets — "

Abigail wrote a note of sympathy, and got on with her work. The next week an acquaintance stopped her on the street.

"Too bad you didn't feel up to the Major's party Saturday. You must look after that health of yours — probably working too hard — "

Although no one in Franklin seemed to know it, Burt was seeing Mollie again. It was Carl who discovered them one evening in a back booth up at Sun City, population 147, on a broken-down bus road. He didn't see them as he settled with the newspapers in an eatery for his supper and to wait for Stephani, who might be in later. After a while he found himself listening to a voice, moving smooth and steady as the flow of the limestone springs that empty into the Wakoon River. It was Burt Parr, in the booth behind him, the cadence suggesting poetry instead of talk. So Carl listened idly as he waited for his steak to be fried, as a man who deals with cows the year around will have it, fried done.

After a while the rhythms began to sound familiar. With closer attention the farmer found he could catch a few words: "The wild gander leads his flock through the cool night . . ." He thought he could remember that in the voice of his eighth-grade teacher, and when Burt got to the line "The sharp-hoof'd moose of the north, the cat on the house-sill — " Carl Halzer was certain. It was "The Song of Myself" that his teacher had assigned to be read with the *Deserted Village*. "Ill fares the land — " Yes, the land fared very ill here, where wealth had indeed accumulated and its men decayed beyond anything Goldsmith had ever seen. But in the booth behind him were two for whom Whitman spoke, a young farm boy from the Wakoon reading to the girl he loved: —

. . . My face rubs to the hunter's face when he lies down alone in his blanket,
The driver thinking of me does not mind the jolt of his wagon —

and a little while later: —

. . . whoever walks a furlong without sympathy walks to his own funeral drest in his shroud,
And I or you pocketless of a dime may purchase the pick of the earth, —

Mollie's soft voice repeating "the pick of the earth." After a long silence the boy started again, reading lower now, so Carl had to lay his ear against the beaverboard of the booth to hear.

This is the female form,
A divine nimbus exhales . . .

He moved his head away, flushing red with the shame at the hearing, for so should the young husband speak to the wife, and none to know. Quietly Carl paid and went out. A long time he stood in the darkness of the little town, trying to hide his shaken heart from himself, knowing now that he should not have asked Stephani to meet him, not even for a talk about the situation up around Stockholm, where she was going. It had been casually done, he told himself, as though she were any of a dozen women he knew, certain that there was nothing in it to bring uneasiness to him or to his friend in Herb's Addition, whatever was between him and the girl whose picture hung over his fireplace. But now, suddenly, Carl saw that it was not so. Now suddenly, because of a woman with eyes like November clouds and hair that made wings at her temples all his life seemed a vast, empty room, seen only in the momentary striking of a match.

It was an hour later that the repair man from the garage found Carl on the dark street. "Oh, Halzer — " he called. "I thought that was your old crate standing out there. A trucker coming by gimme the number of a party down to Franklin trying to get in touch with you — been calling you at every filling station along the road — "

Carl looked at the telephone number. "Thanks," he said, folding the paper into his pocket.

"Nothing tough to take — ?" the man asked sympathetically.

"Oh, no, nothing important."

"Well — you shore got them truckers looking out for you — "

Finally Stephani came in, dusty, too tired to talk until she had eaten a little, drank some hot coffee. But Carl was content just to sit beside her as she ate, Hamm Rufe down in the capital city forgotten, and the call from Marylin Welles in his pocket. Even when she finished there seemed little to say, except that she was going into Franklin instead of to Stockholm.

It was Abigail that Stephani came to see, for there were things she wished to know, personal things. Because this friend of Hamm's seemed so serious and earnest about it, Abigail told what there was, diffidently, apologetic for its insignificance.

She had come in from the little Congregational College

at Walden to take her doctorate in the history of the trans-Mississippi country. She would have preferred Wisconsin, with John Hicks, to a Kanewa degree, but her George was being transferred from the veteran's hospital in Nebraska to the new unit set up at Kohl, near Franklin. George was the neighbor boy back home. They had been eighteen together, with nothing much in the world except each other, but it had seemed a great deal then. By the time they were old enough to marry there was the war. It was ten years before she saw him again, always in the presence of an attendant. The boy of her youth was much changed, slow, dark and brooding, with only a vague recollection of her or any of the past. It wasn't tragic, Abigail hastened to explain. "Not any more than having someone you marry grow into a stranger. That happens all the time, you know — "

So Abigail had kept on teaching, and three years ago she came down here. On his better days they called her, and she went out to see George as she would a sick neighbor. He seemed happy, was always pleased to have her come, told her all about his cabbages — he was particularly fine with cabbages, they said — and always sent regards to her folks, who, like his, were dead years ago.

"Does Hamm know? You seem very fond of him — " Stephani said casually. Abigail laughed. "You can't pretend to be worried about me — "

But that wasn't what Stephani meant. Hamm was a fine, sensitive person; he had the right to a home, to companionship. Would he become interested in anyone if she divorced him? Abigail didn't think it would matter much. It wasn't only that he loved his wife —

No, Stephani admitted slowly, there was more to it — perhaps it was as though a plump, white drake, eating his corn in barnyard warmth and safety, had tolled a wild duck from the dark sky.

"Yes, or a young mustang deserted her free range for the

fenced pasture of her mate," Abigail said. "Soon the high places would call her, and the knee-deep grass would not be enough. Yet behind her the pasture-bound stallion would keep hanging along the fence, head over it, eyes on the hills, waiting, but unwilling to leap its top wire to freedom, to leave the lush feed grounds behind."

Yes, perhaps it was so, Stephani agreed, and went away to Herb's Addition.

CHAPTER XII

CASSIE had big exhaust fans set up and running night and day at Welleshaven, to carry off the building smell as fast as possible. She had helped to wear Cees Hammond a little greyer and leaner this last month with her demands for this change in drapes and that in carpeting, all immediately — all things made up special, most of them shipped in. She kept him running back and forth to the house so much it started a rumor among the less informed that the leftovers from the town's two big suicides were consoling each other. Those who knew them well thought not or at least hoped not. Cees was such a defenseless bit of a man and with his need to pursue each little rabbit of a word as though it were a broad-antlered stag escaping, rattlebrained Cassie Welles would have him envying Cobby and his own little Penny in a week.

But Cassie did get her house open for her birthday. Of course there was talk, with poor dear Cobby buried only seven, eight weeks, but the feature writer's story in the Sunday *World* tried hard to make it look all right: "With the completion of the long contemplated remodeling, the worn old roof has been replaced with the gleam and charm of white glazed tile; the antiquated heating plant was removed to make way for a more adequate system of all-season air conditioning, while two guest rooms and three baths add greatly to the modern facilities and practicability of the old place as a home."

"God, I'd never realized that our fellow townswoman was

such a victim of bad housing — " the Coot told the men about Joe's old heater out in Herb's Addition. They crowded around the paper to see the pictures, were awed by the half-block front elevation of Welleshaven.

"Yeh," Cash Overtill agreed. "If we'd a knowed her privations we'd a offered her the charm of our conveniences long ago, or at least the hospitality that Joe dispenses with so much practicability here among us — "

"It must be hell to live in that wedding cake," one of the old Okies said. "I been tractored off a farm in Kansas and burned out of a hooverville in California, but I ain't had no call to live in no such dump — "

However, Cassie would probably manage all right now, with the income from Cobby's $900,000 insurance, in addition to all the family interests and the rebuilt Welleshaven, with thirty-nine rooms, eight baths, and a stone court, the whole thing painted buttermilk white with the iron grille fencing around the grounds and across the second-floor balconies, front and back, white too. The shutters were painted a pale, dusty rose, Cassandra rose, the architect called it, and others besides the Okies of Herb's Addition took to calling the house The Wedding Cake.

In addition to the page spread of pictures there were enough smaller ones to scatter through a whole extra section of building-trade ads, from architects to sodders and gutter men. Below the cut of the double-winged, balconied front of Welleshaven was a picture of the living room, with twelve mirrors described as pale Cassandra blue, set into recessed panels behind strip-tanks of slender, graceful water plants to reflect in the glass as in garden pools. The furniture was set out from the wall to suggest vastness of space, and made the room look like a cool and expensive hotel lobby.

What interested every woman of the capital city was Cassie's boudoir, with its two bathrooms walled in flesh-colored mirrors, the toilet stools recessed out of sight. The boudoir was in ivory tufted satin — walls, furniture, and all, with a touch of Cassandra blue in the drapes, the floor thick strewn in white rugs, the low wide bed on its shallow platform like a snowdrift under its swirl of throw-spread. Two doors opened upon the back balcony and the sunken garden where Cobby's Dalmatians had walked so forlornly the day of his funeral.

Cassie managed to get the two children together for her little fire laying as she called it, although the fireplaces were all electric now, and there were so many cars that the curved driveway was a dark moving stream from four to seven o'clock. Not even the Harv Ellerses were left out, although they weren't asked out so much since Jimmy's party at the Buffalo Hotel. Cassie wore a fish-tailed velvet dress of warm off-black and a rosy red camellia in her newly glinted hair. Her electric vibrancy, which she called to the attention of her guests, wasn't due to the new house, but to a week of instruction under her new Yogi.

"Oh, yes, my dear, of course, you shall meet him. But not here, with all these people. It would really be too disturbing for the gentle soul," she told the curious ones, planning all the time to keep him to herself, as was only right, for it was she who had him come from California; really paid his way, but she never put things so crudely. He was to help keep Dachel in hand. But he turned out to be so young, his eyes sad night-black in his brown face, and his lips a soft, dark bow, that she wondered if, after all, there weren't higher things in life than the poetry to be written by a vain young man really only from Michigan, no matter what he called himself.

By the time Dachel heard her bring up the wonders and the vibrancy of yogism a dozen times to new arrivals, the cocktails had been around almost as often. So the young man unlimbered his slim legs, smiled his even-toothed most agreeable, and told Cassie, loud enough for everyone to hear, "You

know damn well you said the breathing made you dizzy!"
The women around her fell back a little, making the small, hopeful noises of a flock of chickens at the sound of the grainery door. But Cassie just laughed it off. "This is our poet's temperamental day — " she told them, managing an eyebrow for the white-coated Filipino passing the drinks. So Dachel went to the kitchen himself and, coming back with a full glass in each hand, deliberately picked Eloise Johnson, crammed tight into a black velvet dress, for his long-lashed, caressing glance.

Cassie pretended not to see. She was talking about Marylin, really becoming quite a studious girl this fall, a real reader. That's where she probably was this minute, hidden away in the library, with the whole wall of new books Cassie just got from a little place in Chicago, a Jew place, Harold said, and threatened to take the whole lot out to burn. Noticing the usual little smile on the lovely face of Mona Stone, Cassie gulped her martini and, coughing, laughed that Harold was incomprehensible; all one's children were incomprehensible nowadays.

But the new books really looked beautiful; all first editions, and cost enough to be pretty old. They were the one thing about the house that Marylin liked. They ought to hear her go on about the electric fireplaces, acting like smoke and ashes were essential to the greatest happiness. It was her crush on the barnyard and the simple life just now.

And wasn't it too funny — her daughter, with a platinum fox throw, at least it cost enough to be platinum, and an imported car, sticking off there in the library wing, with all these people here, just to get away from her mother? Daughters of a certain age were like that nowadays, she told Ellie Groves, as Ellie would discover when Helen got a little older. "Keep her away at school as long as you can, my dear, for your own sake," Cassie advised.

Harold was around somewhere too, hid out with the less

attached men, from twenty-year-old Frankie Doover, back from California after the funeral of José and Isaac, to old Billie Bamper. All who could escape the crush of women were in the Men Only wing, as Cassie called it, in the leather-furnished lounge, with its wooden bar and Cobby's guns racked along the bare pine wall. At Harold's suggestion most of them were drinking straight rye with beer for a chaser, and in fifteen minutes or so the lounge was noisy as an auction, with Harold taking a good going over about the stories around town, especially the Tyndale girl running out on him at the cat house. Or was it a married woman he was planning to crack that night? At first it made him feel big, like a devil of a fellow, but with another round or two of rye the fun seemed to sour a little, the questions getting around to the tree-tying business out in Dakers woods. "You wasn't getting jealous over a filling-station punk's floosey?" somebody asked, with still enough sense to look around that no Tyndales were near.

"Hell, no," another answered, pointing out Harold's bald spot. "Women come a nickel a dozen, but not hair, not pretty, pretty hair that burns so nice with a match — "

Now there was silence, and Harold slowly turning his flushed face about the room for a sign of derision. Far back in the corner he noticed Harding Wood, step-nephew of Josina Black, a quiet little youth who had dropped out of the Gold Shirts. Harold saw his thin lips quiver, his full glass splashing, and laughed out loud, the room taking it up as a roaring echo, in relief.

Little Harding straightened up, gulped deep from his Tom Collins. "Yes," he asked deliberately, "why did you tie the pretty boy to the tree? Wouldn't he come across — "

It was Joe Willper who jerked the little revolver from Harold's hand and pulled him back into his chair as he motioned young Wood out. The boy fled, leaving the room behind him silent and appalled; for almost they had seen a murder right here on the Ridge, in the best home of the capital city.

It was Bamper who set out another round of drinks but while here and there one was gulped down fast, others were examined thoughtfully as new opinions of Harold took form. Some of them began to see him, not as the little blowhard but as a man of violence, a few with concern, a few admiringly; others with contempt that he had let a convict lay hands on him like that. Some looked upon Joe in envy and admiration. There must be more to that little squirt than showed — more than just a mustache like half a fuzzy red caterpillar stuck under his nose, and a loud arrogant mouth, extra so from whiskey and from knowing that he was at Welleshaven against Cassie's protest. When she said she wouldn't have the ex-convict in her house, Harold reminded her that Blockert was of the same fraternity, only he did his stealing by the front door, like a true Blue Ridger. So Willper was asked, and sat as big as his five foot four allowed in the host's chair of the lounge. And when young Harding was gone and all the others who couldn't countenance anything of the affair, including even Milo Groves and Harv Ellers, Joe Willper began to talk of mysterious events to come.

"Things is beginning to break," he said, "and with my managing, and his tie-up, I can make Harold Welles the big man of the state before many months!" he announced.

Smith Bridges looked in at the door, at the weasel-chinned Willper, the vain little Harold sweating and smirking, and went away. His own father had really been a big man in the state, the Populist senator who helped carry Kanewa for Bryan and scare the big money men of the east to filling their pants. Even after the sell-out he kept roaring against the big interests until he dropped dead in the Bull Moose campaign, out for old T. R. Fellows like Willper and Harold Welles would give a real man like old Tod Bridges a gut ache.

As Smith left he saw Samuel Tyndale, with a glass in his hand, passing the lounge door, looking for a nook of escape from the woman crowd. When he saw Willper inside he tried to slip away, but not soon enough.

"The Goddamn Jew — " little Joe was saying, "and stinkin' lousy with money — "

As the nights chilled, the Okies gathered in Herb's Addition like fall flies on a warm windowpane. Somehow they dragged their rattling jallopies from as far away as Rhode Island and California. Not in droves, for no one was putting out handbills to coax the dispossessed to Franklin, where labor was still free, as the employers called it. For ten years the Handee garage, with all the downtown business trade, had been getting most of their help for around a dollar a week in cash, a non-transferable meal ticket on the greasy hamburger stand on the alley, and a cot with the rats in the basement. They worked twelve hours a day, subject to further emergency calls. Even so, Bill Witlow of the Handee had a waiting list, as he loudly told the reporter he ordered down from the *World*, when the father of their steadiest helper went on WPA. Went on WPA when he was offered the same as his son here. Dollar a week and found wasn't bad these times. No, old Jim Stanton had admitted, but he had three boys in school who liked to eat too, and besides he was kinda used to sleeping with the old woman. Of course the *World* didn't quote Jim, but the story got some good belly laughs down at Old Horsemeat's, and Pete's pool hall, and at the Labor Temple.

Usually the Okies didn't find Herb's Addition until they were around town a while, and had been moved on several times. Not even the relief people would tell them about the place, not openly. But the chilling nights sharpened their noses, and the old cars came stringing in past the little signboard, one after another, the children spilling out and running wild, much as their grandparents at the same age spilled from covered wagons over the free land of Kansas or Nebraska or the Dakotas. They were met by the three young Dillards, waiting to show them everything: the cliff swallow nests in the upper banks, Sophie's red tiger cat that mustn't be touched, and particularly the WPA privy. "You can use it too, when you has to," they offered the newcomers grandly, "but you got to keep it clean, no doin' anything on the boards no place — "

If the sun was out the day after a new settling there was usually early water carrying from the shelterhouse, and a great boiling of clothes in the old gasoline barrel cut in half and set up on four brick legs. With a smoking fire underneath and a water-bleached stick for stirring and lifting, it was much like the old wash kettles of the Ohio Valley, used by grandmothers of many of these women. But here there was none of the sharp clean smell of soap made from cracklin's and home-leached lye, although Joe at the shelterhouse somehow managed to buy up big lots of yellow soap to sell at a penny a bar, and started a howling around town.

In the afternoon, when the clotheslines sagged with shirts and bedding and towel rags, hung out from perhaps their first good boiling in months, the Coot would come down, puffing at the old pipe almost lost in his beard, and giving out advice. "A tablespoon of kerosene for every bucket of suds, does wonders for the duds, as my maw used to say. Takes out the grease of workingmen's hands, and the smell of the young ones' wetting, or a cat kittening on the bed — "

Before long Joe always came to stand on the porch of the shelterhouse, shouting, waving the old man away.

"Well, I better get going," the Coot would grumble, starting to go. "There comes old Hitler Joe. He can run anybody off this place anytime he wants."

When this news had caused sufficient consternation among the travel-weary women, the old man would slap his thigh and roar out with laughing. "Yeh," he'd say, "Joe can run you off right enough, but he ain't never done so to anybody, not so far as I know — " Then the Coot would go on to his cave, humming maybe "Buffalo Gals," as the new children looked after him, planning to sneak up that way to look in at the tarp-hung doorway when dusk came.

As soon as the squatters could believe in the security of Herb's Addition, they piled sod around their tents or scoured the dumps for material for shacks, trading anything they had to spare for slabs of salvaged tin or boxwood to the Coot or Dillard, or the others. If they could manage no tent or shack, they borrowed a shovel from Joe and dug into the earth for warmth. Two weeks of chilly nights with a little snow flurry increased the habitations of the Addition to sixty-two. The flops at Joe's were already full, the showers splattering much of the evening. Looking at his tobacco can filling with pennies from the coffee and doughnut sales, he predicted a hard winter ahead.

Evenings the new men wandered up to the shelterhouse to sit around the old heater, passing the evening papers among them, playing checkers or a game of pitch. Some just sat hunched over on the benches along the wall, elbows on knees, hands together, hoarding their memories of things past; others kept them alive by telling and retelling, counting jobs held, and money and property owned, as tangible in the palm for counting as the paper in a banker's vault. Those of the capital city or the region about it took a great interest in the growing Franklin National, the Kanewa Investment Company, Josina Black's Equity Life, and other Franklin financial firms, as contributors to the cause. This one had given a store, that one a hotel, or a garage or an office building, or perhaps an acreage. A dozen had given their farms, almost all of them their homes to the greatness of capital city business. Those from out in the state had contributed too, farms, stock, everything, and years of labor.

Hamm talked to most of them. Here and there he found an Okie who thought it was all new, this migration of which he was a part. Chuck Overtill, cousin of Cash, who was long a squatter in Herb's Addition, had other ideas. Twenty-five years ago he sold his farm, went into business, and was squeezed out in the early twenties. Returning to the farm as a renter, he found himself in competition with the thousands of others who had failed recently: schoolteachers, bookkeepers, preachers, bankers. But Chuck knew the ropes, found a little place he could buy and was almost paid out on it by the winter of 1929. In thirty-two he lost the seven-thousand-dollar farm for the two hundred left against it. Since then he's farmed there as a renter, until last week, when Gilson, the farm rep for the Kanewa Investment Company, came by with a long face and gave him a song and dance about things looking pretty bad. Unless the election cleared out the crackpots in Washington and kept Dunn Powers out of the governor's chair the company was shutting down all its farms. It was too bad for good farmers like Overtill, he said, but the investors had to be protected.

"Investors, hell! They've only got two hundred dollars in this to my $6800 and the interest, besides my labor. I make that much for them if it don't rain from June to August, and you know it. What this amounts to is coercion at the polls!" Chuck told the man.

Oh, no, no, Gilson was only saying what would happen if crackpotism in government weren't curbed. The K.I.C. was shutting down its 2500 farms, and other companies were finding themselves in a like position. Of course Chuck knew it was all a bluff, but telling a man with a family that he and thousands of other tenants will be turned out throws a scare into him. His head knows better but a wife and a houseful of hungry kids are good convincers of the heart.

"So I just called their bluff," Chuck said. "I moved off and left my share there. They always get the cream anyhow. By damn, says I, let Gilson, the old tripe-gut, bust his own back getting the corn out. I'm a lifetime resident of this county, and when we get too hungry I'll get grub."

He had given the relief business a lot of thought lately, too, he said. He'd always considered paupers loafers, but when the best workers, the closest savers around him, lost everything in the banks and had to go on relief, it got to looking different. So he started reading up on history books from the library commission. They showed plain that American democracy was founded on relief, most of the colonists coming over on one government relief scheme or another. Some worked for it, like WPA; some got it outright. And the first mess of soldiers returning from the Revolutionary War went bawling straight up to Philadelphia like weaning calves to the cow corral. They got relief, too, in the form of free land, so far away over the mountains that congress figgered they'd heard the end of them. But the howl never stopped until they had given the last piece of public land away to the unemployed, the dispossessed, about thirty years ago. And the whole time there were folks yelling that giving a man a chunk of land big enough for a house would kill his initiative but not if you give him enough so he could steal millions in timber, coal, iron, gold, or oil. And business? Why, before the first Revolutionary soldier could throw his old gun away, business had grabbed up government relief, been getting it in subsidies and tariffs ever since, and using the power the money gave them to buy up anybody in their way.

Now a lot of the down-and-outers were spending their last penny for gas to carry them on west. But the west was gone, nothing left but the Pacific Ocean, bounded by what their grandfathers ran away from on the Atlantic, starvation.

"In the meantime the big fellow can't see that if the laborer and the farmer's out of money, they got something worse than a sitdown on hand — a consumers' strike, consumers that ain't able to buy bread for the belly or rags to cover the backside. Then what the banks is got is only bales of paper.

"They can't see that a dollar spent once a year pays for a dollar's worth of stuff, spent a thousand times it pays for a thousand dollars' worth," Chuck ended, stretching his leathery neck to lick the cigarette he was trying to roll.

By now a couple of Townsendites had moved up closer, and a slope-shouldered little man beside Chuck lifted his voice, accusing him of preaching immorality. It was sinful to spend; godly to save.

"Well, what about *your* savings?" Chuck demanded, and the little fellow dropped his head and looked at the floor between his ragged knees.

Some of the squatters remembered the early Franklinites as common, friendly people. Like the time when a prairie fire threatened the bottoms, everybody, even the soft-handed women with their stylish skirts pinned up, came whipping their horses out, their bouncing buggies loaded down with buckets of water and sacks to help fight the fire. The time typhoid hit the town it was the same. Nobody went unnursed, and nobody asked if the bills could be paid. But as soon as a few got a little taste of the money to be made in rising real-estate values, it was like giving a bunch of lean cows a taste of green corn. All hell wouldn't hold them, and anybody that got in the way got tromped on.

"It's always the same underneath, human nature is," old Cash Overtill told them. "Only the soft parts been getting covered over with stuff like that stucco and them newfangled indestructible wall shingles they puts on their houses; the honest look of it lost under buttermilk paint and kalsomine."

Maybe so, a dump picker admitted, but it would take a hell of a lot of excavating to get to it here, or a lot of bloodletting.

The stories of Cassie's house party were scarcely cold around town, particularly the one about Harold Welles drawing a gun on little Harding Wood, when there was more excitement in Franklin. The weather man predicted a change and all one night the sky glowed with northern lights, from the pale pink dusting along the horizon until it was reddened high over the capitol. The few late Franklinites who ever noticed anything beyond the scattered lights of their quiet streets thought there must be a prairie fire, an old-time one, out on Wild Horse Plains. They even sniffed the air, but the smoke they found had nothing of the clean sharp tang of burning grass, but the damp, heavy stench of smoldering city dumps. Long before midnight the short-wave radio fans shut off their squealing sets, looked out towards the north and went off to bed in disgust.

With the morning a few grey clouds slipped out of the northwest and circled the horizon both ways, finally closing in overhead. Towards noon the wind rose, sharp as an old Sioux woman's hunting knife, as Horsemeat told the few who were out today. Yes, Hamm agreed, it would be hot coffee and chili more often than beer from now on under the old picture of Custer's Last Stand. Already the regulars were beginning to warm their hands around the cups, look up at the fly-specked battle scene and talk about the spring to come and another beer time.

Towards evening a little snow began to fall; thin, grey flakes, like the chaff blowing from a corn sheller. It ran along the streets in little puffs of pale smoke, settling behind the fire hydrants, in the empty doorways, and against the idle taxi wheels while the drivers pulled up their collars and read of summer in their Western Story Magazines. The dark came early, without a change in the wind, except that it whitened, blurring into halos around the street lights, sending the workers hurrying homeward, many wondering about the coal bin, and winter coats, and shoes for the children. The Salvation Army stopped at the corner of Fifth Street, their playing softened by the falling snow. Then, suddenly there was a fire siren, snow-muffled too, down towards Station I, in old Franklin. Drivers craned their necks, ready to clear the center of the avenue. But the sound retreated, and the honking traffic moved slowly on with the changing lights.

On its way across the Polish section the red fire truck picked up a following, and far ahead boys were running across the bottoms towards Herb's Addition that seemed to be one bright blaze behind a veiling of powdery snow.

Hamm's shack had gone first. He saw the flames leap up out of the night just as he turned in off the highway, and ran with a dozen other squatters, but they couldn't save his radio, any of his books, or even Stephani's picture. Before Joe got there with his water buckets Sophie's shack was gone; the last thing everyone remembered was the pretty red tiger-striped kitten running wildly on the window sill, with no one near enough to break the glass. Then the Dillard shack was burning too, the mother, with a homemade batter spoon forgotten in her hand, was herding her children out before her, the youngest held securely on her hip, his leg across her apron, already lifting high with another coming. In a little knot, with the heat of the fire on their faces, the wind and snow whipping their thin clothes, the Dillards watched their home go, their WPA privy with it. For a moment it stood proud and aloof in the red light. Then the white paint blistered, blackened, and burst into flame, the children crying, clinging about the mother, wailing, "Where'll we go now, Mama, where'll we go out?"

Suddenly, halfway across the Addition from the rest, Old Connie's shack broke into a roaring blaze. Everybody ran for it, thinking of the same thing, of Old Henry; bedfast, helpless inside.

Nobody made it in time, although Hamm pulled his coat

up over his face and plunged at the door. But the wind carried all the thick, black smoke that way, and the heat of the many tar-paper layerings Connie added through the years drove the man back. They heard Old Henry just once as they ran up; no words — a single trapped cry. Then there was only the crackling of the wind-whipped flames and the pungent smoke. With their faces turned from each other the squatters stood helpless, silent, as the shack fell in around the old iron bed, and the sparks flew high into the snowy air.

Six more shacks burned, the two Overtills' among them, by the time the fire equipment from Station I came roaring in at the signboard, sliding along on the wet clay slope, the highway behind them solid with cars. The bottoms swarmed with people afoot, the Polish football and track men well out in the lead, running between the burning shacks. But there was nothing they could do, nothing beyond helping to tear down the tents too near the flaming shingles and boards carried by the wind, sizzling as snowflakes hit them, even after they fell into the mud. Then suddenly the deserted shelterhouse was burning too, the flames sweeping in arcs up the old log walls, like the fires once set to the trail stations by the Indians, only this time it was with the smell and the swift high blast of gasoline that lit all the side of Grandview Hill, and the dark figure of a man slipping rapidly up a draw.

"There's the fire-setting son-of-a-bitch!" the Old Coot yelled out, starting to run. A dozen of the longlegged Poles passed him, chasing the fleeing man out of the dusky draw towards Stone House, the ground white enough with snow so the smallish tracks showed up plain. Near the old house they lost the footprints in a dozen of others and while they pounded on the door to demand the fire bug, and could see lights inside through the cracks of the boarded windows, the old plank door stood unyielding against them.

The thickening snow settled and fried on the ash piles of the shelterhouse and the ten shacks, while the homeless huddled together in the darkness about them and wondered where they were to go. The rest of the crowd, almost a thousand by now, although the road patrol shut the highway off completely to cars, pushed up around the sheriff, a couple of deputies, and the fire chief. They talked, grumbled, began to mutter to each other. The officers didn't seem to be doing anything, said there wasn't much anyone could do after thousands of feet had churned up the wet clay of the Addition. Into the light from their cars they had gathered scraps of burnt rags and several empty cans that smelled of gasoline. It was arson all right, the sheriff admitted, but the man or boy who made the tracks in the draw could have been any curious fire-goer, like most of the crowd here, who ran when he thought he might be suspected.

"Ran to the Gold Shirts — ?" someone asked sarcastically.

"Well, you can at least investigate — " someone else suggested.

"Yeh, why don't you go get him — " a dozen demanded. But when the sheriff turned slowly upon the protesting men they vanished into the silence and darkness of the crowd behind them. Somebody here probably would have to be the goat — and one would do as well as another.

An ambulance, siren going, crept up the packed highway, swung in and around to direct its light upon Connie's pile of wet, black ashes. Once more everybody pushed and shoved to see, until a dark object was scooped from under the twisted iron that was Old Henry's bed, put on a stretcher, and carried around to the back; then they were still, unmoving.

But just as the doors were being closed a woman broke from the crowd. It was Old Connie, panting, wheezing from the run out when she heard of the fire, her grey hair down, wet and matted. She stopped short at the ashes of her shack, looked around into the faces of those in the car light, at the dark figures farther back. "Henry, my Henry — ?" she asked. When no one answered she stiffened, pushed those who would touch her away, and walked alone past the ambulance to the sheriff's car. "I think I have some things to tell," she said quietly, and got in to wait. With her face turned straight ahead, the old woman sat without move or sound as the ambulance plowed off through the wet clay.

The next morning all the cars left out stood hub-deep in snow, with a peaceful whiteness over them, like horses hock-deep in hay that had fallen upon them from the mow above. The capitol tower was tall and grey and friendly against the darker sky. Sparrows were out early, scratching, and young dogs looked back at the steam that rose from the fireplugs and the bushes they had passed.

But the morning *World* carried a front-page streamer: FRANKLIN'S EYESORE DESTROYED BY FIRE. Farther down it was admitted most of the habitations at Herb's Addition unfortunately remained, all potential death traps. The story took the reader back to Eli Jiles, "The antisocial and malicious creator of a park that has always been a menace to the health and morals of the community, as it proved to be to the life of one poor cripple last night." While there were many wild accusations of incendiarism, and perhaps some suspicious circumstances, the paper said no one was being held, although there were plans to investigate the whole community at Jiles Park, without doubt the refuge of petty robbers and quite possibly a fire bug or two.

Hamm read the account in anger, the blood throbbing through his scar. Throwing the paper down he went to his coat pocket to look over the rough draft of his own write-up of the story. He would let it ripen today, and tonight it should be finished and sent off. He not only was making charges, he was demanding an investigation, federal if the local officers refused to act. Of course nothing would come of it. The Grandapolis papers might do a nice bit of muck-raking, but without a suggestion of the real situation. He was right; not even Old Connie got a hearing.

In the meantime Joe had managed shelter for everyone but Sophie. When she didn't show up last night he and the Coot took the flashlight down to prod the ashes of her shack, their faces pale and angry. But they found nothing, and the dump pickers said she was still there when the fires broke out, even ran up with them. So the young woman vanished as she came, leaving behind her only the memory of a pretty red kitten crying against the windowpane of a burning shack.

One casualty, the papers said, a cripple called Henry, last name unknown.

No rub doctor setting up campaign headquarters in the old American Bank offices could drive the Coot and his cronies from their leaning wall. They still hung along the sunny west side of afternoon, or moved around to the south before the chilling winds, keeping their hands in their pockets and their greasy caps back from their eyes. It was the Coot who told Hamm about a man who dropped his taxi around the corner and came slipping up to the old bank doors several days before the fire. They all noticed him because he looked both ways before ducking in, doing it without turning his body, an old army trick, Joe said. His cheeks hung down loose as a bloodhound's, and he leaned over an egg-shaped belly growing on him like an old maid six months along. The rest of the day there was a steady stringing into the bank building like back in boom times and now it was said that the man got off the shuttle plane at the airport and sure smelled like dirty work.

The day after the fires in Herb's Addition someone else noticed the new activities about the Stetbettor headquarters. Hallie Rufer Hammond had been to the courthouse to report on Jamie. She admitted that the boy was out last night at Stone House, and she was beginning to wonder about them up there, tolling youngsters out every night the way they did.

It was good for the boys, good discipline, building mental and physical efficiency, the judge said. Or was there some other reason why she was suddenly uneasy about Jamie's activities up there; say something about last night?

A long time the head of the Hammonds and her county official faced each other. Jamie wasn't home, and she had said so, and if he was involved in anything it was through that vicious group up there, many of them grown men and years older than he. The boy was shocked by the things of last night and would not go again; that he had promised. If he was taken up now she would see that they all were — all.

Oh, of course, of course, and only fair, the judge agreed, smiling again, for his youngest son was an officer at Stone House, due for advancement, and palling as equal with men far above his station.

So that seemed settled, and yet Hallie Hammond was worried as she came down the steps of the courthouse, anxious to get to the quiet of her office to think of many things. Cutting across the street she passed the side door of Old Stet's headquarters and almost ran into Glen Doover coming out — Glen, the father of Frankie, accused of killing the two refugee boys, and for thirty-five years married to her sister-in-law, Celia Hammond. Puzzled, Hallie walked slower, glancing back. As soon as the man was lost on the avenue, she saw Billie Bamper come out too; the manager of Senator Bullard's campaign, in with the old rub doctor.

During the two hours of errands Hallie made around the bank she saw enough to send her hurrying up to her office. She found Cees at least safely at his desk, weary, but at work.

By the evening after the fires there was considerable anger even in the local papers. Abigail saw the *World* first, and called Hamm. Somebody important seemed to be pushing a demand for a real investigation. Or was it a plan to brand the whole Addition as a nest of Communists, as the day's special edition of the *Christian Challenger* did?

That wouldn't be a new label, Hamm said, and scarcely worth the bother of an investigation, not even just before election. He didn't tell Abigail but he had received a surprise that afternoon, a call from Hallie Rufer Hammond, asking to speak to Mr. Hamm Rufe, please. For a moment her voice had carried him back to his childhood, to the days at home, and he found himself as ready to say, "Yes, Mother," as ever. But the cool voice at the other end of the line went right on. There were some things that should be done about last night's fires. Perhaps he, as a dweller in the Jiles Park Addition, might be willing to help. Could she see him for half an hour this evening? Her driver would call for him at eight.

When she was gone from the wire Hamm went to stand before the washroom mirror to examine the unscarred, the recognizable side of his face. The hair at the temple had greyed considerably since Cobby's death — certainly it wasn't much like the soft, thick boy-mane of the night he caught a freight away from Franklin, his family, and his name. Nor was there anything to recall the smooth skin of the boy in this strong, leathery brown of a healthy midde-aged man who seldom wore a hat. The forehead was lining, a fold lay down the cheek, the grey eye in its cluster of wrinkles was guarded by a brow much heavier, but still straight, the brow of George Rufer. Several times Hamm had talked of starting a mustache, a sort of game with Stephani, who always complained loudly that now soon it would give the wild Polish beard and the husbandly beatings of her homeland. But today he wished he had something to cover the clear-cut Rufer lip.

Then there was his mother's sensitive ear. While his voice had deepened some, probably, Hamm decided to hoarsen his throat. At closing time he hurried out for a volume of Aristophanes' *Comedies,* and in the storage basement of the Co-op strode up and down under the bare ceiling light roaring out "The Knights," from

> Oh! alas! alas! Oh! woe! oh! woe! Miserable Paphlagonian!
> may the gods destroy him and his miserable cursed advice!

until he could hardly speak at the end: —

> — let him go sell his sausages in full view of the
> foreigners, whom he used formerly so wantonly to insult.

Then once more Hamm went to the washroom mirror to inspect himself, particularly the injured side of his face, the one he decided he must turn to his mother, the cheek and nose cut by the thick, drawn welt of scarring that pulled the lower lid of his eye down, giving him a violent, a menacing look. After twenty years it still shocked him, and yet he had made no attempt to have it improved. As he stood there, rubbing his fingers over the harsh corrugation, he recalled what he overheard the Coot say once to some newcomers: "Yeh, that Hamm feller does look like a squaw buster, from the scar side, but the other, the one he keeps hiding's the one he was born to, dough-soft, stinking soft, as a rabbit's belly — "

Suddenly he saw more than sarcasm behind the Coot's words, and for a second the two eyes in the glass before him were alike, violent in their hatred and contempt for the man under the ugly red rope of scar.

So Hamm Rufe went out to his mother, in her house that was much the same as the day he left it. Not until he had stepped down into the long living room, with its comfortable couches, its deep chairs, low and soft with much sitting, the fire burning warm, did he remember how beloved it was, all this time. There was the deep old window seat overlooking the frog pond on the far side of the Ridge. Between the half-drawn drapes he could see a string of lights down the middle of the old pocket. It had been drained too, as everything else in this region, drained and subdivided, with a couple dozen houses, mostly started in the twenties, and several new ones — the old frog pond where he used to skate with Cobby Welles being sold on the installment plan.

There was a step behind him, and a woman's voice calling something to a maid. Hamm turned.

"Oh, I'm sorry I was detained — the telephone — " Hallie Hammond explained as she came in. She wore an untrimmed tweed suit; her hair, not so much greyer now than Hamm's, was trained close to her fine head. Behind her came a German shepherd dog, standing, waiting at the door. When they were seated, their cigarettes going, the dog got the nod and came straight to Hamm, laid his head to the strange man's knee, his eyes unwavering on the scarred face.

"Well, Kaiser — " the woman said in surprise. "What have you found? You aren't usually so friendly — " But the dog made no move at her voice, not even of the eyes. Clear and steady and sad, as dogs' eyes are, they remained upon the face of the man.

"You call him Kaiser — ?" Hamm asked, worrying an erect ear a little, but looking up to the woman, wondering, remembering her aversion to everything German when he last knew her, in those unfortunate days of war hysteria, so shocking to the son, who loved her so greatly that he could never forget.

"Oh, yes. Kaiser's alone, too, with nothing much but his own woodchopping to do here — " she laughed. But she must not take up too much of a busy man's time. What she wanted to discuss with him was the fire last night and all those poor people — the poor people who insisted upon living out there in their squalid surroundings. She supposed Mr. Rufe knew they had spent the whole day throwing together more shacks to take the place of those burnt, and that the man called Joe was already planning to rebuild the shelterhouse. When she had tried to reason with them, get the lone ones, at least the older, the more helpless, to go to the county farm, where they would be secure and comfortable, they hooted her out of the Addition. Perhaps he could talk to the poor, misguided people.

She had more to say but Hamm wasn't listening beyond that. Poor people, misguided — Yes, that was the way the capital city and its kind would look upon them: the Dillards, an honest workingman with a wife, and the four children who had one great pride, a white-painted WPA privy; Joe, who had fought the war that had driven this woman's son away; the Overtills, good farmers, who had been torn from their earth like sound oak trees by a hurricane; and Old Connie, who walked three miles and scrubbed floors all night to care for a crippled old man who never got to give her his name. Poor people they seemed to Hallie Rufer Hammond, misguided; people for charity —

Suddenly something rose up in Hamm Rufe like a flood that would not be contained, the waters of a cloudburst that swept all the careful little man-made fences away. He found himself on his feet, the dog standing hard against his knee.

"Poor people they seem to you!" he shouted upon the astonished woman. "Misguided, people for charity! Have you forgotten that this was once the land of refuge for such people as these? A refuge from the need and the tyranny of charity? There was a man here once — a man who founded this town, who believed in the preservation of the earth for the common people; a man who fought to the end of his life against the selling out of his state. He was ostracized for his belief in human rights; he had his print shop smashed, his desk rotten-egged for expressing this belief. Fortunately he died before he had to see this town, the city he named for a man whose greatness he could understand, protecting a lot of lawless hoodlums who openly whip and burn and murder, hoodlums that are backed by his own flesh and blood!"

The woman was up, too, now, her eyes angry, but her face controlled.

"You say these things to me, you — you tramp, knowing the man was my father!"

Hamm Rufe bowed his head, and with his hat in his hand he went to the door, the dog still at his heels, squeezing out between his legs, following him down the street. Once the door behind them opened, Hallie Rufer Hammond a dark figure against the light of her home. But if she called there was no answer, and no wavering at all from her dog. And when Hamm finally opened the door of his room, Kaiser pushed in ahead of him, stood waiting for the man's choice of chairs, and stretched himself beside it.

CHAPTER XIII

WINTER seemed to be coming with November this year, the capitol tower standing grey and alone all day long. Often at night it was only a pale, unrooted column rising among moving clouds, sooty black shadows thrown among the stone figures about its top by the cold, steady lightning of the ground beams.

The dampness brought heavy chest colds much earlier than usual, with clots of spit on the morning sidewalks, an unseasonable thinning in school attendance, and a jump in the patent-medicine ads. The city was dull. The big fall weddings were over, the formal season not yet begun. Business had slumped; even the radios were turned off, outwaiting the flow of promises and invectives, for this was the week before election.

By the day of Old Henry's funeral the snow was only a few dirty patches like crumpled wet newspaper where it had been scooped off the walks. But already the northwest wind was blowing again and a few grey clouds rode the horizon, holding off until sunset to spread and cover the earth. Somehow Old Connie had managed to keep her Henry out of the pauper patch. She had a little trouble about his name too. Henry Burns was all she would give the authorities and stuck to that solidly when they tried to browbeat her into admitting that it was a fabrication, and a libelous fabrication if it got into the public records.

"Just wait till I get the money together for a tombstone — Henry Burns is what's going to be cut on it!" she promised them.

There was a nice crowd at the funeral, enough to make Connie fumble at the handkerchief in her water-skinned old hands. Everybody from the Addition was there except Eva Dillard, pretty far along for public appearances, so she sent little Evie and the boys, the baby crying to go too. Hamm and Abigail came with Kaiser tagging the man's heels, and Lew Lewis with two old trucks, the beds full of standing strikers he gathered up at the Labor Temple. Joe of the shelterhouse spoke, not so much of the dead man as of the living. "We lost something the other night, when a man right among us was burnt to death worse than any criminal, worse than I would do to the crumbs in the seams of a flop bum's pants, — a man like you or me, a man who never done anybody any harm, — helpless, crippled. Henry only lost a trap that held him to his bed. We lost something better than bank accounts or full pocketbooks that night, all of us, and we won't get it back until the man who set the fire and all them who's aiding and abetting his kind in our country are caught up with."

Perhaps because of the fall's campaign habits in speech-listening a few clapped, and then, remembering, pushed back behind the others, while the little man from the shelterhouse who believed in God and a savings account said a prayer. They stood with patient heads until he finally finished and then Old Connie went around to take them all by the hand, her pale eyes milky with tears.

Outside the fence, Hamm and Abigail saw a blue coupé parked, with a woman and a youth in it, looking out over the cemetery, watching the little group scatter from Henry's grave. It was Hallie Rufer Hammond, with Jamie beside her, his boyish face pale, his hand gripping the edge of the open window. When Hamm saw them his eyes flooded, and he looked quickly away, out over the bleak fall hillside. Abigail noticed his sorrowed face; she could only keep walking beside him but Kaiser pressed closer to his knee.

There was no mention of Henry's funeral beyond three agate lines among the death notices in the papers, but a protest against a WPA building project out in Herb's Addition made the front page of the *World*. Every right-thinking citizen would protest to his congressman against the fifty houses going up out in that moral sink-hole. Of course, the WPA headquarters denied all knowledge of the houses but if the government wasn't putting them up, who was?

At first Hamm wondered too. The morning after he went to his mother's house, two men in high-laced foreman's boots had come out to find Joe and get a poll of the Addition's workmen. He listened impatiently at first, later with interest. The houses, twenty, not fifty, would be located just above the bottoms, in reach of electricity and water, on soil that would grow a little grass. The houses would be small, most of them with living room, kitchenette, bunk room, closet, shower and toilet; four larger, with kitchens, and two bunk rooms each; all with friendly front stoops and covered with composition shingles to prevent another bad fire. If the management would permit the building, the unit was to become park property, material free, all work on the ground to be done by Addition dwellers, and to start immediately. So Joe left his shelterhouse excavators and came hurrying in for the Overtills and Hamm. Dillard was away on his WPA work, but he was a good hand with level and square and would be glad to help, his wife promised; the children, already tired of their one-room existence, were big-eyed and silent about her.

By one o'clock a truckload of shovels, wheelbarrows, and cement turned in off the highway, followed by a tractor with scraper blade drawing a cement mixer. That evening Hamm stood around with the amazed squatters. Under the direction of the two foremen the ground was already leveled for the foundations, the sites laid out. At seven the next morning trucks brought out the lumber, ready cut, with windows, doors, toilet fixtures, and so on. At noon Hamm found Cash Overtill whistling for the first time in years. "This is going to be fine," the old farmer told him, "and if I hadn't lost my seed corn in the fire I might be getting a chance to try it out, if it wasn't too old — You know we're going to have garden plots on that strip down there along the river — "

Hamm hadn't known. That strip, unless it had changed hands the last twenty years, belonged to the Hammond estate, part of his father's land. So he just grinned and pulled the ear of Kaiser, still sticking close to his side. The Coot came by, not humming this time. He watched the work for a while and then started away.

"Too bad Old Henry couldn't a lived to see the dust a dirty conscience can kick up," he said.

But there were other things than the WPA building shacks to think about by next morning. At every door in Franklin, Grandapolis, too, and the larger towns outstate, was a pink folder, called *In-the-Know*. It was sponsored by forty-five named reporters, including several from the capital city's own *World*. Here, they announced, they were printing information they had failed to get into their papers — mostly things that Hamm and his friends already knew or suspected, such as the financial backing of the Farmers' Association and the *Midwest Farmer* by the Associated Manufacturers of America through their representatives, mostly in the capital city. There was the list of those who attended Cole Dringer's annual fall dinners at Grandapolis, both the general one, and the smaller ones, including even the university staff guests. There was a whole section on Senator Bullard, listing his shares in power holding company stock, with value and date of acquisition, totaling approximately $150,000, underlined with the question: WHERE DID FARM BOY BULLARD GET THE HUNDRED AND FIFTY GRAND? And was that enough for turning against public power development, labor legislation, and tariff and monetary reform?

There were cuts of letters showing that he had a hundred-thousand-a-year job waiting if defeated in the line of duty. Compared to a senator's annual pittance, that was real velvet. Perhaps the voters owed it to their faithful senator to see that he began drawing the salary at once.

The folder took up the one term of Johnson Ryon as governor: the militia out most of the time, against strikers at Grandapolis and at Sheffield, all over the state against the farmers holding up foreclosures; and finished with a cut of his son in a Gold Shirt uniform.

For Dunn Powers the newspapermen dug into the standing obituaries: —

> . . . A man of unusual vision and courage, he missed re-election in 1928, a Republican in a safe Republican year, because, like a man at a drunken party who talks about the morning after, he got up in congress and demanded a halt in government-fostered speculation.
> — Grandapolis *Inquirer*

For Carl Halzer they quoted from the accounts of his term in the legislature: —

> The Bellowing Bull . . . a true man of the people. With the proverbial unwillingness of the horny-handed son of the soil to accept defeat, he won an apparently hopeless battle for a farm mortgage moratorium in spite of all the forces Grandapolis and the capital city could align.
> — Liberty *Standard*

The folder ended by a triple black line: —

WILL THE STUPID INTIMIDATION METHODS OF THE EMPLOYERS AND LAND COMPANIES AGAINST POWERS BUY MORE THAN THEIR MONEY'S WORTH?

An hour after he saw the pink folder, Billie Bamper chartered a plane and headed east, destination unannounced.

But after a few drinks Jack Balton, his state committee man, was telling loud-mouthedly around the club why he went. "The Cole Dringers got to keep themselves out of the public eye — any public eye. The minute the contact man gets conspicuous he's done with the big boys — "

But Billie came puffing back without Cole Dringer's job, or anything else for his expense. "By God, they had the face to say they never heard of me, or Cole Dringer either, but I hear he's being shifted up to Montana, just small potatoes for a man like him, with everybody big up there tied in solid through the copper outfit years ago — "

Farmers clear out to the state line found the pink folders tucked into their mailboxes with the *Midwest Farmer,* or twisted into the wire of their cream-can tags. To many all this election reading matter was confusing. They could understand two things: that the mortgage moratorium had been a good thing where it didn't come too late, and that any company that could take a man's deeded land out from under him sure could be dumping him in the road easy enough if Powers was elected governor, now that the land was theirs.

As soon as Marylin Welles heard of the folder she gathered up half a dozen, threw them back of the seat of her car and cut out on No. 6 for Liberty, where Carl was to speak that noon. He ought to be glad to see her today, or at least the campaign ammunition she was bringing. Her gas foot was heavy with self-contempt. Here she was, following the advice of all the magazine ads; her slip not showing; Teddy Ball wiring invitations for a Caribbean cruise; even Cassie's dumb Yogi trying to sing Spanish love songs to her, and she was tearing out into the country after a dirt farmer with hair wild and bushy as bear grass.

In the cities there was speculation about the action the papers would take against the folder and their insubordinate employees. The editor of the *World* did a little discreet telephoning around to people who might be able to put out a paper. He even called Abigail and Hamm, not saying anything specific, just that there might be "a good opening for an ambitious worker." Neither of them was interested, and by noon the typographical union had rallied to the support of the newsmen. A shut-down the week before election was more than the publishers could face and so there were some wry-mouthed editorials about "the pink sheet from the bed of parlor Reds," and nothing more. Of course, Old Charley Stetbettor ranted against the Communists "controlling our press and papers." But he didn't overlook the possible ground the folder might be cutting away under the feet of Ryon. Now all he needed was something solid in the hand to offer the voter, so he came out for a $30 old-age pension every Thursday.

That caused a flurry over at the Republican headquarters, and another back-door visit from Billie Bamper, who had an unpleasant half hour with Hallie Rufer Hammond yesterday, calling for smooth talk and promising. What in hell did they want, these bosses of his? Work with Stet, the men tell him, and he does; then a damned woman like the Hammond comes horning in, with her "We want nothing of a dangerous demagogue like Stetbettor."

Billie found the rub doctor set. Thirty dollars he was promising, on the advice of La Belle Rose. Of course the legislature had the say on pensions, but who stopped to think about things like that election time? By evening all the Townsend clubs of the state were endorsing Charley Stet, disapproving, as their public statement put it, of his radicalism, but applauding his economic understanding.

"Understanding, hell — " Billie complained, wiping his bare pink head as he thought of Hallie Rufer Hammond. "If that bastard polls enough of the wheelchair vote from Ryon, the radical element among the farmers and laborers may elect Powers. Something's got to be done."

It was. By next evening every local-owned truck slipping past the pickets carried the placard: —

RYON

FOR GOVERNOR

$30 EVERY WEDNESDAY

OLD-AGE PENSION

The day after Marylin brought the pink folders up, Carl stopped at Hamm's new shack. He had it put up himself on the old site, just like the other except that the walls were fireproof shingle instead of tar paper, the books under the windows were gone, and the picture from over the fireplace.

It was about Stephani that Carl came in, to speak to Hamm of her if he could, and the pink folder too, of course. Marylin found him at Liberty yesterday. Even the old Indian in a lumberwagon on Main Street stood up to whip his ponies to the curb as the long car ran the traffic light. The town marshal came yelling from his office, waving his arms in the swirl of dust. "Flaggin' the Streamliner?" the loafers inquired of him with serious faces, and then slapped their thighs with laughing as the marshal ducked back into the firehouse. "Right-hand drive — an import — " they told each other, getting up to stretch their legs and follow the car down towards the high-school auditorium where it turned off. Carl walked right into Marylin as she was getting out. The loafers all stopped to see the pretty girl with the grey fox bustle on her suit. They snickered, flipped up their coat-tails, mincing slowly past. Marylin held out a handful of pink folders.

"Or shall I give them to you less publicly — " she asked, "so's not to queer you with the proletariat — as your Russian lady campaigner would probably call them."

There was no use pretending that he didn't know who she meant, so he just tried to grin it off as he looked through the folder that he saw the evening before. "It was nice of you to bother stopping by with these — "

And he was sorry but he couldn't take her to lunch — had to talk to the Farmers' Union this noon. No time afterward either, not even for coffee with one of the capital city Welleses, for he had a meeting on. The girl got casually back into the car, started it. "Oh, of course," she said, lighting her cigarette, "an important meeting. I seem to be forgetting the weakness men have for Slavic women — "

Carl didn't hear the roar of laughing from the crowd gathering about the strange car. He was thinking of Marylin's father, the Cobby who had a fondness for a Slavic woman too, and this gleaming-haired daughter who could make light of it. Suddenly she was like the tinfoil he used to save for the hot winter stove. A fine big ball would shrivel and blacken with a great stench and smoke and leave one tiny droplet of metal; sound, and bright, but very tiny.

So now he had come in to talk of Stephani, which should have been easy enough, with Hamm asking about her the first thing. Had Carl seen her, and how was it all going for both of them? So the farmer sat bowed over his clasped hands and told the matter-of-fact things there were to say. Stephani had been from Franklin up the Grand to Stockholm and Minerva. Of her work he knew little, for it seemed to be her way to get others to talk of what they were doing. Hamm nodded; yes, it had always been so.

It seemed she was shocked at the great bins of wheat, the cribs of golden corn, the elevators full at every siding, and everywhere school children in patched and ragged clothes, some with lard on their bread, for the cream must be sold against the mortgage or the rent.

Yes, it would be new to her, and shocking, for the farm slums of the middle west got little publicity. But the election, how was it going?

As to be expected, Carl thought. To educate a horse was a long, slow process; to scare him took only one loud yell and a waving of the arms. The public was like a horse. "What wouldn't we all give for one good man able to sway a crowd like the old-timers tell me Billy Bryan could — "

Yes, that was the need here, and it would be long unfilled. Smart young Ohio lawyers weren't moving into trans-Mississippi capital towns any more, as Bryan did to Lincoln. The current was running the other way now. Perhaps, as Abigail said the other evening, they must look towards labor, or the farm. Carl wasn't doing so bad, Hamm pointed out. "All you lack is rolling words. You have the ideas, and people will follow you. Complete strangers followed you into the muzzles of cocked rifles last Labor Day. The words will come."

"Even if you were right, it would be too late," he said wearily, pushing his hands through his thick hair like through the fur of a shaggy dog. "Much too late."

If only Stephani had been of Kanewa, he said. He believed she could have done it. She could rouse both labor and the farmers; rouse them to intelligent action. Out at Minerva she went to one of the Farmers' Association meetings at a schoolhouse. It was packed, mostly with patched-pants hard-ups and a sprinkling of politicians wearing coats. When some of the old fellows got to heckling the strong-arm boys from down at Franklin who were running the show, they tried to shut them up with parliamentary tricks; make them feel like fools. But Stephani hopped up on a desk, and in a minute she had the crowd with her, turning the meeting into a good old debate right from the middle of the floor; handling the lot like an old freighter an eight-horse team in a thunderstorm. Even Harv Ellers, who just happened to be hunting in the vicinity, as he called it, and intensely interested in getting the farmer organized. She let the old fellows ask questions until the Franklin boys tried to stop her by getting some roughhousers to tip her off the desk. So half a dozen of the grey-haired sod busters grabbed Harv and threw him out by the seat of the pants. Purdy Gilson didn't wait for his turn, just jumped through a window and cut off across the broken country afoot in the night. That Stephani, she was the one. She could do it.

Suddenly Carl realized where his enthusiasm had carried him, and stopped, a deep flush rising from his collar to the roots of his bright hair, his eyes dark on his clumsy hands. But Hamm didn't seem to notice. "Why don't you get her to speak for you, places where she's going anyway; not formally, or they'll raise the old Red issue again, but just getting up unannounced like that, in that old spelling-school forum method? The Association investigations have probably blown up for this election year anyway, with the pink folder out — "

"I've done some thinking about asking you to help on my talk for Grandapolis, and I'll even try one here for the League of Women Voters, if you say the word — "

Oh, he'd be fine with those who'd come out at Grandapolis, the workers. And here the Women Voters were the best group of the town, much better informed than their husbands. Carl would do well with them, even if loyalty made them vote capital city. So he went away without telling Hamm what he must say; that the struggle for justice had suddenly become one wide as all humanity and greater than even life itself. And this had happened because a girl in Poland once saw her straw tick run fresh red from bayonets seeking a wounded soldier she had hidden inside; because a woman with wide cheekbones and dark hair sweeping up from the temples had suddenly made it so.

Saturday afternoon the gunmen of a strikebreaking truck saw an old sedan parked along the highway near the Lasseur bridge. Thinking it was a signal post for the pickets a hundred yards beyond, they poured bullets upon the two bobbing heads in the back. When the wife of Sid Dawson, cartoonist of the Grandapolis *News*, returned to her car with a box of late fall leaves to decorate for a church supper, she found her small twin boys dead, the tops of their heads blown off by rifle fire.

The Capital City *World* called this a bad break for the operatives; it would make a fine talking point for those sentimentalists who favored the continued misguidance of labor by outside agitators. Sunday the angry *News* replied with the stories of a dozen eyewitnesses, pictures of the dead children, the striker that was shot and the two who were wounded as the angry pickets rolled the truck over the bank to a sand bar and beat the four gunmen, two already identified as ex-convicts, almost to death. There were pictures of the inside of the sheet-steel carrying body too, with comfortable seats and slits for rifles and machine guns.

The whole state, even the national press and the radio commentators, was aroused, and by Sunday night it was clear that the supreme court would have to act on the anti-picketing law. Monday morning the earliest clerk at the chamber of commerce found the strikers already gathering at the temple. They were very quiet, mostly settling on the steps as soon as they came; silent, motionless, the chewing, smoking, and friendly talk of the Labor Day gathering almost gone. The faces of the men were leaner; their clothes loose with nine more weeks of striking for a contract the operatives of the surrounding states had signed long ago; the shorter driving hours already credited with the big drop in night highway accidents. Yet here they were, kept sitting on their bony asses, while outside firms were taking over all the long-haul trucking of the state; the holdout operatives not only losing money every day but customers for the future.

Quietly the men took their places when the placards were given out. Once more Lew Lewis, not so broad or so gay as back in September, started up Philadelphia Avenue with his flag. Nora watched at the window for him, waving her apron, her eyes always afraid since the night Lew was carried in, a thin line of blood leaking to the walk behind him.

Slowly, very solemnly the strikers marched into the capitol rotunda with its imported pillars of marble about them and high overhead the frieze of the Peoples of the World. Their overalls were faded, patched, swaying loose as sacks around them as they moved down the stone corridors past the supreme court. Above them the marble railing was dark with people, mostly women, products of pioneer ancestors, drawn to these men who still found a cause worth the starving.

The decision came, five of the seven against the anti-picketing law.

"When we have a governor strong enough to enforce such a law, it won't be needed," Billie Bamper said in his talk to the pre-election dinner for the Republican candidates at the City Club.

Monday night there was the big Republican torchlight parade, with free dancing and free coffee for everybody at the fieldhouse after the speaking. The program was in charge of the Young Republicans Club, Harold Welles, chairman; the parade in four sections, each with a topless old car full of torch holders, red fire in front, the back ones pine sticks dipped in tar, flaming and smoking like in the old days. It started out beyond the capitol somewhere, a little late because Dix, the Republican candidate for senator, thought he should lead the congressional section instead of Bullard, a Democrat and really an outsider here. But when the parade came down the avenue, Senator Bullard was directly behind the torch car, standing to his full chunky height and bowing to the Franklinites. Dix, in the second car, was so unnoticed that he sat down after the first block and stared straight ahead as though he were in the line by mistake.

There were statehouse and county sections, each with a band

and a torch car, ending up with the Sons of the Veterans' Drum Corps for the Legion vote, and a slogan-covered old frat taxi full of tarred sticks blazing and smoking the eyes. It was exciting enough to those who could not remember the torchlight parades of the nineties, with their wild and jubilant hope born of desperation. The night was mellow as May; the avenue crowded. At the fieldhouse shocks of corn stood in the entrance and on the stage, with fat golden pumpkins around them; the ushers were extra men from the Handee garage and a few yardmen from the Ridge, in overalls; and the reserved sections were roped off with strips of red calico, to show the laborer and the farmer who was taking cognizance of their existence this election.

Usually the better people didn't go to hear candidates, for, after all, they knew where their men stood. But tonight they were setting examples, as Josina Black explained to her nieces, who had made other plans. And when so few of the lesser seats were filled, she pointed out how urgent was the need of the public stand that right-thinking people were taking.

When it was clear that the audience was all there, the chairman arose, read a stack of greetings through the microphone, and then spread into an exalted introduction of the two speakers of the evening as the saviors of America. Bullard spoke first, then Ryon, but both demanded a re-establishment of rugged individualism, with business freed from repressive taxation, labor from union domination, the farmer from government control, and a balanced budget to bring a return of Coolidge prosperity to all. Nothing of the irrigation and power projects, the $30-every-Wednesday pension, or any other current problem.

There was some muttering among the ushers, but nothing loud enough to call for attention, and when Ryon at last sat down, the applause was warm but not raucous, softened considerably by the genteel patter of gloved fingers. The few with dark, outdoor faces and hands shelled hard in toil had

melted away long before the end of the Bullard speech. No one
waited for dancing or for coffee. Josina Black couldn't find her
gardener and Cassie was disturbed too. The Yogi had slipped
out for a cigarette and apparently left her to walk through
these people of her town alone. One's children always seemed
to be away nowadays, she complained to Eloise Johnson, who
was sympathetic enough. She didn't need to find out about
Dachel, who had been set up in a room by one of Cassie's
maids. Only ten dollars a month, but it had all a poet really
needed, he told the girl — inspiration. Next thing she would
be stealing food for him.

Out on the avenue most of the people kept waiting after
the torchlight parade passed, holding their places for another
show — Charley Stetbettor's America for Americans parade,
led by Old Charley in his white sound truck with a hillbilly
band on the platform broadcasting their songs from the loud
speaker. That was about all, except the astrologer's car and
several jallopies full of yelling boys and young men with
Christian Crusader buttons in their lapels. But the crowd
followed down the avenue in a double current, to jam and
mill about the old auditorium only designed to hold a thousand or so.

"Discrimination against a true American!" Old Charley
Stet roared over the crowd, just to let his listeners know he
was for a comfortable seat for every patched pair of pants.
Of course he hadn't expected to get the fieldhouse the night
before election, and the real heat and hoarseness of his anger
was being saved for Dunn Powers, a turncoat Republican,
a Red in league with Russia and their Communist labor agitators.

"Standing up talking about saving your schools from the
fists of the absentee landlord!" he shouted. "What Red
Powers plans is to put a Stalin primer into the innocent white
hand of every boy and girl of our blessed state, to revaluate

your property and tax it so high you'll be glad to give it, kit and caboodle, to the Reds!" Then, looking towards the wings, and dropping his voice as though with caution, he told them he was going to say what might make him the first casualty of the Jew-Communists. He was going to say what no one else dared say — that if Dunn Powers got into the governor's chair, there would be an Esther, Esther Powers, ruling over the fair womanhood of this state.

"And where did you hear the name of Esther before?" he demanded dramatically of the confused faces before him. "From the Bible at your mother's knee, that's where. There she is, Esther, the tricking Jew husband stealer, the lewd seductress of a noble king!" pointing to his cartoonist's drawing of a beak-nosed, evil-eyed witch. Violently he tore the sheet down, jumped on it with both feet, ground it with his squat heel as the crowd yelled, stamped, and laughed.

When it was over and the American flag picture was saluted and passed out to a pretty blonde girl, Carl Halzer arose from the crowd to speak to the independent rally.

"Who are you? — Who?" Old Charley Stet demanded, climbing back to the stage, turning with his question not to the man but to the crowd.

"Ah, let him talk, Stet," somebody called from the back. "He's O.K."

"Yeh, let's hear him," another urged, and so Old Charley's peace-keepers, in a row across the front, sat down reluctantly as Carl, with Hamm and Abigail, went up on the stage.

Most of the crowd had come particularly to see Stet put on his show, the old people among them to hear the promise of thirty dollars every Thursday. But as they pushed out, here and there one looked back curiously toward the tall, shock-headed farmer, stopped, finally settling into a seat to listen. The auditorium was noisy but the Bull of Bashan still bellowed well, and as word of his talk spread out along the street, more and more slipped in, until there was no hole left, not even right behind the row of Christian Crusaders.

Almost at once Hamm saw that Carl couldn't stick to the speech they had planned for tonight, but wisely dropped back into the expressions of his neighbors down the Little Grand. He held up one of the pink folders, told them to read it, to see how they were being sold out by their fellow citizens. "You know," he roared so the old balconies echoed, "you know what happened at the Lasseur bridge Saturday, an armored car with baby-killing gunmen used against labor. You know what they are doing out on the farms. You have it straight from the company farm reps — threatening to shut down all the places if Powers is elected governor, the renters thrown on the road.

"That's bluff, plain damn bluff, and you know it. The K.I.C. or the rest can't afford to let their investments lay idle, any more than the factory owners who threatened to shut down back in 1936. Nobody gives you anything in this world unless he has to. You got food for your starving children by walking out of the stores with full baskets you couldn't pay for back in 1933. Oh, you were dumped in jail, sure, but they couldn't jail five thousand of you and so you got relief. The same year when you farmers were losing your little patches of ground, you took your pitchforks to the foreclosings, and you got the mortgage moratorium. Try taking the pitchforks to the ballot boxes tomorrow and see what you can get — All of you, — laborer, farmer, reliefer, clerk or little business man being squeezed out, every last one of you, — and see what you can get; for when the common people walk together the ground has to shake!"

By this time six policemen were coming up the aisle. Once more the Bellowing Bull was taken to jail — incitement to violence this time.

They took Hamm and Abigail along. The police judge frowned upon the man from Herb's Addition. "You're getting mixed in a mighty lot of trouble here lately," he warned. Hamm thought idly of telling him why it was so, but there was no longer much joy in the contemplation of a capital city officer falling on his face before the great name of Hammond.

Abigail, the outstate realist, was more direct. She looked with naïve awe upon the officer, told him impulsively that she just had news which he as a civic-spirited citizen would like. Dubiously the man chewed at his surreptitious little cud of tobacco as he took the telegram she laid before him, glanced at it, and then read it carefully.

"Congratulations!" he said, reaching across the desk for her hand. "I hope you will insist upon the picture being made here where something of the spirit of the pioneers still lives on — "

Abigail let him make his speech out, thanked him gratefully for the good advice and got herself and Hamm escorted grandly to the door. On the street he stopped her. "What on earth did you show that man?"

"Oh, I just happened to have the telegram confirming the sale of *Anteroom for Kingmakers* to Goldwyn."

By the time they got to Abigail's house the judge had done his duty by the town. Two reporters were leaning against the walls outside her door, Grandapolis was on the telephone, and in fifteen minutes Carl was with them. Turned loose, just like that. Probably afraid to make a martyr of him.

Oh, no, afraid it might annoy the city's noted citizen, Dr. Abigail Allerton, Hamm said and told him about the telegram. They laughed a little over that, not much, for there would be little reason for joy tomorrow night, with Ryon governor, and calling his militia out against the strikers, Wagner act or no Wagner act.

By this time the better people of the town had all moved from the fieldhouse to Josina Black's Norman living room.

In spite of the empty chairs at the rally there was the quiet confidence among them of a job well done outstate; where it counted, the men told each other over their glasses. Somebody mentioned the strikers' placards of the morning, the supreme court decision.

"The courts have been degraded by yielding to a capitol-steps pressure group," was the opinion Harv Ellers expressed, hoping to regain some of the ground lost by his son's hotel party.

Yes, degraded, but, thank God, only temporarily, Susan Welles said, Josina agreeing emphatically, thankfully. Hallie Rufer Hammond wasn't there to express her opinion and some wondered if she might have gone down to hear the bush-headed farmer, maybe with Marylin Welles. But it wasn't a joke when somebody told of hearing that the WPA really wasn't putting up the shacks out at Herb's Addition, that Hallie was paying for the material, cut at cost in the Tyndale Lumber Company.

"One of our people buying wholesale from that damn Jew?" Bamper demanded, taking up Joe Willper's way of talking.

There was a front-page write-up of Abigail's sale to the movies in the morning paper, with a good picture of her holding the book in her hand, "an enthralling story of which the old Frontier House in the capital city is the main character." By noon there was a big sign up before the hotel: —

FRONTIER HOUSE
LOCATION FOR NEW MOVING PICTURE
ANTEROOM FOR KINGMAKERS
SHOOTING TO BEGIN SOON

Because the telephone company put the howler on Abigail's phone she had to hang up the receiver, but a wad of cleaning tissue between the bells kept them to a soft buzzing that she could ignore. And in the evening paper was an item from the university: Abigail Allerton, frontier history teacher, granted indefinite leave of absence for writing, was being recalled for second-semester work. "Dr. Allerton, who has just sold a historical book to the moving pictures, may find her classes popular," the paper added. Abigail tore it in two and took it out to the incinerator.

That night a pretty girl came to her door. It was Cobby's little Hattie. A confession magazine had written for her story. They would give her a lot of money, five hundred dollars, and if she wouldn't sell they would write the story anyway. It was to warn other girls, they said. But it wasn't she who had a bad life; it was poor Cobby, who was so like the rabbit in the box traps her brother used to set. It didn't kill him, or even hurt him while he ate the carrots, but scared him bad when he found there was no door to get out. Anyway, she could not have things about her Cobby in a magazine for people to read and laugh.

So Abigail wrote a letter on some university stationery she had left from her job. That would settle the magazine. Still the girl didn't go, talking a while of other things, of shows and her little beauty shop. "They all come and look at me like I am something freakish — " But what she really minded was the side line people expected beauty shops to carry, not only contraceptives but other things "for — for perverts," the girl finished, blushing, her white skin the swift, shy red of a prairie rose.

There was evidently still more on her mind, and finally that came out, too. Harold Welles and his lot were bothering around. He was stopping his car across the walk at the intersections when she came along, trying to get her to go with him.

"What I should do — ?" she asked. "Our boys, the Polish boys, they saw him once, and they want to gang him, but that is bad — "

Election day came in cloudy over all of Kanewa, with an afternoon drizzle that started in the northwest counties and spread down along the rivers. By ten at night it was snowing in Franklin, the wind rising, and by morning all the east and west highways were blocked, with only the doctors shoveling through. "A snowstorm shells out kids like a hot day does your beans," one of them told a seed-grower up near Stoddard. Two days later most of the trains were running again, the paved highways deep cuts between the ridges of snow thrown out by the plows. The vote was slow coming in, and the victory cake in the Ryon refrigerator was getting pretty stale.

Franklin, of course, went Republican, except for the sen-ate, with Bullard well in the lead. A strong independent vote from the middle wards put Charley Stet up close to Ryon for the governorship, even on the Ridge. "The Grand Old Party's sure shot to hell from the inside," Dix and Ryon admitted to each other as they ordered up more Scotch for the long wait. Charley Stetbettor showed no uneasiness. "The stars never fail," he told the capitol reporter as he took his astrologer on a tour of the governor's suite. It would do, with extra locks and a guard at the doors. The mansion he called an old shack as he tramped from attic to basement. "Burn like a tinder-box. I'll put up a fitting stone building, with a deck for machine guns," he told the guide.

Plump La Belle Rose, puffing alongside, laughed to show that the doctor was joking.

As the middle county precincts came in Powers climbed a little, held the lead for the governorship for two days, the operatives hurrying to call another meeting with the striking truckers. Bullard weakened in the river counties, the con-servative vote going to Dix as at least not openly for the power companies, the rest to Halzer as an irrigation man. Thursday evening the gathering at Abigail's was gay over the grand protest vote Carl was drawing. But Hamm seemed to be getting more and more silent as the three-way tie for the governorship lengthened. It seemed incredible that people of his state would vote for the demagogic rub doctor; people of his city, of the Ridge, perhaps even his own mother and brother. He couldn't forget the warning of the pink folder in his pocket: —

WILL THE STUPID INTIMIDATION METHODS OF
THE EMPLOYERS AND LAND COMPANIES AGAINST
POWERS BUY MORE THAN THEIR MONEY'S WORTH?

Crowds for the homecoming football game began to move into Franklin from Thursday on, the gamblers, souvenir sellers, cripples, pencil men, and extra women — all in early, like mountain lions settling themselves for the coming of the herds at a waterhole. There was another lot of early arrivals from as far out as Wild Horse Plains, the K. U. alum' scalping squad, and they made no secret of the situation: either Coach Bowdon won this game against the murdering Mickmen, or he was out on his fanny. Kanewa wasn't nursing along a losing football squad forever, and the Buffaloes who fifteen years ago were candidates for a Big Ten membership weren't to be called Beef Bulls by sports writers without somebody getting it in the pants. So they gathered at the Buffalo Hotel, kept the 'hops busy dragging up bottles, called up a few handy women, and talked big. First it had been the eligibility alibi that Chuck Bowdon trotted out, and so they put the heat on the chancellor, got Hipp Dunkin back in center and Loco Rosky packing the ball. But still the team didn't click.

There was inside dope about the Mickmen flying around the hotel too: rumors of practice injuries, a break in team spirit, fraternity politics, and general overconfidence; but still not much Kanewa money came out of hiding. Down at the Labor Temple Lew Lewis was putting a couple of dollars, all he could raise, on his team, but none of the others would risk anything.

"Hell, what's the good of high odds if you lose?" they argued.

Friday night Greek Row was blocked for three hours with cars and pedestrians, all trying to see the houses decorated for homecoming. There was the usual showing of floodlighted cardboard figures in purple moleskin and buffalo horns, tearing to victory across fraternity lawns, or Mickmen trying vainly to ride bucking, stampeding buffaloes. Before the glassbrick paneling of the Siggery a herd of the snorting, wildnosed animals was trampling the Mickmen, tossing them up to lose their masks, showing caricature Pole, Negro, and Jewish faces under them, with a twenty-foot sign across the second story: "Win for Kanewa and America!" That, everybody said, would win the frat prize for the Sigs, anyway.

The sororities always were a little more restrained and literary. On one lawn Red Riding Hood, a scarlet-caped buffalo with a basket of tricks and a skinning knife, was flirting along with a Mickman, a poor little sheep in a mangy-looking wolf hide. The Kay Dees, with their floodlighted white house that reminded Hamm of the Kress building behind a lawn, had a whole string of buffaloes, all curly-lashed Ferdinands, smelling the flowers of the lost ball games: Kansas, Pitt, Minnesota, Nebraska, but the one nearing the pansy labeled Mickmen was tossing his tail and snorting two steady beams of red light from his nose.

As the cops at the intersections whistled and yelled, and the cars wormed slowly by, the houses along the Row filled with students and grads, the men shouting greetings and loud insults to newcomers, the women holding their party dresses high as they dodged through the traffic to the walks still lined with dirty snow. One after another the orchestras struck up inside, and the homecoming parties were under way, as though there were no double tie in the Kanewa election returns at all.

In Abigail's apartment Hamm Rufe sat at the radio waiting for word on the governorship, concern deep as a hatchet
stroke between his brows, the dog at his knee almost forgotten. The three-day seesaw had seemed unbelievable enough,
with Ryon up and then Powers. Now the roads were breaking out on Wild Horse Plains and towards the Indian Hills —
the drouth sections where the land companies had taken most
of the farms the last ten years. Voters who had seen homes
they owned go could well believe they'd lose the leased ones
if Powers was elected. Unwilling to vote for Militia Ryon,
as they called him, they went independent, and as the far
precincts came in Charley Stet began to climb fast.

While Abigail understood the seriousness of this thing, she
felt that Hamm Rufe must be in some personal danger, for
today he had brought her a leather case of papers he wanted
put in a safe place, with a list of the contents and instructions for her in case anything happened to him.

"A joint safe-deposit box?" Abigail asked.

No, in her name, so there would be no red tape about getting to it at once, particularly to his identification papers.

So she took the case down to the bank and put it far back
behind the documents and evidences of her book, wondering
that Hamm didn't choose Stephani. It couldn't be anger with
her, not even over Carl — that wasn't like the quiet, generous
man on her hassock, hands in his greying hair, listening for
the reports and hearing nothing at all of the symphony between.

It was true that Hamm was troubled about Stephani. He
knew that it wasn't right to let her go without a cent and
yet anything else would mean announcing himself as a Hammond, with all the capital city mess brought down upon her,
and Carl too. So the will and the identifications in the deposit
box had to remain the best thing.

At last Abigail went to the kitchen to put on the coffeepot.

Freed, momentarily, of the necessity of making words that were like an overlarge drink of water to his throat tonight, Hamm looked up. Before him, through the wide, unblinded window the capitol tower stood high against the far darkness. Down there, at its foot, was a statue of Franklin, heavy lids shading the tired eyes. Behind him, carved in stone, were his wise words on the place of property in society, and about him lay the grey, sooty snow of the capitol grounds, unbroken by any tracks except those of a timid cottontail that dared come out only with the cover of dusk.

By Saturday morning news floated thick as fall cobwebs over the city. It seemed Marylin Welles got tired of her hog farmer and ran away with her mother's Yogi, who was really a Mexican cabaret singer wanted for a string of no-fund checks from California to the Franklin National. There was talk about Harold, too, going around with a black eye and a cut lip, and Hattie Krasinski taking the daybreak train for New York, to visit her cousin Gerta, who was studying design there. Almost no one recalled that ten weeks ago Gerta was Miss Kanewa, and flying off to Atlantic City. Some said that Harold's fight was really with Joe Willper, that ex-convict from Stone House.

"Yeh, if old Charley Stet gets in, the Ridgers won't be finding the Americanism boys so willing to suck their asses," the Coot predicted, and today there was no humming.

At Johnson Ryon's the victory cake went into the garbage, for the precincts still out were mostly in the Calder and the Minerva regions, where, as the *Thunderbolt* reminded its readers, he was named Militia Ryon by the foreclosed farmers. Of course there were still the thousand or so votes from Grandapolis but Ryon knew what that meant. The returns were held up to swing a tie vote the right way, his way in 1932. Today he wasn't forgetting the votes for Old Stet from the Ridge at Franklin. So the cake went out. . . .

It took two hours to get a bite of lunch in the homecoming crowd Saturday. Even Hammond's first floor was buzzing a little, in a dignified sort of way, of course, the scrawlings in the guest book near the west entrance the only real evidence of the immoderate world outside.

At Tiefel's and at Penney's the crowds tore the visiting fat women from their friends; at the dime stores they stalled around the souvenir stands, only the smell of water-soaked hot dogs and pale mustard moving freely. But in the clear, sharp air outside people hurried along with blankets and cushions or comforted themselves with a reassuring pat at the hip flask. Pretty girls wearing huge yellow chrysanthemums centered with K's of purple chenille dragged their escorts along, laughing, greeting the followers of the Mickmen with their white flowers and pennant canes, in by special streamliner that morning. Towards one o'clock the university band came down the avenue from their serenade at the Franklin House, the opponents' hotel. Brasses gleaming in the sun they played "Land of Kanewa March" as they headed the regular movement towards the stadium, traffic all one-way, four cars abreast, the crowds of the walks following along with them, down the flag-hung avenue; here and there a group singing as they walked.

By noon the outlying counties were coming in fast and as Carl Halzer moved toward the lead his room at the hotel began to fill, many with a right to be there: Victor Heeley, spokesman for those who came to Carl's tent at the fairground ten weeks ago, booked all his campaign talks since; the labor and farm representatives, with a swarm of job seekers already outside the door. Not until Bullard sent congratulations did Carl believe anything of it. Almost the same minute Stephani burst in, stopping at the door, suddenly shy and reserved before this man who towered a whole head above all the rest.

"I'm very glad," she said.

But Carl couldn't let her go. Following her clear down the hall, he made foolish talk. They must celebrate, hunt up Hamm and Abigail; tell everybody the news.

By the time they got through the crowd to the Co-op Hamm was gone. The shack was empty too, the door open, the room full of new smoke. And on the couch lay an envelope addressed to them both, two football tickets with a note: —

> Congratulations, and a long and happy
> life together, my two most beloved.
>
> HAMM

Carl read it through a second time, holding it in both his hands, and when he looked to Stephani his eyes were dark with uncertainty and pain.

"He can mean it — to be?" he asked in wonder.

Yes. Hamm had talked to her. It was his generous wish.

Once more the man looked to his hand with the slip of paper, saw how strangely it trembled, and then to the woman before him; her warm brown skin, her eyes dark as shadowed water. Slowly, the color draining from his face, the young farmer gathered her into his arms, and because he had never held anyone so, he could not know how powerful they were.

In the offices of the Red Line Conveyor Company the truck operatives and the union reps were to sign the Twelve State agreement at last. It was reported ready every day this week, but with the governorship ties undecided there were delays, day after day, the operatives stalling. If they got Militia Ryon, the negotiations would collapse. Otherwise they'd sign. It was a hell of a note.

While representatives of the two sides sat across the table from each other in the Red Line offices, a couple dozen finks loafed in the high-fenced old Hammond warehouse lot across from the capitol, where material had been stored during the erection. They were watching the fifty loaded trucks impounded during the negotiations and holding themselves ready to lead a run through the pickets any instant the conference might break down. In the meantime they listened to the game on the radio, turned too low for the pickets to hear.

Outside the strikers kept up their slow march but they were uneasy, watching the street for a messenger from the conference, listening for the telephone bell in the warehouse. Lew Lewis walked along the curb beside them, talking football, sure of his team, his line; confident as though he were in center position instead of Dunkin. If Loco Rosky ever got loose with that ball it was all over for the Mickmen. "You watch — it'll be all over."

Somebody came putting up the avenue on a motorcycle, swung his leg down. No, no signing yet, he said, but it was Buffalo seven to the Mickmen's six at the quarter, and the Hippo just coming in.

"My God, what is the coach trying to do — ? With the Hippo out of center you can drive a Red Line truck through and turn it!" Lew cried.

Yeh, maybe — but they hadn't done so bad, seven to six, favor of the Buffaloes —

All week there had been an uneasiness in the Tyndale home, Old Samuel at the office as usual, with perhaps a little more long-distance telephoning. Margaret went about getting her hair done, taking her turn at ladies' day at the club, planning for guests for the homecoming dinner tonight. Mollie, too, was going around more, even with the annulment suit coming up Monday, now that Parson Sam was legally the Marryin' Man, and her departure for England set for Monday evening. But it had been put off so often that she couldn't believe it would happen, and besides, there was a note from Burt that morning, a very dear one, and small enough to slip into the pocket of her suit when it wasn't folded in the palm of her glove.

They were all going to the game but at the last minute Samuel had business on, very urgent, he said, homecoming or no homecoming. So he kissed his women and waved them on with their guests, promising to come for the last half if he could manage. From his office he got the Associated Press, saw that things were going fast, and put through a dozen rush calls. He got the answer to one in five minutes — Burt Parr, panting a little with hurry and embarrassment, come to stand before the walnut desk of Samuel Tyndale.

"This day is an unfortunate one for us all, our state and our nation," Mollie's father said with slow formality, his eyes upon the intricate pattern of light in the glass paperweight he was pushing around with his stubby fingers. Burt nodded miserably. Yes, indeed, the man went on, an unfortunate day, but it had brought them all to a new realization of the true values of life, to a reappreciation of old and tried friendships —

Suddenly Samuel stopped, looked up into the boy's dark, disturbed eyes, and came around the desk. "You and Mollie love each other," he said, as quietly as though he spoke of egg gradings, or of sparrow nests in one of his barns. "Today we are glad that this is so, for now it is children like you, with the blood and the heart for battle, who must rescue what we have lost." He stuffed a roll of money into the boy's pocket. "Mollie is at the stadium, west stands, you know. Get her out of Kanewa before they are upon us. Take her car, get her across the state line the shortest way and call me tomorrow night. If we are not here, try Omaha."

" — Omaha — !" The boy's face was appalled. "So it's Old Charley Stet and the Gold Shirts — " he said, as though somehow guilty. Suddenly he thought of something else. " — And England — ?"

The small man drew himself up straight. "England is not what it was when we Tyndales knew it, or there could have been no Chamberlain and no Munich to help make this possible here — "

Slowly Burt started away. But suddenly Samuel Tyndale's meaning came to him and in one moment the whole misery of the last ten weeks was gone, his boy face like swift sun upon a shadowed hill. With no words he could make he grasped the hand of this old friend from up on the Wakoon and then loped out through the empty offices, calling for the elevator to wait, wait!

When the boy was gone Old Samuel answered his telephone that seemed to have been ringing a long time. It was Stockholm calling; his brother. Yes, it had come, Samuel said. Martial law and worse; they must be ready for anything. But Mollie at least was safe.

For two days Hamm had watched the trend of the returns from the drouth counties. The plan of the Ridgers was working; the tenants were afraid to vote for Powers, but refusing to accept Militia Ryon, were going independent. It gave Carl his incredible victory but probably at the price of an incredible defeat for them all. The swing towards Charley Stet had set in strong.

As Hamm waited at his little radio in the Co-op basement he was like the rabbit in the trap of Polish Hattie's young brother, with the only door closing. Suddenly he could stand it no longer. Calling to his assistant, Hamm tossed the man the keys. "We'll probably be shutting down the Co-op permanently tonight anyway — " he said, and cut off across the bottoms towards his shack, Kaiser sneaking along through the weeds, sensing that this was no time for intimate walking with his man.

When Hamm reached the shack he saw that the couch was bare, the white envelope he had left there gone, Stephani gone. And now at last he was empty, empty as grey night, and with his hands over his scarred face he dropped to the edge of the couch.

Almost at once the telephone rang, the voice of Hallie Rufer Hammond asking for Halzer. It was most imperative. Jamie had just called from downtown that the governorship was conceded to Stetbettor; the strike negotiations had collapsed and the Gold Shirts were heading for the truck lot across from the capitol. There would be trouble.

Oh, yes, trouble — and scurrying around to find the tall farmer, scurrying like parasites, like cockroaches with the heat under their bellies, now they could see what they had done.

Hamm's scar began to throb. "You try stopping the trouble!" he shouted into the telephone. But the line was dead. It was as well. Nobody could stop it now, not Carl Halzer, or anybody.

Suddenly the scar cleared, cooled. Swiftly Hamm dug under his couch, brought out the revolver he had never used. Dropping it into his pocket he closed the door on the whimpering Kaiser and started down towards the capitol tower, gleaming high and aloof in the November sun that cast only the faintest shadows on the frieze of the Peoples of the World around the top.

At the bridge over the Little Grand he met a trucker coming to look for Halzer. Hamm shook his head. Carl couldn't help them today; that time was past. So they started to town together, the driver stepping up the rattly old truck, shouting over the noise that the Grandapolis bottom votes had come in but thrown no election this year — with Bullard defeated too bad, and Stet already in by the tricks of the capital city outfit. He'd took over the statehouse, had a man at the radio station and the newspapers, the national guards called out, and Harold Welles and Frankie Doover under arrest. Hell had broke loose sure. At least that's what the trucker'd heard.

Philadelphia Avenue was very quiet, even for the emptiness of game time. Once or twice there were far chants and shoutings, from the stadium, Hamm knew. Finally they rose into a long, high cheering and then settled to steady waves of crowd noises that seemed to follow them up the avenue. Towards the capitol square the traffic thickened, with no policemen in sight anywhere. Horns squawked, two fast shots echoed and died as the men reached the intersection. Seeing that it was blocked by Gold Shirt cars set crosswise, the trucker shifted to his old extra low to buck his way through but Hamm was already out, his little revolver awkward in his unaccustomed hand, pushing through the milling crowd for the high wired pen where the trucks were held. And just ahead of him, from the south, loads of strikers roared up, swarming out in a yelling, overalled stream as they hit the jammed cars, plunging, fighting into the dun color of the Gold Shirts and the dark suits of the Crusaders about the truck yard as the clear current of the Wakoon hits the roily, slow-moving waters of the Lower Grand.

Inside the yard the finks had their loads lined up, gunmen in the cabs, engines going, ready for the run. Outside, as close to the fence as possible, the pickets were still trying to keep marching, Lew Lewis busy among them, slapping their buttocks, encouraging, talking, talking under the rising noise, as in a stadium. "Hold it, fellows, hold that line," he chanted low, calm, once more a great center, the roving keystone of a great wall.

Then the Gold Shirts charged the pickets, the trucks roared and started to move. As the Hammond watchman unlocked the big chain inside the fence, a woman came fighting through the crowd, waving, shouting to the man. "Wait!

wait!" she cried, running directly into two Gold Shirts stomping down men with their boot heels, swinging the butts of their rifles upon them.

"Here comes an old she-Red!" one whooped, and hit the woman across the shoulder with his gun. She went down on one knee, her sun goggles flying off. A man jerked her back, shouted a warning to her in a familiar voice as he tripped, the fall knocking a revolver from his hand.

The Gold Shirt saw it. "You gun-toting son-of-a-bitch!" he yelled, and sent his rifle butt into the man's face.

" — It's Mrs. Hammond!" a high, boyish voice warned over the rising roar as the rifle was lifted against the woman. The Gold Shirt hesitated, let the gun slip from his hands and was gone. Somebody tried to pull her away but Hallie Hammond jerked free and threw herself over the motionless man as a great swell of cheering that had been coming down the avenue swept into the intersection. Cars honked, hoarse voices chanted: —

> Yea, Boes!
> You were on your toes!
> Buf-fa-loes!
> Victory! *Victory!* VICTORY!

Before the mob of twenty thousand wild football fans the jam in the avenue gave way; the fighters were carried along like loose grass in a flood-roaring gully. Cars were rolled aside, turned over completely into the gutter. Gold Shirts, Crusaders, strikers, loaded trucks and finks — all were swept along towards the Franklin House, where the Mickmen must come from their crushing defeat.

Then the crowd was gone, leaving a dozen or so scattered men behind in the torn avenue, mostly strikers pulling themselves to the curb, bending with their injuries, moaning, swearing. Lew Lewis sat up, his hands to his head, looked around him, and shouted towards the blank houses for somebody to call the ambulances. But there were no faces at the windows, no one showing at all.

Near the gate of the empty truck yard one man lay still as the bloody Gold Shirt rifle beside him. His eyes were open, looking down the avenue, not seeing the shadow of the woman bent over him. With her garden glove, forgotten when Jamie called her, Hallie Hammond wiped the blood from the crushed temple, the scarred cheek, and then turned the face up. In its repose the deep lines and folds were gone, the ruddiness of the outdoor skin. It was a face singularly untouched by life, the boyish face of Rufer Hammond.

Steadily the mother looked down upon it, her eyes long dried of their tears for this beloved first-born son. She barely noticed the three heavy trucks of the national guards rumble up and turn into the lot, into her property, without ask or permission, more and more cars full of uniformed men, the strikers dragging away into alleys as they came. Or that Joe Willper and an older man with an egg-shaped belly growing in him were giving the orders, the armed guardsmen sullenly obeying. Finally a long column marched to the capitol, left sentinels with rifles stationed at each side of the entrance, and passed in through the great bronze doors.

At last the woman lifted her head. Except for the guards everything across the avenue seemed much the same as always, the white stone tower lifting its frieze of the Peoples of the World high into the clear, calm air of November. At the foot of the capitol the last rays of the sun gilded the outlines of the figure of Franklin and the granite plaque behind. Over it, from the wide window of the governor's suite, hung a new American flag, best-quality imported silk, ordered through Hammond's. And from up the avenue, toward the hotel, came one faint burst of cheering.